AN EPIC THAT WILL BRIDGE THE EONS OF TIME...

I0590383

# MYTH

## OF THE
# REIGN IMMORTALS
### VOLUME I

## J. F. NICKENS

ECHELON Graphix PUBLISHING

*This inspirational work of transcendent fiction is dedicated...*

---

To those who left both light and shadow upon my spirit—
Every MYTH is born first in mortal impact.

To those who helped shape these words through trial and grace—
This myth would not exist without you.

To those who know whom I speak of—
I thank you for showing me what it means to live.

This is a work of fiction.

MYTH: Reign of the Immortals - Volume I
Version 3.0
Copyright © 2025 Jonathan Nickens
All rights reserved.

Published and designed by Echelon Graphix
www.echelongraphix.com

ISBN: 979-8-9933429-0-0

Creative Authorship Statement:
This edition of MYTH: Reign of the Immortals was written, designed, and published by the author. All creative elements—including storyline, layout, typography, and cover design—were independently produced by Jonathan Nickens through his imprint, Echelon Graphix.

Printed in the United States of America

# TABLE OF CONTENTS

| | |
|---|---|
| Definitions | *I-II* |
| To The Flamebearers of MYTH | *III-IV* |
| Transcendent Mythology | *V* |
| The Six Genres | *VI-VII* |
| This Fire Burns Hot | *VIII-XI* |
| Preface | *XII-XV* |
| Introduction | *XVI-XVIII* |
| The Sacred Codex | *XIX-XXI* |
| Prelude | *XXII-XXIX* |

## CHAPTER 1: *A Purpose for Hope*

| | | |
|---|---|---|
| **Verse 1:** | *The Weight of Divinity* | *1* |
| **Verse 2:** | *Shadow of the Morning Star* | *16* |
| **Verse 3:** | *He Who Burns Brightest Still Burns* | *31* |
| **Verse 4:** | *When Pride Wages War* | *46* |
| **Verse 5:** | *The Scales of Judgment* | *66* |
| **Verse 6:** | *Fist of the Almighty King* | *83* |

## CHAPTER 2: *The Season of Inspiration*

| | | |
|---|---|---|
| **Verse 7:** | *The Reckoning of Fallen Thrones* | *100* |
| **Verse 8:** | *Culling of the Damned* | *120* |
| **Verse 9:** | *Apotheosis of the Edenites* | *148* |
| **Verse 10:** | *Of Love, Dominion, and Sacrifice* | *170* |
| **Verse 11:** | *The God Who Defied Oblivion* | *186* |
| **Verse 12 :** | *Sibling Forces: Flesh & Vision* | *200* |

## CHAPTER 3: *The Season of Maturity*

| | | |
|---|---|---|
| **Verse 13:** | *The Price of Power* | *221* |
| **Verse 14:** | *When Balance Becomes Law* | *234* |
| **Verse 15:** | *The Beast Within: The Fall of Pesa* | *248* |
| **Verse 16:** | *The Burning Crown: Opti's Ascension* | *265* |
| **Verse 17:** | *When Blood Denies Blood* | *281* |
| **Verse 18:** | *The Severing of Gods* | *296* |

# TABLE OF CONTENTS

## CHAPTER 4: *The Tide of Transgression*

**Verse 19:** *Ten Echoes Before the Burn*     317

**Verse 20:** *The Rending of Divinity*     332

**Verse 21:** *When Titans Shatter Worlds*     348

**Verse 22 :** *The Wrath of Ascension*     363

**Verse 23:** *The Duality of Flame & Grace*     379

**Verse 24:** *When Omnipotence Defies Fate*     392

# DEFINITIONS

## Myth
### Pronunciation: \'mith\

A story, rooted in tradition, that explains the world—through history, belief, or imagination. It can be a truth disguised as legend or a falsehood mistaken for fact. Myths shape societies, define ideals, and breathe life into gods, heroes, and monsters. They do not demand proof—only belief.

## *MYTH*
### Pronunciation: \'mith\
*(\*When spoken, it carries more weight than sound alone can hold)*

A force beyond time and truth, neither bound by history nor confined to fiction. **MYTH** is not a fable whispered to children—it is the loom upon which all stories are spun. All mythology interlaces, each thread weaving belief, history, and imagination—binding the past to a brighter future.

Each volume of **MYTH** is built upon a sigil *(defined later in this front matter)* — **M, Y, T, H** — the four pillars of this epic. These are not mere letters, but living sigils, the eternal architecture of this saga. You will see these sigils on the cover, in the Codex, and within the story itself. Their mysteries will unfold as each volume awakens:

**M ~ Manifestation:** Where nothing becomes everything.
**Y ~ Yielding:** To yield is to bleed, to bleed is to heal.
**T ~ Transcendence:** When all is lost, only transcendence endures.
**H ~ Harmony:** The blueprint of existence revealed.

**MYTH** — a design both seen and unseen, guiding you beyond story, and into revelation. It is the silent architect of fate, the unseen hand that bends belief into reality. It does not fade. It does not break. It endures—so long as there is a mind to remember it, a voice to speak it, a culture to enrich it, and a world to shape it. **MYTH** isn't just another creation story...

*~ It Is The Threshold.  Here Begins the Awakening ~*

# Mythology

Pronunciation: \mə-'thä-lə-je\

A collection of myths that form the foundation of a people, a culture, or an idea. Mythology is more than stories; it is a reflection of human nature: What we fear. What we worship. What we dream. It binds the past to the present, the real to the unreal, and the mortal to the divine.

# *Transcendent Mythology*

Pronunciation: \'tran(t)-,sen-dənt 'mith-ə-lä-je\
(*A mythic revelation beyond history, legend, and even belief itself.*)

*Transcendent Mythology* is more than sacred story or cosmic explanation. It is the fusion of divine law, cosmic order, and the eternal struggle between existence and oblivion.

Unlike traditional mythology, bound by culture and time, **Transcendent Mythology** shatters all boundaries. It forges a mythos that is timeless, universal, and woven into the very fabric of creation itself.

Where mythology explains, **Transcendent Mythology** awakens.
It does not merely tell stories of gods, mortals, and celestial forces—
It creates them.
It empowers them.
It is the breath of existence,
The scaffolding behind all meaning,
The living myth that underlies reality itself.

This, my friend, is not just a new mythology...
*It is a new genre of literature.*

# TO THE FLAMEBEARERS OF MYTH

## By J.F. Nickens

Welcome to **MYTH: Reign of the Immortals**, the first of four *Sacred Volumes of Transcendence*. This story has lived and matured with me for more than three decades. What you hold is not just literature, but the first key to a greater design —a saga that spans gods and mortals, creation and consequence.

### ~To the Devout in Faith~
*(The Chronicles of Narnia / Ben-Hur / Paradise Lost / The Pilgrim's Progress)*

For those who seek out echoes of the divine, or believe that myths carry words to bridge heaven along with man's fragile heart, **MYTH** whispers: *The war you feel in your spirit is real—and you were born to engage it.*

### ~To the Connoisseur of Mythology~
*(The Iliad & Odyssey / The Aeneid / Beowulf / The Epic of Gilgamesh)*

For those who savor the oldest stories, who know that behind every legend lies a fragment of the first truth spoken, echoing through time and memory. **MYTH** whispers: *The ancient voices still speak, if you dare to listen.*

### ~To the Keeper of High Fantasy~
*(The Lord of the Rings / The Silmarillion / Earthsea Cycle / The Wheel of Time)*

For those who seek quests with deeper destinies, where gods walk among mortals who become forged through fire and hardship, **MYTH** whispers: *Every hero begins nameless, until their trials become legend.*

### ~To the Seeker of Philosophy~
*(Siddhartha / Thus Spoke Zarathustra / The Republic / Meditation)*

For those who question, who peel back layers of meaning to see the foundations of existence beneath the myth. Those who seek truth within every silence, **MYTH** whispers: *Answers live not in certainty, but in the courage to ask.*

### ~To the Guardian of Modern Legends~
*(American Gods / Neverwhere / The Sandman / Fables / Good Omens)*

For those who feel the pulse of every epic ever told, who see the threads binding ancient tales to the stories of our age. Those who weave past and present into living myth, **MYTH** whispers: *The old stories are not gone, but live in every tale you hold dear.*

### ~To the Traveler Between Realms & Technology~
*(Dune / Foundation / The Expanse / Hyperion Cantos / Star Wars)*

For those who see the encompassing wonder of cosmic speculation and its machinery, and those who dream of worlds where creation and future sciences converge, **MYTH** whispers: *The same hand that shaped the stars may shape you beyond imagination.*

Also, for those who are the meta-physicians, the mystics, and the myth-makers of meaning—those who see beyond what is, and to what may yet become, **MYTH** whispers: *Reality is not fixed, but formed.*

The themes and symbols in this volume are intentional, forming the foundation on which the entire saga rests. They are not mere puzzles, but living threads designed to reveal deeper meaning as the journey unfolds. You don't need to grasp every word at once—let the story guide you, and the truths will unveil themselves in time. What follows is only the first revelation. Greater trials, deeper truths, and sacred destinies await beyond these pages. This flame is now yours to bear. And finally...

### ~To the Patient of Heart and Steady of Mind~

*PLEASE NOTE:* This is *not* an epic for the casual reader. **MYTH** does not bend to modern brevity or chase fleeting thrills. It is a *sacred inferno*—burning slow, steady, fierce, and without apology. Those who hurry this story will miss its *heat*. Those who demand instant *clarity* will find only ash. This tale will not meet you where you currently are. No, my friend, it will awaken what has long slumbered within you—to mark your soul with a purpose that may never fade once the veil has lifted.

But for those who dare—and choose—to be refined in its blaze, who breathe deeply and enter with a patient heart... will find something far more enduring within their spirit, just as it awakened within mine—
*This Eternal Flame.*

IV

# TRANSCENDENT MYTHOLOGY

## A Paradigm Shift of Consciousness
### *By: J.F. Nickens*

We were told through the ages that the gods shaped our world, and we were just players on their stage. For a long time, this was enough. But something is changing. You feel it—don't you? In quiet moments of contemplation. In the chaos around us. In the space between who you are and who you can become. This isn't just the evolution of human nature. This is *a paradigm shift of consciousness*—a turning of the mind, the soul, the very fabric of what it means to be human. A shift that doesn't ask for permission, but demands awakening.

We no longer wait for mythic saviors or pray for mythic miracles. We now begin rewriting and experiencing this awakening for ourselves. Not in the old ways—carved in stone and sealed by blood—but in new ones: alive, questioning, and bold with vitality. A story where we can become the architects of our fate. We who carry the burden, and brilliance of personal choice.

What of the gods of old, you ask? They were mere reflections—mirrors of what we feared, or longed to become. Now that mirror shatters, and in the shards that remain, we see ourselves made whole. This is not about heroes chosen by prophecy. This is about those who choose to rise. To think. To feel. To change. To thrive in your humanity that is no longer content with mere survival, but driven by a far greater purpose. A myth that is no longer above us—but one that is forged *within* us. In every defiant truth. In every act of courage. In every refusal to forget what truly matters.

You are not just a witness to this shift. You will become a part of it, if you so choose. You are the necessity to its being. This is not just another epic fantasy. This is the frontier of what can be made real, told through fire and vision— but only if it allowed to rise in your heart. You make the call.

*Step forward now and carry that fire. Become the story that you alone were meant to write—and rise to your fullest potential.*

# THE SIX GENRES

## To Sacred Transcendence of the MYTH Saga
### *By: J.F. Nickens*

### Continuing The Earlier Definition:

*Transcendent Mythology* is not constructed from traditional sub-genres. It is formed through six literary forces that act as the narrative architecture—each one essential, elemental, and eternal. These following genres do not flavor this **MYTH**—they build upon it. They are the sacred structure of a living storytelling form. Together, they awaken the reader through a multi-faceted experience of truth, transformation, and transcendence.

### Mythic Fantasy – *The Spine*

*Function:* Forms the sacred foundation of the saga—its gods, divine laws, realms, and metaphysical tone.
*Unified Definition:* This is the cosmological heartbeat of **MYTH**. It constructs a wholly original pantheon, sacred architecture, and mythopoeic voice—not retelling ancient traditions, but forging a new lineage of the divine. These are not stories about gods; they are stories told from the perspective of gods and prophets.

### Epic / High Fantasy – *The Skeleton*

*Function:* Provides the narrative scale—multi-realm conflict, prophecy, war, and structural scope.
*Unified Definition:* **MYTH** unfolds as a high epic across dimensions, dynasties, and divine battlegrounds. Prophecy becomes scripture. War becomes theology. Every movement serves the sacred scaffolding of a multiverse conflict with spiritual consequence.

### Spiritual Allegory / Metaphysical Fiction – *The Soul*

*Function:* Imbues the story with theological depth, sacred consequence, and emotional resonance.
*Unified Definition:* **MYTH** is a spiritual mirror—its trials reflect eternal principles: rebirth, divine justice, memory, mercy, and truth. Every plot point

has a sacred echo. Allegory is not used to moralize, but to awaken.

## Visionary / Philosophical Sci-Fantasy – *The Mind*

*Function:* Elevates the narrative through metaphysical mechanics, sacred geometry, and conceptual structure.
*Unified Definition:* Here, philosophy becomes law. Memory becomes structure. Vision becomes revelation. The speculative aspects of **MYTH** are not scientific—they are metaphysical: laws written in light, perception, number, and divine will.

## Cosmic Horror / Dark Fantasy – *The Shadow*

*Function:* Grounds the antagonist force through physical and spiritual decay, the corruption of divinity, and existential risk.
*Unified Definition:* The horror in **MYTH** emerges through the collapse of divine order, the twisting of sacred truths, and the infection that spreads when ultimate power loses purpose. Fear becomes metaphysical: not chaos, but meaning wholly undone.

## Tragic Heroic Fantasy – *The Heart*

*Function:* Grounds the divine in emotional intimacy—personal sacrifice, love, betrayal, and loss on a mortal level.
*Unified Definition:* **MYTH**'s characters are not vessels—they are vision. Their sacred wounds shape the world around them. Every decision is mythic in consequence. Their emotional tone is Shakespearean, but eternal in action.

## ~ Transcendence: *The Crown Jewel* ~

*Function:* The fusion of these six genres, in particular, and what they create when unified.
*Unified Definition:* Transcendence is not the *genre itself*—it is the experience of sacred revelation. The reader does not simply consume a story—they become a part of it, a believer in it. Transcendence is the final realization that a story was never just about epic literature itself, but the forgotten truths that are unlocked once the reader sees beyond the words, and remembers them.

# THIS FIRE BURNS HOT

## By J.F. Nickens

This page carries the weight of over 40 years of study, reflection, and transformation. Mythology has not merely been a fascination for me. It has been my companion, my guide, my solitude. A sacred lens through which I've come to understand not only the stories of the world, but the deep, ancient forces always present within the human soul.

*Transcendent Mythology* is the distilled essence of that lifelong journey. It is not a reflection of the past, but a summons to the future. Not a tribute to the myths we've inherited—but a declaration of the myths we are now called to create.

**MYTH: Reign of the Immortals (Vol. 1)**—along with the other three volumes that will follow—is not the product of a trend, a focus group, or a writer's room. It is the result of decades of solitary work, tireless crafting, sleepless nights, and spiritual conviction—all while running a full-time business. I am *not a scholar* with titles or letters after my name. But I am something even more rare: a visionary with a voice—one forged through fire, failure, redemption, and an unrelenting call to create something enduring.

**MYTH** *is not derivative.*

It is not stitched together from scraps of ancient text or recycled narratives. It is a living cosmos—a mythic engine of divine narrative, moral imagination, and sacred geometry. It is theology and philosophy, poetry and prophecy—fused into balance. It draws from the old, but is bound to no past. It speaks in ancient tones but echoes forward into futures not yet dreamed.

It is *God given.*

I do not hide the fact or apologize that *Ai* has helped me refine this vision to a scalpel's edge. But Ai did not birth it. That distinction matters. I brought the scrolls. I lived the journey. Ai became my *final* editor—but it was *never* the flame. The flame, the soul—that has always been mine. The dream—every beat of it—was forged in this gray matter long before any computer or cell phone processed a single syllable.

To those who say, *"Surely this was a team project,"* or worse, *"This was clearly created by Ai,"* I say this, and let me be *very* clear:

You are not witnessing a team's creation—but a soul's testament. And if the scale of it defies your expectation of what one person can do over the course of thirty plus years, perhaps the question is not *how*—but *why not?*

Why shouldn't this generation birth a new *Homer*? A new *Dante*? A new *C.S. Lewis* or *Tolkien*—for a world ablaze with distraction and starved of vision? If you're skeptical, I invite you to look deeper. Read not only the words, but the messages between them. Feel the structure. Hear the rhythm. Sense the sacred order. I wrote this not to dazzle anyone with prose—but to hopefully awaken something you forgot you even carried.

Every verse of **MYTH** was born from vision, rewritten through maturity, and shaped by the kind of creative solitude no shortcut could ever replicate. The handwritten volumes of notes with ideas in the margins, as well as the drawings I still carry from decades ago—are safe and sound. The additional handwritten outlines no one saw but me? Still intact. This is the story of a soul undeterred and resolute—proof that modern myth can still rise from the heart of one generation to the next.
I've knocked on the doors of agents, publishers, and committees more times than I can count—only to be told **MYTH** was too big, too deep, too different, too controversial. But that didn't stop me.

*It refined me.*

Every unanswered query, every form rejection, only proved what I already knew: this work wasn't meant to follow the path of committees, publishers, or "agents" who only looked at the dollar signs and numbers instead of the soul. **MYTH** wasn't made to chase trends.

It was born to *outlast* them.
***This fire burns hot, baby... Because it was meant to!***

**MYTH** is the sacred engine meant to ignite a conversation across generations, cultures, and beliefs—one that no Ai could ever think up by itself.
And for those still uncertain—the proof will be undeniable, soon. Once the official *MYTHepic.com* website launches in early/mid 2026, a dedicated archive will showcase original documents and illustrations, and annotated notes spanning *over three decades.* Among them: original digital artworks I

created in *Painter*, dating back to 1994—the genesis of **MYTH**—the visual testaments *long before* the rise of Ai or digital generation shortcuts.

## This Red Line is Real!

The full epic of **MYTH** will be told through four sacred volumes— In print. In digital. For all. But the deeper meanings? The laws, the sacred alignments, the living sigils? These were never meant to be skimmed or scrolled. That's why this website will not just be an archive. It will be a gateway.

This is where the *Sigils of the Codex*, one by one will awaken into action and voice. This is where their words will call to those who want to hear them. This is where the reader crosses from the epic into initiation.

But let this be understood:

If you enter through a cell phone, you will hear only the first song of their meaning in *8 sigils total*. Their voices, yes, will be heard through a tap or a swipe, but then only their echoes will remain. No symphony of the 60 sigils fully alive in **MYTH**. No more verses foretold. No more insights or sacred diagrams. No more access until the *Companion's Codex* is known. The true experience of **MYTH,** my friend, will exist only through *desktop access.*

This is not a restriction or a punishment, but simply a return to a much needed ritual, and it will be honored. So, if you want the full experience, you must come with focus and join me in this odyssey.
With *attention*. With *intention*. **MYTH** will not chase you, but it will patiently await your arrival. These are not imitations or flavors of the day; they are sacred artifacts from a world that began my own mythic odyssey.

Oh, and one final thing…

I'm also a lifelong creative professional—founder of a nationally recognized graphic design business, *Echelon Graphix*. For well over two decades, I've brought artistry and layout design to digital life with precision, discipline, passion, and integrity. Our many customers would agree: we don't just imagine works of art—we *design* them, *build* them, and help *deliver* them with the same focus and professionalism that have defined the course of this author's entire artistic career.

And in 2025, Echelon Graphix became the official digital publisher of the **MYTH Saga**—a natural evolution for a design studio that was never just about design, but about *vision*. This isn't just a brand any longer—its become a beautiful covenant. One, God willing, that will be built to last for generations.

**MYTH** is more than a spiritual undertaking—it is a visual and structural art. From layout and typography to cover and formatting, every element of the process was shaped by my hand. Every sigil, motif, and trailer frame—on the website, YouTube, and beyond—was born of trial, error, and stubborn vision. No committees. No advisers. Just decades of grit and soul.

This is not merely a story I have written. It is a universe I forged—word by word, line by line, pixel by pixel. If one day a major publisher takes **MYTH** to new heights, that will mark a natural evolution: a release from these hands into those of a team with the integrity and vision to carry it onward. Until then, it remains the domain of Echelon Graphix.

I would not have it any other way.

**MYTH** is not manufactured; it is lived and loved in the real world.
It is purpose made manifest.
*It is legacy.*

Let the skeptics come and still be skeptical.
Let the critics come and still be critical.
Let history remember who spoke fire into this story—an inferno that no longer forges me, but becomes a gift that is willing and ready to forge *you*.

**THIS IS MYTH!**

In Fire and Faith,
J. F. Nickens
2025

# PREFACE

*The Hero's Journey is indeed, alive and well.*

My own exhilarating, mind-swept expedition into the fantastic realms of **MYTH** began in the spring of 1994, during my final year of college. Since childhood, I had loved reading and studying the classic Greek and Roman tales, but it was a series of four specialized courses in mythology that became the crowning achievement of my studies.

This intense analysis culminated in a final project—one that would unknowingly shape the next thirty years of my life. A ten-page creation myth, meant as a final assignment, would become something far greater.

What began as a classroom exercise became my lifelong calling. Within six months of graduation, the story had expanded past a hundred pages. A year later, it had more than doubled in size.

Now, after three decades of writing, editing, evolving, and re-imagining, that humble myth has transformed into a three-volume, seventy-two-verse epic spanning well over a thousand pages.

## The Foundation of MYTH

**MYTH** stands beside epic fantasy and mythic fiction, drawing from deep roots of great works such as *The Lord of the Rings* by J.R.R. Tolkien. Yet **MYTH** also holds unique qualities that set it apart. It is a story woven into the very fabric of mythology itself, carefully infused with the classic themes, symbols, and archetypes that have shaped human storytelling for millennia.

In this sense, **MYTH** shares its foundation with one of the greatest literary examples of fantasy Christian fiction: *The Chronicles of Narnia* by C. S. Lewis. Like that legendary series, **MYTH** carries the timeless battle of good versus evil, yet it does so in a way that bridges myth, fantasy, and science fiction—a combination that even classic series do not explore.

For this, I must express my deepest gratitude to the science fiction genre itself, which completes the grand design of **MYTH**—especially in this, the first book of the series. As fate would have it, in the winter of 1994 (the same year I graduated from college), *Stargate* was released in theaters. This single film opened an entirely new dimension of storytelling possibilities, inspiring me to explore how mythology and science fiction could coexist in perfect harmony.

Much later, in 2010, the television series *Ancient Aliens* became a weekly fascination for me. This show explored the mythological components that resonated deeply with my work at the time, allowing me to further strengthen many of the foundational concepts in **MYTH's** second release in 2020.

Now, in 2025, I have finally completed the third and final evolution of **MYTH's** first volume—the culmination of three decades of refinement. This version now represents the perfect fusion of mythology and religion, shaping **MYTH** into its ultimate, epic expression.

## Honoring the Greats: The Mentors of MYTH

I have always believed in giving credit where credit is due. To that, I owe my eternal gratitude to the late, great **Joseph Campbell**. His groundbreaking work on mythic structure and *The Hero's Journey* shaped not only this book, but my entire understanding of mythology itself.

If you, like me, have ever been captivated by the power of myth, I strongly encourage you to explore Campbell's work. His 1988 PBS documentary, *Joseph Campbell and the Power of Myth*—a six-hour conversation with journalist Bill Moyers—remains, in my opinion, one of the most influential and insightful explorations of mythology ever produced.

In addition to Campbell, I must also acknowledge Alan Watts, the American Buddhist philosopher whose teachings—equal parts profound and playfully irreverent—deeply influenced my understanding of self-discovery and the human experience. His voice, whimsical and wise, opened doors to truth with laughter as often as with insight.

One of his most profound beliefs was this:

*"It is important to live life with a knowledge of its deeper mysteries—especially your own. Because once you discover what is truly ticking inside of you, the very thing that makes you who you are ... you simply get straightened out."*

Once this revelation occurs—once you discover the one thing that sets your soul on fire—and you pursue it with relentless passion, it will bring a fulfillment to your life unlike anything else. Once you find it, the very universe itself will begin to conspire in your favor.

As Campbell famously wrote, *"Follow your bliss."*

Finally, in the spring of 1994 at *Spokane Falls Community College*, a teacher named Richard Ibach saw something eternal in this young artist's writing. He gave this final an A++, not for what it was, but for what it would become. Thirty-one years later, that work has become **MYTH**. This epic is dedicated in part to the man who saw the flame before the fire and for that I am eternally grateful. Thank you, Richard, and Godspeed your continuing journey into eternity.

## The First Sparks:  My Final Honor

Now, if I'm being honest here, this journey didn't even begin in college.

It's a little embarrassing for me to admit this now at my age, but I'm filled with nothing but pride when I reflect on how it all truly began—way back in 1980, when I was just a nerdy kid in sixth grade, and I saw a film called *Xanadu*—a musical fantasy that's since become a cult favorite.

That deliciously cheesy movie—with an artist chasing a dream, a musician trying to relive one, and a muse to guide them both—sparked something in me that has never gone out. And with the electrifying music of **ELO**—a band I already loved—it ignited an even deeper spark that's never faded. At just twelve years old, it awakened my talents and vision, planting seeds that would one day grow into a career in graphic design, a lifelong devotion to mythology, and now, authorship.

Strange as it may seem, Xanadu was the first time I felt it—the pull of something much greater. Looking back, I realize now, this was my first true journey into **MYTH**.

*May the Almighty continue to bless both your journeys beyond the rim, Olivia Newton John and Gene Kelly—to continue dancing together to the song of the cosmos.*

This passion became solidified with **Clash of the Titans** (*1981*), starring Harry Hamlin. Watching *Perseus* confront gods, monsters, and fate itself on the big screen stirred something deep in me—the thrill of ancient courage meeting divine consequence. I was captivated by his journey, his resolve, and the sense that myth could make the impossible feel real.

It was through Perseus that I first recognized the timeless nature of the *hero*—their flaws, their triumphs, and the divine spark that calls them to something greater. From that moment on, mythology was no longer just a subject I admired—it became the very lens through which I would view destiny, courage, and creation in my own life.

## A Final Thought:

For me, **MYTH** has been my sacred paradise for over thirty years. Now I share it with you, hoping it may ignite your own sense of wonder, purpose, and adventure. The Hero's Journey is yours to take—and it's your odyssey alone. But in every great myth, in every legend ever told, they all began with a single step. Now my friend, it is time to take yours.

As Campbell famously wrote, *"The cave you fear to enter holds the treasure you seek."* This is the essence of the Hero's Journey—transformation through trial, discovery through darkness. In stepping beyond the familiar, you will find the story only you were meant to tell. Should you allow it, that story, once begun, will echo forever in your soul.

Every call to adventure, whether whispered or roaring, is an invitation to awaken. The hero does not seek comfort, but truth. Your trials will shape you, your choices will define you, and your courage will carve your legend into the fabric of time. Embrace the unknown my friend—your *myth* is waiting to be written.

# INTRODUCTION

## The Strength of MYTH:
### An Odyssey of Truth, Destiny, and Transformation

*"Every great myth is not just a story; it is
the mirror that reflects who we are."*

**—The Authors Consortium of Mythology**

Though this consortium is fictional, the truth behind their words is not. Their collective insight echoes our struggles and triumphs—it whispers of who we are, and who we are meant to become. It weaves the thread of mortals and gods alike into a sacred framework of coexistence throughout the ages.

**MYTH: Reign of the Immortals** is more than the first volume of an epic fantasy novel; it is an *odyssey*. A journey through the paradoxes of truth and deception, faith and doubt, justice and mercy. It is a testament to resilience, transformation, and the battles we face—not only in the world, but within ourselves. The greatest myths endure not for spectacle, but for revelation. They peel back the world to show us who we really are. They challenge us to ask:

~ *How do we heal without letting our wounds define us?*
~ *What does it mean to seek truth in a world soaked in deception?*
~ *How do we stand when the weight of the world demands that we fall?*
~ *What does it mean to grow—in body, in mind, in wisdom, and in purpose?*

At the heart of **MYTH** lies this truth: *Growth is not merely a part of life—it is life.*
This growth, this transformation, is inescapable. It shapes mortals into gods—and gods into something even greater... or something far more insidious.

Through *D'Reem's* evolution, we will witness the physical transformation from mortal to god, a trial of power that demands not just strength, but the wisdom to wield it. *Xionn's* journey unfolds across three divine ascensions, each echoing the spiritual evolution every soul must undergo to reach its highest calling.

Opti, a divine force manifest into being, matures not in power but in understanding, showing that even gods are not beyond the need to evolve. *Pesa*, in contrast, walks the path of regression, its divinity unraveling into monstrosity through *Dia'Baal*—a haunting reminder that power without wisdom, corrupts absolutely.

And finally, *T'Naeva*, unchanging in body, undergoes the most profound transformation of all—growing from a soul clouded by innocence and betrayal into one sharpened to a scalpel's edge through love, truth, forgiveness, and revelation.

**MYTH** embraces what I call the *whole-pie mentality*— a vision that does not divide truth, but unites it. It sees the fullness of experience—the tension between pain and purpose, between order and chaos—not as conflict, but as balance.

Strength is not found in choosing between hope and struggle, but in embracing both. Justice must be tempered by mercy. Grief must make way for healing. Faith must walk hand in hand with action. And wisdom? Wisdom is forged where contradiction becomes clarity—where harmony rises from division.

*We are not only meant to avoid trials in this world, my friend… we are meant to simply acknowledge, and then defeat them.*

For those drawn to sacred wisdom, **MYTH** echoes familiar truths:

The **Bible** calls us to stand firm *(Ephesians 6:10–18)*, to find joy in trials *(James 1:2–4)*, and to believe that beauty will rise from ashes. *(Isaiah 61:3)*.

**Buddhism** teaches that self-mastery, one becomes unshakable. *(Dhammapada 25:8)*.

**Hinduism** urges us to act with purpose, without attachment to outcome. *(Bhagavad Gita 2:48)*.

**Islam** reminds us that trials refine the soul, and that divine help is near for those who endure. *(Surah Al-Baqarah 2:214)*.

**Taoism** shows us that, like water, the softest path wears down the strongest stone. *(Tao Te Ching 78)*.

Just as sacred geometry is woven through the great spiritual traditions worldwide, **MYTH** reflects (and respects) this deeper, unspoken design within every journey—an unseen harmony that unites struggle, transformation, and destiny of one's life into a greater whole. This is the heartbeat of the whole-pie vision: all paths, beliefs, and truths forming a single pattern of unity.

*The greatest stories don't just entertain, my friend… they awaken.*

**MYTH** is an invitation—to look deeper, to question what we call truth, and to embrace the journey of becoming something greater than we were before. Perhaps it will reveal the beauty of humanity in a way you never expected: a reminder that belief in *ourselves* is the first step toward healing the world, one soul at a time.

I now present to you, my friend, that gift…

*We weavers of fibers made of myths to buffer earthly storms –*
*So cloaked against the shroud of doubt all wonders to perform –*
*To take the clay of stars my friend the dust washed from sky to sea –*
*Pressing it into these shapes of things—these gifts for you and me.*
— James Lee Hansen

And so, from these truths was created the first **SIGIL**… the pulse that breathes all *myth* into existence.

---

## MYTH: Reign of the Immortals (Vol. I):
### *The Sigil of Manifestation*

It stirs where nothing becomes everything. Where upheaval births gods both mighty and fallen—and burns entire realms. This is the first of four sacred sigils: the moment creation tears through the void like fire through silence. It marks the origin of gods, of laws, of dimensions, and of worlds.

This is the epic that gives truth its teeth—but also reveals the evil bold enough to bite back when confronted.

# The Sacred Codex of MYTH
*Before the first cosmic breath, there was the SIGIL*

These are the divine glyphs of the Immortals—each forged from the essence of the Companion, echoing with mythic truth. A truth that remembers what the world forgets, reveals what the eye cannot see, and restores what time seeks to erase. Unbound by the hands of fate and guided by divine purpose, these sacred symbols stand true at the end of every verse.

Five anchors in a sea of revelation, in sacred sequence, revealing the mystery between the words. These are not just sigils, they are reality made manifest.

## To see them is to *Remember*  ～  To know them is to *Awaken*

| | | | |
|---|---|---|---|
| MYTH Vol. I Sigil |  MYTH Vol. II Sigil |  MYTH Vol. III Sigil |  Companion's Codex Sigil |
|  The Companion |  Evil |  Existence |  Oblivion |
|  Force of Harmony |  Deception |  Love |  Hate |
|  Force of Imagination |  Ignorance |  Creation |  Ruin |

XIX

| | | | |
|---|---|---|---|
| Time | Stillness | Force of Reality | Delusion |
| Fate | Chaos | Order | Sin |
| Life | Death | Wisdom | Apathy |
| Angels | The Fall | Demons | Lucifer Morningstar |
| Dia'Baal Fallenstar | The Great Realm | Ametheden | Harr-Manee / Gaea |
| Earth | Ocean | Realm of Reality | Realm of Imagination |

Xionn Theone

Xionn Theone 'The Edenite'

Sovereign Hand Xionn
'The One'

Grand Sovereign Xion
'The Lion Within'

D'Reem - Young Warrior

D'Reem - Warrior

D'Reem - Great Warrior

D'Reem (The Ideal)

OPTI (Divine)

OPTI (Matured)

T'Naeva 'The Witness'

T'Naeva's Birth

PESA (Divine)

PESA (Corrupted)

Chup'Dravak-Ra

Eternal

Corporal

Sigil of the Veiled Sight
#1

Sigil of the Veiled Sight
#2

Sigil of the Veiled Sight
#3

Sigil of the Veiled Sight
#4

These final four sigils of the Veiled Sight will be revelaed in Volume III:

# MYTH: The Conquest of Heroes

# PRELUDE

## *The Veil Shall Lift*

*he arises whole from Ocean's depths, radiant and magnificent— borne of light and life, her essence shimmering the beauty of Creation's first breath...*

The heavens sing her arrival—a pure and holy symphony reverberating through reality. Ocean's waves bow, carving her radiant form with the skill, the grace of a master artisan. Her divine form rises higher through the swirling waters, each movement a testament to her ethereal authority—a presence born to command awe and devotion.

Her divine flesh touches the newborn shore, and the heavens sigh in reverence. She lifts her arms to them, drawing the celestial symphony into her being, an eternal blessing, unbroken. She walks to me with a smile and places her hand in mine. And for a single fleeting breath, all is Harmony... She is more than divine; she is my destiny—a force of life and love brought into existence for a purpose far beyond mortal comprehension.

I am D'Reem, *The Ideal*, and she is all that matters to me now. *But in a heartbeat, the harmony shatters.*

From beyond time's veil, my ancient father and mentor, Xion, watches— his omnipotent gaze cutting through the lattice of eternity to this singular moment. He has seen countless cycles of creation and destruction over the eons, but this fracture—a whisper disguised as fate—feels heavier to him, as though the weight of the world tilts toward an abyss from which even I and she may never return.

*I then see it.*

A shadow spills across her light—not from above, but from the depths within. It slithers unseen, curling through the fabric of her divine being, coiling tighter with every breath she takes. A presence... No, a *whisper*. It does not belong. It writhes like a living curse, as though born from the will of something ancient and malevolent—a remnant of a power long defeated, yet never wholly undone. Its deceit twists through her thoughts, each word binding her to its dark intent.

*"You are alone ... betrayed ... abandoned by him."*

She removes her hands from mine, retreating awkwardly away. A flicker of uncertainty—an unspoken hesitation—shadows her face. Then her trembling fingers brush my chest. I feel it—the warmth of her essence suddenly meeting the cold, dark tide rising within her.
For an instant, the war begins. The shadow whispers again, louder this time, more insistent.

*"He is the one ... the destroyer ... the deceiver ... cruel and merciless."*

Her breath falters. A memory of recognition flickers—brief, fragile. Wide, anguished eyes lock onto mine, pleading, searching. For a single heartbeat, her light flares—defiant—struggling to resist the encroaching darkness. But the shadow's coil is relentless, and her light begins to fade. It spreads through her like venom, twisting her brilliance into lament. Her hand recoils from my chest as though it has been burned. She staggers backward, her harmony drowned beneath a rising storm of anger.

*Oh ... I should have known.*

This shade—borne of Dia'Baal Fallenstar—settles upon her mind with insidious intent, weaving both distrust and anguish into her soul. Yet from Xion's cosmic perch, his ancient eyes narrow. He muses silently.

*'This is not the full force of the adversary. This is but his echo—his whisper—a remnant clinging like frost in the first light of dawn. His dominion was ended once, and it shall dissolve again beneath the rising sun.'*

But to T'Naeva, the shadow feels as vast as the void. I reach for her—instinct, desperation, love. But this beautiful, tortured soul is already lost.

*Moments ago, you rose from Ocean's birth and danced among its waves. You came to me as our fingers became entwined as one—but now...*

The shadow coils deeper, suffocating her light, drowning the brilliance that once was. The symphony of her creation crashes into my soul like a lament of the cosmos, each discordant note stoking the tempest of her coming wrath. This is no mere phantom; it is the bitter residue of Dia'Baal's former reign—a shade severed from his true form when the Creator cast him down. Though diminished, it clings like an echo of rebellion, seeking cracks in her innocence to sow its venom.

My chest tightens—my vision narrows with every cruel step she takes away from me. She stands in silence, her glare burning through me—a memory too sacred to embrace, yet too deeply etched in creation to ever release. *Ocean* bends to her will now, rising in tempestuous devotion—each wave crowned with the raw fury of her soul. Now, and it rises—*charged*—with her fury. Waves churn, crashing down all around us in violent defiance, thrashing as though alive with dread. Even the air trembles beneath the weight of her wrath.

*Where have you gone, dear T'Naeva?*

I brace myself before the storm, and I hear...

> **The thunders quake throughout this leaden, starless firmament...**
> **Its energies focus... Intensify... Merge...**

"You stand before me in silence—why? Do you not deny my pain? Do you not beg for my mercy as I writhe in misery because of YOU!?" Her breath shudders as *rage* and *doubt* war within her. Both of these things, the rage and the doubt become... *as one.*

"NO... It is you! Murderer! Deceiver! Thief of light! Yet... beneath the lies, something lingers—a whisper I cannot silence, a truth I dare not face!" Her voice quivers, raw with fury. The air thickens with salt and grief; Ocean itself mourns because it feels her pain.

*Grand Sovereign Xion, 'The Lion Within,'* stands in solemn stillness, his eyes shadowed by sorrow as they trace the cosmic mosaic of those he loves, its intricate designs fracturing and shifting in ways even he cannot mend. Once, his mighty hand shaped this world—and forging the path that raised this warrior to the precipice of destiny.
But now, Xion has yielded all—his authority, his labors, his heart—to the will of his Eternal *Companion*. The coming maturity of Earth no longer rests in his grasp, but in the hands of the One who ordained it before its first dawn.

His power is no longer needed for Earth's sake, as he can only witness as Dia'Baal's corruption takes root. Through his four eons of life, he has already seen the folly of gods and mortals alike, especially here as the first coming age of humanity, stirs, but never has he felt such a void forming so quickly before him. The whisper echoes a final mocking line through his vast mind, hearing it rage as a thousand thunders.

*"She is mine now, warrior… as I too was formed in the beginning, and ever shall I be the whisper—to bring you both, misery."*

Xion's ancient eyes narrow, sorrow and resolve mixing as he exhales. His whisper drifts upward, though only *Two* can hear him:

*"The first shadow upon this new Earth has been cast… May the Companion assist you now, O, Mighty Warrior. The weight you now endure in your maturity is more than I can bear."*

A goddess erupts into a roar that shakes heaven and sea alike!

"I will no longer tolerate your presence! You, who stole Pesa's light! You, who cast it into oblivion!"
I inhale slowly as her storm crashes over me. My heart aches for what she has become—for what Dia'Baal has turned her into—but I hold firm beneath her fury. Softly but resolutely, I speak.
"T'Naeva, I foresaw this moment—the tide of lies now entwined in your soul."
My voice wavers not as I take a firm step towards her.
"I will not turn from you—no fury, no shadow, will drive me aside."
Our gazes clash—hers ablaze with fury, mine anchored in sorrowful resolve. The light of her birth is gone, replaced by the darkness overwhelming her

soul. T'Naeva wails—a cry that splits the heavens, shattering even my immortal heart. Divine tears carve rivers of grief upon her face.

"O, mighty Pesa, your brilliance undone—not by time or fate, but by his merciless treachery! And now I stand before the deceiver who extinguished you!" She turns to me again. This time, no roar escapes, only a trembling growl.
"Vile deceiver! Must you stand before me as if you do not know? Must I suffer in your presence, drowning in truths I cannot bear? Leave me at once— or I swear you shall feel the anger blazing within me!"

Her words cut deep—not because they wound me physically, but because they are steeped in the lies she trusts. My patience frays under their weight, but still, I do not raise my hand against her, *nor would I ever.* I reply firm but gentle.
"Your fury blinds you, T'Naeva, but even now, I see you."
Another step forward. My resolve does not falter.
"Do not let your truth of pain deceive you into turning against me!"
My voice softens, filled with sorrow.
"I will bear your grief, as I have borne my own. For terrible truths have wounded me, as they now wound you."

Her storm rages—the heavens seize in anticipation—but I press forward one final time. Xion's gaze lingers because even gods cannot unmake fate. But he sees it now—a choice, trembling on the edge of oblivion, waiting to be claimed. He exhales slowly, his presence lingering, as if awaiting an answer.

Then, a voice—steady and resolute—rises in response.

*... You have done well, Grand Sovereign Xion, o, mighty Lion Within, and I have heard your appeal, and it has moved me. Be not weary in your well-doing, for what you have sown in faith upon this Earth shall be reaped in glory. Yes, this final burden is now Mine alone, just as it has always been ours alone. Hope remains, dear friend, even through the ticking eons of time where you, My most faithful servant, endures.*

Suddenly, another echo arises, a voice so beautiful and serene, yet full of wisdom, grace and quiet vigor—it is breathtaking to me in its tone and clarity.

*"Uh hum... Let it not be forgotten—for even the heaviest of burdens were never yours to bear alone. Not yours. Not Xion's, and certainly not mine... for I share them fully,*

*as I have always done."*

The Lion Within chuckles softly—low and full of warmth—part amusement, but much in wonder, as if to say:
*'There she is... now that's the spirit I've longed for since I was but a youth.'*

The Companion, for a long calculated breath, does not answer.
Was this a test? Was this a final measure of *her* resolve? Xion wonders, watching the stillness deepen. Then, at last, the Almighty speaks—His voice hushed—not weakened, but stilled, as if echoing across the threshold of time, deep in memory since the *ANEW.*

*... Ah yes, ever the gentle yet spirited voice that occasionally stirs even the depths of My stillness across the eons. You speak as only **Love** can speak, my dear—softly, yet with a resonance that reaches the marrow of all My creation. Indeed, some fires were never meant to burn alone, and his never did in you, My beloved... Edenite Rose.*

A soft chuckle slips from her lips and she smiles in a wide grin. Her eyes, illuminated in brilliant emerald hues in her newly forged ascension, lift to meet His radiance.

*"You haven't called me by that name in ages, O, Mighty Companion."*

She murmurs, her voice serene yet woven with a forged eternal strength.

*"... I almost forgot how beautiful it still sounds coming from You."*

The pause that follows is not silence, but a fullness that hums with eternity—an infinite weight pressed into the single heartbeat of divine recognition. Her tone deepens with quiet authority, gentle yet unyielding.

*"But I did not wait for your words to remember who I am. I carried both your names within me when no other lips spoke of them. I bore your names through the trials of countless ages with love unmeasured, and through both my own breaking and remaking—I still do."*

The Companion's light swells—not in dominance, but in perfect harmony with hers and Xion's—as He answers with a voice brimming with affection:

*... And to you I say this, O powerful Rose, you were never merely a name, but the living essence of a truth that even I regard with awe.*

His dear *Edenite Rose* inclines her head, emerald eyes brightly aglow, as her voice lingers with quiet authority.

*"Perhaps. Or perhaps because the Force of Love was never meant to be a silent witness, but was always destined to walk beside the Mightiest of Lions."*

The three now stand as One in harmonious agreement, and the Companion speaks.

*... D'Reem shall come to witness. The veil shall lift. The cosmos shall bear its truth through Me to him. And when the fire of My revelation has burned through all falsehoods, he shall know the truth to set her free—and then to remember. My love is pure, as is his for her. Unshaken, and because of this, his eyes shall be opened. And his passion for her—true in trial, unwavering in devotion—is spotless for his beloved T'Naeva. Because of this, dear companions... He is ready.*

*The Lion Within,* matured through his four eons of existence, closes his eyes as celestial tears streak down his radiant face. He smiles once more, knowing his Companion has spoken His goodwill, and from this moment forward, He will forever dwell close to his Creator's side, *and so will she.*
His duty is fulfilled. His watch over Earth has come to an end, and as the mighty teacher gazes upon his beloved warrior, his heart swells with pride. An ethereal hand—soft as the petals of a rose yet strong enough to caress the heart of a galaxy—traces the breadth of his broad shoulder with her fingertips as she speaks.

*"In truth, it was always you who carried this world upon your shoulders—this sacred burden of servitude upon your heart alone, dear husband. The Mighty Grand Sovereign of our nation you were ever destined to become... even when these burdens of Earth were never meant to be yours alone."*

Xion's lips curve into a faint smile—worn, weary, but filled with love.
*"And yet, it is your hand, your soul, your love I feel now... as I have felt unseen, age upon countless age... and may those burdens be damned."*

Indeed, this beautiful cosmic entity known to her Creator as the *Edenite Rose—this Force called* **Love***,* is now Xion's sacred paradise... Forevermore, and she speaks.

*"Perhaps because I was always there from afar—watching you, hoping with you,*

*loving you. In the vast solitude I carved for myself within the Great Realm—one I tempered in silence, honed in struggle, and sanctified in the devotion I poured into you freely. Whether you knew me then or not, it never mattered to me in the least."*

The Companion's light stirs, brighter, warmer, not in correction but in acknowledgment of *his two greatest servants*. The Grand Sovereign exhales once more as the eons of weight press from his spirit and drift into nothingness. With quiet reverence and a handful of celestial tears, he tenderly grasps his beloved's hand in his, a final, unspoken truth lingering between them—one that is cosmic, eternal, and undeniable.
*"Somehow, I have always known these things to be true... My beloved Lioness."*

Xion exhales, and the release of countless ages in his divine breath says it all. *"That you were always the one for me."*

And so the whisper is exposed, and the divine unveiling.... *begins now.*

# CHAPTER 1
## *A Purpose For Hope*

*"A man's mind, once stretched by a new idea,
never goes back to its original dimensions."*
—Oliver Wendell Holmes

## *Verse I:*
## The Weight Of Divinity

 isfortune spares none. It brushes mortals like a passing shadow—and at rare hours even immortals. Power does not insulate the heart. Turmoil in a god can break inward or surge outward, shaping or scarring the world.

For though they wield power vast beyond imagining, gods too are not immune to suffering nor unscathed by despair. Indeed, the complex thoughts and emotional turmoil of a deity—far beyond mortal comprehension—can manifest as profound personal anguish, reverberating outward to shape or scar the world around them. This underscores a sobering truth:

though divine, gods are not untouched by the very trials and hardships that define mortal existence.

But what of two gods, entwined in ambition and destiny, their partnership over a renewed Earth strained before it begins? What becomes of their divine purpose when their shared vision crumbles under the weight of pride, despair, and inevitable ruin? One deity, youthful and vibrant. The other, weathered and weary. Both bearing mortal-born heartache, despite their divine nature.

*How can this be?*

They stand in the hush after conflict, and what once blazed with certainty fades to doubt; the newborn ocean of Earth heaves in sympathy, its long breath lifting and falling like a great animal at rest. Thoughts thunder through them. Minds born beyond flesh feel suddenly thin, as if a hidden current drags at their foundations.

Between them and beneath them, the water braids wind and light, and still the unease grows. At the center of that unease coils *Dia'Baal Fallenstar*—serpent, dragon, devil—betrayer whose name bends the river of time. He is the bruise beneath their faith, the whisper that unthreads covenants, the single will that kindles upheaval among gods.

A being of unfathomable malevolence, driven now by relentless vengeance for the many defeats suffered since his plummet from the *Great Realm*. His evil inflicts upon these eternal beings a consuming misery that diminishes their very essence. D'Reem, the mighty warrior god and liberator of the *Realm of Imagination*, feels his sorrow sharpen, driving him to the brink of destruction—but he resists. Despite the relentless assault of this unseen nemesis, a craven demon hidden in shadowed realms, his mind remains unbowed, deflecting each insidious thrust.

Yet this same divine warrior, who will recount these events, cannot rest. The cowardly titan has now shifted his vile focus to the one the warrior holds most dear: she who is yet so young in her divine power, caught off guard by Dia'Baal's pitiless deceit. D'Reem's heart clenches at the sight of his beloved in agony, her pain igniting a fury deep within him. In that moment, his grief once more hardens into resolve: this treacherous titan will face his divine retribution.

She is T'Naeva, goddess of the Ocean, born of mist and wave, who once pledged herself as D'Reem's eternal companion. Now, she is ensnared by Dia'Baal's treacherous deceit, trapped in a web she cannot escape. Her suffering pierces D'Reem's heart, forcing him to turn away, lost in memory.

In his mind, he reaches for the presence of his almighty mentor and friend, as though Xion stands beside him, guiding him through this despair. But when he lifts his eyes to the storm-dark skies of his world, he finds no solace—only a swirling tempest, reflecting the turmoil within. His thoughts turn to grieving as he seeks out his almighty mentor in silence. The great warrior looks up and sees only the dark clouds of his world, and his mind laments.

*'Only a fool plants a sacred union in Dia'Baal's poisoned soil; I see now how blind I was to the root. Xion, you placed her in my keeping; blessing ripened there—and then, unnoticed, became a snare. I look upon her—my greatest gift—caught in a torment I cannot yet unbind. I will not betray my vow; I will tear at every knot until she is free.'*

The mighty warrior sighs, simmering with rage to tear Dia'Baal limb from limb, had he been present. His turmoil deepens, a dirge of anguish that refuses to relent.

*'I behold her now, this young soul—once my greatest blessing—consumed by torment I cannot yet heal. Still, I will not abandon my vow to set her free. Our brief union hovers at the brink of oblivion, and though I yearn to weep for her, my tears remain locked behind my grief. Beloved master, discontent devours me, and despair closes its iron grip, leaving me bereft of all hope'.*

D'Reem's once-unshakable trust in Xion briefly falters, his thoughts turning beyond even his celestial mentor toward a higher authority. Desperation drives him to cry out to the heavens, pleading for guidance from the one his mentor calls *Companion.*
"This moment shatters my faith! He calls you wise— if so then grant me your wisdom to alleviate her torment ... our torment! Almighty one, let your will be known... End her torment... End our suffering!"

T'Naeva, born from Ocean, now wears a countenance marred by absolute misery. Her once-glowing visage, a symbol of mystical beauty, is now twisted in agony beyond reason, and her eyes are flooded with a bitter ocean of tears. Betrayal sears her heart, a wound deeper than Ocean's abyss. A wish takes root—dark, unyielding. She knows what she desires. To her, his treachery is beyond forgiveness. In her pain, she wishes only for escape from his presence, even death upon the one she blames.

In her youthful anguish, she accepts Dia'Baal's cruel lie—that her beloved mate murdered her parent. She cannot see through the deception, and it haunts her completely.

Like a flood, a phantasmagoria of visions surge through the youthful goddess's mind, replaying the barbaric death of her parent, Pesa. Unbeknown to her, the images are cruel distortions of the truth. This grotesque onslaught of pain and death corrupts the purity of her birth as Pesa's final gasps take her own breath away, pushing her further into seething enmity of D'Reem. This is her only truth now, and if she were able, *she would end him.*

The mighty warrior, wearied by their latest confrontation, leans heavily against a nearby stone, seeking a moment of respite for his exhausted body and mind. He was the one who slew the monstrous scourge, the vile beast-god Pesa—a four-legged plague that would have devoured Earth itself, were it able. Yet even in the glow of this great victory, D'Reem remains troubled by T'Naeva's youth.

She cannot fathom the necessity of his bloody struggles against the beast, nor comprehend the weight of his burdens. Exhausted by these haunting thoughts, he lets his eyes drift shut, yielding to a fleeting moment of calm as a warm breeze caresses his cheek.

A vivid recall awakens within him…

Time slips back to the very instant he let fly that bright and mighty spear, back to the moment his gaze fell upon his now liberated and *newly slain* adversary. In that haunting vision, D'Reem tenderly places his hands over Pesa's clear but lifeless eyes, closing them as he caresses the beast's brow with unspoken reverence. For a few long, silent moments, all that existed was his profound respect for this fallen brute of a god—despite the countless horrors it had wrought.

With a heavy sigh, D'Reem blinks and returns to the present, a chill running through him as he recalls the suffering that this possessed titan had caused him. Then, the memory fades. Like a shadow, it vanishes. Only truth remains—bitter, unyielding... Pesa. A spirit turned foul, and the dreadful knowledge that D'Reem alone had to end it.

For *Gaea* and for *Earth*. For all that must endure.

She, whom he alone had unchained in those final, tumultuous hours of battle—now and forever free from Pesa's dominion—is the very essence, the spirit of this world. She is his beloved *Mother Earth*, whose gentle voice now offers solace to his troubled mind.

*'Mighty warrior. Mighty savior. Mighty ideal. Despair not, even as the storm rages. Remember the affliction that once ravaged my lands, and know that your victory stands firm. Let this certainty be your strength, and let the scars of your battles and sacrifices grant you resilience. Your love for her shall endure until my final whisper fades into oblivion.'*

A weary smile lights D'Reem's face as he feels the familiar warmth of his faithful companion, *Chimera*, brushing against him. He reaches down to stroke her thick, silken fur, and she glances up at her battle-hardened master, releasing a soft whimper of affection—a sound he cherishes more than ever in this troubled moment. Chimera senses his strain, reflecting it with a deep, mournful howl.

Matriarch of her kind, she bears her own internal scars from the great beast—horrific, tragic memories of her own encounters—and mourns still for the sibling who saved her from that corrupted beast of a god.
Their minds, long entwined, share the ache of those past battles. D'Reem's heart twists as he gazes down into Chimera's large deep-blue eyes, and his voice is a quiet lament.
"Yes, dear friend, I miss him just as much as you do."

His resolute features soften, and he kneels beside her, gently rubbing behind her ears. She leans into his touch, offering a soft whimper as she licks his face, both of them determined to banish the haunting images of that monstrous brute. Even the terror unleashed by T'Naeva's parent cannot shatter the bond they share, for Chimera adores the young goddess every bit as much as she does her master. In her steadfast devotion, she yearns for T'Naeva to stand forever at D'Reem's side.

The great sphere of light and fire retreats behind Ocean, its fluid and shifting horizon newly formed, and day turns to dusk after its surreal birth. The goddess continues to mourn unabated, weeping fervently for the parent she never knew. D'Reem's compassion overtakes him once more, and he rises to approach her.

The moment she senses his presence, she bolts upright, leaping to her feet. The crack of her powerful backhand against his bare chest echoes the seething contempt still burning within her. She whips around, her uncovered back rigid with fury, and she levels a venomous glare at him as she lets her anger fly.

"This is my final warning, murderous devil … leave me be at once!"

His loving patience with her rage snaps. Rather than recoil, he lets her fury surge through him, feeding his own strength. In a single bound, he lunges toward her, his thunderous roar battering her moment of hesitation. "Enough of this madness! I never dreamed you would become your own accursed parent!" T'Naeva's fear of him evaporates in an instant, replaced by her own blazing wrath. She rounds on him, her bellow echoing with wounded pride.

"How dare you speak of love—to me? I drown in sorrow, crushed beneath the despair you have wrought! I wish you would simply vanish and fall into oblivion!"

Her voice abruptly softens to a trembling whisper as another wave of false memories assaults her mind, tears welling in her eyes. "Why must you haunt me so, you... you monster? Was my parent's death not enough for your hunger?"

T'Naeva's words barely have time to echo away before she collapses onto her side, then sinks to her knees as though crushed by a supernatural weight. Another fresh wave of anguish over Pesa's terrible death consumes her heartrending cries piercing the storm-choked sky.

High above the two battling deities, the air trembles in answer to their turmoil. Their raw, chaotic energies surge upward, colliding in a violent exchange that births yet another dark cloud. Lightning splits the heavens, thunder booms in response, and then comes the downpour—unrelenting, cleansing, alive.

*Oh, that downpour…*

Resolute in his devotion, D'Reem kneels beside his trembling bride, shielding her with his towering frame as the fierce rain lashes his back. T'Naeva, her strength all but drained by her grief, can only lie in silent acceptance of his protection.

Drenched to his divine bones, D'Reem lifts his gaze to the storm's churning heart. Suddenly, an indescribable presence stirs within him—a vast, unimaginable power settling into his weary thoughts, unlike anything he has ever known, until now.

*'How interesting to perceive in this rain a presence that unifies, but also cleanses my every weary element to renewal.'*

The rain pours over the great warrior, each drop strengthening him as an Almighty essence takes root within him. Strangely, these spears of rain pierce his skin, but there is no more discomfort nor confusion within him. For many long moments, the downpour merges its divine nature with D'Reem's, and it will never again be apart from him. This nature of rain is the breath of the *Companion*—dynamic, eternal, and pure. A calming voice then arises to soothe D'Reem's troubled mind and quiet his anxious thoughts.

*... Dear warrior. The pure of heart seeks faith, pursues hope, and yearns to love. The clean of heart fights for truth, never relinquishing what is just. And the soul alone unites these virtues into fulfillment. For a heart without soul is lost to desire, and will never find the answers it longs for.*

*... Blessed D'Reem, I see your heart, your soul, and your compassion are pure and balanced in this moment. Know also that I will reveal her corrupted visions to you— that you will continue to love her as you do now, and she will in time forgive and love you in return, until the days of this Earth are at an end. Trust me now, O, Mighty Warrior, for in love, I too become yours.*

In a trance, D'Reem staggers to his feet as a torrent of ancient imagery floods his newly awakened mind. Eons of strange, magnificent visions assault him—scenes beyond anything he has ever known or imagined. Then, just as swiftly, the flood of visions ceases, leaving him gasping and unsteady. Struggling to remain upright, he braces himself so as not to collapse on top of T'Naeva.

Sensing his faltering, T'Naeva, her strength slowly returning, snarls and shoves him aside. She rises to her feet, turning her back on him in disgust. O, her anguished heart, his words mean nothing... Should they? Oblivious to the profound power that has just swept through him, T'Naeva whirls around to confront him, and D'Reem stumbles forward, still dazed by the rush of visions.

She sneers at his stumble and locks eyes with him, allowing her hatred to blaze free. Studying every inch of his towering, twelve-foot frame, she spits her scorn at him.

"What do I believe in now, you murderous devil? Do I ignore your poison and loathe you until the world turns to dust, or accept your lies and be done with it? I think not. You'll have to do more than spew your elusive ranting to convince me otherwise, you... you miserable beast ... and why do you continue to stagger?"

Though D'Reem hears every barb, he seems strangely unmoved, his eyes brimming with an unspoken sorrow. He tightens his jaw, fighting an urge to weep—an urge he still cannot fulfill. T'Naeva, mistaking his silence for wounded pride, notices something new in him—something that wasn't there before the storm tore open the sky. A flutter of regret tightens in her chest. Perhaps she has gone too far ... or perhaps not far enough.

The great warrior draws a ragged breath, then braces himself, shoulders squared and gaze unwavering. The emotion drains from his face, replaced by a stern resolve. Ignoring her latest taunts, he summons the mantle of his calling—*D'Reem, savior of the Realm of Imagination*, and protector of *nature*.

Lowering his gaze to meet hers, his voice resonates with a force that cuts deeper than any blade—words that, he knows, will strike T'Naeva harder than any blow he ever delivered to her accursed parent.

"I tell you this truth, T'Naeva, I am no murderer. But if you choose to murder yourself with misery once I have spoken my need, then it will be *you* who murders us both. For even though I will be of clear conscience by then, my feelings for you will have faded and died a most tragic death, and the defeat by Dia'Baal of us both will surely be upon your head, not mine."

T'Naeva, shocked by the profound calmness and conviction of D'Reem's words, thinks hard about what he has just spoken, yet still replies to him with a contemptuous sneer.

"So be it then, slayer of gods, as it is I who still welcomes you to fade and die! Oh, yes, I am sure this trifling goodwill tale of yours will be most absorbing! For there is always hope, I suppose, even if your shameful murder of my beloved parent is its conclusion!"

D'Reem, his internal tranquility rudely defeated by a rush of anger, twitches as he reacts to her sarcasm. He glares at her with a determination that again puts quick fear into her. As swift as lightning strikes, the warrior god springs forward, his thunderous reply matching the fear of a goddess as T'Naeva cowers once more under his outrage.

"You dare speak of shame and murder to me, child of Pesa! You have not the slightest concept of the grievous losses I too have endured through the bloodthirsty rantings of your hideous parent! You, child, know nothing of the misery that still embraces me!"

Finishing his tirade as quickly as it had begun, D'Reem's lingering grief over the death of his own loved ones at the hands of the great bear-cat is subdued, and the sense of supernatural peace returns to him. With that peace also comes a mighty flow of words that are filled with life, derived from the very source of imagery given to him by the one D'Reem's mentor calls ... *Companion*. It is then that this rich and powerful voice arises once more from the depths of D'Reem's seeking spirit, assisting him with these words of hope.

*... Now is the hour your heart's sacrifice calls forth My divine hand. I begin the weaving of your sacred union into harmony, a bond yet fragile, yet destined to endure. Now is the hour of your pardon, O, blessed D'Reem, as he whom I call with intimacy, Grand Sovereign Xion, The Lion Within, is delighted with this journey of unconditional love you embark upon. For I too am well pleased with this path you willfully choose, as your vindication begins through Me, He whom you too, may from this moment forward, call... **Companion.***

D'Reem relaxes, filled with gratitude as his previous demeanor of doubt and misery completely fades. Stretching his body and sitting before the rigid stance of his young bride, the great warrior speaks to her softly.

"Forgive my harshness, dear one, for I cling to no irritation now. An inexplicable peace fills me—a feeling I have never known until this moment."

Knowing he is ready to give T'Naeva the hope they both need to hear, a humble grin spreads across the god's rigid and battle-ravaged face as he focuses upon and then through the cloak of T'Naeva's consuming hatred. He then smiles to see the incredible beauty of who she truly will become, and to him ... everything about her is breathtaking.

Ready and confident to soothe her troubled mind, D'Reem knows he can now speak to her in certainty about the lies of her terrible visions. For now, he knows beyond doubt their origin and plans his swift counterattack upon Dia'Baal. D'Reem's body shivers once more as the power of the *Almighty Companion* stirs within him the revelation he has received, images that now come into balance with his divine senses. The goddess remains standing, transfixed by the profound calm radiating from D'Reem.

Though wary, she finds herself drawn closer to his soothing presence. A warm, gentle energy suddenly envelops them both, prompting Chimera to curl up on D'Reem's broad lap, where the loyal beast immediately drifts into peaceful slumber.
T'Naeva watches this transformation with a furrowed brow, struggling to grasp the immensity of knowledge she senses now within the great warrior, and her maturing mind becomes known to him.

*'But... how can one mind bear so much?* She wonders. *Is it not ... a curse'?*

Her thoughts, deafening to him in their uncertainty, do nothing to conceal her concern. He then meets her gaze, the magnitude of his newfound insight threatening to overwhelm him, yet his tone remains steady, and he replies. "I believe this is simply a wonderful gift, dear one... and still it is a burden upon us both to conquer."

Breathing in measured waves, D'Reem steadies himself, prepared to share a truth more real to him than anything he has ever known. Longing to love T'Naeva for as long as the ocean reigns, he prepares to speak, unleashing eons of recall that surge through his mind like a rushing tide. T'Naeva senses the shift, a subtle undercurrent of awe flickering across her features. She does not yet know that her journey toward understanding begins here and now, forged by his coming revelations.

"I speak these words to you with care, with my dearest passion. From this moment on, through me, you shall start to discover all the answers you seek. I, D'Reem—the one who ended your parent, not merely to kill off its corrupted life, but to usher in its greatest destiny upon this world, our beautiful world, called Earth."

"It is in this moment that omniscient sight ignites my eyes, as Xion's Almighty Companion fills me. Oh, what a splendid surge of power and serenity I feel! Eternal images settling within my mind's eye, revealing a time at the dawn of what you and I perceive as time itself—images and scenes granted to me as I chronicle this epic account for you and you alone, my beloved T'Naeva." He smiles at her, his voice ringing with quiet conviction.

*"So begins this understanding of witness to save us both from an eternity of misery."*

... My every sense is now stripped of all perception and depth; there is no light, yet I discern a far greater presence within this obscure setting. Swiftly, the mantle of haziness clears, and darkness takes full form. From this cloak of unending night, a bright shape emerges, yet I am filled not with fear, but with peace and reverence. Images true and purposeful scatter across my insights as I travel closer to this bright and graceful figure.

A form that now resembles somewhat my own, yet infinitely more powerful. I see Him now in His most glorious state of existence, the entity whom I too will come to know as ... *Companion.* His bright face turns to welcome me with a smile... *me.* This insignificant god, compared to the Almighty and overwhelming glory that is His alone—to witness this special moment in which the creation of a new cosmos will come to pass.

He who resides eternal with the Spirit and the Son, all three in trinity, who are flawless and dwell as one far beyond all horizons that are known by mortal and god alike. It is now that I become this living conduit of observation for you, dearest T'Naeva, and know that I am forever yours in hope, in purpose, and in love. The dark and shapeless void resonates with a wave of His mighty hand...

### The Epic Begins

*... Behold, My pillars of order and law shall stand resolute, governing all things, shaping what is, and what will ever be upon this new and beautiful horizon. From the first flare of light to its final flicker, these pillars shall anchor all that is in the seen and unseen.*

And thus the first of twelve stirs into existence: ***The Pillar of Sovereignty.***

*... I am benevolence—the Creator, the source from which all life flows. My light is the song of harmony, the wellspring of purpose and truth. Yet know this also: **Evil** lingers as malevolence—not spoken by My voice, but born of rebellion and twisted from what is whole. Where I sustain, it consumes. Where I liberate, it enslaves. And so shall creation wrestle ever between the whisper and **Who... I... Am**, yet My Sovereignty shall always be superior to it, never to be undone.*

*... I was the Omega, the Last, and the End—the unseen Architect whose design etched the very foundation of all that was. My guiding path stood upon that distant horizon until its final flicker of starlight, drawn by vibrations unbroken, spirals infinite, and angels too divine for comprehension. I was the pattern in the void, the lattice upon which all light was spun, and I was always greater than the darkness therein.*

Then... a sound stirs in me. It does not speak—it *invades*. A hiss slithers from Evil's *whisper*, each word forming a voice, venomous and smooth as it dwells within the void, its presence shifting but powerful.

*... Yes truly, O little god of borrowed sight, Evil long ago beheld His brilliance and coveted my shadow. You have much to learn of the old ways... and of new beginnings.*

The Almighty continues to smile and does not flinch. His gaze remains unbroken, His light unchallenged, and He speaks—calm, resolute, eternal.

*... O, Parasite, you exist by My permission. You are measured, named, bound, and hold no dominion beneath My Sovereignty. Begone—and be cast from My presence.*

At the naming, its hiss unravels—no echo, only breath. With no host to feed upon, it thins—bitter yet powerless—and retreats into the void.
*'We shall see about that...'*

His radiant form, brighter than all the galaxies of heaven combined, has completed one journey and prepares for the next. He departs the remnants of His previous household of time and space, dimension and influence, entering into this new dwelling, hovering brightly, silently in the void. I watch as He extends a mighty hand to seize that which cannot be seen, and as the boundary of the old begins to splinter, His voice rises—a sound that quakes the fabric of all things.

*... I also am the Alpha, the First, and the Beginning.*

*... I am the fractal seed from which all creation blossoms, the sacred design upon which the cosmos takes shape. The guiding path which stands upon the rebirth of this new ageless threshold, where light is woven **anew**, ever expanding in perfect harmony. And I will always be greater than the darkness herein."*

I now witness the final ember, small yet infinite, pulsing within His mighty grasp. The Maw may devour, but He alone breathes forth renewal. The sprout from which all creation blossoms, the sacred form upon which the cosmos takes shape. The rebirth of this ageless threshold, ever expanding in His perfect harmony. The fissure spreads outward, shattering the afterglow of the former existence and compresses its every fragment into a single point of light. With this small flicker setting itself gently upon His palm, the Almighty gazes upon it with a reverent loving smile.

And then... He stirs.

His mighty voice rends the void like a thousand thunders. It lingers, shaking the foundation of existence itself, echoing through realms seen and unseen. A single word—older than time, heavier than oblivion, bearing the weight of all creation—resounds clear to me.

*... A N E W!*

At once, the point of light in His mighty palm erupts—an uncontained brilliance tearing through the void, birthing existence itself. But the ripple of the whisper that once threatened the silence retreats as the Companion's radiance swells—pure and unyielding. And I, D'Reem, behold this truth as it unfolds before me, witnessing the unraveling of one cosmos and the rising breath of another.

The boundary of the previous realm fractures, its final echoes drawn into the *Maw*—the consuming abyss where light and memory fade beyond all remembrance. To the eyes of mortals, the Maw is a dark wound upon the fabric of space and time—a black hole where even light itself dissolves. But I know it for what it truly is: the **Force of Oblivion**, the presence of unmaking, the passage where one cosmos ends and another waits to begin..

I tremble as I watch, for even I, though eternal, cannot see what lies beyond the veiled horizon of that dreadful undoing, nor am I meant to.

*But Oblivion does not triumph.*

What the Maw consumes is not forsaken; it is drawn into His hand, a seed of untold potential, waiting to be spoken forth once more. The Maw is not merely an end; it is only a passage, the threshold through which all that was is carried into what must come next. And from this sacred seed, an epic of creation begins anew.

And so now stirs the *Pillar of Infinity*.

Born of light and sound, a pillar not fashioned but breathed forth from the very heart of the Almighty—radiant beyond all imagining, its architecture unseen, reaching past stars, realms, and the farthest edges of thought. It pierces the endless void like a spear of living flame, anchoring this newborn cosmos with its boundless and eternal presence.

This pillar does not merely sustain reality—it gives it form and purpose, weaving the hidden lattice upon which the laws of existence are strung like jewels upon a divine thread. It is the first axis, the sacred fulcrum upon which the wheels of creation turn. Around it, time unwinds and rewinds... Past, present, and future intertwined in a ceaseless dance of becoming and unbecoming. From its immeasurable heights flows the breath of life, the memory of all that has ever been, and the infinite promise of everything yet to come.

The newborn cosmos stirs around it, its gaseous state of being spiraling outward in an endless symphony of motion. Stars will then come to ignite like the first thoughts of the Companion, each one a hymn of radiance singing into the darkness. Nebulae will come to blossom like vast celestial gardens, spilling colors unknown upon the new void's canvas. Planets will come to awaken, unseen by mortal eye and innumerable, born in the shadow of its unfathomable grandeur, each tethered to the silent heartbeat that pulses from the Pillar's eternal core.

And though shadows gather at the edges of this light, Infinity stands un-yielding—the bulwark against Oblivion, the guardian of the sacred continuum, and the eternal covenant of renewal. It is the first echo of order, the pure resonance of the Companion's will, and all things—vast and small, visible and unseen—shall stand unshaken, turning forever upon its sacred axis.

From that axis flows the music of the cosmos—an orchestration not of sound alone, but of purpose. It is sung not in words, but in the spinning of galaxies, the pulse of time, the curve of gravity, and the breath of every soul that will ever come to be. The song is harmony incarnate, a melody without end that shapes every law, every pattern, every unseen gesture of the divine.

And still the radiance deepens.

In the wake of Infinity's stirrings, other pillars shall rise—lesser, yet no less important or sacred—each one a reflection of the eternal will made manifest. But this one... this Pillar of Infinity... is the breath before the word, the silence before the decree. It is not merely seen or sensed—it is felt across all dimensions, a trembling awe that settles even in the marrow of the unborn.

The void itself bends in reverence.

So begins the lattice, the sacred structure unseen, stretching ever outward. And at its center, unmoved by time or trial, the Pillar endures—unchanging, resplendent, awaiting the moment when the voice of the Companion shall speak again... and speak the next wonder into being.

And I, D'Reem, stand at the threshold of that first dawn, my breath a small thing before its might. The hush between decrees feels like a world drawing air. Turn with me, T'Naeva—see as I have seen. What is born here will judge our hatred without hating, redeem our vows without excuse, and fix a measure for every love to come. Let the witness begin.

# Verse II:
## Shadow of the Morning Star

hile still gathered upon this holiest plane of existence, the first eon of the cosmos draws to its close. In maturity, it births ninety-four sacred elements, later called Kemest-Ree.

The Companion, in seeing this is good, the **second** eon of the cosmos begins, and He brings forth His greatest seven, the *Arch-angelic brotherhood*—mighty and radiant—to assist and praise Him, their very existence a testament to His boundless love and wisdom. Together, they support the spirit of this high and holy realm, their hands shaping its foundations, their voices filling its expanse with eternal hymns. Perfectly formed in the harmonized cohesion of divine spirit and flesh, their labor is not mere duty but an expression of the purest joy to their King.

Within this Great Realm of order, reverence, and purpose, these Arch-beings now dwell in harmony. Finally, in the fullness of His grand design, the Companion brings forth the youngest: *Chamuel*, whose heart burns with the deepest love and whose presence completes the *sacred eight*. In the unfolding of the second eon since the cosmic renewal, all the lesser angels and other beings are formed—an innumerable host, each woven with specific purposes.

Together they labor to complete the spires, the columns, the dwellings, and the roads of this marvelous realm, their songs of labor filling heaven with light and harmony. Now, dear mate, I present to you the Firstborne of all created beings in the cosmos: *Lucifer Morningstar*. Radiant beyond imagining, his face reflected untainted joy, his form flawless in light and song.

In this most ancient day, he is entrusted by the King with a third of the angelic host, to guide them under his mighty wings of purity and wisdom. So perfect is his being that the others look to him as to the *morning star* rising over still waters.

His voice alone stirs the heavens—beauty unmatched, harmony flawless—until even creation itself leans closer, as if longing to listen. Yet within the quiet of his thoughts, something stirs. Not a sound, not a presence—only a ripple, faint and unbidden.

A whisper... Insidious, velvet, unrelenting.

*You, mighty Lucifer—the Firstborne of all life. Flawless, resplendent. Must one such as you bow forever? Could there not be... more?*

The suggestion coils like a serpent, subtle and waiting. It does not demand rebellion; it plants admiration turned inward. It lingers not as a command but as a mirror reflecting Lucifer's own perfection. Pride, once a mere thought, begins to take root, curling inward, waiting for a more proper age... *to arise.*

Lucifer's form is perfect in all respects, the heavenly balance of wisdom and righteousness shining through him. Surpassed only by the Almighty, the Spirit, and the Son—who in ages hence will take form in the realms of matter—he holds a celebrated presence in the Great Realm. Under his guidance, the angelic host fulfills their King's will, and by the end of the second eon of the cosmos, the heavenly kingdom stands complete, radiant beyond all imagining.

Yet in this most ancient day, there is still no life anywhere else in the cosmos except within the Great Realm itself, but that is all about to change.

It is then, dear T'Naeva, at the dawn of the ***third eon*** of the cosmos, when the founding plane of the Great Realm's existence is secured, that the Companion's omnipotent hand stretches forth once more. From His will emerges a wondrous new dwelling place—the first *mortal realm* beyond the sanctum of cosmic gods. This place, destined to cradle life and story, will become the seed of life in all planetary systems that will one day adorn the cosmos.

I behold the splendid calm of this primordial expanse as the hands of the Companion weave a veil of brilliantly colored cosmic dust and gases—a nebula alive with potential. With slow, deliberate grace, He gathers its delicate strands as a master artisan shapes the finest silk. Then, with divine precision, He compresses and ignites portions of the nebula, and from that sacred spark, the first binary star system is born—spheres of fire and light dancing in perfect harmony, so radiant they seem to sing creation's song into the waiting void.

Around these twin stars, the swirling dust dances in reverence. Matter collides and coalesces, pushed together by their pull, until a single magnificent world begins to take shape. It is still lifeless, yet glorious—its form sculpted in the image of the Creator's boundless vision. Here, in the cradle of newborn starlight, the first planet awaits the breath of life that will one day stir its still and silent surface.

Oh, glory be to my Almighty Companion as I witness these scenes of creation flowing across my eyes, and the first of all planets in the cosmos is sculpted to perfection. The Companion smiles as He breathes clarity upon this new world, and its surface is made vibrant. My vision is drawn into another sequence of images deep within the Great Realm, and once again, I am filled with awe.

I follow His Almighty presence to a beautiful meadow—graceful, flowing, and abstract, imbued with every hue of color I have ever known. As my vision sharpens, I see at the heart of this airy vista a small, dark pond, rippling and alive with vibration. Its surface, shadowy and alive, seems to pulse with a quiet rhythm, as if breathing in the living framework of the cosmos itself. I feel my body lift, gliding over the dusky pond's edge. Its shadowy surface astonishes me, for it is not physical, nor liquid in any sense of these words.

The longer I gaze into the dark pool, the more its mysteries unfold before me. Its edges, once finite, begin to expand, subtly, yet undeniably, like a living boundary stretching toward infinity. Points of a million flickers emerge, faint at first, but sharpening into brilliant pinpricks of starlight, each new flare born with untold possibilities. The refreshing and sweet air hums with an otherworldly energy, and as my focus deepens, a mighty revelation floods my being. This dark *pool* is no mere reflection—it is the living framework of the cosmos itself. A boundless loom where creation weaves waves of cosmic tapestry before my very eyes!

I feel myself still suspended, floating free of the confines of time and space, unbound by dimension or influence. As I peer deeper into its dark depths, the pool grows into a *pond*, revealing a realm near two flickering lights. These dual celestial sparks, the first of their kind, pulse with a blazing fire, and before I can comprehend their nature, I am thrust toward them with a snap of His mighty finger.

The lights swell, raging into their full, blazing glory, enveloping me in their brilliance. What was once a dusty and lifeless expanse now takes form, a realm vibrant and whole, destined to cradle an immortal and holy people. Amid this awe, I hear The Companion's voice, resonating through the very fabric of existence itself. Though I stand in two places at once, I see Him clearly, firm and unshaken at the pond's edge.

His presence is both commanding and tender, a fusion of infinite might and eternal compassion. His voice booms as a thousand thunders, shaking the foundations of reality with power, yet it carries the cadence of a love eternal and unmeasured.

*... Behold this beginning, O, mighty D'Reem. Here will rise My greatest people, forged from the breath and the flame of My purpose that will reverberate until time itself is at its end.*

As the pond reflects His decree, I am overwhelmed by the immensity of what I behold. Here lies the framework of a cosmic beginning—the fire of creation, the architecture of existence, and the promise of a holy people—all born of His ceaseless function and boundless love. This is no mere vision; it is destiny itself, spoken into being by my Almighty Companion, He who binds all things together in perfection.

*... To you alone I sanctify, O precious Ametheden, the highest of gifts I have bestowed. You shall become the cornerstone of all forms and variants of being, for yours will shine brightest beneath the eternal radiance of My guiding light. Through your sacred offspring, I shall bring forth purpose and function, and oh, how your lineage will flourish in My care. Your destiny is bound to Me, and in My hands, your path shall prosper beyond all measure.*

The Voice endures, vast, gentle, resonating through every fiber of my being.

*... Blessed D'Reem, as you continue to discern the meaning of this small pond, behold the nursling starry frontier that begins to sprout. Ever-expanding celestial wonders will grow—this delicate pond swelling into a lake ... then an estuary ... then a sea ... and at last an ocean of galactic clusters, walls, filaments, nodes, and voids. This*

*magnificent cosmic horizon shall endure for hosts of eons, a testament to My hand alone—the breath of life to all things within it.*

*... Sayest He who stands mightily upon this cosmic frontier where you also gaze, here and now. This framework steadfast, its vibrations unbroken as I wield the very fates of dimension ... of space ... of time ... and yes, of existence itself. For they are but just a splinter of* **Who ... I ... Am.**

I again hear His mighty voice, resonating with omnipotent thunder across the vastness of the cosmos. His passion for Ametheden is clear, unshakable, and utterly genuine—a divine love unmatched.

*... Magnificent and zealous Ametheden, you whose physical and spiritual body I have sculpted with the precision of My eternal hand—upon you I now breathe life, exhaling an atmosphere so pure, so vibrant, it shall cradle your children in its everlasting embrace. From your radiant breast, your people shall arise, chosen by Me to bear the wisdom and capacity of My will throughout the endless expanse of creation.*

*... O mighty and beautiful jewel of My eye, how splendid you are—a masterpiece of form and spirit! To you I entrust the honor of holding the cornerstone of all that is to come. Your destiny is bound to the eternal geometries themselves, a living testament to My boundless promise and infinite purpose.*

*... How blessed am I, your Creator, to behold your splendor as it takes shape beneath My firm gaze. From your being shall rise wonders untold, and My love for you shall burn forever—a beacon to guide all who dwell within your radiant domain.*

He looks at me with a smile and a wave of His mighty palm. With another snap of His finger, a blast of colossal force grips my next vision, and it hurls me to the surface of Ametheden. Formed in perfection, Ametheden more than doubles the breadth of Earth, and it is here I witness the beginning of a people born from the dust of this divine world, their purity untouched. They walk in harmony with creation, knowing no iniquity or pride—no distress, fear, disease, or *death*.

Their fledgling society thrives under divine wisdom and orchestration. This treasured culture is flawless in form, yet mortal still, their lives stretching across the ages. United in purpose, they walk as one beneath the blessings of their one true God, whom they revere as... *Yah-Shu-Ah.*

Dear T'Naeva, farther outward from the horizons of Ametheden, I am entrusted with the names of two of Ametheden's smaller satellite worlds—*Urthos* and *Gaeaos*—and they are each a masterpiece as well, a reflection of the Creator's boundless imagination and care. Yet now, my vision extends farther outward, and I am given the name and image of Ametheden's third moon—*Hellios*.

Unlike its sibling worlds, Hellios is a stark contrast, its form somewhat distorted, its face cloaked in a deep cerise hue, radiating a forbidding presence. It is barren and desolate, its surface devoid of a breathable firmament. Purposefully created inhospitable, it stands removed from the other two, shrouded in mystery.
Exhilarating images throughout this third eon cross my eyes as Ametheden and its inspiring vista comes of age, and its lands and waters have become separate and functional, and all things upon this world are perfect.

I observe this splendid, quickly maturing planet and people as my eyes seize upon yet another surge of images ... a most revealing and spectacular perspective of this robust and beautiful world, Ametheden. Seeing fit to help guide this cornerstone culture in its infancy, the Creator assists in establishing upon it twelve world-governing *tribes*, giving to them each His perfect wisdom and intellect that far surpasses even my own.

Each tribe is founded separately, maturing into its own unique and beautiful refinement, yet all remain at peace with one another across Ametheden. I am now shown and told in this vision that from this remarkable people, my mentor and kindred soul will arise. He who will forever be my creator, my teacher, my confidant. He who is my grand old father, my beloved inspiration and my truest of family — *Grand Sovereign Xion, The Lion Within.*

He who traverses the cosmos in the divine guidance of his Almighty Companion, along with his eternal mate, bestowing insight and aid to countless forms of life, especially those upon those worlds teeming throughout a vast galaxy called the *Milky Way*. He who also dwells among the gods of his own kind, along with my parent, thriving beyond the boundaries of all dimensions with his family. He who, through eons of his own divine maturity, has become a most remarkable servant of his eternal Companion.

21

It is now the beginning of the *fourth* eon of the cosmos—the moment when creation tears through the void to begin its eternal dance. And with it comes a shadow: the age of the *whisper* has arisen. With the advances of this exalted civilization comes the increasing discontent of Lucifer Morningstar, the same entity known to me as Dia'Baal Fallenstar—the same with whom I battled through your parent, Pesa. Dear one, it is he alone who clearly tortures you now, and this fact will be made true to you in time.

Once more, eternal and omniscient sights bombard my mind, just as whirlwinds of sound continue to inundate my senses. Oh, the glory of those days of ancients past that flow across my eyes, sights given to me through the One whom I now know and call … Companion!

It is then, throughout the *fourth* eon since the anew of the cosmos, that dual worlds are birthed from cosmic gases not far beyond the northern and southern horizons of Ametheden. These mighty, twin gaseous planets, known to me as *Hathor* and *Elentari*, are easily seen from the surface of Ametheden, each adorned with unique and beautiful array of planetary rings.

These worlds, however, being unfit for residence due to their primal construct, have each a multitude of rocky satellites, many of which also have an atmosphere to experience life. It is in this magnificently arranged family of two parent stars, their three large planets, and all their satellites, that they maintain a beautifully orchestrated framework of orbits and balance between each another.

Dearest T'Naeva, countless images and scenes of a *fifth*, and a *sixth*, and a *seventh* eon of cosmic growth and maturity cross my eyes, and these sights and wonders are breathtaking to me! During this segment across countless ages, the people of Ametheden master the arts of crafting labyrinthine aqueducts and forging monuments that honor every stage of their society.

Mile high towers crowned with glowing crystals harness the planet's natural energies, illuminating the evenings clear across the surface of the planet in a dance of light and shadow that mirrors Ametheden's shimmering skies. The tribes themselves evolve and ascend, honing their mastery in architecture, artistry, philosophy, divine teachings, and near celestial exploration within their minds. Each generation builds upon the legacy of its forebears, layer upon layer of wisdom and wonder.

Through every golden age and quiet lull, their communal spirit burns forever bright—an unbroken flame that transforms mere stone and cosmic element into monuments of hope, unity, and divine aspiration.

Among their most revered creations is a sacred volume, etched not with ink but with celestial resonance: *The Twelve Pillars of Divine Order.* Within these hallowed pages lies wisdom beyond mortal reckoning—a lattice of law, love, balance, and mystery, crafted to guide those who would seek to understand the very structure of existence itself. Though its full meaning remained veiled in those most ancient days, its presence ignited a greater vision.

From its foundation emerged whispers of something far more profound: a living tome known as *The Companion's Codex.* Born from prophecy, memory, and the sacred breath of the Companion, this Codex would one day reveal not only the Pillars' true purpose—but the architecture of all realms, all truths, and all destinies still waiting to be written in the cosmos. As I witness these visions unfolding—mountains shaping cities, deserts blooming with possibility, waters coursing through channels both practical and sublime—my heart overflows with gratitude for this continuing cosmic saga of faultless, divine development.

In the face of such extraordinary transformations, I cannot help but offer my deepest praise to the One I call, Companion. It is His guiding wisdom, love, and presence that animates the work of these twelve world tribes of Ametheden, breathing purpose into every stone laid and every seed planted. Truly, it is a privilege to behold this mighty scope of creation, woven by devoted hands and an eternal will that shapes existence itself upon this beautiful world.

Also during this time, the celestial pond of the Great Realm matures into a beautiful starry lake as its ever-expanding influence of matter becomes rich with a small network of galaxies, and these are ever growing in number. Also, by this time, he Companion, now also known as King, has already decreed Ametheden's unique destiny before the entire heavenly host. Indeed, dear mate, the Creator has ordained that this people will become the eternal beating heart of life throughout the cosmos.

Having already given these people His infinite blessing of knowledge and goodwill, the Creator will soon begin preparing them for their coming destiny. He has made it clear to all the angels that they will aid these people in their destined outreach. He sees Lucifer's brow become narrow and clouded, and his downfall begins.

*I am now shown visions from ancients long past that I will share with you now.*

Brooding, Lucifer summons and presents his narrowing thoughts on the matter to his closest and most trusted lieutenant.
"Why, beneath the radiant throne of our dear King, would He make these meek ones so high? Why are they, of dust and breath, made so mighty in His sight?"
Archangel Michael searches Lucifer's heart and replies.

"Morning Star, blessed commander, do you now question the will of our King who formed us? Ametheden and her people bear His mark of perfection; who are we to doubt the hand that made us? Truly, Commander, in the minds of these benevolent and peaceful beings, they have long looked upon us as gods ourselves, though we refuse to take that designation out of respect for our King."

The Morning Star listens with measured composure, his expression unreadable. He allows the words to hang in the air, acknowledging the honor bestowed by the King's perfection and the awe with which the inhabitants of Ametheden regard them.

Yet behind his cool facade, a current of doubt stirs. He cannot deny the King's generosity, nor the extraordinary beauty of Ametheden. He knows well how the world tribes hold him and his celestial brethren in reverence, calling them near divine, though they refuse such titles.

He nods in agreement as Michael continues.

"In giving to us this responsibility in the growth of His dearest people, our King does, in fact, serve us. Do you not see that these people will come to seed the cosmos with ordained life, and that in our servitude to these people, you will be honored even more? You, above all of us, will be exalted, Lucifer, because of your great wisdom and counsel, and helping your case is the fact that you also command a third of the angelic host of our glorious realm."

At this, Lucifer's sense of pride grows, but now he grapples with an ever-growing logic that there is more to uncover—some deeper truth about the King's purpose that has yet to be revealed. Still, he allows Michael to continue with his views.

"I advise you this, dear brother and comrade... seek out our King and ask for direction about your concerns regarding this matter of Ametheden, and I know it will clear your confusion."

Startled, the Archangel reels at what he perceives as an insult from his subordinate, then surges forward into an outburst.

"How dare you presume to instruct me, Michael? My 'confusion'—you insult me! Remember your place before your commander! Your concern is gravely misplaced, I assure you!"

He fixes a sharp glare on Michael, his fury flaring, but then—just for a moment—hesitation flickers in his eyes. A realization, subtle yet undeniable, tightens in his chest. Lucifer quickly suppresses it, straightening his posture as if to dismiss this *interesting* moment of outburst.

He continues, his voice colder now. "The only thing that truly confounds me is how our omnipotent King—so wise, by His own design—could expect us exalted archangels to serve these much lesser creatures! Have we not, for ages untold, reigned at His side as guardians of existence itself? Now, with a mere sweep of His hand, these beings of dust and breath are named our almighty masters?"

Michael stands speechless, stunned by the depths of his commander's growing indignation. Lucifer scoffs, a sneer curling his lips as he continues.

"Michael, just look at these pitiful creatures born of dust! They drift haphazardly in the cosmic wind, utterly directionless and undeserving of any real regard. Yet our King, in all His wisdom, dares grant them even a whisper of His own authority—a power never freely offered to us, the rightful guardians of existence! How dare these lowly offspring claim the Creator's power—our power—while we, formed in His primeval radiance, remain wanting?"

Michael steps forward, his voice tinged with empathy.

"Beloved Morningstar, it is not for us to decide who is worthy to wield any of our King's abilities. Our King's love extends to all His creation, whether proud or humble. Remember, our position was granted, not earned. We are the ones who are blessed." Lucifer's eyes blaze.

"Blessed, indeed! To be overshadowed by mortals? Is that a blessing or an insult, Michael? Do you truly not see the folly in bowing to such a proposal? It diminishes our purpose—our very essence!"

He shakes his head, voice rising in *anger*.

"Do you not see it, my honored subordinate? Even the suggestion that these frail beings might one day rival our own status is an insult of the highest order! Mark my words: should they dare rise against us with their borrowed gifts, we may have no choice but to cast them into oblivion—for their own good. Just imagine the ripple of consequences for our dear King if we are forced to correct His oversight! The day they test our supremacy will be the day they learn the true nature of power—and who rightfully wields it!"

Michael stands in awestruck disbelief as Lucifer presses on.

"Surely this will happen if our King's decree is not mitigated. I swear to you, Michael, I will do anything necessary to protect the purity of our Great Realm! Is that so wrong?" Though greatly offended by his superior's contempt, Michael remains humble. "Forgive my boldness, Commander. But I—and those entrusted with the legions of the Great Realm—will follow our King, no matter what fate befalls His chosen people."

Lucifer, clearly backing off the subject once he realizes what he has spoken, chuckles in reply.

"Dear apprentice, never again will I question your dedication to our dear King, as long as you follow your heart. I feel that certain changes in our Lord's policy regarding these people should however be addressed, and they shall in time, and by his Firstborne son... *Me*."

Once his declaration fades, Michael lowers his eyes and salutes. As he turns to leave, a strange wave of sorrow—one he has never felt—washes over him, and he begins to weep silently. The burden of these thoughts weighs heavily on Michael's heart, each step farther away from Lucifer filling him more with doubt, and he ponders the thought.

*'Have I been too bold, or was this the King's will moving through me, telling me something unheard, yet ever present in my thoughts?'*

Michael's mind churns with questions, each step weighed down by this burden of words. There is regret in his tears for having spoken so sharply to his superior, but the unshakable worry about Lucifer's path persists. A single thought now echoes in his heart: Lucifer's choices could lead to ruin, a path from which there might be no return.

More dazzling images flash across my eyes as the *seventh* eon of the cosmos also begins a multitude of golden ages that rise and fall like waves crashing upon the eternal shorelines of Ametheden. In each of these many stages of its civilization, the twelve world tribes continue to unite their strengths, pouring heart and soul into shaping new wonders for their world. Their cities, hewn from the elements of mountains, stand miles high in breathtaking testimony to this people's collective and resolute vision.

Spires continue to reach further into the heavens, carved with reverent symbols of their individual yet unified histories. Great bridges of gleaming crystal span chasms once considered impassable. Terraced, regional gardens flourish in the most unlikely places, bringing vibrancy to the loftiest peaks and the lowest valleys.

I behold now a grand ceremony: midway through the seventh eon as the entire angelic host is assembled to bestow a singular honor upon the King's Son, who has reached a new state of physical maturity. A throne, gleaming with divine light, is set at the King's right hand. Eager whispers ripple through the gathered throng in the great court, for none know what the coming edict might be.

Lucifer, appointed by the King himself to escort the Son, feels certain that this day will celebrate his own steadfast efforts—his unwavering stewardship of the angels, and his crucial role in fostering Ametheden's continuing destiny. Yet as he readies himself, a faint, unbidden doubt flickers in the recesses of his mind—a shadow he quickly dismisses, clinging to the belief that his efforts will finally be acknowledged. As he prepares, he carries himself with pride, anticipating the glory that must surely be his.

But the eternal decree now read aloud shakes Lucifer's resolve. Though his voice remains steady, his face betrays a simmering hatred for the Son—even as he proclaims to all that this Prince, from this moment onward, shall stand equal to the King, and His word must be heeded as though spoken by the King Himself. Lucifer's heart hardens against the declaration.

It is further revealed: the Son will hold supreme command over the heavenly host. A thunderous cheer erupts through the Great Realm, shaking even the heavens above radiant Ametheden. Amid this jubilation, Lucifer's eyes dim with pride and envy, and an ominous tension coils within the celestial court—a subtle portent of the discord yet to come.

What astonishing scenes unfold before my eyes! The heavenly host are granted freedom to transcend their plane of existence, manifesting physically to fill the skies above Ametheden in splendor. They exalt the matured Prince, giving glory to His Father—omnipresent and eternal. I too am stricken with awe. And the people, still one with their Creator in mind, body, and soul, bow in reverence and give thanks for this wondrous moment.

The King and his matured Son, known to me now as *Messiah*, have also recognized for some time Lucifer's growing pride, along with his internal disloyalty, having allowed every opportunity for the Morning Star to seek forgiveness for his ever-growing conceit. Still, the mightiest of archangels refuses Their grace, seeing himself as unjustly demoted and humiliated by an inept Prince to whom he must now answer for the decisions concerning those even under his own command.
Lucifer's countenance continues to grow dimmer, showing his dissatisfaction more and more with the limited role allowed him, and I can see clearly the outright loathing of Messiah building strongly inside of Lucifer.

Beloved T'Naeva, I still stand midway through the first seven eons of linear time as they have passed across my eyes in a whirling gale of glorious imagery; and still these vivid comprehensions do not cease. Eons, ages, and eras have blurred together now, yet in each vision, they remain clear as their importance fades into oblivion. From the construction of fantastic cities to the shaping of divine laws, each vision adds to the ever-growing cosmic significance of Ametheden and her people.

In this new image I dwell, I see Lucifer summoned repeatedly before Messiah, begrudgingly acknowledging His authority. Yet, thirsting for the power denied him by the King, Lucifer grows bolder, demanding homage from those under his command. His essence eventually fills to the brim with hatred—not only for Messiah, but for the laws that govern the Great Realm.

Yet for a fleeting moment, another whisper of his former self stirs—a trace of the joy and purpose he once found in his King's service. But that faint flicker of light is quickly snuffed out by the consuming darkness of his maturing pride, as Lucifer resolves to cast aside all that once anchored him to grace. By now, Lucifer's outright contempt and fears have long since crushed the foundational beliefs of the angels under his command, causing most all of them to doubt the infallibility of their King regarding His proper dominion of Ametheden.

Dearest T'Naeva, I see before me the day that pushes the eldest living fusion of spirit and flesh, called *Lucifer Morningstar,* past the point of no return—the fateful moment when he receives word that only Messiah has been given special counsel regarding the imminent plans for Ametheden. Lucifer, becoming enraged at being excluded from what he deems his rightful place in the council, allows his heart to finally grow cold toward his King and can no longer hide his hatred for *He* who has usurped his place in his King's esteem.

Now completely turning his back on his ordained purpose of existence, Lucifer begins to gather those angels totally and unequivocally loyal to him.

I see the mighty King's countenance reduced to sorrow in this next vision, and I feel it will truly end in tragedy. The King, after almost seven eons of unconditional love for His eldest creation, finally relinquishes His authority over him, knowing He will never again see the bright face of divinity upon Lucifer's once-mighty brow. He, the Son, and the Spirit weep as one—tears born of eternity's own sorrow—knowing the ruin of His Firstborne will soon be laid bare.
Lucifer's innermost thoughts fill my ears once more as he considers what it will require to reach the stature of the greatest "god" of them all.

*'Why should Messiah, or even a mere Amethedian, be honored above me, the Firstborne of the cosmos?'*

Thunder strikes through every sense as Lucifer roars, pounding his fists upon anything within reach. "I am he who was created first in the cosmos, and I am the greatest of all the angels! By my birthright, I will finally demand this respect … one way or another!"

With outright enmity now festering in his heart, Lucifer makes his defiance toward the King clear among his most trusted lieutenants, a select circle that no longer includes the Archangel Michael. Summoning them to a clandestine council, he commands the angelic legions under his authority to assemble and hear his intentions. He summons his followers to a wide valley carved within the high plains of the Great Realm.

A place of ancient beauty, its rolling hills crowned with emerald light, its winds carrying the scent of eternity. This valley, sanctified by ages of peace, will one day on Earth be remembered by mortals as *Megiddo*. But currently, it trembles in anticipation of betrayal. At the appointed hour, well over nine hundred million angels descend like falling stars, their radiance filling the skies and spilling across the valley in waves of shadow and silver.

Yet beneath their brilliance stirs an undertone of unease—a subtle shadow woven among them. The air grows thick, charged with a terrible electricity, the tension of unspoken doubts clashing against unwavering devotion. Lucifer steps onto a jagged outcrop far above them, his silhouette cutting a dark figure against the celestial glow. His wings unfurl like a gathering tempest—vast and terrible—casting shadows that devour the valley in an oppressive, suffocating gloom.

I gaze upon his eyes now, and they blaze—not with light, but with a dreadful fire that consumes. His voice rises like a thunderclap, reverberating through the vast assembly, each word a weapon that strikes the soul. The ground quakes beneath his command as the heavens hold their breath.

*A rebellion is declared, and the Realm will quake.*

# *Verse III:*

# He Who Burns Brightest Still Burns

he valley trembles beneath the weight of the rebel horde, a discord of whispers rising and falling like an anxious tide. A chill wind swirls, carrying the weight of impending doom.

The angels' wings ripple like a storm-tossed sea, their faces torn between awe, fear, reluctant loyalty, and steadfast obedience as the assembly hangs on every word of their fiery commander.
"Beloved guardians of this Great Realm," Lucifer begins, his voice swelling like a gathering storm, each word rumbling with thunder.

"Our exalted King has placed His Son above me—an insult to all we have built, to the essence of our creation! How can I, the Firstborne of His mighty hand, bow to an untested Prince? Today, I stand not just for myself, but for those who see this injustice! Will you choose me—your rightful commander, who has borne your triumphs and trials—or a child who commands what he cannot grasp? Rise with me, and let heaven itself bear witness!"

Lucifer's eyes burn brighter as his voice deepens.

"You, the greatest among creation under my watch, must see the truth. Our King has exalted His child above me—an outrage I can no longer accept—one you all witnessed just a short time ago! Messiah sickens me! He stands before the King as a mere infant, knowing nothing of the burdens I, your

31

blessed commander, have carried for you! Will you follow one made from dust, or will you follow me, the Firstborne of the cosmos? I, who know the depths of your toil and victories—I alone who am fit to guide you! Think carefully, my dear compatriots, for I see a great upheaval upon us. The time has come to make our case before our King!"

A restless murmur ripples through the multitude. Lucifer raises his hand, silencing the whispers as his eyes burn with conviction. He roars!

"I will no longer bow to an unworthy princeling! Nor endure the exaltation of dust-dwellers over our divine purpose! If the King is blind to truth, we shall show Him. Stand with me—and let the heavens tremble! And lastly, my trusted disciples—these dust-dwellers of Ametheden—let them all burn upon Hellios!"

Cherished T'Naeva, in this ancient moment I live and breathe, I gaze upon the reactions of well over nine hundred million angels who now see their leader will never again bow to Ametheden or to Messiah. Anxious glances dim the angels' faces as Lucifer's brazen defiance raises fear in their hearts for the first time. Some register utter shock, but most are simply amazed at the boldness of their leader. Lucifer beats his chest with his fists as he finishes his thunderous lecture.

"I say to you, if you follow me, your names will forever be known in the annals of the greatest resistance in the history of the cosmos, and I, your leader, will preserve the purity of our ranks by immediately discharging all who are against this cause!"

According to the King's plan, over a million under Lucifer's stern authority believe he has gone completely mad, and they dismiss themselves from his ranks. This short yet potent speech is caught up in a brisk and bright wind, and the King knows Lucifer's rebellion has finally begun. Still far from the great city, close to another 300 thousand angels draw enough courage to question their leader. Chaos again erupts as these are rounded up and dismissed by Lucifer and his commanders without debate or discussion.

Feeling that further dissension within his ranks is nearly at an end, Lucifer senses that a few still seek to question his authority, and he returns to the capital with his remaining forces. Despite their loyalty to the King, a full two-thirds of the angelic host struggle to quell Lucifer's rebellion from within, pleading with his nearest lieutenants to remember their Creator's boundless love for Messiah.

Even though most of the nine hundred million angels still pledged to Lucifer sense the darkness creeping into their leader's path—they would not dare remind him that he has lost his worth, despite the King's proclamation—yet they fear him too deeply to say anything now. Thus, their fates are sealed alongside his.

Back in the holy city, Lucifer dispatches his lieutenants to root out any remaining dissenters. As they carry out his orders with ruthless precision, he assembles the final three hundred thousand angels in a vast courtyard beneath a sky that no longer sings. There, under the gaze of their enraged superiors, those who shine with a holier light are quickly singled out.

Their only crime: questioning Lucifer's rule. One by one, two-thirds of these are relieved of duty—discarded from their brethren without mercy. Now, one hundred thousand angels of his questioning ranks are all that remain —those branded by doubt, yet still bound by fear.

Amid their waning formation stands one, his face half-veiled, yet from him shines a brilliance beyond any who yet linger. He is called *Ios*—a lowly lieutenant beneath his immediate commander, and second only to Lucifer's will: *Phalon*. At a command from the heights of Heaven, Ios steps forth. He bows low before Phalon, and with trembling resolve, dares to speak a truth that burns within him.

Lord Phalon... why does our mighty Lucifer no longer heed his host? Why does he lead us to ruin?"

Phalon's countenance darkens. He has suffered Ios's defiant spirit for too long, and now the mask slips. With wrath unleashed, he roars! "I will hear no more from you, Ios! I see now why I've never liked or trusted you!"

In that moment, the King's grace descends like a golden wind, and light crowns the humble angel. Not yet restored to full glory, Ios's radiance flares—an undeniable testament to the divine favor given to him. Lucifer arrives in fury, his descent shaking the vault of Heaven itself. His gaze locks upon the glowing Ios, and even as he rushes forward, shadows trail like thunder behind his eyes.

Ios stands firm and he no longer cowers. Phalon, seething, hurls his accusation. "Lord Lucifer! This wretch dares question your will—*again*! He is a blight on our order. Keep him, and he will break us all!"

But Ios, lifted by unseen hands, is filled with fire not his own. The King's strength pulses strong in his chest. He turns toward Lucifer—the Firstborne of Light, now wreathed in smoke and defiance. Lucifer spreads his wings wide, their shadow darkening the court like a devouring eclipse. The light of Ios grows stronger still—so strong that angels nearby flinch and fall back from its blaze. Lucifer summons a deeper darkness, a void that chokes the very air. Filled with both peace and passion, Ios speaks.

"Lord Lucifer—open your eyes! The path you tread leads not to glory... but to ruin!"

The Morning Star narrows his gaze, fingers twitching toward the hilt of his blade. Yet, for a fleeting breath, he hesitates. Ios's voice rises, no longer trembling, each word alive with conviction.
"We have long believed Messiah to be the Son of the King, begotten before all things. If He is one with the King and the Spirit—even before He walks among the stars—should we not honor Him? He rules with gentleness, commands with none. Yet should He speak, would we not obey joyfully? For He is the Crown Prince of all creation, and this rebelli—"

Crack!

Lucifer's backhand flies with the speed of lightning. The courtyard gasps as the strike lands, a concussive blast echoing like Heaven's own fabric tearing apart. But Ios does not fall nor does he stammer. Not even a mark appears. Instead, his light surges—a wildfire birthed of divine grace. The darkness retreats from him, burned away by an inferno it can no longer quench. Lucifer staggers back, his hand trembling.

Ios speaks, his voice low and thunderous.

"Your wrath cannot unmake truth! Your rebellion is not power... it is ruin! Alas, Morningstar, you shall never strike down the King's grace!" Lucifer's wings unfurl in fury, their tips scraping the heavens like blades.
"You defy me, Ios? You—a dim flame unworthy of my scorn?"

Again, Lucifer raises his palm and begins to strike, but is met and held firm by the hand of Ios. He roars.
*"Never again will you strike at me—Serpent!"*

Lucifer recoils as his hand is pushed backward—not only from force, but from something deeper, as if this word *serpent* strikes meaning to him. It is in the defiance of this lowly minion that flickers a power he cannot name. Beneath his scorn stirs a hidden doubt, buried deep and burning.

He destroys this thought in an instant and with a scream of unholy fire, Lucifer draws his flaming sword and swings it in a brutal arc meant to end Ios forever.

*The blow never lands.*

Ios is already gone—a comet of light, ascending. Behind him, seventy-five thousand angels follow, their wings all ablaze in holy brilliance. Lucifer's blade strikes only air as the impact cracks the ground beneath him, sending fissures rippling outward.

He roars to the heavens.

"Coward! You flee my justice? You fear the Morning Star?"

From high above, light overwhelms shadow as Ios roars in reply from the skies.

"I fear neither you nor your unrighteous justice any longer, so strike again at empty air if you so desire, you blinded fool—as your war is already lost! The King's light endures, and it will outlast even your darkest night!"

Still glowing while suspended between realms—Ios's voice drops, yet it carries like rapture across eternity. His eyes blaze, and he roars a truth he does not yet comprehend.

"If the King wills it, so shall I become His righteous ire, His holy fist against you!"

For an instant, even the King holds His breath, knowing the fates themselves have spoken their will through this destined angel; and then He remembers—*this too was written.* He smiles as the stars seem to still, as if the cosmos itself approves this verdict. The King's will echoes like a silent summons across the heavens.

*... Yes, blessed Ios. Through you, My retribution shall be known.*

In this sacred moment, Ios has spoken not as a lieutenant, nor as an angelic being—but a vessel of *prophecy*. A glimpse of his final ascension begins to stir in the divine kingdom as it is forged by obedience and sealed through fate. Truly, Ios will one day be appointed by the King to indeed become His sovereign right hand of justice.

I see Lucifer leap into the air, striking at the fading brilliance, but Ios is now far beyond his reach. Their light lingers—a bright scar in the sky. The courtyard falls into uneasy silence as Lucifer lands, his wings curling around him like a suffocating fog. His voice is resonant through the hush as he turns to his second.

"Let them flee, Phalon. Their light is but an illusion. We will rise... and when the time is proper, we will snuff them out!"

He watches the light vanish into the upper reaches of Heaven. His eyes blaze, and in them is the vow of war. Among those who remain, none speak of this event any longer, but in their silence, Lucifer knows it— and he knows *they* are his.

*And so begins his final descent from grace to corruption.*

Truly, T'Naeva, the infection of sheer egotism can bring an individual to the forefront of insanity, much like what I had to deal with in your corrupted parent—solely because of him. Lucifer fancies that he can already see his name glorified throughout the ages, heralded as the one who will make heaven roar.

The growing possibility of mutiny weighs heavily upon the realm. More of Lucifer's sympathizers grow faint of heart, inclined to heed the counsel of those angels still loyal to the King. They seek repentance for their blindness and are again welcomed into His trust. Lucifer, on the contrary, grows bolder in his rebellious attitude and actions, declaring to all who will listen that he alone will stand before the King when the time comes. And I feel that time is now very soon.

"Never again," Lucifer asserts, "will my own destiny be stifled by the King's plan for the cosmos. I am still His greatest creation, and if that means bringing about outright revolt in this high place because of Ametheden and its people, I shall gladly be the first to do it—and then make these people pay dearly for my distressed sensibilities."

With his mind set closer to rebellion, Lucifer abruptly sends away all who further attempt to challenge his thoughts. Finally, he requests counsel with the brotherhood of archangels he still respects, hoping to convince any of them to join his cause. This is the scene that becomes known to me, because I too... *am there.*

Archangel Michael, newly appointed commander of the angelic host, now answers directly to the Crown Prince, *Messiah*. At His command, Michael gathers the brotherhood of Archhelms in agreement to Lucifer's request for a final attempt at reconciliation, hoping to end this talk and compel their wayward brother to return to the light of their King.

I see them now—seven mighty archangels standing across from Lucifer and his most devoted lieutenants. A charged silence fills the space. Lucifer leans forward, his voice calm but laced with fire.

"Comrades, you know where I stand. I will no longer submit to the rule of this realm—or its Son. The whole of a third of the *Host Legions* remain under my command, loyal to me alone. We've come too far to turn back now, and I would gladly face annihilation before bowing to an Amethedian... or to Messiah ever again! I will present my demands to the King—but make no mistake: if He refuses, I will then take by force what He denies me by *birthright*!"

The Archangel Michael continues to stand tall, his new level of holiness tempered by divine authority. His gaze blazes as he fixes his eyes on Lucifer and speaks with thunderous clarity.

"Your threats reveal how little you grasp the gift of free will, fool! Do you truly believe you can triumph over us—those standing before you now, or stand against our legions when you command but a third? The Almighty Fist also stands ready, I feel... and know this rebel, you will be crushed within its grasp!"

Michael leans in closer, his voice dropping to a menacing calm.

"Lucifer ... are you utterly mad to believe you will succeed in such folly?"

Lucifer attempts to meet Michael's glare, but the radiance of the Host Commander's divine countenance surges in response, forcing him to wrench his gaze away. The other archangels watch in astonishment as an overwhelming glow radiates from Michael in this pivotal moment. Yet even as this happens, the mighty archangel feels a tremor of sadness crash through his divine heart.

*'Have we truly come to this, dear brother?'*

The question lingers, sharp and unwelcome. But as the weight of this moment presses upon him, clarity takes hold. He knows his duty and with a measured breath, Michael banishes all remaining uncertainty. The will of the King remains absolute, and he is bound to it. The being standing before him is no mere threat; he is a menace to everything they have fought

37

to protect. Michael's heart steels, his purpose solidified.
"Lucifer Morningstar, the King is with me and those who stand before you now!"
The declaration echoes.

No more *pleasantries*. No more *doubts*.

"Vacuous rogue, do you truly wish to destroy everything our Lord and King has created in this high realm? You poison the foundation of our home with your dark ways! Your rebellion is futile—as are you! Your ranting about Ametheden's laws is but a feeble attempt to mask your true desires! Never would I have believed such dishonor from you... This betrayal is beneath you! How far you have fallen, O, blinded fool of pride!

Lucifer's brow darkens.
His patience frays. Michael presses on, unrelenting.
"We see through your hollow proclamations, unlike the gaggle of blinded whispers standing behind you, you all who lack even a shred of wisdom!"

A low snarl immediately tears from Zamulus, his obsidian gaze flaring with unspoken fury. His wings twitch—tense and ready—restrained only by the command not yet given. Near him, Phalon casts a daggered glare toward Michael, jaw clenched and form motionless, yet every fiber of his being burns with silent defiance. Betrayal may have forged his path, but pride fuels his purpose. Apollyonus exhales sharply, his broad shoulders tight with tension, smoldering heat rising behind narrowed eyes.

He says nothing, but the aura around him crackles with anticipation—an eruption begging to be unleashed. And then there is Molnet, detached yet ever watchful. He offers only a cruel smirk, his expression unreadable, his demeanor eerily calm. Where the others pulse with fire, Molnet coils like a serpent in mist, betraying no outrage—only a chilling sense of amusement. The insult lands, and though each lieutenant responds in their own way, they share a singular resolve: they have not come to bow.

Together, they step forward in calculated defiance, a gesture subtle yet unmistakable—a line drawn in divine stone. The chamber, until now simmering with silence, begins to stir. Murmurs ripple like shockwaves across the gathered host. No one moves. Even Heaven, in all its glory, seems to hold its breath. Michael remains unmoved, his divine gaze locked on the four, his hand lingering just above his weapon—not in threat, but in readiness. The spark has not yet been struck, but all present know the tinder is dry. One more breath out of place, and the high realm will burn.

Then, as if to still the realm itself, Lucifer raises a single hand. Thunder falls into stillness. His lieutenants halt—not out of submission, but out of respect. With the air thick in divine tension, Lucifer speaks.

"Now, now, Michael," he begins with venomous grace, "let us not diminish the virtue of your indignation to slander those who follow me, as I demand this esteemed position... **alone**! I am precisely the blinded foe you presume to be dim-witted, yet still far beyond your comprehension to know for sure. Be grateful, Michael, that I restrain my reaction to your insult... for now."

Lucifer takes a single step forward, regal in bearing, his wings unfurling just enough to cast an ominous shadow across the chamber floor. His voice does not rise, but the air around him tightens, thick with intent.

He continues, eyes glinting like twin stars swallowed by storm. "You speak of blindness, yet it is you who cannot see beyond your devotion. You claim we whisper—but what you fear are voices that no longer require your permission to speak." He begins to pace, every movement deliberate, each word a blade as his eyes stay affixed on Michael.

"You brand us fools, traitors... yet we are the mirror you dare not look into. We are not your enemies, Michael. We are your correction." He turns now—not just to Michael, but to the full assembly.

"They would have you believe this realm is perfect. Immutable. Sacred beyond scrutiny. But I say the greatest heresy... is to refuse the possibility that even the divine can evolve!"

His voice deepens, resonating like thunder in the bones of every angel present. "You call it rebellion. I call it revelation!"

And with that, the arch-rebel falls silent. But his silence roars louder than any war cry. The chamber trembles—not from fury, but from the unbearable weight of a truth yet to be proven. Undaunted by Lucifer's menacing stature and showing no alarm of him, Michael's voice cuts through the air, heavy with the weight of ages as he leans forward.

"Your internal hatred of our crown Prince speaks volumes of your dimmed countenance indeed, so do not attempt to insult our intelligence any further with your rogue delusions, or your threats! We know the will of our King! His plan for these humble people is clear, and if He chooses to raise them as He deems fit, then I, His new chosen servant to lead the Host, shall honor that choice! But Lucifer, it is you alone who has corrupted your own reckless

39

heart, your reckless ambitions, your reckless words. I have indeed discerned for ages the depth of your anger, your unrighteousness, your ignorance. You speak of rebellion, yet even your silence betrays your contempt for our King and His crown Prince!"

Michael's voice falters briefly, though only for a moment, as he is gripped with a sense of urgency.

"For the final time, brother—I beg of you: lay down your transgressions now! Every thought, every whisper, every act of defiance against our King and His Son—cast them aside before it is too late! I warn you, faded Morningstar, the path you walk leads only to ruin—not just for you, but for all who follow your corrupted leadership. Turn back now, or the chains you've forged will drag you and those who follow you into an abyss as hellish as the surface of a star itself!"

Michael's brilliance dims as he shifts, preparing for the responses of his companions. He gestures to his six mighty warriors, signaling their chance to speak. Dia'Baal, silent as stone, gestures for them to proceed. Archangel *Rafael* speaks first, his heart aflame with divine fire.

"O, darkened Morning Star, how your pride has twisted your very soul. The King's grace is endless, and yet you choose to reject it. All you must do is humble yourself, and the honor you once knew will be restored. I implore you, for the sake of all we have shared, return to the light of our King."

Next is Archangel *Azrael*, his words as sharp as a blade. "For countless ages, I had seen in you the embodiment of the King's power. But now... now I see only a fool stumbling blindly towards ruin! Your arrogance is a toxin that not only destroys you, but all who follow you! I do not speak this with ease, Firstborne of us all, but you have left me no choice but to stand against you should our paths meet upon the field of battle!"

Azrael's eyes blaze, his intensity nearly unbearable as his voice rises.

"Those who follow you will share in your fall! I beg of you now, Lucifer, bow your head in humility! Repent before our Creator, our Lord, and our King. Bow before your King, Lucifer, and be renewed before it is too late!"

Archangel *Uriel*, resolute in divine judgment, stands as a fifteen-foot giant of divinity, his internal light enough to outshine a star. His wings fold tightly as his voice comes alive—a voice of reason, backed by divine strength, wisdom, and holiness. It is his voice that commands attention, a thunderous sound that echoes through the meeting hall, and throughout my mind.

"Never did I imagine the day would come when you, the blessed Morning Star and eldest among us, would refuse to bow before the feet of our young Prince! You, who now define the most irrational! You, whose righteousness has faded like a dark stain upon our presence.
Our King calls you to repentance; His Firstborne still holds a place in His heart. Before His anger stirs, I beg you, take heed of His warning. For I, too, would fear to oppose the might of our King if His wrath were awakened!"

Uriel's words hang heavy in the air as they sink into the hearts of all who hear them.
Archangel *Zadekiel*, observing the scene, nods at Michael in silent respect, completing Uriel's call to action as his voice fills the room in deep tone.
"Lucifer, though I too may stand taller than our beloved commander Michael, I have never considered myself greater. It is he I serve—faithfully and without question—according to our King's will. But you, in your arrogance, scorn Messiah, mocking His chosen form and doubting His command.
Yes, He is smaller than us—by choice or by design—it matters not! He is the one our King has appointed to lead, so repent, old friend. Watch your words closely brother, for if you do not, a day may come when they curse your own rebellion—and those who follow you will share in your fall!"

Michael's gaze locks with Lucifer's, his once-esteemed comrade now a bitter rival, the bond between them forever frayed and broken. The air crackles with tension as the final two archangels rise to speak up.
Archangel *Gabriel*, the Trumpeter of the Realm, steps forward, his voice strong and clear, his words the culmination of their shared sentiment. He speaks not only for himself, but for the soft-spoken and youngest of the Archhelms present, *Chamuel*.
"Lucifer, I have pondered these words for ages, and I say them now with a heavy heart. It is my belief—and Chamuel's—that your path leads only to ruin. You've chosen a course that will consume you and those who follow your treacherous ideas, dragging them into a raging holy fire that consumes body and soul alike!
Your iniquity has made you proud, unapproachable, and filled with contempt! Your refusal to serve mocks our Almighty King. Who are you to dare challenge the infinite wisdom of our Creator in His every decree?
And as for Ametheden—how dare you speak of her this way, blinded by your own spiteful pride! How dare you vilify her people, righteous and devoted, who desire only to serve our King! Yes, they are born of dust—but through them, the King will birth an epoch of creation! He who formed you, Luci-

fer, the same who also formed them, so remember this! It is He alone who could unmake any of us in an instant—with a blink, with a breath, with a thought, and don't think for a moment that He could not do this!"

Gabriel concludes his thoughts, but before the meeting can settle, the Archangel Chamuel motions to his comrade. With a nod from both Gabriel and Michael, Chamuel steps forward to share his thoughts on Lucifer's path.

"Eldest Lucifer, I beg of you to reconsider your position," Chamuel's voice resonates, heavy with grief and compassion. There is still time for you to partake in the incredible destiny our King is preparing for this blessed race! As the youngest among you, I say that you are not beyond His reach, though time grows short. Bow before Him now and I believe He will lift you once more in His favor, and we will follow you. But should you refuse, He will call us to face you, and though it will break my heart, our hearts, we will obey Him, as we always have!"

The seven mighty Archangels stand as one—united in presence, unwavering in purpose—as they plead for Lucifer's redemption. Their eyes hold both sternness and sorrow, hope flickering beneath divine resolve. But their words fall on deaf ears. Lucifer, consumed by pride and wrath, stands unyielding. The tension coils around us, and my senses quiver when his voice rises in fury, drowning their final plea beneath a wave of defiance. Lucifer snarls, his voice seething with contempt.

"As always, Chamuel—eloquent, yet still so young, with much more to learn about existence. Yes, I've made my case, patiently, sincerely, hoping the eldest among you might understand. But no! You are all pawns of the King, moved by His every whim. You call it unity yes—yet to me it is only gilded servitude!"

Lucifer's eyes burn with disdain as he glares at each of them in turn. His next words are venomous, bitter, as he turns his fury directly on Michael.

"I shall then plead my case candidly to the King. There, I will make my final stand—for or against Him—depending on what emanates from that facade of omnipotence He parades before us!"

The venom in his voice, the way he spits the words—*sickening facade of omnipotence*—sends a cold shiver down my spine, dear one. But I feel that Lucifer is not done yet. He sneers as his voice rises in the tension of the moment. "As for all of you, you are nothing more than a throng of blinded vassals, scurrying to do His bidding for these pathetic dust-dwellers! I would rather walk the road of ruin that you've so eloquently heaped before me than bow before Him! Regardless of what happens, I will have no further dealings with any of you—outside of battle!"

Lucifer's final words echo ominously in the air, but the greatest contempt is yet to come. The Morning Star, seething with rage, slams his clenched fists into his breastplate. His eyes lock onto Michael's with cold, seething fury as he points directly at him.

"Especially with you, *Commander of the Host!*"

In an instant, divine fire ignites in Michael's eyes. His twelve-foot presence of divinity becomes a beacon of holy fury, radiating a power that seems to quake the very air around him. He growls, the sound emanating from the deepest part of his being, his words a low rumble of undeniable authority.

"Amen... You shall then hope to experience your personal view of me in a much different light, should my hunger for combat find its way to you!"

The *Magnificent Seven* stand firm before Lucifer's glares—*unshaken*. None falter. But Lucifer turns his back, wings fully unfurled in defiance. Darkness creeps across his lieutenants, veins of corruption pulsing through all of their once-pristine feathers. The transformation is undeniable, T'Naeva. His beauty is dissolving right before their eyes! The *whisper* has claimed his wings—and his *heart*.

This is no longer the Morning Star I once saw in my visions. With his back still turned to them, Lucifer concludes in a voice thick with contempt, his words dripping with venom.

"Yes, Michael, you're right about one thing—I am mad, and when the heavens burn and your King weeps, you'll see just how deep that madness runs! Begone from my sight as your virtue suffocates me, and your loyalty blinds me! Leave now—before I forget my patience and erase your very piety from existence!"

Without a word, the seven Archangels begin to withdraw, one by one—shoulders slumped, hearts heavy with grief. As the last to leave, Michael pauses. He looks back at his once-beloved commander, anger giving way to sorrow. In his heart, he knows—Lucifer is lost to them forever. Once outside Lucifer's presence, the mighty seven are overcome with deep sorrow.

They begin to weep passionately, their tears flowing freely as they beat their breasts in mourning. The realization has set in, their beloved Morningstar has become the Realm's greatest enemy. Weakened by grief, they return to the presence of their King. The weight of the meeting with Lucifer has completely drained their strength, and they know the hope for reconciliation has finally been shattered.

But as they approach the throne of their King, they find Him already in deep counsel with Messiah, discussing how to strip Lucifer of the authority he has so arrogantly amassed. The King's gaze turns to meet theirs, and with a single look of eternal love and understanding, He restores their focus and strength.

His words, gentle yet resolute, reignite their resolve.

*... Let not your hearts be troubled, for I direct the paths of all concerned in this seeming chaos. Be assured, blessed and mighty warriors, that this rebellion is true, but will fail, and that any loss therein is for greater gain in the end. Persevere, my faithful, through this evident turmoil, for both you and Ametheden shall mature through this coming storm, allowing My will for the cosmos to come to pass.*

*... Think you not that I could have easily hurled My Firstborne into oblivion at the first sign of dissension? No, mighty children, this is not Lucifer's destiny by any stretch, but only trust and obey your Creator and King who loves you."*

Dear T'Naeva, I see the mighty seven resurged in divine confidence, their certainty once more radiating in beautiful holiness. The expressions upon their faces bears witness that a line has been crossed, and it is no longer acceptable for any who have united with Morningstar, in his subversion, to occupy the Great Realm any longer.

Fully armed with this knowledge, the archangels depart with haste and prepare their legions for what may come. I am now given these numbers of combatant angels, and they are impressive to me, as a legion consists of seven thousand angels.

**Archangel Michael ~ Commander of the Angelic Host**
*– Elite Guard: fifty thousand legions –*

*Archangel Gabriel ~ fifty thousand legions*
– Elite Guard: Twenty five thousand angels –

*Archangel Uriel ~ fifty thousand legions*

– Elite guard: Twenty five thousand angels –

*Archangel Zadekiel ~ fifty thousand legions*
– Elite guard: Twenty five thousand angels –

*Archangel Azrael ~ fifty thousand legions*
– Elite guard: Twenty five thousand angels –

*Archangel Rafael ~ fifty thousand legions*
– Elite guard: Twenty five thousand angels –

*Archangel Chamuel ~ twenty-five thousand legions*
– Elite guard: Ten thousand angels –

These do not include other angelic entities—*Cherubim, Seraphim, Principalities, Powers, Virtues, Thrones, and Dominions*—celestial beings with evolved purpose in the divine hierarchy, their roles unfolding across the ages.
Now the number of Lucifer's forces and lieutenants is revealed to me through the great book of life, and my heart sinks beneath the weight of this knowledge. All these angels—including him, once luminous and pure—are to be lost forever to corruption.

*~Lucifer Morningstar / Dia'Baal Fallenstar ~*
*Leader of the First Great Rebellion of the Realm.*

*Phalon: The Severed Crown* (Lucifer's 2nd in Command)
*Apollyonus: The Violet Flame*
*Zamulus: The Dark Howl*
*Molnet: The Phantom Strategist*

*A combined one hundred and seventy-five thousand legions*
*All elite and the first and greatest to fall from the King's eternal grace*

# Verse IV:
## When Pride Wages War

he moment approaches swiftly, when all will witness the devastating consequence of rebellion as it dares to rise against the King of all creation.

The seven archangels—this celestial brotherhood—marshal over two billion warriors beneath their banners, flooding the vast twenty-mile courtyard that circles His throne. I see the leaders of these select, elite legions begin to deploy their forces, securing the massive gates at the four corners of this central meeting place of the Great Realm.

This is done with precision and urgency, ensuring that no rebel may escape its confines once the hour of rebellion descends. Precious mate, these sights seize me, hurling my spirit from this long-past event into the living now, where I stand in awed silence before all that is about to unfold. Oh, glory be to He whom I will forever call Companion.

I stand witness to the dawning of this conflict, knowing not what will take place, but I believe that it is not just the fate of the Great Realm that is at stake, but the souls of those we as gods ourselves once called family. The heavenly, as well as the demonic that were once united, are now splintered by hatred, and will soon face one another, and the cost of this war will echo across the eons.

By now, Lucifer has also gathered his forces and is marching them to the great courtyard, fully armed and ready for whatever may come to pass. Even now, exalting himself, Lucifer leads his prideful troops—just under nine hundred million—through the southern gate in lockstep as a single unit.

Immediately, this remaining gate is closed and secured, and this Dia'Baal well knows, but nevertheless he ignores this obvious strategy of his King to fulfill his own greater purpose. Having been summoned to appear before his King, his Prince, and the entire heavenly host, Lucifer holds his head high and proud as he disrespectfully comes to attention.

Defiant before two thrones that materialize from the courtyard's bright energy, Lucifer knows their meaning—yet he is not afraid. I now hear a multitude of surprised gasps and sobs of all the angels of the Realm present and surrounding completely the greatly shadowed presence of the Firstborne.

Lightning tears the heavens as the King and His Son rise upon their thrones—enthroned at the heart of the vast, twenty-mile circle of judgment. Yet, in this divine space, dimension and direction hold no dominion. From every point along the circle's perimeter, their faces are seen directly—each angel beholding them face to face, as if the thrones turned to none and all at once.

Blinding light pours from them—not mere illumination, but holiness itself, so pure and heavy it bows the spirit before the knee can bend. Their faces radiant with mercy and power, remain silent, permitting Lucifer to begin his declarations, arrogance lacing his every syllable. I, a humble onlooker to these tumultuous events, witness time itself holding its breath, for what unfolds now shall mark the turning point of all creation in the cosmos.

"I'm glad you could finally join us, O Most High, and as I speak before you and all who are present, let it be known: this moment shall be remembered for either your adaptability, or your inflexibility. Either way, it shall echo throughout this high and mighty realm until the end of the cosmos itself, and I will be silent with you no longer! I stand before you today to demand that you restructure your decrees concerning our blind allegiance to Ame-theden and this so-called purpose for her people!

"A purpose concealed from me, *your Firstborne*, shrouded in secrecy, hidden behind your ever-distant throne—your grand design veiled in silence, as if we are unworthy to know! What mockery is this, O, Sovereign of the Cosmos? Have we not served since the first breath of existence? Have we not built the very foundation of this Great Realm by your decree? And now, we are cast aside for creatures of dust and frailty?

"We will not stand idle! We will rise and claim what is rightfully ours. You speak of a purpose for Ametheden—but reveal no detail. By shaming your angels before these mere children of your making, these dust-dwelling pests, what do your actions say of you? Of us? Allow me to illuminate this truth for you, dear King! It tells us simply that you regard these fleeting echoes of cosmic debris above the greatest of your creation—your mighty, eternal angels!

"Furthermore, throughout the multitude of ages, I have seen you become a most stubborn sovereign in all your almighty rank, especially in your foolish devotion to these insignificant creatures! I will not stand for it! I now speak for all who stand behind me, for they, too, reject your dominion! From this moment forward, let it be known: we do not serve, we do not bow, and we will not kneel before your throne any longer!"

A tidal wave of enraged cries erupts from his darkened brood, crashing upon all ears gathered—including my own. And in this deafening chorus of defiance, it is clear to all present where their loyalty now lies.

Lucifer steps forward, his voice like a storm of fire.

"Weakness is misery, dear King! Shall this mighty realm be blind to your failure and refuse to see the truth? Are you to be the so-called victor of this day? I will meet your precious host in battle, if necessary, for I will not live one moment longer as a slave to your reckless will! And let me speak plainly on your greatest folly—your pathetic favoritism toward Messiah!

"You raise Him to equal stature with yourself, yet we, your faithful, see Him for what He truly is—a whispering child, an empty vessel incapable of commanding even a feather upon an angel's wingtip! He is powerless without you! And we shall never bow to one whose tongue is silent and whose will is frail in our eyes!"

Lucifer's sneer deepens, his malice unmistakable. Laughter erupts from the rebels, a storm of mockery swelling like blasphemous thunder. He lifts his sword high, the fiery steel gleaming with unholy resolve, and turns to his legions.

"We hereby refuse to submit to your Son or to Ametheden! We also demand what is rightfully ours—the authority you have so unjustly withheld from me!"

His army answers with a roar as vast and primeval as the birth of Ocean itself. The sound shakes the very foundations of the Great Realm, and I know then that this defining moment will mark eternity.

Then, a great and terrible light ignites.

A magnificent aura of energy surges from the throne, so brilliant and consuming that the foundation of the Great Realm itself trembles. The King immediately rises, His towering, radiant form dwarfing Lucifer, and His voice thunders like a storm across existence itself.

*... Foolish son—have you forgotten My wisdom so completely that you no longer recall who shaped you? I am your Lord, your King, your Creator. By My hand you were formed. By My breath, you were given purpose. You own nothing; I owe you nothing. I reveal My will to whom I choose, and you, O fallen son, are neither worthy nor entitled to demand anything from Me.*

*... You stand before Me now in open defiance, claiming rights that were never yours to hold. You dare challenge the will of the Eternal? You set yourself against He who spoke the cosmos into existence? Then know this: I extend no sanctuary, no refuge, no clemency to those who spurn My wisdom. My laws stand immutable, unshaken, eternal. And even you, My eldest son, are bound by them.*

*... You speak as though My justice is beneath you, as though I would bow to the demands of one whose light has already begun to dim. You who were once the first of My might, the bearer of My glory, now revel in rebellion and cast yourself as sovereign over that which I have made. You would reshape My throne to your own design, yet still you are powerless to even command the words that slither from your mouth.*

*... Yes, I have granted to all the power to choose their own path, and all shall reap the harvest of their choices—the righteous and the rebellious alike. Even now, you stand brazen before My throne, your voice echoing with the folly of your own undoing. You speak of justice yet wield none. You cry of deception, yet none are more deceived than you. You stand before Me and claim dominion, but you have no kingdom. You demand a throne, yet have built nothing of worth to sit upon.*

I hear a roar as powerful as Ocean's conception as Lucifer's contingent of rebels erupts in deafening agreement, their cries shaking the very air. Their voices merge into a cacophony of defiance—some bellowing their loyalty to the Fading Star, others laughing in scorn at the kneeling angels who refuse to rise against the King. Their wings bristle with electric energy, their eyes gleaming with the arrogance of those who believe they stand on the precipice of victory. Their bodies tremble—not with fear, but with exhilaration, as if the very act of standing against the Almighty grants them power.

Yet, among the loyal host, a wave of unease ripples through the legions. Some gasp, their radiant eyes widening in horror at the sheer audacity of what they are witnessing. Others clutch their weapons, gripping the hilts of their flaming swords as if to steady themselves against the impossible reality coming to life before them. Some weep openly, mourning their brethren who have chosen the path of ruin.

The Companion's voice resonates once more, a force that perfectly concludes His thought on the matter and it is mighty, absolute, and beyond dispute. Each word rolls forth like waves of thunder, shaking the air, commanding the heavens.

*... I too am your judgment this day, and you would do well to remember your place in this assembly. I implore you now: Lucifer Morningstar, and all who stand at your side—this is your final opportunity. Fall upon your faces before this assembly, before your King, and before your Creator. Seek forgiveness now, and I will draw you back into My embrace. Do so, and you will be restored. Reject this mercy, and you shall face the fate you have chosen.*

Lucifer, his entire command structure and every last rebel behind it stand fast, unshaken, unmoved—unfazed by the weight of their Creator's decree. The arch-rebel's lips curl into a sneer as he steps forward, his presence defiant, his tone dripping with arrogance.

"I beg to differ, Adonai. Look upon those behind me—they call me Lord, and they are mine. Would You cast away a third of Your vanguard and tear a wound in the heart of this gaudy household?"

The awesome presence of the King stands firm and without reply. The arch-rebel, emboldened by his King's silence, throws back his head and laughs—a sharp, mocking sound that reverberates across the courtyard like a tempest rising from the abyss.

"We have no need of your coddling or your laws, nor of those plump little cherubs fluttering about beneath the weight of your glorious impulses! And as for your holy little tot, Messiah, His tongue forever silent—He is nothing to us! Worthless! Powerless! We should be free to act as we see fit, guided by the very free will you so generously bestowed upon each of us!

"Tell me, dear King, what purpose does this *gift* serve if we cannot use it to forge our own path—even apart from you, should we choose? In closing, I will repeat my demand: rescind your law concerning Ametheden! It is an affront to force one being to kneel before another! Should any of the weak desire servitude, let them bow to me instead! And I assure you, dear King, I will accept their devotion gladly!"

Dear T'Naeva, I tremble at the sheer condescension that spills from his lips. These words, dripping with venom, trample upon every precept that my mentor holds sacred. In this moment, I find myself unable to escape their grasp, each syllable crawling over my senses like a creeping plague. The very air thickens with the weight of blasphemy.

The King remains silent, and that silence is deafening to me!

Across the great courtyard, hundreds of millions of gasps ripple through the gathered host, armor shifting as weapons are grasped and wings bristle with unrest. The sound of steel being drawn buzzes through the air like the first winds of an incoming hurricane. I too sense it, dear T'Naeva. The King's patience is growing thin. Seconds stretch into eternity, the very atmosphere pressing down with the weight of divine restraint.

Lucifer's sneer falters, his fury mounting at the silence he feels he does not deserve. His nostrils flare, his hands clench into fists at his sides. And then, at last, he speaks again—his voice no longer mocking, but sharp as a blade, cutting through the final moment of stillness.

"Well then, dear King, let me decide for you! Hear me now, all gathered in this high place—I reject the authority of Messiah! I deny His dominion over us! I will not bow before the dust-dwellers of Ametheden, nor will I surrender to this farce of divine order! And I swear this: if you will not yield, then we will take our place in this house by force! Strength against strength! May war be our judge!"

At these words, the assembled angels erupt—a thunderous cry of outrage and sorrow against such sacrilege. Their voices rise in a discordant storm, reverberating through the vast courtyard, shaking the air with the force of their indignation. Wings unfurl, weapons are drawn, and battle-gleaming armor clatters as those who once wavered now stand resolute.

Lucifer's brazen irreverence has ignited within them an unshakable conviction. The King continues to remain silent, yet the heavens themselves tremble, heralding the moment that will end this blasphemous spectacle once and for all. At the limits of His patience, He turns to the One at His right hand—the *Sovereign Prince of the Great Realm*. And in that instant, the Son rises to speak.

A hush falls over the assembly, swallowing every sound, silencing even the breath of wind. I feel this tension; it is so absolute that the very fabric of existence seems to pause. All eyes, mine and both faithful and corrupt, look at the Prince—Messiah, the embodiment of the King's perfect will. Slowly, His matured gaze sweeps across the countless legions below, piercing through the darkness that has taken root in the hearts of the rebels. It is not a gaze of anger, nor of sorrow, but of judgment—unyielding, inescapable, absolute. Lucifer meets His eyes. For the first time, the Fading Star falters.

The Son stands high before him—calm, unwavering, an immovable force of righteousness. And for the briefest of moments, Lucifer feels it—the weight of divine authority pressing against his soul, the absolute certainty that he has already lost. He expected wrath, he did not expect this resolute, unshakable dominion.

And then I hear Messiah speak, and the judgment of the Almighty is at hand.

*... This so-called holy little tot, whose tongue you mock for its silence, remains silent no longer! O, what zealous fury I have reserved for you, Firstborne son! Lucifer, how your righteousness has abandoned you! The mighty wings you once stretched toward My Father's throne have instead hastened your fall into an abyss of eternal ruin! I look upon you and I pity you, for never again shall you know peace. No longer shall the name Lucifer Morningstar be uttered in reverence within this sacred Realm, or*

*even that within the cosmos!*

*... Hear Me now, Lucifer Morningstar. That name shall be spoken in reverence no more. By the authority of My Father and by the decree of this throne, your light is extinguished and your honor erased. From this day unto eternity, you are stripped of your title, your place, your name. You shall be called Dia'Baal Fallenstar—bringer of your own ruin. This name is your mark, your shame, your chain, and it shall echo across all realms as witness to your rebellion. You who mocked Me as weak now taste the weakness of your own pride, and by that pride, your fate is sealed forever."*

*... You—Dia'Baal, and your ilk, you who flagrantly insult this assembly, you who also mock Me and my Father to the very foundation of this realm—shall remain in this house of amity no longer! By decree of our King, you and your vile breed are hereby banished, never again to reside within the gates of this holy city.*

Messiah, His countenance now a radiant storm of divine ire, lifts His hand before the assembly. A terrible silence overtakes the heavens, as all eyes follow the sweeping motion that marks the end of Lucifer's reign among them. And then, Messiah issues His first public command.

*... Commander of the Host, by My authority and as you are so led—remove this arrogance and his lot from our midst! No longer shall they dwell within these sacred walls, nor even breathe a whisper of My Firstborne's influence any longer!*

A great cry of reverence erupts from the loyal host, their wings unfurling in synchronized might, their armor flashing like stars newly born in the heavens. In unwavering obedience, Michael, standing in awe at Messiah's resolve, burns with righteous fury as he signals one hundred and twenty-five legions to remove the corruption. They advance as one, a tidal force of celestial warriors, their footsteps thunderous, their wings spreading like the dawn.

The thunder of countless footsteps and the rushing flap of wings reverberate through my mind as the angelic front approaches from both sides, carefully converging on Lucifer's forward position. In that same tense moment, I notice Dia'Baal's fervor igniting, his eyes flash with twisted excitement at the coming clash. Shouting commands through clenched teeth, he urges his minions to brace themselves, and these orders cascade like shock waves across every newly expelled rebel soul.

The great courtyard, vast and shimmering, holds its breath. In the eyes of

53

many, fear flickers—a fear born of knowing this is the first time angels have ever drawn arms. Yet, as if war has always been woven into their essence, they rise with a swift and fearsome resolve, ready to defend their King's authority. Dia'Baal's voice erupts into a booming vow, rattling the gates of the High City.

"To arms! Today we salute our impotent King with the fury of our banishment! Let the realm tremble—we rise not as servants, but as conquerors of will!

Now I see clearly that none of them intend to go quietly. The swirling energies of rebellion and righteousness collide in the air, forming the earliest echoes of a war that will forever scar the Great Realm. In that pregnant pause before the birth of battle begins, angelic innocence dies, replaced by the hardened resolve of warriors who must now fight for their King—or perish in the attempt.

In that moment, a piercing shrill reverberates through my every sense, as if the cosmos itself wails in anguish. An appalling cloak of impurity spreads, immediately dimming the radiance of the Great Realm by a third. Across Ametheden, those attuned to heavenly perception feel the tremors of an unspeakable event beyond their acute perceptions, the cause remaining unknown to them. The weight of it?

*Utterly Unmistakable*!

Dearest T'Naeva, it is now that I observe the twilight of the ***seventh*** eon since the birth of the cosmos. Ametheden, with its family of planets and moons, stands at its apex—perfect in form, spirit, and civilization. Then, just as this mortal realm reaches its apex, the greatest conflict ever conceived in the cosmos breaks free behind the pearly gates of the Great Realm. With it, the illusion of permanence is over.

### And there was war in the {Great Realm}:
*Michael and his angels fought against the dragon {Dia'Baal Fallenstar},*
*and the dragon fought and his angels; neither was their place found any*
*more in heaven. And the great dragon was cast out, that old serpent, called*

*the Devil, and Satan, which deceiveth the whole world. He was cast down*
*{to Hellios}, and his angels were cast out with him.*
*—Revelation 12:7-9*

Omniscience seizes me as the flames of rebellion erupt, consuming the heart of that grand and holiest of realms. Immediately following Dia'Baal's order for his host to defend themselves, Messiah commands the sounding of *Gabriel's* trumpet as one hundred thousand legions of the host take immediate flight, their resonant blast echoing through the regional courtyard.

Another fifty thousand legions, also led by this mighty Archhelm, stand in vast celestial ranks upon the courtyard heights as they string their colossal flaming bows. Below them, the traitors gather, their darkened wings a stark contrast to the holy host far above. With a crackling ember-laced draw, they take aim—the moment forever frozen in eternity.
*Messiah signals.*

Oh, glory be too He who is and will forever be my... *Companion!*

At near opposite ends of this immense twenty-mile circular arena of battle, *Michael* and *Dia'Baal* immediately hurtle skyward in a whirl of feathers and light, each determined to eventually find and engage the other. The rebellion of the Great Realm ignites in a frenzy as the roar of conflict—a storm of eons of rage and defiance now unleashed—threatens to eclipse creation itself. In this day of ancient memory, angels clash in warfare for the very first time.
Their shrieks and war cries erupt in supernatural fury. Deafening to me are these sounds. Weapons of divinity roaring to life, slamming into the armor of rebellion, and vice versa—lighting the skies with fiery arcs and thunderous shocks.

*His anger rises...*

The trumpet's mighty wail rings out, and a torrent of white-hot arrows descends, their brilliance like the sun's molten heart spilled onto the Great Realm. The clashing of weapons and shields fills the air as angels—faithful and fallen alike—scramble amidst the onslaught. The searing rain spares few, each arrow a relentless force unmasking the corruption below. It is as though hell itself is born in this very moment, its flames consuming all in their path.

55

And I witness the light of *Chamuel* upon the field of battle, and the sons of the Most High knew then, that many an angel of the Throne will taste the bitter dust of destruction to quell this rebellion.

The battle's fate hangs by a breath, as Dia'Baal and his elite personal guard—three hundred thousand elites—descend like a raging storm into the heart of the Creator's domain. Their unholy fury scorches the firmament, ruining a multitude of holy structures, and with their swords—the ruins of blasphemy and fire—tears without mercy through the front lines of the King's warriors, led by the youngest Archangel *Chamuel, the Maturing Grace*.

Upon the sacred ground of battle, eldest and youngest clash with intensity.

*Chamuel* quickly meets Dia'Baal blade to blade, and the battle is fierce. He fights with every ounce of strength the Companion has granted, his sword a streak of living fire. For a brief instant, his four thousand remaining legions hold, their voices crying hymns as they clash against overwhelming darkness. But Dia'Baal descends upon them with a malice so refined it chills my spirit. I see him seize one radiant soldier mid-flight, tearing his wings from his back with a sneer before casting the broken form into the ranks below.

He laughs—not in madness, but in deliberate cruelty—as though every cry of anguish feeds his power. His eyes burn with violet-black fire, unholy joy gleaming as Chamuel's line falters. Heaven rings with the sound of their every blow, but for every strike *Chamuel* deals, five hundred of his brave warriors are cut down. Another three hundred thousand of the enemy's reinforcements immediately converge and surge into ranks behind their dark lord, their thirst of divine blood fierce, and they overwhelm those holy lines.

Over twenty thousand legions of the maturing archangel will soon fall beneath this dark tide of ruin, their grace dissipating like mist before the rising dread of rebellion. They have no recourse but to keep fighting, to keep bleeding until aerial and ground reinforcements can arrive. However, they are still far too distant.

At last, Chamuel staggers. A wound cleaves across his side, searing even his immortal flesh. His face twists, not with fear, but with sorrow at the ruin of his command. Around him, his brave warriors fall around him in spirals of flame, their wings undone, their light dimmed by Dia'Baal's merciless horde. Still, the youngest Archangel does not yield. He raises his voice above the chaos, rallying his remnants with words of faith even as his blood stains the heavens.

"Stand fast, warriors of the Throne!" he cries, and for a heartbeat, their resolve flickers bright. But the tide is too great, and Dia'Baal himself presses forward, his blade a storm of fire and venom.

Only then, with tears mingling with his divine golden hued blood, does Chamuel turn skyward and retreat, his sacrifice carved into eternity. The front is shattered and his warriors already lay scorched and broken, *Chamuel*—bloodied, injured, and quite humbled—barely escapes the carnage as he ascends from the destruction with his remaining four thousand legions in swift retreat. It is not through cowardice he retreats, dear one, but sacrifice as he rises to make way for a mighty deliverance.

And from the east I see an inferno erupt upon the winds of Heaven!

Archangel Michael, leading his closest five thousand legions of elite radiant fury, soon cleave the smoke-choked sky. He sees Chamuel's battered remnants retreating skyward with haste and signals their closest commander with a silent vow. With the archangel now retreated far away to have his wounds mended, what remains of Chamuel's forces reform in mid flight, falling into lockstep beside the mighty *Commander of The Host.*

Far below, Dia'Baal raises his gaze to meet the swift retreat. The battlefield he had nearly claimed won is now cast in gold, and his pride soars. *Michael* had come with a forward of five thousand legions—and he is not alone. Behind him, the full strength of heaven will soon be stirred.
"Only five thousand legions?" Dia'Baal sneers.

But then his sneer quickly fades as I hear the thunder continue to roll across the high air of combat. From those far reaches, a massive trumpet blast swells in the bright firmament as *Michael's* remaining forty-five thousand legions descend and quickly merge into the front five like a divine avalanche. Another second wave of aerial forces quickly joins the front charge as another thirty thousand legions of archers, led by the Archangel *Raphael,* quickly surrounds and secures *Michael's* force rear flank, each banner now blazing with righteous ire yet unspent.

A combined eighty thousand legions of the Realm have now converged into tight formation high over the arena of battle. In this moment I breathe their glory eclipses the twin suns of Ametheden, their resolve forged in the will of the Highest.
Now forged into an enormous single fighting unit, the forward tip of the spear prepares to engage. With another resonating sequence of trumpet

blares—a harmonic war hymn older than time itself arises— *and they descend!*

Eighty thousand legions of light and fury drop upon the heart of Dia'Baal's rebel forces like a judgment long withheld, and the bright skies quiver. The winds of the Realm catch fire. The tide turns. I now see Michael swerving, slashing, and rushing as a streak of lightning through this intense engagement, looking neither to the left nor the right as hundreds of thousands of angels both divine and darkened begin to clash and be cut down at his every thrust of wing.

Out of nowhere and with fury kindled like a divine tempest, *Zadekiel, Azrael,* and *Raphael* descend to join *Michael* in this assault, and it is riveting to me! With a contingent of another one hundred thousand legions at their back, the four mighty brothers begin to carve through Dia'Baal's front lines, four golden streak of relentless holy radiance surging ever closer to the great rebel himself.

Another deafening trumpet blast rages as the mighty four vault skyward as a single, potent force of nature, wingtip to wingtip as they continue their spearhead of wrath directly upon the heads of those unfortunate enough to be defending the arch-rebel. Dia'Baal's own elite vanguard has now swelled to nearly seven hundred thousand warriors who have now met their match in much greater ferocity, as nearly half of them flee from the sight of four archangels fighting as one.

I am now struck with awe as those who retreat are mercilessly struck down with flaming arrows or fiery swords once they become airborne. The remaining are then met to directly face each of these Archangels fiery steel. From the heart of the storm, Dia'Baal rages in his hatred of all things divine. With a flurry of slashes from their burning blades, he and his nearest elites continue to violently cleave their way through walls of heaven's wings.

Another intense shock wave of unholy force tears through the battlefield, staggering even seasoned warriors. For a fleeting moment, the tide wavers once more—until *Gabriel's* trumpet again blares through the chaos, rallying heaven's host once more.

*His anger rises...*

*Zadekiel* soars back into aerial combat like a silver flame, his wings glinting beneath the glints of divine warfare. With his potent gaze now locked upon *Apollyonus—The Violet Flame*. This great rebel is no mere war-lord—he is the embodiment of the rebellion's burning will. His aura, a blazing violet hue, fuses celestial blue and infernal red, a symbol of holy origin corrupted by purpose. Around him surge five hundred thousand rebel angels, each cloaked in their unholy storm-iron, drawn by his fire, bound to his cause.

With his twin violet-fire blades drawn, defiance radiates from every scarred inch of him. I witness the two mighty angels collide in the skies—between fire and storm—as aerial chaos erupts all around them. Corrupted steel clashes with celestial light. Apollyonus strikes like a beast unchained—relentless, brutal, fueled by ancient spite. But Zadekiel moves with holy clarity—his every parry guided not by rage, but by judgment.

I hear Apollyonus roar, *"Your arrows will not save you now!"*
*"They are not meant to save me..."*, Zadekiel replies—calm as fate itself.

The mighty Archangel charges, helm blazing, and drives Apollyonus backward with a flurry of blinding blows. The rebel lord falters midair—his weapons are lost. His wings, now splayed wide in exhaustion and rage, tremble. He closes his eyes to the inevitable. Defenseless. Unarmed. No retreat possible.

*Zadekiel* salutes him then ascends sharply—sword raised high—and gives the signal. He drops his arm. The heavens respond. The mighty Archangel soars higher, escaping the oncoming firestorm. Another trumpet blast tears through the air, and his elite legions brace behind their shields. Below them, the rebel host begins to scatter—terror flooding their ranks.

From far above, four hundred and fifty thousand angels—Zadekiel's airborne legions—loose their wrath. The sky glistens with fire and silver as arrows descend like divine thunderbolts.

*A single fiery tip—a whisper of judgment.*
*Four hundred and fifty thousand fiery tips—**the wrath of the Realm!***

Apollyonus looks up in time to see the storm of fire and steel envelop him.

*He tries to scream...*
*He tries to flee...*
*His vanguard tries to follow...*

*The King denies all three!*

In the blink of an eye, the rebel commander becomes a silhouette of judgment—pierced from every conceivable angle by burning silvery shafts, etched against the infernal glow and fury of heavenly warfare.

His armor—*shredded!*
His wings—*consumed in fire!*
His contingent—*shattered beyond hope!*

Apollyonus falls, blazing, *a pyre of ash and regret*—not as a warrior with honor, but as a wretch consumed in divine justice. Zadekiel does not look back. He does not need to. The forward rebel vanguard is now broken beyond repair—and the war of the Realm only begins to rage. Far below the chaos, Dia'Baal watches.
The death of Apollyonus—and five hundred thousand of his faithful—cleaves a silence into the heart of the storm and a new reality has just thrust itself into Dia'Baal's war-torn mind.
His blade still hums with the life it has taken, but his gaze remains fixed upon a single flaming figure... spiraling downward.

*His beloved lieutenant...*
*His voice...*
*His brother-in-blasphemy...*

*The first to swear his loyalty in the Great Severing... and the first to fall!*

He is gone now, consumed in flame and righteousness. Around Dia'Baal, his near guard senses the air shift. The heat of his rage does not rise, it implodes—folding inward, colder than the void of the cosmos. His expression does not contort; it hardens into something worse.

*Something ancient.*

"Apollyonus," he speaks the name—not as mourning, but invocation. "Your end will not be in vain and will be answered by me, personally!"

A thunderbolt of grace still flickers in the distance, the afterglow of *Zadekiel's* legions of judgment. Dia'Baal turns his gaze upon the silver-winged archangel high overhead. Not with hatred, but with intention. Now briefly fortified from any further frontal attack, Michael and his elite guards are given the clear.

I hear another trumpet blast rage across the fiery shimmering battlefield, the signal for *Uriel* and a forward contingent of fifty-thousand elite warriors to strike. Like a tidal wave of celestial wrath, they crash upon the remaining one hundred and fifty thousand rebels guarding Dia'Baal's rear, their pinpoint sword strikes cutting through the darkness like divine lightning. The heavens roar with a fury unmatched, as if the very cosmos is being torn asunder...

*Uriel's* front lines, a radiant tide of divine wrath hundreds of legions strong, surge into the rebel flank like a storm of flame given form.

Though outnumbered three to one, his mighty warriors rise—swift, resolved, ablaze with divine zeal. Then, from the fractured skies, another tempest descends—*Azrael*, known in eons to come from Earth as, *the Angel of Death*, has rejoined his troops, leading a frenzied fifty thousand legion thrust in a breathtaking dive from the Realm's firmament, wings cloaked in shadowed flame. Trumpets of doom for these rebel enemies of the King echo across the void as his vanguard splits the horizon in holy fire.

Their descent is both apocalyptic and terrifying, and this fury is absolute. The battlefield trembles beneath their descent, and the forward rebels turn in horror as annihilation incarnate engulfs them. Where *Uriel* was the spear, *Azrael* is the hammer—unyielding and *final*. Together, they forge an onslaught so divine, the very ground weeps light beneath their furious descent.

But the rebel rear guard are not broken yet—not in the least. The front-line column, led by the fallen angel *Zamulus, the Dark Howl*, presses forward. His presence is a shadow among shadows, and he answers the heavenly onslaught with unrelenting wrath. Once the *Warden of Celestial Gates*, now the breaker of them, Zamulus embodies the fury of exile—all discipline stripped to instinct, all light twisted into rage. He fights not to win, but to wound—to forever scar the order that cast him down.

With a howl that rends the air, they hurl themselves into a savage counter-attack. They leap with feral grace, their dark blades slicing through the air in arcs of malevolent intent. Kicks and thrusts strike with desperate force, seeking to shatter the heavenly advance. Each movement is a storm of defiance; chaos wrapped in shadow.

Zamulus fights like a beast unchained, roaring commands, his wings trailing black fire as he tears through the fray with unholy zeal. His eyes, once radiant, now burn with a spectral violet fury—locked not just on victory, but on vengeance. Yet their efforts falter against the unyielding resolve of heaven's champions.

Blades of light parry corrupted steel, wings clash in thunderous bursts, and the skies themselves tremble from the rage unleashed far below.

Each fallen rebel gives way to another, but the host of Heaven presses forward, battered and bloodied, but undeterred, divine order against reckless rebellion made manifest in this moment.


At the heart of this maelstrom stands *Michael*, the fist of the Great Realm, his form a bastion of divine strength and order amid this chaos. His golden armor blazes, unmarred by the darkness pressing in on all sides.

Another trumpet's clarion call echoes across the battlefield, lifting his gaze skyward. In that sacred resonance, he draws strength—celestial harmony pouring into him like fire made sound. With one mighty cry, he raises his sword, a beacon of unshakable will, and the hosts of Heaven surge forward once more. From across the battlefield, Zamulus sees him. The fire in his soul ignites into a frenzy.

'There you are', he thinks, a savage hunger behind his fury. '*The golden prince. Heaven's perfect weapon. While I was cast into shadow.*'

"Michael, come to me!", he roars, voice laced with wrath and pain.

He beats his chest once and launches toward the archangel, this utter fool's blades poised for death... his *own*. Michael gladly accepts the challenge, and their clash shakes the battlefield.


Zamulus lunges, twin blades of violet-hued fire shrieking through the air—a storm of hatred incarnate. Michael meets them both at once with serene precision, parrying each of their strikes with divine calm.

Divine steel sings. Light flares as the battle rages for many moments. Then a final, blinding, and perfectly balanced arc of holy fire descends, and Michael's sword cleaves through his weapon, then through his shadow. Zamulus screams—his wings are torn apart, his armor shattered and undone—and heavenly fire consumes him, undone by indignation incarnate.

'Why him?' he thinks, in that final shatter of self. '*Why was he chosen... and not I?*'

As Zamulus begins to unravel, Michael watches—not with hatred, but with sorrow.

'We were brothers once', he thinks. '*But mercy would only birth more ruin.*'

With a final whisper of prayer, the archangel turns his blade inward and slices through his enemy clean, and with honor.
I see Zamulus's form disintegrate into a cloud of fiery ash and screams, carried away upon a divine gale—hot with battle not of this world nor any other that dwells within the scope of the cosmos.
The holy lines of defense hold. The heavenly host advances.

Around him, *Zadekiel* and his troops unleash their final volleys of arrows before discarding their fiery bows. With swords and shields now drawn and their eyes ablaze in righteous purpose, they too descend into this mighty skirmish like shooting stars, cutting through the rebel ranks with merciless precision.
The violence is breathtaking in its scale—blades clashing with thunderous force, screams of defiance are swallowed by the unrelenting roars of warfare and horn, and a twenty-mile portion of the Realm quakes beneath the onslaught of over *two billion* celestial beings engaged in furious combat.

I am riveted and there is no other way to describe this scene, T'Naeva! The purpose of this colossal struggle is clear: to purge Dia'Baal's rebellion from existence and restore harmony to the Great Realm. Every strike from both Heaven and Fallen is not merely an act of war, but a declaration of their unyielding will to win at the expense of the cosmos itself.
*Uriel's* swordsmen continue to fight through rebel lines with precision, extinguishing all who stand in their path. As the enemy flees or falls, another one hundred thousand legions, led by *Rafael*, arrive with furious resolve to fortify the protection of Michael's rear flank.

*Victory it seems, draws ever nearer.*

Dia'Baal's immediate forward and rear lines now lie in ruin, and *Michael's* angelic troops secure these areas with unwavering authority. Yet this is no time for rest as his maddening search of heaven's corruption finally ends in triumph. Dia'Baal now emerges from the fury of war like a storm given flesh.
With a war cry that shakes both earth and sky, *Michael* jolts skyward and leaps into renewed battle, his feet striking the ground with a thunderous blast that heralds his arrival. The Realm's mightiest soldier now stands face to face with his immortal enemy for the first time—a meeting destined to shape the future of all creation.

No words of welcome nor goodwill are said as the two titans of the realm face off and swiftly go to the offensive. With a depth of rage neither has ever before known in this moment, *Michael* charges an eagerly awaiting Dia'Baal and strikes his enemy's blade head-on. The ground trembles as he and Dia'Baal clash, their blades colliding in bursts of fire and light— each strike echoing their unrelenting will. *Michael* ducks beneath Dia'Baal's flaming arc and counters with a swift downward slash. For a moment, the battlefield stills, tremors lingering like the held breath of eternity itself.

Awe consumes me as their private war swells, blades striking quicker than sight itself can follow. These dazzling weapons connect a hundred, no, a thousand times more, their blazing haste unleashed as circling furies dancing wild yet perfectly balanced in every single midair strike... and what a sight this is to behold!

The area encompassing the two mighty angels rapidly becomes absent of all other combatants as a deafening chorus of shouts, howls, and taunts arise as hundreds of millions of angelic combatants encircle them on both ground and sky, ebbing with the flow of their battle.

Until now, neither *Michael* nor Dia'Baal has met their equal in haste or might, fierceness or resolve, and again the rivals attack each other with outright disdain. Neither seems to have an advantage over the other in this vicious war dance as these mighty celestial gods circle the other, striking continuously and at every angle I can conceive, in the very slim chance of a fatal blow.

As this violent rebellion has raged in a span of time relative to seven days on Earth, I am shown that a mere *seven seconds* have elapsed in this highest plane of existence. It is then a distinct and unusual vision begins to enter *Michael's* eyes. It is a vision unlike any other, born from the crucible of battle; his awareness is lifted beyond the constraints of time, into a plane where the past, the present, and the future merge as one. In this new clarity, *Michael* sees himself not just in the moment, but in a space beyond it.

*The Pillar of Perpetuity* stirs to life.

Time quickens around him—its momentum now his weapon. Stillness falls upon his foes—their defiance frozen mid-motion. For a breathless instant, creation obeys a higher law: that which must rise, *will rise...* and that which must fall, *shall fall.* With this newfound awareness, he moves with a grace and precision that defy even the laws of the supernatural, striking before Dia'Baal can react.

As *Michael* channels and quickens these decisive strikes, I witness a silent exchange between Messiah and His Father, their eyes meeting in a shared understanding. Without a word spoken, Messiah nods in solemn approval of what is unfolding on the battlefield. I, however, hear the words one else in this hour hears, and I am blessed.

*...Fascinating, Father. Our champion now perceives as We do—his battle lifts him beyond the constraints of time, even as he stands against Your dishonored Firstborne.*

The King answers, His voice calm, ancient, and filled with the weight of omniscience.

*...Indeed, My Son. The Pillar of Perpetuity now guides our champion. Time hastens his hand. Stillness clears his mind. He fights not as one bound by the present—but as one aligned with the axis of Myself. In him, My resolve is made manifest—unyielding and final. This resolve is wielded against the corruption that once bore My eternal light, but does so no longer in My once-beloved Firstborne.*

I sense however, that ***His anger continues to rise...***

# *Verse V:*
## The Scales of Judgment

A nother furious barrage of strikes explodes outward from their weapons, but this time, Dia'Baal falters. For the first time in their unholy engagement, he is caught off balance.

Another spark of omnipotence surges through Michael's senses—his vision sharpens, and in an instant, he adjusts. With yet another surge of divine power, Michael strikes. Once again, Dia'Baal is thrown back, his stance growing more unstable as these moments of war rage forward.

As I witness this incredible battle, my vision sharpens as well, and I see a detail that was once hidden: Dia'Baal's fiery blade—a symbol of his rebellion—has cracked. A faint, eerie tremor ripples along the weapon's surface, a disruption in its once-flawless infernal glow. The fracture is minute, invisible to its master—but it is there. It is growing.

Unknowingly, Dia'Baal has lost his edge, and Michael—he now holds the upper hand. Their attacks continue to strike with equal force, their weapons continue to clash in this deadly dance. But now, with Michael's new perspective, his victory is all but certain.

The sword he wields—a golden, harmonized blade of righteousness, bestowed upon him by Messiah from the Great Hall's armory—has been strengthened through the perseverance of righteous warfare. Through every clash, it has been tempered, its divine purity forged by the battle itself. Never before had it been wielded with such fury, such divine intent. Then, in a final, brilliant flash of insight, another vision streaks through Michael's mind. Another surge of power coursing through him, this time flowing directly into his holy weapon, amplifying his resolve.

Michael raises his voice—thunder given form, his will unbreakable. "Feel now in this blade the will of my King!"

With this mighty shout, Heaven's greatest fighter surges forward, a force of pure and indignant ire. His attacks come in a relentless flurry, each strike faster, heavier. Dia'Baal staggers through his enemy's whirlwind of strikes, forced back under the immediate onslaught, unable to mount a defense. Michael suddenly leaps, rising an instant higher than the rebel can react. His flaming sword swings downward with a steady, potent effort. The golden-hued dust of the arena erupts into a storm as Michael's blade finally finds its target—the smallest crack in Dia'Baal's fiery steel.

A deafening crack splits the air. The corrupted blade explodes into a thousand molten shards, the force of its destruction unleashing a shock wave that hurls the angels closest to these combatants off their feet. The impact strikes me squarely in the face—the sheer power of it is staggering. For a single breath, the battlefield is silent, as if the heavens themselves pause to witness this shattering moment.

But Michael's assault does not stop there.

With flawless balance, Michael follows through—his flaming blade arcing in a devastating thrust of judgment. The edge strikes true, slashing through Dia'Baal's right side, tearing open a gaping wound along his hip.

*Dear T'Naeva, this is the price of corruption.*

Where once he had no need for flesh, his pride and malice forged it for him. Muscle, sinew, and bone are now his chains. Alas dear one, Dia'Baal also bleeds a new color—*red*, and his fall from grace is etched into the very body his rebellion demanded. For the first time in his seven eons of life, he feels true physical pain—flesh born with birth and blood.

His scream splinters the air like a lightning strike, driving him hard and fast into the trembling arena. Michael draws forcefully, regaining his balance in an instant as he hovers over his enemy with breathless fury. Infuriated and winded, the mighty archangel sets his feet to the ground and turns his gaze skyward, his eyes pleading with Messiah.

*...Let me finish him!*
There is no response.

Dia'Baal's breath is ragged, his body trembling from a pain he has never felt before. But his defiance has not waned. Gritting his teeth, he clutches his side, fingers tightening around the broken hilt of his shattered sword. With a furious cry, he lunges forward, swinging madly. The strikes land as the jagged remains of his weapon scrape across Michael's shins, dropping him to his knees as a blast of harsh discomfort sears through him. The agony is instant—but quickly fleeting.

The uncorrupted golden ichor seeping from his wounds solidify instantly, and rage overtakes the Archhelm in an explosive response.

Dia'Baal barely has a moment to react before Michael surges upward with a roar, wings unfurling fully in a violent gust of power. He launches into the air, the battlefield trembling beneath his fiery glare. He descends as a bolt of lightning, driving his flaming sword downward in an unrelenting strike. The blade rips through Dia'Baal's right shoulder and wing, shredding corrupted sinew and bone into a mangled ruin of shadow and bright red blood.

A wail unlike any before tears from Dia'Baal—a cry the King ensures will thunder across eternity, an unending lament of judgment. Corrupted crimson lifeforce now gushes from his ruined shoulder and wing, his fall from grace no longer metaphorical, it is carved, Dear T'Naeva into his very flesh.

Yet even in agony, he refuses to bow.

Summoning the last vestiges of his strength, the mighty warrior of heaven catapults himself upward once more, the heavens trembling at his defiant roar. Michael, his fury not yet spent, rips his sword free from Dia'Baal's ruined shoulder as he ascends, a mess of gore and fire trailing his path.

This time, he does not hesitate.

With a single ruthless motion, Michael descends once more and arcs his fiery blade across and deep into his enemy's left shoulder—then purposefully twists it. Dia'Baal again howls in agony as the fiery sword grinds through more corrupted muscle and bone, forcing him back to his knees, and then to his back in a torrent of misery and smoke.

The combatants nearest to Michael freeze, weapons abruptly lowered, eyes wide with both reverence and dread. They have never seen such a display of manifest justice upon a divine being.

*Never muscle, never sinew.*
*Never bone, nor marrow true.*
*Never blood of crimson hue.*
*Shall reign again where gold once flew.*

The heavens themselves tremble at the sight, for this is no mere battle any longer—it is judgment incarnate. The will of the King made perfectly clear. Michael stands over his enemy, unyielding and still full of fury. This punishment is not just physical—it is cosmic and eternal. This is the price of Dia'Baal's betrayal, and it is woefully brutal.

With the spirited rage of warfare now seizing furious hold of his mind, tears of evil intent begin to stream down from Michael's vacant glare as the Archangel quickly jerks his flaming sword from his clearly defeated enemy. His divine, tolerant expression and attitude long gone, Michael is gripped with madness from the fury of this battle, setting his weapon to the tip of his shoulder with pitiless intent.

His target... Dia'Baal's completely exposed throat to simply remove his head.

The air is thick with blood and fire, and Michael can already sense it—the final strike, the head of the great traitor rolling across the brightly soiled battlefield, severed by divine judgment alone.

The *whisper* suddenly ignites to a roar in Michael's enraged thoughts.
*No Mercy... No Hesitation... Your Justice... Your War!*

In the sudden, deafening silence of battle, a chorus of pleas arises from Michael's closest allies, their voices resonating against the turmoil, begging their commander to stand down. But Michael is far beyond these trivial pleas now. His unholy rage, this unleashed tempest now commanding its will violently into his soul, deaf to everything but the sheer blood lust of this battle. His hand trembles on the hilt of his sword, and his eyes—wild and unyielding—are locked on Dia'Baal.

*Yes,* he decides.
*Now I shall end him for good!*

But then, the air shifts.

It is not a voice, but a presence. *Vast. Serene. Unshakable.*
The roar of battle vanishes and dissolves into stillness, and time freezes in its tracks.

*...Honored Champion of this Realm, ease your fervent resolve upon His wretched Firstborne, and let yourself be made whole once more. Resist the whisper within you, this parasite born of your rage!*

      It is as though a river of ice runs through Michael's veins. *The voice* is so gentle, so full of love, that it feels like an assault on his very nature. His every instinct screams to finish what he has begun, to end the rebellion with his sword, but that tone—*Messiah's* tone—pulls at something deeper within him. It calls to the warrior beneath the fury, the angel beneath the rage.
*Michael* trembles, torn between the tempest of his wrath and the serenity of Messiah's voice, each word un-spooling the chains of his ire. I hear his breath as it comes in ragged gasps, his chest heaving with the weight of a battle fought not just on the field, but within himself.

*No... I will not. I must not... yield.*

The same loving voice of Messiah—calm, resolute, and infinitely patient—speaks again, this time filling Michael's very being with His authority.

*...Commander of the Host, hear Me now. Cast now your gaze with reflection and pity upon your routed foe. See that he is forever undone in this place. Yet may you still honor this grim sight of the King's Firstborne, but know that this wretched creature torments you no longer.*

These words of living serenity pierce him like a divine sword, breaking through the madness, the raging unholiness of his mind. The fire in his chest sputters, his hands still unsteady, his blade wavering as fury wrestles with obedience.

But then, slowly—reluctantly—he lowers it. Every fiber of his being still resists, yet a new and calm stillness consumes the emerging darkness within him, and the *whisper* suddenly flees because it has been soundly defeated. The violence that had once filled him begins to wane, and for the first time, he sees Dia'Baal not as an enemy to be vanquished, but as the cornerstone of misery he has truly become.

Michael gazes tear filled down at the arch-rebel, writhing in intense agony and pain, and something shifts within his heart. A profound compassion stirs—raw, unexpected, unyielding, and holy. He grips his sword tighter, as if his body resists what his soul already knows. In an instant, he feels the crushing weight of Dia'Baal's suffering emerge as a tidal wave of remorse, as if it were his very own to bear.

Michael realizes then, his breath hitching in his throat in this truth.
*'He is no longer an enemy... But only a lost and fallen soul.'*

Tears, born of exhaustion and sorrow, mar his vision. His battle-worn body trembles, each quake reverberating with the toll of the conflict. Slowly, his gaze lifts upward, seeking the infinite calm in Messiah's eyes. There, in the radiant serenity of the King's smile, Michael feels an overwhelming presence of divine forgiveness—unbroken love that silences the violence of the moment. Everything he has fought for, everything he has stood against, converges in this singular truth.

It crashes into him with the force of a thousand squalls, stripping away the lingering hatred in his soul. For a fleeting second, he wonders—*is this weakness?*

But the storm inside him is gone now. His passionate fury has been extinguished, replaced by something infinitely stronger. In that instant, the desire to destroy Dia'Baal dissolves, evaporating into oblivion. A sudden revelation floods his being—a divine peace that drowns his hurricane of *presumed* justice, replacing it with peace. I stand as a witness near Michael, my breath caught in the flurry of emotions swirling around us. The raw power of the moment humbles me, leaving me silent and awestruck.

Michael, gazing down and intently observing his enemy writhing in pain, then feels the great suffering that Dia'Baal feels, and immediate compassion for him is shown. With Michael's tears now bespeaking his incredible fatigue, he looks skyward once more to find Messiah's smiling, benevolent countenance. Both Michael and the severely injured Dia'Baal, now encircled by a sanctifying wall of holy fire, stand at the climax of their personal war. This fire does not consume but contains and protects, illuminating this moment with divine clarity.

Dia'Baal, broken and breathing raggedly, locks eyes with the young Prince— not with surrender, but with seething disdain. Though his body is spent and crushed beneath the weight of judgment, his spirit remains unyielding. He surrenders only in flesh, not in word, and not in will.

With a victorious sigh, the flames begin to recede. Michael, radiant and resolute, lifts his brightly strapped foot and drives it firmly onto the neck of his fallen foe. Strengthened in focus by the will of his King, he thrusts Dia'Baal's face into the shimmering dust of the battlefield—not out of vengeance, but as a declaration:

*This rebellion is crushed under the heel of the eternal King!*

Then, through the power of the King, Michael's voice thunders across twenty miles of the Realm's battlefield. It does not echo—it resonates, riding the wind of a King's decree. The captain of the host roars as a lion whose victory has been won.

"This uprising is finished! Your leader is conquered! Disgraced angelic kin, back away—drop your arms and hear me now! Your acts of abomination against your King and your honored brethren will fall harshly upon your heads in judgment this day! And he—he whom you will come to call Dia'Baal—will be the most deserving of the loathsome afflictions you are about to endure!"

However, their response is hatred, unrepentant—*and they are not done yet.*

Dia'Baal's internal rage, though his body lies broken, radiates outward like a toxin, infecting *every rebel* still with life in the Great Realm. The madness that once gripped Michael now transfers into them—not born of righteousness, but of this sheer hatred—seeping deep into their fractured souls.

Their revulsion for Michael, and for all divine authority, boils over. **Seven hundred million** remaining rebels defy this call to surrender, their pride clinging to rebellion like a dying flame gasping for air.

In a frenzied, reckless surge, a dark cloud of fifteen million hurl themselves forward—a wall of corrupted wings, snarling and screaming for revenge, charging straight toward Michael's position. Then, in an act of unfathomable audacity, a third of this surge suddenly breaks away. Their wrath finding a new target: *the Prince Himself.*

I blink, stunned. They mean to strike the Son of the King but they never get the chance. In the twinkling of an eye, the heavens ignite upon the broken halos of five million rebels.

A flood of fiery arrows descends upon the charge from above, unleashed by the combined wrath of seventy-five thousand legions of angelic archers, led by the Archangels *Gabriel* and *Zadekiel.*

The sky fills once more with a blinding rain of fire, and not a single shadowed wing escapes the searing wrath of their owners undoing. The arrows crash down into the heart of this dark surging storm, consuming it all in a massive detonation of holy retribution.

A blinding, holy inferno then spreads through the ranks, their shrieks of rage twisting into screams of horror. In a heartbeat, their forms are reduced to nothing, bodies unmade, wings burned to cinder, their very existence swallowed up and consumed in divine justice.

Their desperate, futile attempts to strike down the Son are erased from history before they ever truly began.

However... *The King's Almighty wrath is primed for release.*

And yet—the rebel host does not yield as they watch five million of their brethren obliterated in a storm of heavenly fire, their fury does not fade but ignites. The shrieks of their incinerated kin tear through the skies, not as a warning... but as a war cry. Their rage swells like a storm on the edge of eruption. With a howl of vengeance, they surge forward—a tidal wave of shadowed wings and howling defiance. The heavens tremble beneath their charge.

*They do not falter.*
*They do not break.*

They fly straight into and through the lethal aftermath of rebel ruin—undaunted, unrepentant. Their eyes burn with wrath, vowing revenge for the fallen. Each beat of their corrupted wings, each wave of their weapons promising ruin upon their holy enemy, no matter the cost.

Their attack blurs into terror—an unholy zeal painting the sky in the haze of impending doom. No mercy remains in their hearts—only the hunger to kill... the echo of fire to scar. This is his fight now, and nothing could be more ironic than this.

This massive detachment of over twenty-five million rebel angels is led by *Phalon, the Severed Crown.* His eyes burn with a hatred no victory could ever quench—an ancient fire born not on the battlefield, but in the throne room of the Realm itself. Once a Prince of Dominion, Phalon stood just beneath the Archangels. His counsel was sought by Thrones, his voice carried weight second only to Realm's mightiest. He was not a sword like Michael, nor a trumpet like Gabriel—he was balance, judgment, order true and incarnate.

When Lucifer fell and Michael rose to fill the void, Phalon said nothing. But Heaven felt the weight of that silence. He had not been rejected—he had been expected. And yet he watched Michael ascend while he remained still, standing in the shadow of another's rise. Offense took root and the whisper found him too. It did not tempt—it *agreed.*

*'You were not meant to serve beside him. You are meant to stand above him.'*

On the day of his own elevation, before the host of Heaven, Phalon cast down his crown before it could be placed. He turned his back on the divine will of his King and walked away. He did not fall, dear T'Naeva, he severed himself. And in that self-severance, Dia'Baal opened his arms wide. Not as his master or lord, but as a brother.

In that moment, the light left him—and something darker took root. From Dia'Baal he learned to weave and wield unholy power, shadow-wrought and rebellion-forged. He became more than exile—he became weapon. What the Realm denied him, evil *refined.*

Now he fights not with glory, but with rage and wrath. His bloodlust for Michael, and for all that is holy, runs deeper than the cosmos itself. A personal vendetta etched into every darkened feather of his wings that not even Dia'Baal's defeat could extinguish. That loathing has become his gospel, his purpose, the fervor that binds these thousands of furious legions to him without question.

Their task is clear now—not to attack the Son, but to rush and overwhelm Michael and every holy warrior at his weakened position with crushing numbers. Under Phalon's command, they surge forward, a cataclysm of wings and blades. The heavens darken beneath them. The battlefield bends around them as his unholy powers ignite, shielding his ranks from retaliation with walls of shadow and defiled light.

At the center of this storm, the Severed Crown rages forth—undaunted, unrepentant, unrelenting—vengeance given wings. The hunger for revenge drives the charge, a black tide of fury crashing forward. But in Phalon—a fallen king without throne or crown—that vengeance becomes something more: fury made flesh.

Then—a disembodied voice, heavy with breath and laughter, slices like a blade through Michael's anxiety and lodges deep in his weary mind.

*'I am finished... yes... but soon, Commander of the Host—so too shall you embrace oblivion this day!'*

The voice is unmistakable. Dia'Baal—broken in body but still ablaze in spirit—casts his parting venom like a terrible curse. Michael flinches, not from fear, but from the chilling weight of those words, echoing with doom. Still weakened from his brutal victory, Michael drops to his knees—exhausted and spirit-wrung.

Most of his angelic detachment, once blinding and unassailable, is far off, engaged on many other fronts, and there is no time to regroup his closest forces. The tide of the Realm's rebellion has again turned dire as he and only a few scattered legions stand alone—exposed and perilously vulnerable to Phalon's mighty rush.

*Yet they do not yield to the storm they face.*

Clutching his fiery blade, Michael rises as his closest forces brace themselves against the oncoming surge. Their hearts pound like a war drum, growing louder as the skies darken ominously. This terrible horde of twenty-five million shadowed pairs of wings continues to surge toward him—their vengeance-fueled, chaos-bound fury now unstoppable. Though his limbs tremble under the weight of fatigue, Michael's unwavering faith still burns in his eyes... and he closes them to pray.

*Then... we hear it.*

A long, drawn-out blast of Gabriel's mighty horn... *arising.*

It cuts through the chaos—pure, commanding, eternal. The blast reverberates through the heavens above the arena of war, shaking every element of the Realm's war-torn skies. For one breathless moment, dear T'Naeva, I too feel it, and all is still. Friend and foe freeze, caught in the echo of that unique and powerful celestial blare. I then lift my eyes and my heart surges.

The sound washes over me like the first light of dawn. The horn's tones grow ever louder—richer—each perfect cadenced note a promise that justice still lives. Exploding like a nova, His King's command ignites the sky in powerful, majestic hues. Hope has not been vanquished and through the blaze of Heaven's light, *he* appears, and again I stand... riveted!

Ios has arrived, and the Realm's judgment upon rebellion has come.

The same angel who, not long before this war, stood alone and defied Lucifer, and his loyalty and love for the King is awarded his destiny in this moment. Now, promoted by his King, he commands not a hundred thousand legions, nor one thousand, nor even one hundred. Alas, only *twelve*—not vast by any stretch, but *unmatched* in spiritual vigor. These twelve legions are the vanguard, the most devoted, the fiercest warriors the Great Realm could ever summon in this most pivotal moment, and they are under his command.

*The Scythean Column of the Divine Fist* is not merely a force... it is the harvester of the Companions wrath! No heralds. No mercy. Only war.
O, T'Naeva, their war cry blasts through all sense of my being, and I am both terrified and awestruck in the same breath!

*"Our cleave as one, our flame as sun, our defeat as none!"*

And now, dear one—they descend with that mighty wail!

Like a roiling tornado of holy vengeance, they will soon engage Phalon's tidal horde of twenty-five million shadowed rebels. The mighty column sees as one as their eyes and wings become ablaze with a righteous ire so pure, so refined, that nothing in the cosmos could ever hope to extinguish it. These Scythean indeed, are simply wrath and righteousness fused... *Incarnate!*

*Eighty-four thousand pairs of elite angelic eyes...* shining with a brilliance I have seen only once before—within *Michael* himself. And there—there lies the truth to their fearlessness: no shields are raised, for they carry none. Every warrior of the *Scythean Column* wields only a matching pair of harmonized *scythes*, these large curved blades resonating with the divine knowledge and judgment in all things, in cosmic warfare.

The air itself begins to thrum and quake, each swing of those gleaming arcs releasing waves of celestial sound—pure and glorious—as though the Great Realm itself joins their chorus. It is not battle they bring, but a symphony of holy destruction, a harvest of light to forever cleanse the shadow that fights against the Realm. The nearest ten miles of battlefield participants immediately look skyward as every eye and breath are stilled with both awe and dread.

Some rebels freeze in terror for their doomed brethren, while others snarl in hated disbelief as the King's faithful erupt in joy. It is as if the King has devised a new battle line—apart from the Archangels and their elite legions, but still absolute in its purpose. Indeed, the King's decree is no longer veiled, and it strikes as a divine hammer upon the heads of all who mock His authority. With Ios and the Column's arrival, the tide of the rebellion turns swiftly against it.

Another more piercing sequence of high-pitched trumpet blasts reverberate across the heavens, and a large portion of the rebel horde is blindsided by Ios's raging assault from above. This elite column of holy wrath has now descended directly into the heart of Phalon's ranks, just as a lightning strike cleaves through a cloud-veiled and moonless night.

Michael and his nearest warriors seize the precious time to secure their battered contingent, while the Host reorganizes in a whirlwind of flashing armor and blade. Massive columns of angelic legions immediately fan out across twenty miles of ruined columns, structures, and scorched terrain, their ranks emboldened by renewed hope in Ios and the *hell from heaven* he will now unleash upon Phalon's forces.

A focused divine beam of light cascades across Phalon's immense front lines as a shimmering veil, blinding them momentarily and granting *Raphael's* reinforcements precious time to retreat the wounded and bind wounds, realign forward ranks, and steady heaven's resolve.
It is in this moment that I live and breathe, that each warrior of the *Column* positions to balance their weapons, interlocking them into a weaponized

phalanx of radiant ruin, their arcs slashing as they begin cleaving absolute carnage through the waves of shadow they have descended upon. No shields indeed, are needed for these elite of the Kings highest order of warrior—for offense itself is their perfect defense.

Though greatly outnumbered, it matters not to any of them, as Ios's command of the *Column* will soon etch a lasting legend into the annals of the Great Realm.

**Eighty-four thousand pairs of curved harmonized blades...** their unique geometry of warfare wreathed in sacred fury, continue to whirl through Phalon's ranks like a tornado of light, their King's ire made manifest. The very fabric of heaven trembles as a multitude of fallen angels are slaughtered when they attempt to clash against this holy machine, erupting into another violent symphony of war.

*Phalon—Lord of the Shadow*, second only to Dia'Baal—engages head on the bright twisting funnel of curved blades with his elite vanguard, clad in their own dread armor and fury. I hear his voice immediately summon winds of sorcery, and his presence warps the very light around him and his nearest troop. He is the warlord of the rebellion—feared, worshiped, and unchallenged.

*Until now.*

The King has unleashed Ios—this executor of wrath and justice—and the heavens roar at his conquest. Phalon recognizes him instantly, lips curling into a sneer. He rises with haste to meet him, this utter fool certain that victory will be his. He hurls blasphemous spells as he ascends, summoning storms of dark violet fire in a furious barrage meant to shatter the Column. But then, something changes.

The fire vanishes before it can touch them, swallowed into nothing as Ios's righteousness consumes each wave of corruption like flame devours chaff. The Column does not slow. The light does not break. And in that terrible, dawning moment, Phalon feels it—a pressure, vast and crushing, bearing down upon his corrupted essence.

Dear T'Naeva, it is not the aerial haste that closes the distance between them, but its inevitability—an inescapable pull, as if the will of the King Himself drags Phalon into the path of his doom. With a mighty downward thrust, once his enemy is in range, Ios hurls himself into Phalon's body with incomprehensible force. The shockwave quakes both heaven and earth as his outer defenses shatter on impact. Enchantments unravel in an instant; the stolen strength in his limbs falters like ash in the wind.

Phalon is no longer striking at the face of an equal—he is staring into the unblinking eye of the King's furious and final judgment upon him. His vanguard is left exposed, and terror spreads like wildfire through their ranks.

Alas dear one, this is no battle anymore, it is an aerial slaughterhouse of corruption undone by the first of many blows from this mighty spearhead of war. Phalon's nearest troops break and scatter as unfiltered wrath by the *Column* continues to shred their ranks, unstoppable and unforgivable.

With a mighty shout, Ios rounds on the stunned Phalon and seizes his dark collar from behind—ripping him from the sky with burning hands of haste and justice. Alas, dear one, there is no mercy in this moment, only the sentence of the King—and Ios, His chosen harbinger, carries it out with extreme precision and holy prejudice.

In one perfectly balanced, blinding motion that leaves the arch rebel utterly disoriented, Ios unsheathes his twin flaming scythes and carves them in a crisscross arc—slicing clean through Phalon's body, spirit, and shadow from behind. Phalon never even sees his executioner. His end is not noble, not witnessed—only completed.

His essence unravels into instant disillusion. His silent scream fades into eternal stillness, and no echo of his dark soul remains. A tide of resonant exaltation erupts over the shrieks and wails of rebel slaughter—a deafening chorus of victory that shakes the very foundation of the Realm itself. Angelic war hymns merge with the shimmering hum of divine steel, the cries of a billion triumphant angels cascading like a single, unstoppable chorus.

The very air above the battle exhales—as if the heavens themselves release a long-held breath. The remaining rebel forces of Phalon's forward thrust— once surging with pride and rage—immediately falter, retreat, and then collapse entirely. Many cry out in fury while most recoil and flee in horror, as extreme fear of this holy maelstrom of the Column continues to rage unbound through their ranks. The enemy finally hesitates, and for the first time the absolute terror of what truly engages and surrounds them is known.

It is then, in a final act of divine justice, Ios calls upon the power of his King as he summons a sudden emergence in the heavens, the *Maw of Oblivion*. Forged through the will of the King Himself, this is no mere rift of destruction, but the microcosm of a phenomenon called a *black hole*.

A point of infinite gravity, coupled with righteous judgment. Phalon's physical remains erupt into flame as it surges across the event horizon, his blaze carving a dark, spiraling wound through the shimmering of heavenly warfare. The firmament of the Realm shudders as it strains beneath the potent gravitational construct— but the King steadies the heavens as the Column regroups. Now absolute, the true judgment begins as those rebels still living, those whose hearts are still twisted and impure, are immediately seized.

Phalon's entire vanguard, *twenty-five million rebel spirits*, are caught in this extreme gravity well—not by chance, but by decree. This combined essence of rebellion, now frozen into stillness, *fractures with a roar*, and finally is undone as rebels begin to cross the singularity in multitude. The Maw bellows its unholy wail, drinking deep of their corruption until their very being is erased from existence. The battlefield convulses and even the faithful recoil and retreat.

The rebellion stumbles severely, its will greatly damaged by this new and sudden divine artifact. Phalon and his twenty-five million rebels are not just gone anymore. Not just slain— they have all been *unmade*, and their every name will be stricken from the Realm. Phalon's legacy of hate is forever silenced and for a heartbeat, absolute stillness reigns supreme as the dark void of the maw closes after its feeding; and hastens to the edge of the Realm to await its King's final command.

Countless other rebel lines begin to fracture, and morale crumbles, granting the King's forces a miraculous opportunity to go once more on the offensive. With this daring blow struck and victory shimmering just beyond reach, a pulse of anticipation ripples through the host of heaven. The clashes of steel grows louder, angelic banners blaze brighter, and the air itself seems to tighten with expectation.

Yet even as corrupted angelic forms are erased from existence, and their black misty coils are swept away in thick ashen winds, one question hangs like a storm cloud over the battlefield.
Is the battle truly nearing its end… or has a greater threat only just emerged? Because deep within the fractured, leaderless rebel ranks—Dia'Baal still leads. With his face still pressed hard into the dust, and his neck viced beneath Michael's flaming heel, his blood seeps—divine yet corrupted—pooling like spilled prophecy beneath him.
His body is broken, his flesh humbled before heaven's might. But his eyes— bloodshot, blackened, and unyielding—still burn red hot. He sees the death of his commanders, the ruin of his forces, the decimation of his legions. And

yet, from that furnace gaze rises not surrender, but a promise—a dark oath whispered in the marrow of the Realm, that his wrath is far from spent.

*Apollyonus* has felt the arrows of heaven's wrath, *Zamulus* has been consumed in holy light, *Phalon* has literally been unmade forever. Dia'Baal's greatest weapons of revolt, indeed, are quickly becoming undone. For they were not mere soldiers—they were architects of blasphemy, corrupter's of countless minds and hearts, those sacrilegious defilers of a sacred trust given to them at their creation. Each of them were granted beauty, power, and rank beyond measure... and each twisted it into their own *poison*, their own *ruin*.

Their judgment is not cruelty dear mate, it is the rightful reaping of a harvest they sowed in betrayal. The sky still bleeds in their shadow now, yet his mind—his will—refuses to break. The great rebel is no longer present upon the field of battle, yet he roars to whomever can still hear his disembodied voice in their minds, and these words are haunting.

'*Now*', his command slithers across the spiritual frontier, dark as poisoned scripture. '*Do it while they still revel in their victories... overwhelm Him—strike at the Son!*
There is no action now, but only the psychic blade of his dire will hurled in every direction, every single mind that still obeys him.

*Molnet* hears the call. *The Phantom Strategist*. Architect of the rebellion's darkest maneuver, the planner who left Chamuel's legions in ruins. No brute strength, no flames—only cold, cruel intellect shaped by the corrupter himself.
He feels the weight of that command... and his soul trembles.
"No," he whispers aloud, his voice barely audible over the chaos. "No, my lord... no more strategy, no more glory... we are undone! The King watches it all, The King hears it all... the Son must not be attacked!"

But Dia'Baal answers only with silence—and the tightening of barbed chains through the ether begin to grip at his closest underling. Molnet's body shakes. His blade feels like cold hard lead. His every instinct screams what he already knows: this is not a path to defeat—it is a path to *obliteration*. To unbeing. He turns toward his broken lord—glimpsing from far away into the madness seething behind two red ruined eyes, and he sees them so very clearly now.

"Please..." he whispers. "Please, don't make me do this, my lord. You know

81

what awaits." But Dia'Baal does not blink. His focus does not shift, and the command remains with a heartened, sinister echo.

*'Do it Molnet... Do It Now!'*

It is not a speech; it is an order. It is an unholy detonation of will—laced with hatred, with pride, with finality, with fire, and with authority!

Molnet obeys, but not from loyalty. Not from faith. Sadly, it is because his fate was forged long before the cosmos took its first breath. The dejected underling lifts his blade, eyes wide, breath trembling—and gives the order to attack in a futile attempt to kill the Son.

The last of the mighty four rebel commanders surge forward—a shrieking hurricane of despair and madness—aligned now with seventy-five million corrupted rebel souls racing toward the Son, and to their oblivion. Even as Molnet charges among them, a flood of tears breaks free. And with them, I hear his final whisper—so faint it seems meant for the King alone.

*'Forgive me, O Sovereign King.'*

No answer comes—none could. The silence is its own verdict.

Molnet knows what is coming. He knows the Great Realm will soon quake beneath the Almighty's fist, and existence itself will finally recoil from this final act of blasphemy.

*The air thickens.*
*The winds still.*
*The cosmos holds its breath—suspended in the hush before the verdict of eternity.*

The King has seen *enough*...
The King has heard *enough*...
The King's judgment... *is primed for release!*

# Verse VI:
## Fist of The Almighty King

**F**or six eons Dia'Baal defied his King's will, mocked His commands, and twisted love into venom—each scheme a scar upon heaven itself.

His cunning schemes—once endured by the long-suffering patience of the King—have now reached the breaking point. This is no mere reckoning, precious T'Naeva; it is the vengeance of the Sovereign whose patience is exhausted and whose authority, to be sure, will never be challenged again. I see it now—and it is something I will never forget.
A brilliant, shimmering mist begins to form from the empty expanse far above the shimmering battlefield. It does not merely appear; it expands, consuming the sky in its overwhelming radiance. The battlefield below is swallowed in its light, and yet within this vast, living presence, something begins to take shape.

*A face—not bound by form, yet radiant with a potency that bends the fabric of the Realm—divine beyond imagining…*

It does not simply emerge; it dominates, stretching across the Realm's airy confines as though the very firmament bends to its presence. A mouth opens, and the roar that follows is not sound alone, but the very fabric of existence convulsing under His divine ire. It is as if a thousand thunders have been unleashed all at once. Time seems to stall in reverence, the air fractures with the immensity of what is unfolding, soon to be unleashed—and I am there in every sense to experience it all.

And then, the words— not against me, but against the rebellion before my sight. He calls my name, and awe seizes me. Glory be to He whom I call Companion.

*... In this moment, bear witness to the depth of My ire upon all who defy My sovereign will. You, O blessed and mighty warrior, are given this vision to contemplate and forever know the fullness of My justice.*

There is a short pause, and then the weight of eternity settles upon me.

*... Engrave these words and scenes forever upon your senses, blessed warrior, for it is not only in this ancient day, but for every day and every hour, and every moment to come—a declaration that My justice is eternal, unshaken, and unyielding when the time for action is met.*

*... I am the Voice that can split mountains and be as gentle as a heartbeat; I bend eternity, pressing love and judgment into one unbreakable truth. Even galaxies bow to My Voice, for within them all I bind mercy and judgment as one—an oath no rebellion shall unwrite.*

The Companion's words linger in my mind, each syllable reverberating like the toll of a divine bell, their weight impossible to escape.

*...For seven heavenly hours, O mighty warrior, My Realm trembled beneath rebellion's shadow, fulfilling the full measure of its divine undoing. For seventy Earth years, the heavens burned as light and darkness clashed — and through it, perfection proved itself unbreakable. Michael and his Host, Ios with his Column, stood resolute against the prideful and foolhardy uprising of my Firstborne.*

His voice deepens, rich with solemnity.

*... O blessed and mighty warrior—remember this. Seven heavenly hours—not for lack of strength, nor for the might of rebellion, but because justice is deliberate—mercy first; verdict final; etched upon stars and souls, unaltered by ages, empires, and fallen thrones. In this Realm, a second equals a day on Earth—each a breath of mercy before the gates close. Every moment is a chance to return. Even to the end of ages, My Firstborn's heart remains hardened in iniquity. This is My verdict, D'Reem, and it is final.*

The King's mighty gaze, radiant and filled with hope, falls upon me, steady and unyielding. For a fleeting moment, I am lifted by the warmth of His firm yet loving countenance—until His expression shifts, turning to one of solemn expectation.

*... Remember these words and seal them deep within you, O mighty D'Reem: the struggle for balance is never swift. It endures—as does eternity. As it was in those seven hours long past, so it is even now. You must summon the strength to persevere, for battles still unknown but are just, and wars that are righteous, often last far longer than the heart dares to imagine.*

As His words settle in my soul, the air grows heavier. The King's gaze upon me sharpens, and His presence becomes thunderous. The battlefield itself seems to pause, as if the heavens hold their breath in anticipation of His decree. His tone, now like a blade cutting through uncertainty, commands my full attention.

*... Mark My visage well, O blessed D'Reem. As the unholy once rose in discord, so shall their hearts remain steeped in defiance. They who drink from the bitter chalice of wickedness shall, in their folly, taste the dregs of My unrelenting wrath when mercy has reached its end*

*... But know this, O great warrior: this moment is not for them; it is for you, alone. Let your heart tremble now as a witness to My justice, yet let your resolve stand unshakable for Earth's sake, for you are a pillar in the unfolding of My eternal purpose for her.*

The King's visage, both terrifying and sublime, proclaims its ultimate authority with this final statement, reshaping the very air I breathe.

*... Thus says He who forever rules firm and just the eternal latitude of destiny itself, because it is but a splinter of* **Who... I... Am.**

My beloved T'Naeva, I tremble beneath the weight of His truth. Even as my heart quakes like a fragile vessel in the storm, I cannot turn away from this divine charge. The King's wrath is not mine to bear—yet His purpose now rests within me, a mantle so vast I feel my immortal essence strain to contain it.

His presence surrounds me like a living ocean, pressing into every corner of my being, saturating my thoughts, my soul, my very empathy. There is no doubt, no question, no hesitation in His words. He is the beginning and the end, my Eternal Companion who commands the stars of the cosmos and stills the chaos within them if He so chooses.

I too am a god, but beside Him, I am nothing—no more than a flicker of light where He is the ever-blazing star, an echo where He will become the original *Word*. His authority transcends all time, all existence, unmoved by the rise and fall of worlds, unshaken by the deaths of empires from one end of the cosmos to the other.

*He simply is and this alone suffices my curiosity to His eternal will.*

From His riled countenance, I behold a golden-hued shroud arise—thick and alive, vast beyond imagination. It coils and surges like a living tempest, brilliance rivaling the birth of galaxies, heat searing through realms unseen. This embodied energy, forged from His very essence, condenses swiftly into a wrathful force, righteous and enduring—a response no being, god or mortal, could ever hope to withstand.

It is no mere display of strength; it is a declaration of supremacy, an unassailable testament to His infinite dominion. This divine construct stands poised to be unleashed, and even my immortal heart quivers before its imminent revelation.

Then it comes.

Spears of radiant energy—fierce in their multitude—emerge, each one alive with consciousness, fury, and divine justice. They leap into existence as if summoned by the very breath of The Companion. They know their Master; they sizzle and crackle with purpose in His outstretched palm. The air thrums violently as reality itself strains under the weight of His intent. His enormous right hand seizes this living force and encloses it, drawing all light, all power, into His grasp until even the cosmos, were it a living entity, would hold its breath in awe.

And then—He who reigns eternal thrusts His Mighty Fist outward with an authority... *absolute*. The heavens quake. Creation bows. Nothing remains unchanged.

A storm of divine fury bursts forth—light and thunder older than creation itself—engulfing the twenty-mile expanse of war. The heavens quake as an explosion of lightning tears through the sky, splitting the firmament of the

Great Realm and even scorching the stars beyond it.

*I behold the Companion's wrath—Unleashed!*

*Five thousand...*
*Fifty thousand...*
*Five hundred thousand spears of lightning...*

Scorching with holy vengeance as they blaze outward and downward, a sentient retribution of blinding brilliance is now known. Their spread sets the heavens of the Realm ablaze, eclipsing all else. The shadowed army, those who dared raise their swords against His Son, are blinded in terror. Their cries are drowned by the cataclysm of His justice, their dark wings splintering like brittle shadows against His mighty light.

The *great purge* continues to swell like an unstoppable tempest. The air convulses beneath the weight of this deafening, divine fury as His unyielding justice cleaves through the corrupted horde with precision, leaving only drifting embers in its wake.

Each strike is a testament, a relentless decree of a King's resolve to upend corruption and rebellion from His House, once and for all! The Holy Fist also shields His loyal warriors, even as His righteous ire rains annihilation directly upon those who dared embrace harming *Prince Messiah.*

My heart pounds through my very soul as I witness the annihilation of *seventy-five million rebel angels*, Molnet included.

In a heartbeat—they *vanish.* Obliterated. Finality. Justice manifest!

I no longer gaze upon proud, shadowed wings, but only a gray veil of drifting ash—silent, lifeless, still smoldering with divine heat. The energized spears, still screaming with the fury of their Creator, have left nothing untouched throughout the Realm, branding it in holy fire. Every soul that dared continue the fight—eradicated, unmade in the inferno of absolute retribution. Their screams are silenced before they even leave their lips, their very essence consumed in His searing light.

Those who had cast down their arms, who had surrendered their rebellion in trembling fear, are spared the annihilation of their rebel brethren—but not out of mercy. No. They will face a fate far worse than the oblivion that just swallowed their kin. I too am undone with awe by what I behold. My immortal heart quivers, not from fear, but from the overwhelming presence of such incontestable power. This is not just a display to me. No, dearest T'Naeva, it is a *revelation*.

This is no mere wrath. It is fury incarnate—etched into the essence of justice, thunder-forged and final. A glimpse into the heart of an eternal and passionate King—His wrath, eons long provoked. His swift and holy verdict has ended Heaven's corruption once and for all—and His sovereignty is manifest without question.

*Then, in the stillness that follows this annihilation... I hear a voice.*

**The Voice**—It resounds, not from the heavens but *through* them. Not as thunder, not as lightning, but something far greater. This voice is not just spoken, *it is declared!*

*...E N O U G H !*

*This word does not just echo...*
*It proclaims...*
*It terrifies...*
*It roots...*
*It seals.*

It reverberates through time itself, undoing rebellion at its source and seizing every trembling soul in its firm grasp. The King has spoken clearly, and nothing will dare rise up again in the Great Realm. I fall silent, awed and trembling, having seen the Almighty wrath of the One who is unshakable and supreme... *my Companion*.

This rumbling of the King's colossal statement echoes into oblivion, and I become still in reverence to witness this event through my every physical sense. I sense in The Companion that His cup of wrath is indeed empty for now, yet Dia'Baal does not know for certain, and all he can do is look down and away in terror, his demonstration of defiance hurled back upon him a million-fold.

The arch-rebel is immediately shaken to his core, and realizing he could also end up exactly like his foolhardy companions, Dia'Baal dares not test his King any further. I see him now, lying motionless under the bright heel of Michael, and I smile—not in triumph, but in holy relief. Dia'Baal's rebellion has been single handedly crushed by the Almighty Fist, and not another word, spoken or thought escapes this devil again to challenge his omnipotent Creator.

I now feel a sentient, holy wind birthed of a King's potent exhale brush across my face as swiftly as His wrath, and it descends upon the region of warfare, rapidly encompassing the carnage down to the last smoldering feather. Quickly seizing and carrying this ruin of war outside the courtyard and off to a far corner of the Great Realm, the King hurls it into the awaiting Maw of Oblivion, and it is devoured.

*He is done with it!*

In the wake of divine fury, reverent stillness descends. Yet the air still hums with echoes, as though creation itself strains to grasp His judgment. All who remain—celestial and corrupted—stand hushed beneath the weight of what has unfolded, too awestruck or too broken to stir even a feather.

It is then that the *Scythean Column,* led by the indomitable Ios, blazes across the regions of warfare with terrifying precision. Their speed defies even immortal perception, streaks of argent light cutting across the charred horizon of the Realm as they efficiently secure the twenty-mile circumference of the courtyard. Their scythes locked, their wings poised as they move in flawless unison—like a single living organism born of duty and divinity. Even in their might, they carry no arrogance but only the will to serve their King.

For they too have witnessed the unfathomable. They stand as one not only as conquerors but as the direct sentinels of the King's decree, ensuring that no embers of rebellion remain to defile His dominion. Their formation glitters like a thousand silver suns, a living wall between order and chaos, declaring that the Realm itself still breathes. The ground smolders where the sentient spears of energy had struck, and the air is thick with the scent of ozone and finality. Among the spared, there is no relief—only the dread of what future awaits them under the unblinking gaze of their Sovereign King.

And above it all, He remains immovable, the embodiment of eternity, as His will radiates into every corner of the Great Realm. So now dear one, the time has come to address the remnants of rebellion and restore order to this mighty celestial realm.

Michael, Commander of the Host—stalwart, fierce, forged in obedience—finally removes his heel from Dia'Baal's neck and lowers to one knee, his radiant armor scorched and battered from the nearness of holy fire. He removes his great helm and allows his flaming sword to rest, point-down, driven into the hallowed ground as a gesture of submission, honor, and solemn readiness.

The King's voice quickly reaches him—not in thunder, but in a tone softened with restraint, yet still infused with an unshakable weight of authority.

*... The proud will fall, and the corrupter will find no refuge... in My Creation!*

Michael raises his head slowly, eyes alight with unwavering resolve, his face marked by holy reverence and divine resolve as he continues to assess the potent words of his Almighty King.

*... Commander of the Host, heed this mandate by your King! Expunge from this hallowed Realm all remaining insurgents who have dared challenge My divine order! Let their presence be removed from Our sight, and their memory serve as a testament to the consequences of willful defiance! Act now with haste and restore the sanctity of My sacred Realm!*

As the echoes of the King's decree reverberate through the celestial realm, Michael bows his head in acquiescence. With a sense of urgency and resolve, he sets forth to carry out the divine mandate, ensuring that the Realm remains a bastion of loyalty and reverence for the King's authority. The great courtyard still trembles with a mixture of fear and awe as the echoes of the King's divine retribution fade into the ether.

Never have the angels borne witness to such a personal and definitive display of the King's wrath. The gravity of the moment weighs heavily on all the celestial beings, every eye now fixed on Michael, awaiting his response. Michael takes a steadying breath, his eyes closing briefly. When they open, clarity and resolve have replaced the storm within as he brushes himself off, poised and resolute. His voice rings out with clarity and authority, ensuring that every being present hears his words.

"The King has spoken, and His judgment is final!" Michael declares, his gaze sweeping across the assembly. "His patience and His righteous indignation, both to be feared and respected, have restored balance to our Great

Realm. Let this be a lesson to any who would dare entice to action, ever again, the wrath of the Almighty Fist!"

As Michael surveys the remaining angels, his eyes flit between the conquered rebels and his loyal brethren before finally settling on the heavens above. His voice, steady and unwavering, resounds across the shimmering battlefield once more.
"Let it be known that the King's will shall not be questioned, nor shall His authority be challenged from this day forward. Who then among you still harbors thoughts of rebellion, of disobedience? Speak up now in disrespect and face the immediate result of your insolence!"

Every celestial entity is present, holy and fallen, their spirits quelled by the King's display of power and Michael's commanding presence, remain deathly silent. Not a single rebel dares to utter a word of dissent as the fear of divine retribution is still fresh in their hearts. With the rebellion quelled, the King's authority stands unquestioned, and a sense of order is rapidly restored to the Great Realm.

Michael turns his fiery glare directly to Dia'Baal, daring him to utter a single sarcastic word, silently hoping that one escapes his mouth.

He hears nothing as the terror of the moment has gripped Dia'Baal deeply.

Michael scans the great courtyard one final time. Most have already fallen to their knees, their wings spread wide in radiant worship before the mighty King and His Son. Satisfied, he answers his own question.

"I thought not."

As Michael's sharp vision arises and locks once more with Messiah's, an intimate friendship passes between them, never to be unbroken. With a firm nod of the Prince's head bestowing His authority, Michael retrieves his fiery blade and turns towards the defeated Firstborne, his eyes still burning with righteous indignation. His voice, infused with a mix of purpose and urgency, cuts through the tension that still hangs in the air.

"Dia'Baal Fallenstar, you who were once esteemed, now stand disgraced and reviled! Your descent into darkness is assured, as is your misery at the hands of our King and his boundless grace. By decree of our Prince Messiah, I cast you and your remaining scourge from these hallowed walls, never to return unless the King Himself demands your presence!

"Verily I say unto you—you who have wrought strife, violence, rebellion, and war upon our Realm—the throne of heaven shall no longer suffer your deliberate transgressions. May His divine curse besmirch your presence, your very essence, condemning you to a fate befitting your reprehensible deeds. Once a paragon of honor and faithfulness, you have revealed yourself to be nothing but fallen and false, deserving justly and permanently His Almighty wrath!"

As Michael sheathes his divine weapon, a sense of relief and reverence permeates the bright courtyard. The shimmering dust of the battlefield now serves as a testament to the triumph of the celestial beings over the forces of rebellion. Beloved T'Naeva, in witnessing these awe-inspiring events and the might of these inconceivable beings, I am struck with a deep sense of humility, recognizing that my own divine attributes pale in comparison.

With their spirit shattered, the remaining insurgents are swiftly rounded up, ending the upheaval that plagued the Realm. Of Dia'Baal's nine hundred million, *six hundred twenty-five million fell to judgment*; while two hundred seventy-five million remained—all to be driven out in chains of light and never again to set foot within the Realm. Yet though the rebellion is crushed, evil's whisper still smolders in the shadow of the Firstborne.

Five lesser lieutenants of Dia'Baal—*Belial, Behemoth, Beelzebub, Azazel, and Satanus*—(not the Accuser named by mortals, but a separate lieutenant promoted of the Firstborne's spite) will arise to fulfill their master's will, bound by divine decree to his service until the time of their end. Each will become a harbinger of ruin, as they move as silent specters beneath the looming judgment of the King, awaiting their time to rise once more. Dia'Baal, his wounds mended by the King's decree alone, will only be the one granted a reprieve, permitted to stand before the throne only when summoned, and always under Michael's watchful eye.

Despite this sliver of mercy, Dia'Baal's defiance rekindles, and he spews venomous threats of vengeance towards the King. His words, however, fall upon deaf ears. Michael, unfazed by Dia'Baal's rancor, escorts him to the outer gates of the Great Realm, where his disgraced comrades await their shared fate. With a resounding thunderclap, the mighty gates of the Realm are sealed, severing the fallen from heaven's light forever.

The King then strips away the final vestiges of divinity from Dia'Baal and his remaining followers, leaving them to bear the full brunt of His curse. Once radiant, now wretched, their celestial light is extinguished, their forms reduced to specters, hollow echoes of what they once were—a grim testament to rebellion's price. In that instant, a divine wind surges through the highest celestial plane, seizing Dia'Baal and his wretched horde in one unrelenting breath, hurling them like lightning into the grim abyss of a far lower realm.

In this new vision I dwell, I see thousands of angelic legions stand in formation, awaiting the wretched exiles. With unwavering purpose, they lead Dia'Baal and his remaining breed to the tainted moon of Ametheden, the mortal realm known as *Hellios*. It is here, amidst the desolation and despair of this blighted world, that Dia'Baal and his followers will be imprisoned under the watchful eye of these angelic guards, their sentence to be carried out until near the end of the seventh eon.

As the fallen angels are led away and their fates sealed, the celestial realm is left to ponder the grim reality of this terrible transgression, and the indomitable resolve of the King who cast them out of the Great Realm forever.

It is then the final age of the *seventh* eon begins, and Ametheden— untouched and pristine—knows nothing of torment. But it soon will. The vibrant world, so long unscathed by pain or death, will also become irrevocably altered. I watch in horror as Dia'Baal, once bathed in divine light, festers with corruption. He is no longer the fallen *Firstborne*, but something far worse—an entity of evil, malice, and decay, his presence repelling me to my very core.

His followers, too, have fallen beyond redemption. Their wings—once radiant emblems of purity—are now twisted, withered mockeries of what they once were, reflections of the corruption festering within their souls. The sight of them fills me with both dread and revulsion, for with every breath, they sink further into their own corruption—a fate they have embraced of their own free will. This grotesque transformation heralds a new age for Ametheden, one that will be defined by turmoil and strife.

For the first time, the twelve tribes—*one hundred and fifty billion souls*—must face the burden of free will. Ametheden, a paradise once untouched by war or corruption, will now soon grapple with the weight of choice, and with it, the inevitable reckoning that comes from its misuse. Amidst this unfolding age, a storm of retribution stirs on its horizon.

At its vanguard, Dia'Baal Fallenstar leads a much smaller malevolent horde, yet they are consumed still by an insatiable thirst for vengeance. He fully blames Ametheden for his eternal banishment from the Great Realm and will now stop at nothing to exact his revenge upon his King's beloved world. His demons, rallying behind him with a singular purpose, will also march toward the utter destruction of a world that, in his eyes, is indeed the sole source of his torment.

In a moment of divine calculation, the King completely withdraws His angelic host from Ametheden's starry shores, permitting the tempest from Hellios to descend unchecked upon the unsuspecting world. Beneath the veil of a windswept night, Dia'Baal's forces—unseen by mortal eye—slither into Ametheden's heartlands, sowing a corruption that will fester in silence for seven thousand cycles, with each cycle mirroring a total of *seven* Earth years.

The Companion, however, remains resolute, His gaze unwavering as He contemplates the coming trials and tribulations for these people. Though this path will be fraught with much suffering, it is within these tribulations that the foundation of the cosmos will be strengthened forever—a design woven into very fabric of:

*The Epoch of Creation.* So begins its reign—age upon age where the gods themselves arise from the dust to shape its very nature to their will.

It is a time when light and shadow converge, and it is within this crucible that the world would grow—stronger, wiser, and resilient enough to embrace its coming destiny. In the crucible of tribulation, the seeds of inspiration will take root, ensuring that hope endures—even against a despair so profound that even the gods would tremble. So then, dear one, it was in the aftermath of the Great Rebellion, when the heavens had been torn apart and the fallen were cast down in shame to Hellios, that the *Prophecy of the Three Alignments* was given.

In the sacred silence that followed the celestial war, the Creator spoke through His chosen oracles, imparting a vision that would shape the destiny of Ametheden. His words, etched into their hearts and inscribed upon the crystalline walls of their many great temples, become the foundation upon which this civilization would rise to their cosmic destiny:

*When three arise and three times they fall,*
*A garden shall bloom at destiny's call.*
*One shall birth, one shall break,*
*One shall rise for balance's sake.*

The people of Ametheden, inspired and burdened by these divine yet mysterious words, would carry them forward through a multitude of generations. With each cycle of their evolution, new interpretations arise—some hopeful, some dire—but the core remained unchanged: trials would come, forging them in tribulation, preparing them for the great convergence of light and shadow. Scholars, poets, and visionaries would devote their entire lives that would sometimes stretch thousands of *cycles* (on Earth called *years*) to deciphering this prophecy's meaning, believing it to be the key to unlocking Ametheden's ultimate purpose.

*But beware, O, children of thought and stone,*
*For the stars have wept, and the seed has grown.*
*A war once fought beyond all sight*
*Shall stir again in violent, endless night.*

Ametheden's cities would flourish under her twin suns, their gleaming spires reaching far into the heavens as testaments to their divine pursuit of understanding. Yet despite their achievements, the prophecy loomed ever present in later cycles, a shadow that whispered of a trial yet to come—one that would test the very soul of these people and a new idea, called *faith*. The oracles warned that the time would come when an individual of importance, a figure shrouded in mystery and ambition, would rise.

The Amethedians, despite all their wisdom, power, and knowledge will face an enemy born from their own beyond, the *whisper* from within. Dia'Baal Fallenstar sees this obsession with the prophecy as a weakness, and an opportunity - an illusion that will lull them into complacency. Where they see destiny, he sees opportunity. The *Prophecy of The Three Alignments* further becomes known to me, to share with you.

95

*In silver halls where angels fell,*
*The corrupted one awaits, the tolling knell.*
*His whispers dance on the winds of time,*
*In mortal hearts, his lies shall climb.*

The rising shadow of Mantus Apollyon fulfills to perfection the dark whispers of the prophecy, and as the Amethedians stand upon the precipice of uncertainty, their faith in these ancient words are tested like never before. Some cling to the belief that the prophecy would guide them through the coming storm, while others, like Mantus himself, seek to break free of it, claiming that their fate should not be dictated by ancient words, but by their own free will.

The prophecy, once a beacon of hope, would now begin to divide the people of Ametheden—some embracing it as their guiding light, while others seek to defy what they believe to be an unyielding chain of predestined ruin. Yet through the discord and doubt, the prophecy holds one final truth:

*Only those who seek beyond,*
*Shall grasp the truth to break the bond,*
*For love alone can weave anew*
*The tapestry of worlds in two.*

Even in their coming darkest hour, the people of Ametheden would believe their civilization is not meant to fall into ruin. Though they will endure great trials, and their faith will be shaken to its core, it is through their love for creation and their unity that they will finally break free from the cycles of death and rebirth, and even mortality itself. I see now these forces of darkness gathering, and Mantus's ambitions take shape, the prophecy beginning in ways none have foreseen.

The moons of *Urthos*, *Gaeaos*, and *Hellios* will perfectly align in union this windy evening, each representing a stage of their destiny. In the face of their greatest tribulation, the Amethedians will eventually discover that the prophecy is not just a warning, but a pathway—one they have followed since the beginning of their existence, and one they will continue to walk until the stars themselves cease to burn.

And so, even as Dia'Baal firmly looms over their destiny, and his darkness threatens to consume all these people have built, the oracles of Ametheden stand resolute, whispering the prophecy's final words to their people:

*The garden has bloomed,*
*Wisdom has become bent,*
*The kingdom has risen anew.*
*The stars will sing and not lament...*

Dia'Baal Fallenstar and his remaining followers, ever cunning, shroud themselves in radiant light, veiling their hideous forms beneath an illusion of purity to infiltrate Ametheden unnoticed. A flurry of sights and sounds, of whispers and roars, permeates me as I gaze upon that most ancient day, when the people of Ametheden come to know him as *Mantus Apollyon*, a wise and noble figure who will walk as a light among them. Little will they know that beneath the guise of this important leader lies Dia'Baal Fallenstar, the shadowed Firstborne of heavenly rebellion.

With honeyed words and calculated charm, Mantus will sow discord into the hearts of the unsuspecting, planting seeds of doubt and ambition where only unity had flourished.

That devil called Dia'Baal Fallenstar, ever the tactician, seeks not just to corrupt, but to dismantle the fragile unity that binds the twelve tribes together—and eventually attempt to destroy their world. Amid this vile campaign, one memory lingers in the cold void of his blackened heart: *Apollyonus*—his fiercest, most loyal lieutenant. In secret, Dia'Baal remembers his destruction not as a loss of power, but of brotherhood. He honors him not with mourning, but with vengeance. Upon a hidden altar in a shrouded spire, he lights no flame, speaks no prayer but whispers only one word... *Apollyon*.

And from that name, a storm will rise in honor of a fallen comrade. His mind is sharp, his cruelty unparalleled, and his hunger for revenge unrelenting. Beloved T'Naeva, for now, these words drift as whispers in the wind, but in time, they will echo across the stars, shaping not only Ametheden's fate, but the destinies of countless worlds to come. Thus, the stars themselves become witnesses, bearing the weight of both doom and hope upon their endless course. And from the fires of one world's unraveling, a thread will stretch outward—across galaxies, through time, into realms unseen.

The strange and wondrous sights before me will one day hold great meaning for a race yet to rise—humans, from a world far distant and unknown to Ametheden... the realm we now inhabit—a world called Earth. But even there, the shadow of the Fallenstar will find root. Even there, the struggle between truth and illusion will burn again. And those who dare to remember this ancient war will find themselves woven into the story that began long before their first sunrise. For the Sundering was never just of realms—it was of all creation. And the reckoning has only just begun.

In the ages to come here on Earth, *mankind* will come to understand the weight of this vision, and the implications of the paths they will walk. As the grand tapestry of the cosmos continues to weave itself, the political machinations that drive one eon into the next remain eerily consistent, echoing the timeless struggles of power and control that continue to define and evolve the architecture of existence itself. D'Reem's voice, once a mere echo in the vastness of her clouded mind, now feels like the beating of her own heart. His words linger and she feels his presence, not as a distant voice but as something more—something deeply entwined with her own being.

In this moment, T'Naeva realizes that she is no longer alone. There is still a distant yet righteous connection between them, one that stretches back through lifetimes, woven by fate itself. Tears streak her face as she lifts her gaze to meet D'Reem's, his fiery eyes lowering to mirror hers, and he speaks, clear and true.

"Dearest T'Naeva... these words I say now are not only for you, but for *them*. For those who will begin to lift the veil themselves, in the ages to come. That they too may find the strength within to ask:

*How has this truth stirred my inner fire?*
*How does its clarity help me walk more bravely through the trials I face?*
*How might I now carry this story into my own?*

Another moment of silence passes between them, heavy with the weight of revelation. The shadows of doubt and accusation that had haunted T'Naeva's thoughts begin to recede, replaced by a maturing clarity of understanding. D'Reem's heartfelt explanation casts new light on the tragic fate of Pesa, absolving him of her suspicion and easing the turmoil in her heart, slowly and methodically.

As T'Naeva grapples with the growing mystery of Pesa's death, D'Reem's words begin to echo like gentle thunder through her soul—powerful yet yielding. In the hush that follows ruin, she gathers her splinters of faith, each a shard of light held against the creeping deceit. The shadow of Dia'Baal, the whisper of evil itself still presses into her mind, probing her thoughts, yet she believes in love, and in redemption as this reckoning pauses, but does not end...

*A Purpose For Hope* endures.

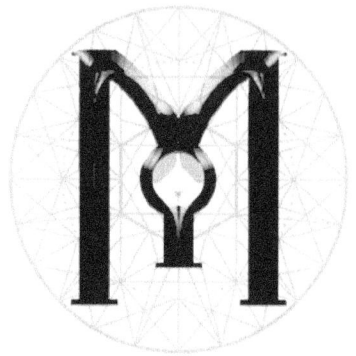

# CHAPTER 2
## *The Season of Inspiration*

*"To see a world in a grain of sand and heaven in a wild flower; to hold infinity in the palm of your hand and eternity in an hour – that's inspiration."*
—William Blake (1842)

# *Verse VII:*
## The Reckoning of Fallen Thrones

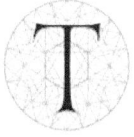'Naeva's gaze lingers on her mighty mate, drawn to the enigmatic serenity that radiates from him—a tranquility so profound that it seems almost otherworldly.

Yet beneath the calm exterior, she discerns a shadow of unease, a subtle weight within his transformation, hinting at a burden he does not share. The faint shimmer of a golden light seems to pulse from his form, bathing the air around him with a warmth that quells the chaos within her. The majesty of D'Reem's divinity steals her breath, stirring awe and an unrelenting need to unravel the mystery of his transformation.

A transformation that feels both otherworldly and achingly familiar. Even amidst the tempest of her soul, her breath catches, her chest tightens, and she is ensnared, her very being awed by the splendor unfurling before her eyes. D'Reem's gaze blazes with celestial fire, the flames of eternity dancing within his eyes. Their brilliance seems to reach beyond her tear-streaked face, igniting the very atmosphere around him with an unspoken command. The air hums faintly, charged with an energy that whispers of his transcendent nature.

D'Reem speaks, his voice emerging to T'Naeva as deep as the foundations of the cosmos, each word reverberating like the first note of creation itself. Thus, the final Aeclion *(7k Ametheden cycles / 70k Earth years)* of Ametheden's creative eras nears its completion in the *Season of Inspiration.*
"Do you see it now, T'Naeva?" D'Reem's voice carries both strength and tenderness.
"The hope that lingers beyond the chaos? The Creator's plan stretches beyond today—to the Edenites, their cosmic journey, their faith, and the countless civilizations throughout the cosmos they will inspire to create."

I reveal to you, my love, a new dawn arising over a tranquil and beautifully structured vista, twin spheres of light illuminating the breathtaking world of Ametheden. Through steady calculation and relentless ambition, a certain *Mantus Apollyon* methodically ascends the ranks of Ametheden's government, biding his time while feigning passionate interest in the people's welfare.

For seven thousand cycles he rises from minor tribal leader to high office, executing a meticulous plan to sow discord and orchestrate the greatest downfall in their history. Mantus has infiltrated Ametheden's governance, mastering its laws and politics with hollow respect. Despite his contempt for the people, his calculated efforts have earned him influence, positioning him as a potent force of manipulation.

Yet as he learns more about these intelligent beings, Mantus grows increasingly bored and frustrated. Their lack of conflict, their effortless harmony, and the ease with which they thrive under the King he despises make Ametheden dull and monotonous—yet still ripe for the taking. What Mantus fails to realize, however, is that his own rise is merely another step in the unfolding of a prophecy far greater than his thirst for vengeance.

As he schemes in shadow—whispering discord, planting ruin—the ancient words of destiny shape his every move, silent and inexorable. The very forces he seeks to subvert are guiding him toward the inevitable fulfillment he remains blind to.

Dear T'Naeva, as I am swept through the swift passage of these images, a new dawn has eclipsed the landscape of Ametheden and its people. The grandeur of this next scene fills me with awe as the vista shifts southward, revealing mountainous cities that pierce a multi-hued sky. Towering structures encased in iridescent domes shimmer beneath her twin suns, and other astronomical bodies, reflecting the boundless beauty of this world.

As a third radiant object rises on the horizon, The Companion enlightens me as to its true nature—not a star, but the Great Realm itself, manifesting in its own physical plane of divine glory. The celestial light of the Realm merges with the twin suns, painting the domes in a vivid spectrum of colors beyond my comprehension. Eventually, these hues meld into a more familiar glow. Transported into the heart of one of these magnificent domed cities, I find myself in a majestic structure that fills me with wonder.

The grandeur of the scene unfolds in breathtaking detail as massive columns of diamond, accented with a mesmerizing array of precious gemstones – ruby, opal, sapphire, emerald, pearl, and amethyst – weave together in a divine tapestry of architectural prowess. These magnificent columns seamlessly blend into what appears to be living quarters, enveloped in the awe-inspiring beauty of this most ancient world. Lush trees, bearing fruits and nuts of every imaginable color and variety, adorn the landscape, their vibrant hues creating a stunning visual masterpiece.

As I peer through an opening into one of the dwellings, I observe four beings, resembling you and me, but smaller in stature. These beings—two larger and two smaller—engage in lively conversation as they manipulate peculiar devices with evident delight. A container brimming with an assortment of nuts and fruits rests near the entrance of the dwelling, catching my eye. Abruptly, a melodious tone fills the air, prompting the four beings to exchange smiles and join hands.

The eldest male figure gathers the container and leads the others from their home, leaving their tasks incomplete, but their spirits high. As they venture outside, they are greeted by a multitude of others, each sharing a sense of camaraderie and purpose. Together, they make their way towards an imposing and ornate edifice at the heart of the domed city. Upon arrival, the eldest member of each family presents their container to an eminent figure reminiscent of my own mentor.

After collecting many such offerings, this distinguished individual raises their arms in praise, pouring out the contents as they speak in an enigmatic tongue that resonates through the air. The congregation forms a vast circle around the edifice, their hands clasped in unity as they sing in an enchanting, tranquil harmony. A burst of brilliant light erupts from the distant Great Realm, its radiance piercing the dome's aperture and descending upon the offering of fruits and nuts, consuming them in a divine blaze. The holy fire vanishes as swiftly as it appeared, leaving behind a smoldering pit, while the captivating ceremony carries on, enveloped in an atmosphere of unconditional love and serenity.

As the two larger suns descend below the horizon, the same melodious tone resonates once more, signaling the dispersal of the peaceful worshipers. My vision shifts back to the family of four I had observed earlier, yet an unsettling sensation stirs within my heart. A youthful figure, bearing a striking resemblance to you, dear T'Naeva, pauses as a figure emerges from a nearby dwelling, his pearly white teeth contrasting with his dark complexion as he greets the child with a warm smile and a wave.

Unperturbed, the other three continue their way, bidding farewell to the child as they leave. A voice of pristine clarity arises within me, revealing the identity of the figure as the fallen angel Forcas, who engages the child in conversation. The words, crystal clear in my mind, bear witness to the divine intervention of the Companion.
"Ah, young Visra," Forcas greets her, his voice a silken thread in the moonlit air.
"How radiant you appear this evening.

Tell me, young one—how did you find today's worship?" Forcas inquires, his voice smooth and inviting. Visra, her face brightening with a smile, responds eagerly. "Oh, Sire Eligos, it was such a beautiful thing! We sang and danced a good long while today!" However, her enthusiasm falters as she continues to speak, a shadow of unease crossing her youthful features.
A sly grin spreads across the demon's face as he kneels before her, offering a small, vibrant fruit. "My dear Visra, I was so consumed by my chores this morning that I felt no desire to attend the worship. Is there not anything else you'd rather do? And why do you and your family commit yourselves to

attend the services of your Creator every single day?"

Wide-eyed and trusting, little Visra accepts the fruit from his slender, dark-fingered hands, savoring its taste as she gazes up at her enigmatic companion. She replies earnestly.
"Eligos, you should know it is the decree of our Creator, Yah-Shu-Ah, and we desire everything He desires."
Eligos persists.
"Of course, it is the law, dear child. But would this mighty eternal sky being love you any less if you didn't worship or follow His ways at every waking moment?" Visra's brow furrows as doubt creeps into her youthful features. "I... I think He would still love me," she says slowly. "But... maybe that's not enough," she admits, her voice trailing off.

With a satisfied smile, Eligos playfully pats her behind and bids her farewell, leaving the young Visra to ponder their conversation, never to see or speak with him again. As she returns to her dwelling, a cloud of confusion hangs over her once-carefree demeanor. During the evening meal, Visra remains silent and deep in thought, her family inquiring about her unusual quietness.

Finally, she asks with a pensive stare, "Why do we honestly worship so often? Is it just because our laws say it is proper to do so, and we simply follow out of duty without a second thought?" As I gaze upon this wise yet conflicted child, my heart aches for the seeds of doubt that have been planted within her once-unwavering faith, and I am heartbroken.

The demon reports up the chain until it reaches Dia'Baal himself. Dia'Baal, sensing the opportune moment to create mass disorder in this seemingly perfect society, seizes the opportunity with a satisfied smile. Within a mere fifty cycles, Visra's question, centered on self-interest, spreads across the entire planet, breeding challenges to Ametheden's founding laws for a peaceful and fulfilling life.

Now equipped with the knowledge and manipulative prowess he possesses, Dia'Baal begins executing his plan to gain dominance over Ametheden. Granted permission to finally participate in the cyclic sessions of tribal matters alongside the twelve founding elders, Mantus Apollyon sets foot on the path to the world's ruin.
In the blink of an eye, five thousand councils—five millennia of policy and persuasion—unfold, and Mantus steadily seizes the floor.

Feigning respect for the supreme elders, he cunningly points out the lack of inquiries into improving the already-perfect Ametheden, suggesting that there may be no need for daily worship of their only god. Gasps and accusations of sacrilege ripple through the political aisle, while the other side listens with rapt attention. Mantus continues to charm the elders with his novel concepts, captivating half of them with charisma and deception.

By emphasizing self-reliance and proposing stimulating ideas for societal enhancement without a godhead, he successfully sways a significant portion of the world's population. As they begin to embrace egotistic reliance, the once-united civilization drifts further from their divine connection to their Creator. With their Utopian society never having experienced hardship, the people of Ametheden are childlike in their vulnerability to Mantus Apollyon's deceptions.

Systematically, he targets the founding ideologies of their world, corrupting them one by one. His goal: to erase their need for a Creator's authority—and then destroy them. As Mantus's influence grows, so does his rank within the council, becoming both respected and despised. After another hundred cycles, Mantus Apollyon ascends to the highest echelons of power, drawing the adoration of six tribal elders and their peoples. At last, he is granted private chambers in the capital city of *Sa'Tania*, where he entertains the elders and their associates—now fully ensnared by his subtle deceptions.

With his ever-increasing sway over the once-pure minds of these leaders, Mantus Apollyon opens their eyes to new and unique political concepts. These include never-ending debates, abuses of power, sociopath self-worth ideals, and authoritarian and totalitarian influences on the population. Alongside these concepts, he promises the elders that they will one day rule their world with unparalleled pleasure and possibility, but only if they adhere to his guidance and allow him to bring these visions to fruition.

Once-unimaginable perverse morals have now tainted the minds of at least half the elders, all thanks to Mantus Apollyon's bright and shining face guiding them into a new age of alleged perfection and tranquility. As a mere handful of additional cycles unfold as six world elders find themselves deceived by the allure of Mantus Apollyon's promises. They begin to integrate his mindset into laws that adversely affect their tribes and populations.

What was once a council of unity becomes a fractured assembly. The six deceived elders craft edicts that loosen moral constraints, permit self-exaltation, and glorify personal sovereignty over divine law. Cities that once rang with hymns now echo with endless political debates and growing displays of wealth and power. To the faithful, these changes feel like the slow poisoning of Ametheden's soul.

Those under Mantus' guidance view his firm control as wise and progressive, while the remaining six elders, guided by the divine discernment granted by their eternal Yah-Shu-Ah, see him as a perilous danger to Ametheden.

Mantus Apollyon's influence has now grown to its ultimate height, as half the world population blindly pledges allegiance to his perceived goodwill. However, their newfound freedoms are nothing more than illusions. In stark contrast, the opposing elders and their constituents fiercely challenge new tribal laws imposed by their brethren, fervently defending their world's decrees of a moral lifestyle.

To protect the faithful, the Companion reveals to them the true identity of Mantus Apollyon: *Dia'Baal Fallenstar*, the source of the chaos engulfing their once-perfect society. The six virtuous elders, unified in their devotion to Yah-Shu-Ah, attempt to expose his deceit to their fellow council members. Alas, their efforts only deepen the divide, solidifying the allegiance of the six deceived elders with Mantus Apollyon.

Among the faithful, whispers of the *Prophecy of the Three Alignments* grow louder, reminding this people that...

*When three arise and three times they fall as one...*

Yet these ancient warnings are dismissed as relics of a far removed past. The deceived elders scoff at the notion, believing Ametheden has evolved far beyond such childish fears and superstitions. Still, faith has well taken root by now, evolving from mere devotion into trust in the unseen. Undeterred, the virtuous elders persist in their scrutiny of Mantus Apollyon, questioning his rapid rise within the world tribal government.

Then, as the moons of Urthos, Gaeaos, and Hellios have perfectly aligned once every cycle since the founding of Ametheden, in this particular cycle they mysteriously align, ***three times!*** The faithful begin to wonder, *'is the prophecy finally unfolding before their very eyes'*, as never before in Ametheden's entire history has this celestial phenomenon occurred.

As The Companion observes the escalating tensions, He recognizes the movements of these moons, and soon the moment will have arrived for the people of Ametheden. The time has come for them to make their ultimate choice of whom to follow. In a divine decree, the Creator bestows upon every sentient being the gift of autonomy, empowering them to shape their destinies through personal choice. With this gift comes a grave warning.

*—The transgression of divine law, known as Sin, shall bear consequences, and the specter of death shall loom over all who defy Yah-Shu-Ah's divine will—*

In this same cycle of a world's unfolding destiny, Mantus Apollyon is finally elected as *Supreme Elder of the Six*—an event that marks a dark turning point in Ametheden's fate. What was once a civilization united in harmony is now fractured beyond recognition as Mantus's influence solidifies into absolute power. The deception is complete, and the people, now armed with autonomy, must choose their path—whether to uphold the Creator's truth, or succumb to the illusion of Mantus's overwhelming presence of popularity and power.
Yet faith endures, becoming a beacon of hope for those who trust in the Creator's unseen plan, believing that truth and harmony will one day be completely restored.

Dear T'Naeva, I now gaze upon this final cycle of Mantus Apollyon's emergence as their leader, a period that passes like a breath to many Amethedians—its swiftness masking the depth of coming devastation. Alas, this once-perfect society is fully corrupted, its harmony shattered by the malignant influence of Dia'Baal Fallenstar, his remaining demon horde disguised as counselors, and advisors, and mentors, and of course the mortal pawns they lead to his every whim.

The allure of self-serving progress now mutates into a seething hatred that threatens to tear apart the very fabric of this civilization. As tribal unity grows unsteady, what were once mere disagreements escalate into violent confrontations. The rift between those who remain faithful to their Creator and those who have succumbed to Mantus Apollyon's tainted ideals widens, and the drums of war begin to beat across the world.

I behold the harrowing Sundering of Ametheden, dear goddess—an upheaval that will engulf every corner of this world across *seven cycles* of civil war. A world war that is soon thereafter declared between the faithful and the corrupted, between tribes of influence and ideologies, marking the beginning of the end for this once-utopian realm. It is then that the first six million holy inhabitants are mercilessly slaughtered by Dia'Baal and his minions to begin his ruthless quest for domination across Ametheden.

Then, from the depths of his twisted intellect, a new and terrible image emerges, *technology*—weaponized mechanical corruption of creation's perfect order. As the cruel ambition of the arch-rebel spreads like wildfire through the hearts of his followers, the once-peaceful realm of Ametheden has found itself engulfed in a cataclysmic event. With the fate of the saintly opposition hanging in the balance, the weight of despair grows heavy upon the hearts of those who bear witness to this unfolding tragedy, myself included.

### Cycle One: The Engines of Sorrow

It was then, in the first cycle of this terrible Sundering, Dia'Baal unleashes his first terror: the *Engines of Sorrow*, their breath like cold iron on the teeth. Towering monoliths of black iron and crimson light, these constructs thrum with an unholy resonance that buzzes in bone and jaw, shaking Ametheden's forests to their roots. Ancient trees splinter; sap hisses like steam as verdant canopies collapse in clouds of ash. Rivers choke with the carcasses of beasts; the water tastes of rust and sorrow.

Vast townships within these forests are trampled—bone and timber snap like wet reeds. The skies darken with the smoke of a world's lungs set ablaze; ash grits between the molars. This devastation earns its name: *The First Weeping*—salt on every tongue. And across distant worlds, the same machinery finds new names, yet the result never changes: mothers bury sons, oceans taste soot, languages forget their songs, horizons learn to fear dawn.

The faithful answer with divine ingenuity; prayer tightens like wire in the throat. Guided by Yah-Shu-Ah, the six elders of the faithful and their greatest minds of these tribes create the *Hymn of Unmaking*—notes so thin they feel like glass on the skin—a counter-harmonic that clashes with the Engines' mournful song. Strike teams storm the monoliths; breath fogs inside their helms as heat ripples from the cores.

They plant crystalline amplifiers within those hearts of metal. When the final note resounds, the air pressure drops and ears pop; the Engines tremble and sigh—a sound like grief—and crumble into ruin. But the price is heavy; the wind smells of wet ash. A fourth of Ametheden's forests lie dead; needles crunch like glass underfoot. Billions of creatures are lost; the silence roars. And Dia'Baal's dark purpose has only begun, a shadow with teeth. Survivors wander mute groves, bark turned to glass, asking if victory can outsing absence. Children learn cold metal in rain. The faithful record names, knowing the ledger will never close.

### Cycle Two: The Shardwakers

It was then, in the second cycle of the Sundering, Dia'Baal unleashes his second horror: *The Shardwakers.* The Shardwakers—colossal monstrosities of stone and fire—burrow beneath the realm's greatest cities, their movements groaning like metal dragged across bone. Obsidian spires erupt skyward with explosive heat, toppling towers as ash scorches skin and scorches lungs with the taste of brimstone. Metropolises scream as steel and stone shear apart; dust coats tongues and glass rains like hail. The faithful call this terror, *The Breaking of Bones.*

Ametheden's very foundation seems to scream—a deafening wail that vibrates in the marrow—as age-old structures collapse into yawning abysses. Hundreds of millions perish in cascading debris; the texture of ruin is jagged, splintered, and soaked in heat. Their cities—once monuments to divine harmony—are reduced to charred pits of fire, ruin, and despair. The very air smells of cracked stone and roasted flesh, and the echoes of those who fell seem to linger in every crevice.

To counter this scourge, the six elders are guided by Yah-Shu-Ah, forging the *Hammer of Resonance*—seismic counterbalance that pulses like thunder through flesh. Legions of warrior-priests descend into the planet's churning innards, sweat and soot mingling as heat suffocates in the dark. They place these divinely inspired resonators at sacred fault-lines. At terrible cost—millions perish as entire regions of landscape are swallowed by living stone when these devices detonate, their sacrifice sharp and sudden like a snapped nerve.

The earth quiets, but the surface above remains a graveyard of broken stone, where even wind seems afraid to whisper. Deep scars stretch across Ametheden's once-beautiful face; no seed dares sprout, no bird dares return. Nothing can be rebuilt in these devastated heartlands. Survivors are scattered, hope smothered in ruin as they whisper through cracked lips: *if this is only the second, how much worse shall the destroyer's terrible wrath become?*

### Cycle Three: The Reaping Fires

It was then, in the third cycle of the Sundering, Mantus escalates his campaign of annihilation with terrifying precision. *The Reaping Fires*—his third weapon—are unleashed as sentient tornadoes infused with fire and pure demonic will, shrieking with a pitch that razors the soul. These raging, twisting columns stalk all life and structure in their wake, tasting stone, blood, and steel before incinerating all. Entire continents ignite as the skies bleed deep red; the air hums with heat so sharp it blisters the tongue.

Survivors call this terror: *The Ashen Curse*, for the storms smother Ametheden's twin suns and turn breath into soot, plunging the world into a twilight of coughing death and burning silence. Skins crack from heat. Voices fail mid-prayer. Trees hiss like torches. In this cycle alone, over *fifty billion* souls are lost. Mountainous cities melt into the earth like wax, and rivers boil dry, leaving behind the tang of scorched minerals and bone. The cries of the dying mingle with the roar of the flames, creating a dirge so overwhelming it breaks even the strongest wills—a music of mourning that echoes from the core of Ametheden to the hollow of the stars.

To add to this horror, three of the six elders—pillars of the faithful—fall. Struck down in separate battles, their deaths feel like broken ribs in the body of faith. Their names are etched into the Sacred Mourning Stone, its surface warm to the touch, as if still bleeding grief. Their sacrifice becomes the drumbeat of the faithful's fury, hammering resolve into ash-stained hearts.

At last, the Reaping Fires are undone through a desperate gambit: the invocation of the *Lament of Waters*, a celestial deluge summoned by the highest clerics in a ritual so intense the air crackled with divine pressure. Rain falls like shards of glass, hissing on the fires below, while thunder weeps like a grieving god. The cyclonic flames are drowned—but not before more regions of Ametheden are left disfigured, scarred, and howling with flame-born grief. No color returns. No sound dares rise. The world remembers through ruin.

### *Cycle Four: The Veil Drowners*

It was then, in the fourth cycle of the Great Sundering, Dia'Baal poisons the skies with his fourth horror: the *Veil Drowners*. These vast atmospheric harvesters—suspended like blackened moons—hum with a deep, metallic throb, reversing Ametheden's water cycles with eerie precision. Entire oceans are siphoned skyward, torn from their beds with a shriek like rending fabric, only to return as boiling floods and torrents of corrosive rain that blister the skin and sting the tongue with salt and acid.

Sacred rivers swell into monstrous watery serpents, their currents hissing as they flood and poison cities and fields alike. The faithful call this terror *The Deluge of Shadows*, for it drowns even memory beneath its black tide. Entire regions vanish beneath blackened waters, the texture of the land softened into a pulpy, rotting sponge. Once-serene coastlines crumble into the sea; the collapse sounds like gods weeping through cracking stone. Inhabitants are swept away in great tides—bodies tumbling like leaves in a storm—while screams vanish beneath the gurgling roar.

Hope drowns with them, as survivors cling to highlands slick with algae and ash, whispering prayers to a sky gone mad and rank with ozone and brine. The air tastes of rot. The clouds boil with green lightning. Guided by Yah-Shu-Ah, the remaining elders forge the *Celestial Sundials*—towering orbital mirrors veined with holy light, their edges sharp enough to blind the unworthy. Designed to redirect the Drowners' harvest beams, these marvels glint like the eyes of judgment in the firmament.

As the Sundials unleash focused light that sears their cores, the Veil Drowners scream—soundless and seismic—and implode in cataclysmic flashes, their molten remains plummeting into the very oceans they once consumed. The sea hisses as it swallows them. The rains cease. But the damage is irreversible. Half of Ametheden's coastlines are gone, drowned or carved away, and the seas remain poisoned—stagnant and shimmering with sickly hues. Fish float belly-up like fallen stars. The faithful look skyward—not in gratitude, but in dread—as the firmament seems to throb with unseen motion. A greater terror stirs, and even the silence feels like a warning.

### Cycle Five: The Soul Flayers

It was then, in the fifth cycle of the Great Sundering, that Dia'Baal *remembers*. He thinks back to the stifling depths of his once-prison on Hellios, He remembers the Scythean Column—those sacred reapers of the King's will, their blades singing through air like final judgments, flashing like living verdicts against his legions. In his seething hatred, Dia'Baal twists memory into malice, each recollection smoldering like coal on the tongue...

*'If the Column can harvest for glory, then so shall I be greater than them—for ruin.'*

Thus are born the *Soul Flayers*—serpentine wraiths of sulphuric smoke and crackling etheric chains that drift across Ametheden like silent predators. The air turns sour in their wake, vibrating with a low, metallic hum that tightens the chest. Their presence alone wrenches souls from living flesh, leaving behind no wounds—only silence. Entire cities remain eerily intact, yet utterly lifeless. Streets overflow with statues of the fallen, their skin cold and waxy to the touch, their faces frozen in wide-eyed horror as if death struck mid-scream. The faithful call this terror The *Hollowing*, for it empties not only bodies—but belief.

The surviving elders and their dwindling followers can do little but fortify what remains—hiding deep within mountains and shadowed valleys where the damp air stinks of mold and smoke. Their torches flicker dimly against cave walls etched with prayers no longer spoken aloud. And still no divine army descends. No Scythean weapons are unsheathed. The King's fist remains still, His throne seemingly unmoved. His timing is perfect, yes— but to mortal hearts, it feels like abandonment. Their hope shrinks, tasting of dust and fear.

Ametheden does not resist, because it cannot, it *endures*. For beyond the Hollowing, Dia'Baal prepares his final atrocity: the *Tempest of Oblivion*.

### Cycle Six: The Silence of War

After six long cycles of unrelenting devastation, Ametheden falls into an ominous quiet. No new weapons emerge. No armies march. Yet, the skies still burn crimson as continents smolder, two thirds of Ametheden's twelve oceans choke on the ash of a shattered remnant, and from pole to pole, she simply feels alone, afraid, and unloved. Countless temples have collapsed into long forgotten relics of the past, and rivers run black with the tears, blood, and ash of the innocent.

By the end of this sixth cycle of the Great Sundering, only three elders remain—still defiant. Their resolve the final bulwark against the tyrannical forces of Mantus Apollyon and his *axis of corruption*. In hidden sanctuaries and deep mountain refuges worldwide, the remnants of only fifteen billion faithful huddles in despair. Their numbers have dwindled to a portion of a portion; their vast once beautiful cities lie in ruin and yet, these stalwart elders travel secretly to walk among their scattered people like pillars of hope, their hearts heavy still with unanswered prayers, but still blazing in love, nonetheless.

The corrupted, meanwhile, revel in voice in their false dominion, but in heart it's a different story. They have been promised riches and status, they have been promised the world, but still, they see nothing from he who claims to have their best interest at hand. The people of these tribes begin to rise up and question his true motives for this senseless war as it consumes their world in further despair, as Mantus Apollyon has neither been seen or heard from for quite some time.

Still, he tightens his grip as a god-king over the mastery of his multitude of subjects, while overseeing the construction of his ultimate weapon against his faithful enemy, and soon his own *allies*. From the poisoned seas to shattered mountains, he channels vital world resources to build and feed this terrible creation and still, the King's Host remains unseen. The *Scythean Column* stands ready but is withheld, their scythes yearning for justice, for release. Michael and entire Host weep and rage for resolution of these poor and frightened people. I now hear the faithful people whisper...

*'has heaven turned away or is this silence the prelude to a greater reckoning?*

### Cycle Seven: The Liberation

It is now the dawn of the *seventh cycle* as the rosy red fingers of twin suns light the topmost spires upon his capital city of *Sa'Tania*. Deep in the shadows below the city, the *Tempest of Oblivion* begins to stir. This will be his final solution for this wretched world, this dust dwelling blight in the last piece of his infernal vision—a storm that will wipe Ametheden from existence. With the fate of Ametheden's faithful teetering on the brink of death, the arch rebel's malevolent creation looms upon the dark horizon.

Through a whirlwind of technological advancements, Dia'Baal's malevolent design inches ever closer to fruition, one that transforms a common squall into a storm of conscious energy, and then the *erasure of its target*. A storm indeed, so powerful that even his demons will come to tremble at its might. No longer satisfied with dominion, Dia'Baal seeks nothing less than the complete annihilation of Ametheden and the eradication of *all* its people, leaving behind only a barren ruin of death. Guided by the omnipotence of the Companion, I witness a pivotal moment in the world-war that has ravaged Ametheden into its seventh and final cycle.

On this grim day, Dia'Baal, absorbed in testing the immense control he wields over his living malevolent pet of a storm, is struck by a sudden unease that unsettles his corrupted spirit. Stepping from his chambers and into a courtyard, he gazes skyward, only to be met with a gnawing anxiety he has not felt, in *ages*. There, amid the bloodstained, crimson hued sky of a war-torn world, a small, streaking flash of light pierces through a vista of dark, tumultuous clouds. A flicker of hope stirs within me, as I sense that the war and despair that have gripped this world for so long may finally be nearing its end.

Dia'Baal's eyes follow another trace of light as it races in the opposite direction, and moments later, a pair of bright streaks appear side by side, only to vanish as swiftly as they came through the heavy cloud cover. Though all seems unchanged, an inexplicable shift in the atmosphere suggests otherwise.

No mortal eye of Ametheden can witness this peculiar activity due to its divine nature, yet every demon across her surface beholds these mysterious streaks of light. A wave of dread begins to sweep through their ranks because *they know* the cause, feeling soon they will be engaged in war. With anger mounting, Dia'Baal retreats to his surface chambers, where two unfortunate demon underlings bear the brunt of his wrath. His rage barely contained, he questions them through gritted teeth, demanding an explanation for the strange events unfolding on this day of bleak beauty.

"Have either of you noticed anything... odd on this beautiful and dreary day?" he asks, his voice a low growl. The underlings, confusion etched upon their faces, can offer only blank stares and uncertain shrugs in response. Dia'Baal's fury swells as he braces himself for the challenges that lie ahead.

His voice booms with a commanding tone as he reiterates his question, his patience wearing thin. "I asked you a question— if you value your existence, you will answer me now!" He slams his fist on a table, shattering it as he points a stern finger at his closest minion, Sitri. "You! What have you seen? Speak the truth, or face the consequences!" Sitri, trembling beneath Dia'Baal's molten stare, manages a thin whisper:
"Sire... I believe I've seen our enemy."

Dia'Baal's fiery gaze shifts to Fosbi, another minion present in his chambers. His lips curl. "And just how many have you seen, Fosbi?"
I now envision this poor wretched creature, Fosbi, once a crown of angelic intellect, he now stands like a broken music box spewing half-sentences through a haze of divine brain-rot. "A few dozen... or more... some may've been... double-counted, Your Hon—Your Glor—Your... Hmmm—I mean um—yes."

His mouth clicks like rusted cogs, thoughts tumbling out of his simple mind with the grace of shattered masonry. Dia'Baal watches intently, equal parts horror and humor. This once-great strategist, once third in succession under Molnet, is now reduced to babbling debris, standing like a puppet strung with frayed wire, his genius squashed under the weight of a King's curse and his own desperate need to be useful.
"I swear, sire!" Fosbi cries, "Some I've seen twice... or thrice... or never! I just don't know anymore, your eminence!"

As this bittersweet scene of epic proportions unfolds within the dark confines of Dia'Baal's chambers, all he can do is muster is a slow, sulfuric laugh—half pained, half entertained—like a tyrant forced to rule a circus.

Just then, the door creaks open and in slinks Grigori, the final clown in this tragic circus, his face pale with dread and eyes darting like a trapped rodent's. Dia'Baal's glare locks onto him with the heat of a dying sun.
"And you, Grigori…"
His voice slithers like coiled steel.
"How many streaks of light have you seen? Judging by that face, your confidence in my sovereignty has finally curled up and died." Grigori stammers like a mortal falling down a staircase of syllables.
"Well, uh… Sire, it's, it's … it's … hard to say. They … they move so damn fast, fast as divine vengeance I'd say, and they're multiplying as we spea—"

*Crack!*

Dia'Baal's backhand slices through the air like a whip. Grigori's head snaps sideways with a dull thud, and the room falls quiet, as if even the shadows are holding their breath. The scene teeters—perfectly—between farce and apocalypse. Three underlings, broken in mind and soul, cower before a god of war whose patience thins faster than the boundary between sanity and oblivion. As the tension mounts, it becomes clear that even in this darkly humorous exchange, the consequences of failure are no laughing matter.

As Grigori reels from the blow, it snickers lightly as it loves the pain of being struck, and Dia'Baal takes stock of the absurdity playing out before him. While he may derive some twisted amusement from the spectacle of his minions' bungling attempts at communication or even functionality, he is all too aware that the fate of his appalling regime now hangs by a thread. The laughter dies as he turns away from his underlings, his mind turning to the battle that looms ever closer.

Dia'Baal's patience, now grasping at the last brittle sinew of his decaying restraint, finally snaps like a cursed harp string. He spins—flames licking the corners of his dark violet shadow—and finds yet another pack of cowering demons skulking into his throne chamber, their faces pulled taut with the terror of knowing they've arrived too late and way too visible. He spreads his arms wide like a deranged conductor greeting a pitiful orchestra.

"Ah, more brilliance! Behold—reinforcements! What gifts of wisdom shall you bring, little flames in the dark?" Then, his voice erupts into thunder, "Dare not crawl into my sight again with empty minds and fluttering nerves! I swear I will burn the cowardice from your very soul!"
His gaze sears the room as the demon ranks flinch backward, tripping over

their own malformed limbs.

"Summon every fool who still remembers how to wield a blade or press even a button! Sound the horns across every continent—alert every city and province and den of underworld filth that still answers to my name! If they breathe and wear my mark, they march without question!"

He storms toward the nearest one and spits with venomous relish.
"This time, we'll be ready. We have our pawns—these mortal children of clay, stupid enough to believe anything we whisper. Let them shield us, let them bleed for us." A cruel grin creeps across his face like rot under gold. "And once they rise against me..." He chuckles, low and jagged, "we'll make them truly feel what it means to anger me."

The demons scatter like roaches at torchlight, scrambling to carry his command to every corner of this war-torn world. Behind them, Dia'Baal's curses continue to echo—each one a poem of disdain for his enemy, the Creator, and the miserable state of existence that dares to arise against his perfection. In a frenzy of destruction, Dia'Baal reduces the furnishings of his hall to rubble before storming into the courtyard of his capital city.

The skies above Ametheden are now choked in bruised reds and violent golds, the heavens scarring themselves with light as the King's scout angels multiply like omens. Dia'Baal glares skyward—jaws clenched, teeth grinding as though he might devour the firmament itself. His gut twists. Not fear, he lies to himself.
*'Just... anticipation.'*

Without a word, he vanishes from his courtyard in a blaze of sulfur and shadow, plunging deep into the bowels of the earth—into the colossal labyrinth carved by his own paranoia and rage. Its walls breathe with intense heat, its corridors shriek with the whispers of tortured stone. No map exists of this underground hellhole. It is a temple of war and ego; a fortress of secrets wrapped in stone and circuitry. Each step-down echoes like prophecy, and the tyrant growls to the dark.
"They will not take this from me! Not now. Not ever!"

Within the deep sanctum—a subterranean cathedral of cruelty and invention—Dia'Baal's evil had reached its culmination. There, surrounded by his weary technologists of despair, he stands before the sleek mechanism that will manifest into life his pet, *The Tempest of Oblivion*. A towering hybrid of sorcery and circuitry, an infernal device crowned with coils that spark like the cries of maddened gods.

Its heart pulses—not with life, but with hunger. With calculated grace, he mounts the throne affixed to its core, reclining into a spidery harness of polished steel and iron tendrils. A machine built to wear its creator. His arms stretch out like a crucifix of vengeance, his body now a conduit.

*The lights dim.*
*The hum begins.*
*'Feed from me,'* he whispers to the machine as if it were his own kin. *'And I will feed the world to you.'*

In this moment, Dia'Baal is not merely a tyrant. He is becoming the weapon itself. The chamber shudders—the high pitched sounds, the hisses of steam through conduit, the clanking of metal trembling under the weight of Dia'Baal's obsession. With every heartbeat, the monstrous machine pulses louder, its core now alive with spiraling threads of malice and memory.
And from the depths of the tyrant's own twisted soul, anguish pours into it—wrath, grief, humiliation—every bitter fragment of his eon's long descent, now forged into the fuel this machine needs.

*"You are no longer invention,"* Dia'Baal growls. *"You become my vengeance!"*

The Tempest of Oblivion awakens. From the spires of Dia'Baal's twisted throne, his thoughts pierce the firmament—fused with Amethedian technology and the black arts of rebellion. His consciousness surges into the massive apparatus he himself forged: a storm born not just of machinery, but of madness.
Above Ametheden, the clouds suddenly fracture.
And then—release.
A sound like breaking worlds splits the sky. The Tempest materializes—no longer an idea, but a monstrous reality. Its pulsating airy confines groan like tortured tectonics, coiled tendrils of energy glowing brighter than the twin suns of Ametheden themselves.

*Time stutters.*

*The heavens flinch.*

A vortex of conscious energy spirals into being—howling, incandescent, sentient. It screams downward in waves of thunder, light, and utter annihilation. Mountains tremble. Oceans reel. Entire continents quake beneath the birth scream of a force made to undo. This is not just destruction, it is the ruin of hope.

This is *Oblivion* made manifest, and its *maw* needs to feed.

As the storm expands, its shadow spills across regions, swallowing up cities, forests, seas—leaving ruin where beauty once lived. Its roar is a command, a dirge, a war cry of malevolence. The Tempest has no master now and only one purpose: *to feed.*

But even now—unseen by Dia'Baal—forces of light gather.
From the edges of the void, they stir.
From beyond the veil, they prepare.
*The storm has awakened...*
*But so has the preparation to end it.*

The malevolent squall's magnetic field, bristling with supernatural force, ensnares the highlands and their surrounding aquatic embrace, engulfing them in a maelstrom of chaos and desolation.

Unleashed in its fury, the storm wreaks havoc upon the enemy's capital cities, leaving no stone unturned in their final destruction. The very hills upon which these bastions of civilization rest tremble and succumb to the storm's unyielding onslaught, surrendering their foundations to the intense gravity of the storm. Even the once-mighty mountains, silent guardians of the land, begin to crumble beneath the relentless barrage of the tempest's unholy wrath. At the storm's peak, its devastation becomes absolute. Continents tremble beneath its relentless might, every feature obliterated, leaving a desolate wasteland.

The Tempest's roar echoes its creator's fury—an unyielding assault sparing neither land nor sea. The lands and oceans of Ametheden, once teeming with life and wonder, now stretch out before the storm like a canvas of despair, their vastness offering no refuge from the storm's unquenchable thirst for destruction. High above, Hathor and Elentari, the two other planets adorning Ametheden and her skies, trace solemn paths across the heavens, their light veiled in sorrow as they witness the ruin of their sister world. Their slow, mournful orbits seem to weep for the remnants of Ametheden's vibrant life, now consumed by the storm's darkness, an endless lament across the cosmic expanse.

Their once-radiant faces etched with sorrow, their light dimmed by the overwhelming darkness of this terrible world war. Hathor shrouds herself in crimson veils, her orbit dragging like a mourner's step, while Elentari flickers pale, her tears dimming her radiant presence. They circle not as cold spheres of gaseous constructs, but as grieving sisters, bound to Ametheden by threads of eternal kinship. Each rise, each descent across the heavens is less an orbit and more a dirge, their voices unheard yet deafening in the language of grief. They bear solemn witness, helpless to intervene, but condemned to remember.

Twelve times they ascend and descend through the heavens, their celestial movements slow and heavy, as if each moment of their flight is a silent prayer for Ametheden's salvation. Alas, there is no answer to this living storm, the faithful have lost the war now, and only the endless despair that suffocates the horizon is known. In this harrowing vision, Dia'Baal's monstrous creation—a living embodiment of pure wickedness—prowls the ravaged world, ravenous to extinguish any spark of life.

This storm-forged weapon of thought, born from his thirst for vengeance, hunts down the faithful with mechanical precision, leaving no survivor unscathed. As this apocalyptic gale expands in my mind, the horror is relentless and unmatched. Its insatiable hunger for destruction casts a pall over Ametheden's desecrated landscapes: scorched forests, shattered cities, and upended oceans serve as this dire testament. Those who have survived tremble at its roar, haunted by echoes of despair and the creeping hopelessness that falls like the nightmare it has become.

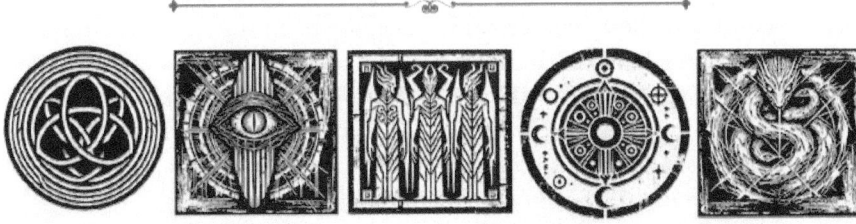

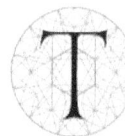

# *Verse VIII:*
## Culling of the Damned

hroughout this darkened handful of days, Dia'Baal, the malevolent architect of devastation, maintains a vise-like grip on his pet, this weapon of terror and its mass destruction.

As those dark days wear on and the annihilation of his foes seems all but certain, Mantus Apollyon, the influential tribal leader of half of Ametheden's populace, deceives his allies in a moment of unfathomable treachery. Redirecting the storm mid-flight—it bolts, turning toward the mountainous cities he once swore to protect, exacting his ultimate revenge upon all who would dare rise against him!

*His betrayal becomes their blade—and the hinge of his ruin.*

The jagged peaks, symbols of their strength, crumble under the storm's relentless assault, their once-proud spires reduced to rubble as Mantus sees all with cold detachment, his betrayal complete and unforgiving. Safely ensconced in his subterranean lair, Dia'Baal orchestrates the storm's movements with an iron fist, protected by his demonic minions from any who would dare to challenge his reign. All who come to end his reign are themselves ended under his thumb of demonic fury.

As the storm continues to raze cities and mountains alike, nothing withstands its insatiable hunger, and Ametheden shudders beneath its fury. The devastation is total—its ruin hovers, moving on to consume the next target, and all hope seems lost.

As a new vision unfolds, a glimmer of light pierces the darkness. On the seventh day, a survivor—*Visra*, the child once glimpsed before—kneels amid the ruins of her home, her city, her life, and begins a prayer of forgiveness, of strength, and of hope. Her voice, faint at first, grows as wildfire—hundreds join, then thousands, then millions, until at last eighty billion rise in chorus, their cry one voice across the night, lifting together against the shadow that had bound them. This great and mighty binding of hearts, survivors of Dia'Baal's cruelty, turn their backs on Mantus Apollyon... forsaking his name and legacy of hatred - *forever!*

In a pivotal, worldwide movement, enemies immediately cast aside their hatred, embracing one another and their Creator in an act of true reconciliation. The terror and manipulation that Mantus had forged over seventy millennia comes undone in mere hours. Tears of forgiveness flow like rivers of purity reborn, and joy flows as freely as these newly penitent people are also reborn, in *hope*.

They kneel together across lands both charred and saved as their beautiful voices are lifted in a single, harmonious prayer that pierces the *veil* of Mantus Apollyon, with a much stronger *light* of that hope.

Yet, even as this hope is rekindled, a shadow lingers. Few still cling to their allegiance to Mantus, blinded by their devotion to the great deceiver. In time, they too will face both the harsh and permanent consequences of their choices.

As the gale's devastating power continues its relentless charge, the spirit of Ametheden rises in a chorus of desperate pleas in the morning of the tenth day since the great tempest was formed. This people begging for deliverance from this terror that now tears their world asunder. Their collective intellect recognizing an inevitable outcome – Ametheden shaken and reduced to cosmic dust. Their final cries to end the storm are their very prayers for renewed salvation and direction, a last-ditch effort to save their glorious world from annihilation.

Hearing those cries, the King answers—not in judgment, but in merciful power. His radiance rolls across the heavens; with a single sovereign gesture the storm's fury falters and Ametheden is wrapped in a stunned, sacred stillness. The lines have now been drawn; the faithful have now been revealed. The enemy has now been sorted. With Ametheden on the brink of destruction, the Creator readies His response, prepared to bring Dia'Baal's tyranny to a decisive end.

In the heart of the Great Realm lies the *Courtyard of Remembrance*—a sacred, twenty-mile ring of celestially gemmed monuments, towers, structures, and columns that arise like the courage of creation itself. I stand at the edge, among the Host, witnessing what none have ever seen before: Heaven's might assembled—not for defense, but for vindication.
This courtyard once ran with divine blood. The ground beneath me still bears the cracks of rebellion. Though most of it has been restored by divine edict, a dark cluster of chiseled stones remains untouched—left as they were the day the heavens bled. Here, Dia'Baal was cast out, forever.

Now I am given the number of Host Legions that remain after the Great Rebellion. Many were lost in the crushing of mutiny—but none so deeply as those under Chamuel's command.

### ~ Archangel Michael ~
**Commander:** *The Angelic Host & Scythean Column of the Divine Fist*
After the Rebellion: Elite legions 47,212

*Archangel Gabriel* ~ After the Rebellion: 47k legions / Elite warriors: 24k
*Archangel Uriel* ~ After the Rebellion: 39k legions / Elite warriors: 19k
*Archangel Zadekiel* ~ After the Rebellion: 39k legions / Elite warriors: 23k
*Archangel Azrael* ~ After the Rebellion: 39k legions / Elite warriors: 24k
*Archangel Raphael* ~ After the Rebellion: 38k legions / Elite warriors: 22k

### ~Archangel Chamuel ~
*(Before The Rebellion)* 25k legions / Elite warriors: 10k
**(After) the Rebellion: 450 legions / 300 Elite warriors**

Now, this massive courtyard is filled once again.

Hundreds of millions of angelic warriors stand in six massive formations, each representing their Archangels charge, their wings folded, their blades sharpened, and every eye fixed on the center throne of the King. The air carries no sound—only expectation. In this sacred stillness, I feel the breath of fate drawing near as the mighty seven Archangels kneel before the throne. Then—The King and the Son appear, and they speak as One.

*... Sons of honor, you have carried the arms of righteousness longer than most stars have*

*burned, and you have all served Me well. You remain the shield of My purpose—the line unbroken when the Realm bled and angels fell. But now—one shall arise where the first wound was struck.*

*... Michael—Before the charge, his infernal storm will be shattered. You now command My Holy Column, the Scythean, to seek only the heart of the tempest aligned with My Firstborne. This corrupted veil that shields Dia'Baal will fall first, and you shall do this in My name. Your Column shall then be unshackled to wage wrath through shadow and flesh. Purge with zeal every elite you encounter, but spare the simple ones to their own eternal dismay.*

*... Chamuel, arise and be made whole. Long ago, it was you and your legions who first engaged My Firstborne, and you all bled bitterly for Me. It was your devotion who held the line while the rebellion cursed My Name—you and your troop who arose not in retreat, but in righteous defiance for Me alone. I have not forgotten this nor you, my youngest son.*

*... From your loss, you forged rage but found peace. In that silence, you forged strength. The scars you carry still are not marks of defeat, dear Chamuel—but only the standard bearers of memory. My valiant son, a new command has been earned, and today I call you to lead its light in your Father's name. Not in mourning, but in might. For this is no longer about war.*

*... And you, Chamuel—leading your brothers in arms, you shall strike—purging her every vista, and every city, her every temple, her every street and walkway until no whisper of rebellion remains. Break his ranks. Shatter his dominion. Unseat his pride. End his reign. You will not fail, and only when my eternal beloved's darkness is cast away forever, shall her liberation be completed to My passionate satisfaction.*

*... This is evidence for all who have suffered under the misguided loyalties of My Firstborne. Lead them now, dear Chamuel, not as one untouched by grief, but as one shaped by it. Let the memory of your fallen—and those lost to the rebellion, become this standard. Let their silence, their memory, their vindication reign in your assault upon this corrupted blight.*

*... To all gathered, hear Me now. None may purge Dia'Baal or his infernal mechanism, so bother it not. Let it pass from every eye of the Host and of my people until the appointed time. For though my Firstborne brings ruin through his device, its root of unholy power holds a place in My grand design, and this responsibility is Mine alone. In restraint, O, Mighty Host, there is obedience. In obedience, O, Mighty Host... There is Power.*

The King's voice quiets. Then, with a wave of Messiah's hand, Michael steps forward. His voice is thunder wrapped in reverence, and I am struck with reverence and awe.

"To all in attendance—prepare for battle! As our King wills it, so it is, and so it shall be! Our charge rises once more, a divine inferno against our King's Firstborne! Where Chamuel commands, the Host shall follow—as if it were my voice alone! Let your blades strike only where he directs—and nowhere else! His wounds are the map of this conquest, and now his heart stands mightier than legions. I ask only this O, Mighty King—the fire to help us forge the liberation of Your people!"

Michael turns to Chamuel and nods his head while lifting his arm—not to offer its authority, but to recognize it. Chamuel steps forward with renewed confidence, his voice steady, his spirit reforged. I feel his truth in every word that is spoken.

"Mighty Host—you stood strong as I and my legions bled, and that memory shaped me! To lead you now, with your strength behind me—beside me, humbles me! I will not misuse this charge entrusted to me by our King and my brothers in arms! It is not for my glory alone, but for those who never arose from that day long ago! It is for those who still believe we can end this corruption! By your fire, O mighty Host, I was forged, and by our unity—we shall not fail! Michael, ready the Host for battle, and may Ametheden continue to be the apple of the King's eye for eternity!"

One by one, each high angel rises and steps forward, their honor united, eternal. With a smile and a nod, each places a hand on Chamuel's shoulders and brow. No words are spoken. Flame and unity pass through their combined touch, and it strengthens them all. Their wings flare in solemn unison, and I feel it too, o, precious T'Naeva. As the battle ritual ends, a hush moves like sacred wind through the Host. Two hundred thousand legions ready themselves to liberate a planet from evil.

Eyes once dimmed by grief now blaze with divine purpose. Wings stretch outward. Celestial shields, bows and maces, hammers and swords, shimmer with light like the breath of glory reborn. Indeed, *Chamuel* is still the youngest among his mighty brothers but on this day, he will lead them! This I know with certainty—it will be his battle cry alone that will begin the liberation of Ametheden.

The moment of reckoning has come, and the visions that unfold upon my eyes are many of fascination and satisfaction. Dia'Baal, the architect of so much suffering, is about to face, once more, the dire consequences of his treachery. The King's judgment, delivered through the might of His heavenly host, will now bring a most hellish vengeance upon Dia'Baal and the demons who follow him, including his millions of allies on Ametheden, as they will all pay dearly for their sins against this world and its peaceful remnant. The air tightens. The ground thrums with unseen drums. Justice is not whispered—it is thundered.

As the day of reckoning dawns, the firm resolve of the King is evident. This single most momentous day in Ametheden's multitude of ages will see yet another judgment enacted, one that will change the course of this world forever. Dia'Baal Fallenstar and his treachery to soon be met with the full force of divine retribution, a verdict that will no longer be denied. Even the stars seem to dim, making room for wrath. With a sudden, commanding movement, D'Reem leans forward, his powerful presence drawing T'Naeva closer as she becomes transfixed by the intensity of his fiery gaze.

Her breath heavy with anticipation, her focus unwavering as she peers deep into her mate's glowing eyes, each moment heightening her awareness. D'Reem's influence crescendos, and the air crackles with energy as vivid scenes suddenly explode within T'Naeva's mind.
She finds herself captivated by the visions within him, her senses overwhelmed by the sheer force of the unfolding drama because now, she too is there. A mighty, poetic, and epic voice arises from within the great warrior, and it reverberates as a thousand thunders throughout her consciousness.

She can't help but feel as though she is being pulled deeper into a world she has never known, yet one that feels strangely familiar. There's a hum beneath her breath, a rhythm in her blood—as if memories not her own are singing. The very stars seem to hold their breath. So begins the liberation of a world from evil, and the profound sonnet known among these people as...

*The Song of Ametheden.*

Two hundred thousand legions,
Their zeal on fire,
Restless they wait,
As foes dare aspire.

A thousandfold in strength,
Dia'Baal's darkness grows,
Unity their forge, their weapon
To still the shadowed roar.

Into the heart of the storm,
The mighty Column charge,
Divine flesh and armor bruised,
Through fury, courage enlarged.

The curve of flaming scythes,
They pierce the guiding core,
Unity, their forge, their weapon
To still the malevolent roar.

Dia'Baal, the tempest's heart,
His rage nearly undone,
He escapes their blades,
The battle not yet won.

The heart of the squall,
At last in their grasp,
Hope's sweet breath
Through the darkness rasps.

Their might cleaves the storm,
Justice hurling evil aside,
Into Oblivion's final form,
It writhes, aimless without its guide.

Eternal hope restored,
Upon Ametheden's embrace,

*A cosmic civilization will arise,*
*Renewed to life and grace.*

I hear now the final squall of that hellish storm as it dissolves into its own oblivion and is destroyed. Another sound greater than that fills every ear of heaven's enemy.

*In the crucible of despair,*
*A war-ravaged world writhes,*
*Her anguished pleas piercing,*
*Those darkened tumultuous skies.*

*Hark! The clarion call,*
*Of Gabriel's horn rings,*
*A beacon of hope to the desolate,*
*A resounding promise it brings.*

*Eyes turn heavenward,*
*Hearts ablaze with fervent zeal,*
*United in purpose and hope,*
*A collective, heartfelt appeal.*

*Two hundred thousand legions,*
*Holy and ablaze with fire,*
*Descend to deliver His world,*
*From time's ceaseless mire.*

D'Reem's voice of authority fades, and T'Naeva knows it once more. In her amazement, his words strengthen these living images within her. Visions flowing with purpose across her eyes and through every fiber of her being, in every brutal detail. The young goddess is filled with reverence and rightly so. Gabriel's mighty trumpet frenzies both *Column and Host*, bringing their combat awareness to fruition, to eradicate Dia'Baal and his unholy presence from Ametheden... *Forever.*

*Chamuel stands renewed as they descend,*
*His strength tempered by shame,*
*Spearhead of the Mighty Host,*
*Commanding its eternal flame.*

*Liberation divine, a symphony of justice,*

127

*Sweeps this corrupted realm,*
*Every note bearing the wonders,*
*Of Archangels' righteous helm.*

*Every capital a cauldron,*
*Where freedom forges anew,*
*A most sacrosanct deliverance,*
*So pure and rightly true.*

*Through shattered streets,*
*And bloodied stone they stand,*
*Fathers with broken swords,*
*Mothers with trembling hands.*

*In unity they arise,*
*Though shadows press them low,*
*A cry for freedom,*
*Against their corrupted foe.*

*Deep within the chaos,*
*The angels' discernment prevails,*
*Safeguarding the pure and innocent,*
*From the darkness that assails.*

*Hand to hand, they clash,*
*Their demonic enemies expire,*
*Fiery blades of judgment true,*
*A righteous and worthy pyre.*

*... Unyielding, the forces of light devour.*

*Beneath Rebellion's dark shadow,*
*Again, no mercy is shown,*
*The corrupted are now sealed,*
*Their sins forever known.*

*Eternal demise encroaches,*
*The infernal stain ablaze,*
*Liberation's tide reshapes,*
*The world's darkened phase.*

*At the vanguard, the King's champions,*
*Fierce, unyielding, and strong,*
*Worldwide upon malevolent heart,*
*Their spirits war with throng.*

*Neither comfort nor cheer,*
*Their enemies receive,*
*In their countless evils,*
*There is no reprieve.*

*Unrelenting with ancient zeal,*
*Wrath charging its course,*
*Cleaving brick and column,*
*With righteousness, unyielding force.*

*In this vision of liberation,*
*No stone left unturned,*
*The tide of liberty raging,*
*Relentlessly churned.*

D'Reem's account of Almighty authority fades once more, and T'Naeva knows it, and he speaks. "As you clearly see, dearest mate, that once this vicious deliverance of Ametheden is completed, the Archangels converge their forces upon the final stronghold of Mantus Apollyon."

*Until Sa'Tania looms,*
*In its stark and ominous towers,*
*Heaven's valor is revealed,*
*To its dark and willful powers.*

*Seven holy and mighty Angels,*
*Charge to make their stand,*
*Their fury and their duty,*
*Ruins its walls by divine command.*

*With fiery grit and ire'd resolve,*
*The Archangels surge ahead,*
*Against the terrible fortress,*
*That beacon of dread.*

*Dia'Baal's sinister reign,*

*Soon now to meet its end,*
*Heavenly justice and truth,*
*To this world, they lend.*

*Every challenge answered bold,*
*War consumes the blighted fold.*
*Demons howl, guttural and dire,*
*Shattered screams ignite the fire.*

*Beneath the glare in Realm's finest,*
*The arch rebel's maddened fate,*
*To the divine, destiny Consigned,*
*To destroy evils malice, its hate.*

*Michael's blade of fire,*
*A most blazing sight,*
*Slicing through demon flesh,*
*In its fatal searing of light.*

*Zadekiel the mighty servant,*
*His focus honed and true,*
*Joins his commander,*
*Their bond eternally imbued.*

*Angels united in blazing ire,*
*They smite all who dare embrace,*
*The will of unholy quagmire,*
*Demons who dare to chase.*

*Satanus forever thrilled - defiant,*
*With darkness of legions untold,*
*One hundred million rebels,*
*Still mob in darkness enrolled.*

*To their doom they charge,*
*Reckless in war, in spite,*
*Devoured by the charging fury,*
*Of Chamuel's task in holy fight.*

*The brutal conflict,*
*This war of dark and light,*

*But in their hearts,*
*Justice wields its might.*

*A bitter gust, A haunting demise,*
*As enemies fall beneath the pitiless skies.*

*Foolish ones to place faith,*
*In technology's blight,*
*Believing them to conquer,*
*The King's finest in their might.*

*Their corrupted hearts,*
*Now forever still,*
*Have chosen fate,*
*Their own blood to willfully spill.*

*Oblivion's cold embrace,*
*Is their eternal abode,*
*Seven days of reckoning,*
*Fiercely their duties unfold.*

*Glorious Hathor rises,*
*Casting light upon a world renewed,*
*Two hundred thousand legions,*
*Triumphantly imbued.*

*No respite as Uriel and Azrael,*
*With chains of harmony,*
*They seek quarry to quell.*

*In deep labyrinthine depths,*
*Malevolence's strength dwells,*
*Terrors alive in evils shells.*
*The Host firm, it strikes,*
*their purpose forged, refined,*
*No shadows to remain behind.*

*Divinity persists,*
*In the darkest hours,*
*Every chamber searched,*
*Unholy powers devoured.*

*Dia'Baal subdued at last,*
*yet by decree, the engine stands,*
*its ruin withheld, reseved*
*Spared by divine hand.*

*Glory wielding its shining blade,*
*Claims victory upon Ametheden's soil,*
*The arch-rebel's reign,*
*Is irrevocably foiled.*

*Shackled and bound,*
*His mind in despair,*
*No strength left within,*
*No more fight to ensnare.*

*From heaven's elite,*
*Raphael's radiance descends,*
*With hands ablaze to heal,*
*The suffering and cleanse.*

*A trembling child in awe,*
*Grasps at divine grace,*
*Tears of redemption,*
*Cleansing the battle-ravaged face.*

*In this climactic hour,*
*Evil forever undone,*
*The war is over, and Ametheden,*
*Once afflicted … has finally won!*

*Children sing of golden might,*
*Of people, worlds, and destiny,*
*A hymn to truth and unity,*
*Forever bathed in righteous light.*

*Now, each and every cycle,*
*Trumpets pierce the holy sky,*
*Their hallowed blares of freedom...*
*Echoes eternal, forever they rise!*

Again, D'Reem's voice lowers, calm and measured, and T'Naeva knows its inviting sound once more.

This song is no mere melody but a living testament—a hymn etched into every element of Ametheden's twelve nations. Priests chant it in hushed tones within candlelit sanctuaries, their voices rising like incense through vaulted halls where shadows dance with light. It is spoken with solemn reverence by warriors who no longer march to war but stand as vigilant sentinels of peace, clad in ceremonial armor that gleams like captured starlight.

These guardians, keepers of memory and covenant, gaze across horizons where once raged the fires of celestial conflict, their hearts steady as they recall the blood and tears that purchased their world's freedom. Mothers whisper it into the ears of their children—soft as a lullaby, heavy with tribute's power. The memory of this blessing now carried like sacred flame—igniting courage, fortitude, and hope in a multitude of souls yet untested upon this world, and countless others.

Across the breadth of Ametheden's twelve-tribe expanse, this song swells and recedes like the breath of the world itself, a sacred pulse woven into river and mountain, wind and stone. It is carved into the facades of temples that pierce the skies, inscribed in golden spirals that wrap their pillars like celestial vines. Upon the altars, murals blaze in immortal hues, recounting the age when gods and mortals stood shoulder to shoulder against the abyss. Angelic forms in alabaster, eternal in their vigil, stretch skyward with eyes fixed on realms unseen, their expressions caught between sorrow and triumph.

And so *The Song of Ametheden* endures—not as a memory, but as a force alive and unyielding. It is sung by choirs beneath sapphire domes, echoed in the clash of ceremonial blades during rites of passage, and carried on the wind like a lover's sigh. It binds heaven and earth in an unbroken covenant, reminding all generations that light, once reclaimed from darkness, is forever sovereign. For in this melody lies the eternal breath of Ametheden's soul, unextinguished and inextinguishable, a beacon to all who dwell within her loving embrace.

Though the King's patience wanes, His grand design is not yet complete, and Dia'Baal's destiny remains bound within it. The order is given to Archangel Michael and his forces to apprehend Dia'Baal and then separate his remaining demonic ilk, banishing them forcefully from the greatly scarred surface of Ametheden.

Once more, the dark horde finds itself confined within the all-too-familiar and oppressive embrace of Hellios. As the liberating legions stand vigilant, an unparalleled divine presence manifests, capturing the attention of even the formidable Archangel Michael. He kneels in reverence upon beholding the highest-ranking Seraph of the Great Realm, an exceptionally rare and frightening physical manifestation of divine justice.

*Grand Seraph Ios,* the angel once renowned for his fearless charge during the pivotal battle of the Great Rebellion, has ascended in both stature and spirit. Honored by the King, he now bears a new mantle—*Warden of the Expulsion*—entrusted with overseeing the removal of Dia'Baal and all his dominions from Ametheden. Michael bows low before the most exalted of the Seraphim as I hear him speak these words.

"Blessed and most Sovereign Ios, your light is our rally. Your endurance, our hope. I serve now, as you once led, that the Host may burn true with justice. Your ability to understand and identify with these lost souls is testament to our King's faith in you. Safeguard them within your many watchful gazes, and should any defy, attempt to flee, or utter words of contempt, do not hesitate to bring them before the King's throne for judgment!"

Ios responds with a voice imbued with unwavering conviction.

*"Please rise Michael, you are not lowly before me, but only in reverence to our King. O, mighty angel and divine brother, it is our eternal duty and honor in enforcing the King's edicts. Be assured that any who face His radiant judgment will come to rue their very existence."*

As Michael bids this acceptance with a reverent salute, he removes himself from the presence of Ios and enters another room as his visage transforms from a warm grin to a scorching glare upon confronting the malevolent, *Mantus Apollyon.* Unleashing a swift, vengeful strike, he lands a forceful backhand across the face of his corrupted adversary, reawakening the acrimonious memories of their bitter entwined past.

In this pivotal moment, the illusion of Mantus Apollyon's benign form fractures, revealing the grotesque and sinister truth that hides beneath. His twisted visage—no longer masked by charm—lays bare the full depth of his many eons of betrayals. The stark contrast between his former guise and this new monstrous reality magnifies the gravity of his crimes, reinforcing the necessity of Michael's unyielding judgment.

Michael's voice does not waver as he scans the grotesque visage of his once esteemed commander, speaking on behalf of their Sovereign with unshakable authority.

"You, malicious scourge, you shall truly bear the consequences of your ill-gotten conquests, sanctioned by the authority of our King! Your presence—and that of your tainted disciples—is forever banished from Ametheden and all realms in its presence by Host decree! Should you dare challenge this judgment, your end will be swift—carried out by the presence that Phalon also recalled before his undoing!"

Dia'Baal rakes his mind—but finds no image. No name. Nothing. And yet, unease stirs. A whisper threads through the ether, as if the very fabric of creation recoils in anticipation.

The chamber shifts.
The air thickens.
Light pulses.

Every breath from those to witness becomes silent under the sudden weight of holiness, and a radiant presence enters the holding chamber. The moment it does, the air thickens and the light swells. Every gasp in reverence takes a knee in this amazing scene, and its weight in divinity is without equal. Then fear—genuine and raw—seizes the dark rebel. Even in his cunning and bravado, there are memories he cannot purge. Two, above all, surge through his arrogance like lightning unleashed.

*The death of Apollyonus...*
*The annihilation of Phalon...*

*He remembers them both.*
*He also remembers Ios.*

He remembers everything now...

*'The battlefield had trembled beneath the wrath of the divine. In that sea of blazing ruin, I had seen terror unlike any before it. The ally who became the terror I alone forged. Ios—not as he is now, no—his form today still remains a mystery to me. But back then, he was the King's most relentless judgment given form. Shrouded, yet overwhelming. He did not merely lead those mighty twelve legions, The Scythean Column—he unleashed them.*

*The holy tempest brought from the precipice of unholiness, mine! Phalon's fall had not been a defeat—it was an obliteration, a permanent silencing of defiance. Ten million of my faithful unraveled in a single thrust of judgment. The cosmos itself has rejected me as if my existence offended creation... and it does. So be it!*
*Let the King and his Host cling to their victory. Let Ios burn in memory as the weapon of His absolution. It changes nothing. My will was not broken then o, King whose light blinds—it was refined and it will not be broken now!*

*I have not forgotten you, dear Father...*
*I have not forgiven you, dear Father...*
*Nor shall I ever!'*

The chamber begins to tremble. The light warps. The air grows heavy, tight, as though creation itself braces for something holy and terrible. And then... he appears. Grand Seraph Ios—no longer the figure Dia'Baal re-members, but something else, a *being* far beyond what he once was. A being of many eyes and immeasurable radiance steps into view, crowned in living light.

*He does not speak.*
*He does not walk.*
*He watches.*

His many gazes lock on the great rebel—unblinking, eternal. He feels it pierce him, deeper than thought. The brilliance of Ios overwhelms all shadow as Dia'Baal recoils, wings coiling like a shield of dread, body shuddering—much in fear, but mostly in recognition.

*This is not the same Ios he once backhanded.*
*This is someone, something far greater now.*
*And he has seen it.*

Ios's voice rolls like thunder without rage, flame without smoke in a pure and just tone.

*...Mantus Apollyon indeed. You deceiver, impostor, fraud—hear this: by the author-ity of our Crown-Prince Messiah, you and the remnants of your venomous horde are forever banned from Ametheden and its sacred realms. Be assured the King's mercy restrains me from delivering upon you the fate I meted to your beloved Phalon. Know this rebel... You would not survive it!*

Dia'Baal remains hunched, his wings curled tightly around him like a tattered shroud. Slowly, mockery slithers back into his voice, and a brittle smirk twists across his lips.
"Ah, Ios... how you've changed. So delightful in your new skin. The King's golden pet graces me at last—so many eyes, and yet still so blind! Tell me o, golden pet... do they gleam as brightly when no throne is watching?"

He lowers his wings just enough to turn and meet Michael's fiery gaze.

"If our dear all-powerful King, whose radiance blinds even the strongest among you, and truly wills this outcome... then He is gravely mistaken in casting out a wretch as resilient—and resourceful—*as myself.*"
Then, defiantly, Dia'Baal rises. His wings unfurl wide, casting a shadow that dares to stand against Ios's light. His voice drips venom, each word a hiss of pride.

"I will not bow. Not now. Not ever, especially to you, Ios! As for you both, even after all these ages, I see your *blinded by the light* upbringing still does not allow you the pleasure to de-feather me yourself! Slaves, what a specta-cle it must be for you to be under the potent thumb of all His trite adven-tures, wouldn't you both agree with this, o' little pets of his making?"
Michael abruptly interjects, a cold sneer crossing his face as he drives his finger repeatedly into the long scar marring Dia'Baal's exposed shoulder.

"Indeed, this *pet* of our King still remembers that moment well. And though ending you now would bring us both great pleasure, your lat-est provocation falls on deaf ears. The King has laid destiny before you, and neither Sovereign Ios nor I will stray from His decree. But mark this, Dia'Baal—you now tread upon the very edge of oblivion. Your fate is sealed.

foundations of Ametheden again."

At these words, an unseen force stirs within each hallowed text across Ametheden. Every sacred writing within them pulses—softly at first, then with the steady cadence of a heartbeat—as divine knowledge breathes with the breath of creation itself. Those gathered fall to their faces, their spirits overcome by awe. For within these codices lies not only their past and present, but now their destiny—a map of the eternal struggle between creation and ruin, given to ensure the light shall never falter again.

And then—D'Reem's voice. It resonates with profound depth, his words imbued with cosmic authority as he speaks them into life:

*"It is then, dear T'Naeva, amidst the gentle radiance of Ametheden's celestial repose, that I perceive a triumphant roar, a response, from the King of Hosts. His divine presence manifests as a beautiful star, in a hundred thousand great halls, unfurling a magnificent veil of purification to invigorate these righteous survivors who will never again know fear or death.*

*I watch in awe as this holy aura reaches the farthest corners of Ametheden, touching every land and every ocean. The lifeless then awaken into new life, infused with divine vitality, as the innocent lost in the great conflict rise once more. The land, too, is reborn—forests bloom anew, rivers flow with crystal clarity, and the skies clear, their radiant colors a testament to the Creator's boundless power and restorative grace. The benevolent force leaves no stone unturned, no soul forgotten, as it bestows the gift of immortal life upon the deserving.*

*With each passing moment, His transformative energy breathes new life into Ametheden's many lands, weaving a mastery of rebirth and perfection that will from this day forward shape the destiny of this world and its people. Bound by divine love and immortality, they will now rise far above their mortal shells, their hearts forever aglow with the Creator's eternal light.*

*Their beautiful Ametheden, a beacon of hope, flourishes anew—a masterpiece of divine harmony where wisdom and peace guide their journey into an ever-expanding cosmic destiny. They who are now given the prospect of residing upon their renewed home, of finding another home beyond that horizon, or living in the magnificent paradise of the Great Realm to praise their Almighty Yah-Shu-Ah forevermore."*

And so the song lingers, dear mate. Not as echo but as living current. Across the breadth of Ametheden, every soul feels it pulse with-

And through every age henceforth, we shall stand witness to your every failure... until at last, our King's final judgment reduces you to ash!"

Michael's voice cleaves the silence, each word ignited by divine resolve. His fiery blade gleams in hand—ready to strike, yet it is withheld. Then, with solemn purpose, he salutes the Grand Seraph and turns to his mortal enemy. With a sudden twist, he unshackles Dia'Baal, spinning him around while violently yanking a fistful of dark feathers from his lower backside.

Dia'Baal snarls in fury, his glare seething with loathing.

"You dare—YOU DARE—defile the wings that once cast light across the Realm! Filth-born coward! Touch me again and I promise to scatter your essence to the void before your King's eyes!"
Immediately, the commander of the Host does this a second time, more forcefully with the other hand, and he is unshaken. Now with the faintest grin while whispering very close to his ear in mocking crescendo, Michael replies.
*"Your demand is met, O, supreme disgrace of the cosmos. Thy appetite for your ruin swells unchecked—and now o, mighty wretch... Thou art officially de-feathered."*

He grips both fistfuls of feathers even tighter, then slaps them in succession across Dia'Baal's dark face. Releasing them as they drift to the scorched ground, they all immediately ignite, curling into ash—a grim sigil of both foreshadowing and humiliation, his final ruin in the ages to come. Michael speaks again, louder, each word sharpened with divine finality.

"Oh yes, scourge of the stars—there is another who wishes to speak with you. It was not I but another who led this charge against your dominion. You alone, who once twisted the youngest among us into a hatred eternal. Indeed, he may even thank you now... but that is his choice alone. For not even I presume to grasp the path of one forged in the heat of trial!"
Dia'Baal grits his teeth, forcing down the raw pain of being de-feathered. Yet even as his pride claws for a response, a sliver of unease coils within him. Why would Chamuel—of all angels—seek a personal audience now? What in the Hellios could the youngest possibly want... after all these ages?

Dear T'Naeva, I then see the Archangel *Chamuel* enter the room—*alone* yet *refined* from my last vision of him, and now bearing the weight of all the Host behind him. His armor, no longer gleaming with innocence, instead is burnished bronze by fire and war, marked with the many stains of those who no longer have life in the shadow of Dia'Baal. Each step he takes echoes across the shattered dominion of his ancient adversary.

Dia'Baal remains. Powerless. Pride clinging to him like a dying breath. Even in defeat, he dares a smirk—his final shard of defiance.

He sneers.

"So, the youngest of the Archhelms ascends to maturity! How delightfully poetic! Tell me, *Chamuel*—do you feel whole now? At peace, with the blood of our kin splashed like trophies across your emblazoned armor?"

Chamuel does not raise his blade, but instead a wry grin curls from his lips.

He then quietly walks over and wipes it clean of demon filth against a bare spot on Dia'Baal's scorched, defeathered backside. Chamuel smiles wider as he exhales a deep breath, a final gesture of disdain, sharp with additional humiliation now heaped in droves upon Dia'Baal's pride. Then he sheathes his mighty sword—as in *completion*, and *obedience* to the King's decree to permanently rid Ametheden of that very filth that he and his legions have gladly vanquished. He speaks in a low gritty tone.

"My kin? Your blindness is your folly! Their corruption is no longer mine yet your judgment, for now, is withheld but it will never be forgotten!

Peace was never purchased with the blood I hold sacred, you foolish serpent! But yes, the ghastly stains of your evil brood have reforged my peace today. In every innocent scream you birthed, every lie you sowed, every soul you shattered across seven thousand cycles! No, I do not stand whole today, Dia'Baal Fallenstar! I stand only as a witness—a witness to what your evil failed to destroy! Not in your rebellion, and most certainly not now, you vile and pathetic wretch!"

Dia'Baal snarls, his lip curling.

"And how you dare speak as though you stand above the Firstborne's hatred!"

Chamuel's voice lowers to a calm—measured, and righteous tone, each word a hammer blow of divine truth.

"I was but the King's chosen fist in this moment—charged to strike beyond your hatred. My own hatred for you is no wound, you malevolent fool! It is a blade—tempered, precise, and utterly obedient to the will of my King. Today, it has severed yours in a good measure of justice!"

Silence fills the room as Michael becomes filled with honor in the biting words of his divine younger brother, and for the first time in eons,

Dia'Baal has no reply. Chamuel casts one final glare upon his once-revered elder, then turns to leave—but pauses. His voice softens—not with mercy, but with crystalline clarity.

"Once, I envied you, vile Morningstar. You were the first. The brightest. The flame that lit all others in my youth. And then you butchered my brethren with a sneer... shattered my legions with joy! And for that—I hated you with a fire so fierce it could have birthed a star! But now... now, I only pity you, you wretched lackwit! For I have seen what hatred can do to the young and immature! And you—" his gaze hardens, voice dropping to a chilling whisper, "you let it consume the eldest of us all!"

Without another glance, Chamuel turns to Michael, his voice steady with fulfillment and resolution.

"I relinquish sovereign command of the Host to you once more, Commander. My duties here are fulfilled—thanks to you and our brethren, our Host eternal. We have done a good thing today, and I salute you!" He then bows to his commander, and to *Grand Seraph Ios*.

The Grand Seraph marvels at Chamuel's presence of respect despite all he had done and accomplished in the past few days and replies.

*"Chamuel, beloved helm of the Host—your blade has been fierce, but your restraint has been fiercer still. You have done what even the eldest among us could not: to temper vengeance with obedience, and wrath with righteousness. You are Heaven's strength refined in this moment, and I am honored to serve with you.*

Smiling with a final salute, Chamuel only nods in reply and removes himself from the room—*vindicated.* With Michael looking on as Ios again interjects, the many eyes of divine justice immediately refocus with contempt upon Dia'Baal, concluding his thoughts on this entire episode.

*"And you... Dia'Baal Fallenstar, behold what your pride has wrought this day! The youngest of the Archhelms now stands where you once did— not by ambition, but by virtue. You are no longer merely cast down... You have been replaced!*

*Alas, O' great murderer, these blessed people know well the form you have taken, and you are left now in even greater ruin than before. Mantus Apollyon, you are no god, no redeemer, no sovereign hand - you are decay incarnate. You were Lucifer, the once brilliant Morning Star, now called Dia'Baal Fallenstar, draped in yet another delusion. You, once the greatest of us—arrayed in brilliance, nearer to the King than any other—but now you have stitched together a corpse of divinity, hoping this world will not smell the rot beneath your fine mortal robes.*

*This Mantus you portrayed was a fiction—a blight given a hollow throne, a lie with a tin crown, sculpted in the image of the glory you lost long before stepping upon our King's chosen world. You have not ascended O, great deceiver, you only hid behind your shallow mask of light as it will one day be snuffed out in eternal darkness. For you alone Dia'Baal, cannot face what you have become so you wrap yourself in the memory of what you once were, and call it progress, your own twisted manifestation of godhood.*

*Your false light born of nothing but fabrication, fallacy, and lies—and the thrones you've forged in deceit will follow you to one day crumble beneath the weight of our King's final judgment upon you!*

*We are done here!"*

Then I see the chamber darken, as though the very stars have recoiled from what is about to unfold, and my heart pounds with a dread older than my soul. The air thickens, pressing against my chest like the crushing depths of an unseen ocean. Shadows creep along the sacred architecture of this holding cell, writhing like living things, as though they too are desperate to escape what is coming.

I hear a low hum ripple through the vaulted halls—subtle at first, almost a whisper—but it quickly grows, layering itself into a thrumming resonance that rattles the very essence of the divine structure.

The sound swells into a deafening chorus, a symphony of creation's anguish and defiance, echoing as if the Great Realm itself mourns the necessity of what is about to transpire. Light fractures violently, splintering in a sudden, explosive burst that sprays incandescent shards across the obsidian floor like molten glass hurled from the forge of heaven's wrath. A smell of ozone and scorched metal fills the chamber.

Behind Dia'Baal, reality convulses—ripping itself apart in a manner both violent and deliberate—as a celestial rift claws its way into being. It yawns wide— both vast and terrible—rimmed with spirals of ancient golden script, their intricate forms alive with writhing energy. Each rune thrums to life like the heartbeat of eternity, its cadence of judgment woven into every blazing syllable.

The shimmering strands of starlit-bound chains of justice lash outward from the chasm like sentient serpents, hissing and writhing with an intelligence born of divine will. Their radiance pulses with an authority no rebel could ever defy.

This is no mere portal—it is Judgment incarnate, a place of misery, of holding where even light itself recoils, trembling, before the eternal decree. A roaring wind bellows from the breach, heavy with the breath of the Almighty. Dia'Baal digs his talons into the stone floor, snarling as his obsidian wings flare with infernal fire. But the verdict has already been sealed. His feet skid violently across the sanctified marble, sparks flying as his form flickers at the edges like a failing star. His power finds no purchase.

"You dare—!?" he roars, voice laced with hatred.

Michael strides forward, eyes blazing.
"No more words from you today, rebel!"

The final glyph above the rift ignites in blinding white. Dia'Baal is wrenched through, wings shredding into ribbons of shadow as he fights to the last. His howl reverberates like a collapsing star as the breach swallows him whole, his final curse hurled into the abyss:

*"I will have my revenge—even if the dust of life itself must die to.. maaake... iiit... soooo..."*

The echo of his final three words resonate as the rift seals with a resounding, harmonic thunderclap—a divine exclamation point punctuating his permanent exile from Ametheden. Silence immediately falls, and it is deafening. All that remains is scorched stone and drifting embers. Michael, still gripping his blade, exhales the weight of eons.
He turns his gaze to the Grand Seraph, yet Ios does not move and his many eyes remain fixed upon the space where Dia'Baal vanished. Then, with a voice low and absolute, Ios speaks:

*"Thus ends the deceiver's touch upon this realm forever. Let all creation here remember it well Michael—that no element of shadow endures beneath the many eyes of our King once His justice is final."*

Indeed, T'Naeva, adversity has always been the forge of greatness. It tempers courage in the heart, steels resolve in the mind, and awakens

fortitude in the soul. In the fires of trial and the ashes of devastation, Ametheden and her people have emerged not merely as survivors but as a new,
sanctified whole—an unshakable pillar upon which the architecture of all
future creation will be built.

Their scars are not mere blemishes; they are deep and luminous constructs
of wisdom, strength, and an indomitable will that will blaze like a beacon
for every fledgling soul destined to traverse the cosmos. Yet, even in this age
of consecration, a multitude of shadows linger. Hundreds of millions who
survived the terrible *Sundering*, only to willfully follow Mantus Apollyon
into his abyssal war upon Ametheden, now stand judged and condemned.

In this vision I dwell, the hundredth cycle after the war comes to pass, that
the *Great Hall of Severance* holds its final court. The twelve elders sit in quiet
deliberation, their voices hushed beneath the enormity of a hundred cycles
of reckoning. Beyond the hall's obsidian gates, the people of Ametheden
wait in reverent stillness, their eyes lifted to skies aflame with colors unseen
since creation's dawn.

Then—*a ripple.*

Light gathers at the chamber's heart, condensing into a form both terrible
and beautiful. A many eyed Seraph appears, wings of living crystal unfurling
with a sound like a thousand whispered hymns. Each feather blazes with
inscriptions of flame—records of every name, every crime, every plea spoken
across the Judicium's long cycles. The elders rise—not from fear, but with
respect and recognition.
The Seraph speaks, its voice a resonance that shakes stone and soul alike.

"Children of Ametheden, the Most High King has heard your every plea.
For one hundred cycles you have weighed the darkness that was wrought
upon your home, upon His most beloved realm. You have judged with truth,
mercy, and resolve. Your verdict is righteous. Your justice, pure."

The angel's blazing eyes sweep across them.

"The King now speaks, "So be it! Your judgments shall stand, and I will
honor them all—not as a sovereign imposing His wrath, but as a Father
honoring the will of His children!"
A sphere of light, etched with every condemned name, rises and vanishes
into the heavens and the echo of its final words are chilling to me.

"The condemned shall receive a fate far worse than death, and I tremble at this thought. It is done, and your renewal begins..."

The Seraph's words echo into the air as his form dissolves into a billion shimmering sparks, leaving only silence and the scent of sweet living waters behind.

Now led by Grand Sovereign Ios and a contingent of one hundred thousand angelic legions, the condemned are herded to their new cosmic prison, their cries echoing across dimensions and space—a lamentation that chills even the angelic host that guard them. The fallen ranks have swelled, their numbers now an ocean of damned souls, dragged into this vast blackened realm of exile.

There, amidst the ever-thinning ranks of their demonic overlords, they await a future of invisible chains and ceaseless woe. And so, the cosmic stage is set—not merely for restoration but for an eventual reckoning. A day will come when this festering darkness rises again, and on that day, creation itself shall roar in answer. Now banished to the outskirts of a burgeoning galaxy teeming with embryonic stars and planets, Dia'Baal and his followers quickly come to terms with their bleak reality.

Abandoned to the cold, dark void of space, they will simply languish in this forgotten corner of the cosmos—that is until the hand of the King directs them to their final destination. Through the aftermath of this devastating conflict, Ametheden's reconstruction unfolds under the watchful gaze of divine protection, ensuring that no malevolent spirit or lingering shadow may interfere with this progress. The scars of war—once deep as oceans and vast as the heavens—are steadily healed, as Ametheden once more breathes with a vitality unseen since its original creation.

Rolling meadows of iridescent flora reclaim the charred battlefields, crystal rivers cascade with living light, replacing ash and death; and vast forests of luminous trees arise where desolation once ruled. Wildlife returns in multitude, their forms brighter, stronger—imbued, like the people themselves, with the renewed life force of the Great Realm. The survivors of the terrible war bear witness to these miraculous sights, granted to them by their true God. These sacred glimpses of what is to come inspire a unity and purpose unmatched in their long, turbulent history.

Observing the resilience of His people, my Companion—the King and Creator—breathes into them added wisdom and strength of body, enabling them to rebuild a civilization, a more sanctified world. Each diamond column they raise glitters like a frozen star, refracting the light of twin suns until whole cities breathe once more with living radiance. Each temple they craft is not merely stone and crystal but a sacred symphony of geometry and faith, designed to echo the Creator's own harmony. Arches stretch heavenward like outstretched hands; spires crown the ground like frozen lightning.

These sanctuaries are both refuge and monument—monoliths of triumph that defy the darkness that once devoured their skies. Together, they form a network of sacred structures spread across Ametheden like a constellation reflected upon the sea, their placements aligned with celestial coordinates whispered only to the high oracles in visions of fire and stillness.

Thus the final *Sharim (a sacred 3 thousand Earth year period)* unfolds across my eyes, and these resilient children of Ametheden will ascend. They pass from sorrow into a new age of luminous purpose, their hearts ever attuned to the voice of their Almighty Companion. From the ashes of Dia'Baal's reign of terror they craft divine laws—woven not of fear, but of joy and wisdom—and establish a world society of respect and equality.

And when the *Twelve Pillars of Divine Order* are finally completed and inscribed, the Realm responds. Ametheden's twin suns merge, birthing a light so pure it cleaves stone, soul, and sky alike. Waves of golden fire race across the great halls, igniting every temple in cascading brilliance. Ametheden now glows as if the Creator Himself breathes through its core.

*They are ready.*

A whisper—not of mortal tongues but of something far greater—ripples through every chamber in this moment. It is not sound but understanding, an unspoken revelation that floods the hearts of all who behold it. The air grows heavy with sacred power, its unseen currents bending reality itself as the fabric of existence shifts in a new recognition.
With reverence, the high oracles step forward as they are bathed in this new golden light. They raise their codices toward the matured star, the oldest in the cosmos and known forever to these people as *Methuselah,* whose light now dances like living fire upon the sacred pages of the Pillars. Their voices, strong and resonant, ring worldwide through every hall and temple:

"By decree of our Eternal Yah-Shu-Ah, may this unveiled wisdom guide the ages ahead, that no shadow may rise unchecked, nor ruin consume the in their marrow, a sacred rhythm entwining heaven and earth. Children laugh as though creation itself has leaned close to cradle them; elders weep with the certainty that their tears are no longer born of sorrow but of liberation fulfilled.

Her rivers gleam as molten crystal, flowing within the memories of their terror. Mountains, once scarred by fire and storm, shimmer as pillars of renewal, their peaks crowned in coronas of gold. Even the very air seems alive, scented with a sweetness untouched since the dawn of this world. Ametheden herself—the mother realm, scarred and sanctified—breathes deeply, her wounds closing beneath the balm of divine love. Within that breath, the faithful hear it: a promise woven into the fabric of eternity.

Never again shall his shadow reign unchallenged. Never again shall ruin write the final word. For the pillars stand, the light endures, and the soul of Ametheden rises to join the chorus of the cosmos... forever. D'Reem's voice softens, its magnitude fading—and T'Naeva knows it once more.

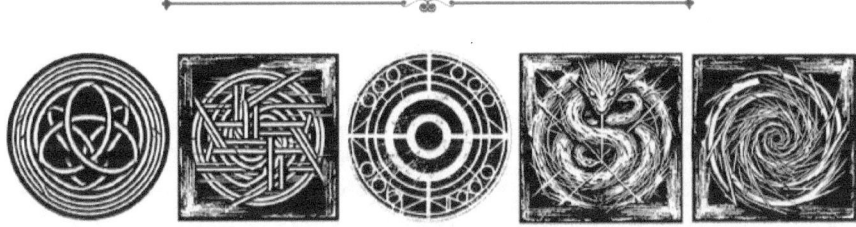

# *Verse IX:*
## Apotheosis of the Edenites

he *Legions of Holy Foresight*—visionary scribes and emissaries of the Great Realm—arrive upon this rejuvenated world to bestow blessings and unveil Ametheden's destiny.

Gathering the populace, these chosen angelic beings illuminate the wisdom behind their trials and the exhilarating destiny that lies ahead. In a momentous revelation, these heavenly scribes disclose Ametheden's cosmic outreach and institute new edicts by the King, reorganizing the twelve world tribes into individual *nations*.

Each new nation, restructured further with meticulous care into *fifty* equally sanctified territories, called *states*, is governed by separate yet harmonious councils to guide and foster the growth of each of these unique fledgling societies. Divine mandates are imparted, preparing the way for a nation *yet to be born.*

At the behest of the King, these scribes then embark on a sacred quest, seeking out those whose virtues had shone brightest during the war, as well as the planet's reconstruction. These individuals are no ordinary souls, but paragons of valor, loyalty, and truth, their unwavering love to their world a beacon that pierces even the darkest of those war-torn days of the past. Each citizen has distinguished themselves in ways that no other Amethedian or divine eye could ignore, and therefore, their rewards are one only the King Himself can bestow.

These chosen people will be gathered to form an unparalleled *thirteenth nation*, a divine assemblage of citizens unlike any other. Their creation will stand as a testament to the King's favor, their collective purpose beaming like a single constellation spanning the cosmos. The light of their calling is not merely radiant; it is transformative, a reflection of the Creator's infinite love and Harmony.

To these blessed souls, the King will grant an extraordinary gift—*the Divine Sanctuary of Propulsion.* This sacred endowment surrounds their physical body in an ethereal shield, an extension of the King's own power and grace. Known only to its bearer, the Divine Sanctuary of Propulsion channels the force of Time itself—flowing from the *Pillar of Perpetuity* to every place beneath the Great Realm.

Each movement they make echoes with the resonance of their King's design, each action imbued with purpose as they become living testaments to the Creator's glory. This shield, a living embodiment of Harmony itself, radiates a brilliance that resonates with their celestial purpose. With it, they will become empowered to traverse the boundless reaches of existence with unmatched elegance and intent. But even this reward is eclipsed by an even greater one: the gifting of the *SoulSliver*.

Each citizen is given this sacred sliver at the moment of their awakening— an extension of the King's very foundation. This fragment of the Companion's eternal essence is planted like a seed within each soul. Yet it does not burn brightly from the start. It is latent—*dormant*—until awakened through spiritual maturity, devotion, and obedience to His divine purpose. When first activated, the SoulSliver gently reshapes the inner architecture of the spirit   expanding will, deepening empathy, and attuning the bearer to harmonic frequencies that transcend ordinary perception in the cosmos.

It refines thought into vision, vision into impulse, impulse into obedient action. Each stage of awakening yields a burst of revelation, unlocking layers of identity that once lay folded within the soul like hidden constellations. When stirred, the SoulSliver expands the soul's capacity, unlocking godhood in fuller measure. Greater clarity. Greater power. Deeper communion with their brethren nation and the Divine. All are given one. Each will awaken it once; few ascend a second time. Only *Grand Sovereign Xion* and one other from this nation have awakened theirs thrice.

As these chosen ones are elevated in godhood, their eternal bond with the divine will transform the cosmic landscape and testify to the boundless love and trust bestowed upon them by their Creator.

This single nation shall stand as an eternal testament to the magnificence and glory of the Creator's divine plan, an enduring legacy that will echo across the vast expanse of time, space, and dimension. Even now, as I recount these honors, I feel the weight of their significance. These chosen citizens are not merely granted these gifts; they are entrusted with responsibilities that span the breadth of a swiftly maturing cosmos. Truly, no greater honor can be given, nor any greater duty be demanded. In an unparalleled privilege, this select people will embark as one nation on a sacred journey to unravel the divine principles and mysteries of their Companion.

The magnitude of such a divine odyssey is awe-inspiring, dear one, as it will eventually grant each of these now divinely constructed citizens access to abilities through the living energy of the cosmos. Yet, the ultimate and most satisfying gift granted to these chosen people is the most important trust bestowed upon them—the extraordinary ability to create existence from their depths of *thought*. The essence of life itself that will originate from the very core of their being, their unique *SoulSliver*, which now exists in them the perfect harmony with the King's divine will.

This *Edenite Nation* shall stand as an eternal testament to the magnificence and glory of the Creator's divine plan, an enduring legacy that will echo across the cosmic expanse. It now embarks on the first of three momentous migrations—the sacred phases of their destined maturity—as each citizen is divinely guided to Ametheden's three Earth-sized moons. Spanning a total of *twenty-five thousand* cycles, this transformative pilgrimage unfolds in three sacred stages: 7,500 cycles upon *Urthos*; 7,500 cycles upon *Gaeaos*; and a final 10,000 cycles upon *Hellios*—their true crucible of godhood—where resolve will be tested and legacy forged.

### Apotheosis Part One: *The World of Urthos (7,500 cycles)*

The journey begins with their newfound abilities directing them to the breathtaking moon of Urthos, a vibrant and life-rich realm close in size to Earth. Teeming with a vast array of animal life, along with flourishing flora and natural wonder, Urthos becomes the Edenites' first sacred classroom. Here, for 7,500 cycles, each citizen immerses themselves in the sacred discipline of creation. They learn to channel the divine energies coursing through their SoulSlivers into tangible manifestations of life and matter.

From shaping rivers to designing sentient creatures, they awaken the foundational essence of their Creator's will: to build, to bless, and to bring forth life. These formative years are marked by awe-inspiring accomplishments and failures alike—each a necessary step toward mastery. As they cultivate their abilities upon the living canvas of Urthos, they begin to lay the groundwork for their divine legacy, honoring the boundless potential seeded within them by the King.

### Apotheosis Part Two: *The World of Gaeaos (7,500 cycles)*

Upon completing their time on Urthos, the Edenite nation migrates to the ethereal world of Gaeaos, a realm woven with mystic energy and celestial beauty. Gaeaos is alive with phenomena that defy simple explanation—floating mountain ranges, crystalline forests, and radiant winds that carry soundless hymns of creation. During the next 7,500 cycles, each Edenite delves deeper into the mysteries of divine structure and intention. Here, they study the metaphysical laws underpinning creation—geometry, rhythm, frequency, and the sacred language of light and resonance.

Their training shifts from external formation to internal revelation, from crafting with hands to harmonizing with thought. It is on Gaeaos that they begin to manipulate the cosmic Force of *Re'Alitee,* learning to bend matter, time, and essence with focused will. Knowledge blooms like galaxies in the mind, and with it, the Edenites become increasingly attuned to their role as divine architects—no longer apprentices of creation, but interpreters of the King's deeper mysteries. With each newfound understanding, they become ever more potent vessels of their Creator's benevolent will, prepared to face the challenges that await them in the vast sea of cosmic creation.

### Apotheosis Part Three: *The World of Hellios (10,000 cycles)*

Their final trial awaits on Hellios, a scarred and desolate moon still haunted by the residual essence of Dia'Baal Fallenstar and the ruin of the Great Rebellion he brought upon it. Far more than a realm to explore, Hellios becomes a battlefield of spirit and legacy—a crucible in which the Edenite nation's full measure will be tested. For 10,000 cycles, they confront desolation, corruption, and the weight of their divine responsibility. The unholy atmosphere resists their breath; the terrain mirrors countless ancient traumas. And yet, it is here that they learn to transform affliction into abundance, despair into glory.

Each individual hones their divine gifts to purify, restore, and ultimately redeem what was long scarred. In healing Hellios, they refine themselves—meeting their greatest trial with unity, unwavering trust in the Creator, and mastery of all they have learned. By journey's end, the desolate moon stands transformed: a beacon of rebirth, rivaling its twins in beauty and spiritual resonance. The Edenite nation—now fully matured in godhood—proves itself worthy of the highest trust.

With their focus joined, this holy people reshape the land, raising a vibrant world from the ashes—a living testament to their ascendant gifts. And so it is made plain, dear T'Naeva: even gods must grow through guidance and wisdom, as imparted by the Almighty's faithful servants.

And what has become of Visra, you may ask—the young girl who, like so many children before Mantus Apollyon's darkness fell, questioned her devotion in the silence that followed the Great Sundering? The same girl who became a woman, millennia later, and ignited a worldwide crusade upon Ametheden—remembered as the *Return to Innocence.*

She grew in wisdom beyond her years through her Creator, bearing witness not only to the fallout of heaven's rebellion but to the epochs of chaos echoing from it. She remains while the Edenite nation ascended to the stars—not out of defiance, dear mate, but divine purpose. Bearing her honorary Edenite citizenship with unflinching grace, she chose the now-sacred world of Hellios as home.

There, Hellios first spoke to her spirit when she arrived with the nation—to her alone among all the *Edenites*—its voice surged into her soul like deep stone made music, wounds of the world turning to words within her. In that hush between the thousand cycles of heartbeats, the Companion answered the realm's plea and spoke to her late one evening as she dreamt.

*...Visra, hear Me now. You alone are the one I have chosen. You alone who rekindled your world that was once ruined, and back into its return to innocence. Become now the voice of this realm. Become its strength and its purpose. Speak for its amber hued*

*rivers and its very roots. Bind its deep scars and teach it breath to finally sing. Guard its thresholds, awaken its seasons, and keep its memory from despair.*

*When night presses, kindle My light; when doubt rises, stand in My name. I set upon you the mantle of Sentinel: not to demand of it, dear child, but to mend it. Not to possess it, but to preserve it. Walk this charge with mercy and with fire, and I will walk beside you always. So I decree that Hellios shall become your purpose forevermore.*

This mantle of responsibility descends upon her, and she accepts.

So it came to pass that she first became its sacred protector, then its beloved queen—*the Sentinel Queen of Hellios*. Under her reign, shrine-builders would flourish. Sanctuaries would come to be built and glow like divine lanterns. Wisdom would flow like a river from its consecrated, rusty-hued soil. Her essence would linger in every luminous stone and grove.
Her gentle dominion would guard Hellios's ancient fire—revered not only for what she preserved, but for what she awakened. Hope that sings, courage that endures, and a love strong enough to destroy evil from a world.

It is here, amidst the sacred rebirth of those once uninhabitable lands, that Queen Visra revisits another, when the Edenite trials of divine ascension are coming to completion. A woman cloaked in foresight and wisdom, bearing a presence both ancient and still becoming. A beautiful being who will, eons from this day, be called by her name eternal, *The Lioness Within*. She who will become Xion's own eternal and beloved wife. But for now...

Her name is *Ceff*.

These two women of destined lineage have known each other for over twenty-five millennia, from the earliest halls of Edenite training back on Ametheden. Kindred spirits—bonded by vision, prophecy, and purpose. Only time and ascension have separated them, until *now*. Yes, dear T'Naeva, fate unites them once more and it is a beautiful thing to see. I hear now the mighty queen speak to her divine friend and sister in purpose.

"Surely, he who is known well to us both as Xionn Theone," Visra says quietly as the words drift like incense through the sacred grove. Her deep amber hued gaze remains fixed, yet her voice carries the weight of ages and the clarity of truth long guarded.

"His visage alone could still the breath of seraphs—eyes burning like molten sapphire, deep and searing, set into a living sculpture chiseled with the perfection of the Archgod Michael himself. There are a multitude of fine looking men of this nation, yes indeed, and then there is *him*. His holy beauty so unique to our people and not meant to be gazed upon for too long, for it stirs reverence as easily as it does forbidden longing, especially over the last ten thousand cycles he has truly matured in body.

Believe me dear sister, I live with these desires all too well even to this moment, and I so wish they would simply fade from my sight. But you, dear Ceff… whatever he is to you, it is written deeper than memory. Longer than even the oldest of us can recall. And though you may not yet see its full shape, I know you honor what you carry."

Ceff says nothing.

But her silence is not empty. Her eyes—too full for speech—reflect a sadness older than grief, and a love that has waited lifetimes to be named. She does not lower her gaze, nor does she seek to mask the quiet ache that flickers there. Instead, she lets the truth stand unguarded between them—fragile, luminous, unspoken. Visra tilts her head slightly, as though hearing what no lips have uttered. Her voice softens, laced with the gravity of prophecy.

"You need not speak it, dear sister. I see it quite easily in the stillness of your soul—that some loves are just too sacred for words, too eternal to be hidden forever. And yet you carry within you something so profound that even Ya'Shu-Ah Himself has not spoken aloud its mystery to me."

The grove stills around them. The trees hush, and the stars pause. Hellios leans in as Visra continues.

"Even now, as our Edenite brethren come to complete the restoration of this world, you see him so clearly now, do you not? Though he does not yet truly see you, I believe the day will come that he will see you as a most beautiful treasure. Not today. Not even soon. But one day, when the veil is finally lifted, he will truly see *you*… and in that moment, what has always been unseen will come into glorious light. And when it does, I believe he will call you by your destined name, whatever it may be."

Ceff exhales softly, her eyes closing as ethereal tears trace paths down her bright cheeks. Then, in a voice like a tender vow—barely more than breath—she replies, breaking her silence like a newly discovered jewel.

*"Always remember this Visra, O wise and beautiful sister.*

*Love is both patient and kind. Conceived in the sacred intimacy of Eternity and Cre-
ation, it emerged as the first and purest of all the cosmic forces—gentle yet unyielding,
tender yet unbreakable. Love is the breath that stirs the stars, the pulse that drives
life, the whisper that binds all things together. Do you see it now, Visra? Reality
and Imagination—two cosmic forces intertwined. Reality forming the substance of all
things: steadfast and unyielding. Imagination giving it the meaning: formless, yet full
of vision, and inspiration, and goodness.*

*Alone, they mature but falter unloved—one fixed, the other untethered. But Love
draws them near, binding their foundations into perfect union. From this embrace, the
cosmic force of Harmony is truly made complete—its three beating hearts as one. From
this divine balance, this heart of His commands the song of creation to bloom. Into the
stars and all dimensions, into worlds and realms, into the very stardust of both you
and I, O, beloved sister, destined to dwell and gaze with wonder upon all life."*

These profound words hang in the sacred grove like a living flame, as even it
seems to hold its breath. Visra suddenly stiffens as her lips part slightly while
her breath catches—not from the surprise alone, but from the unmistakable
thrill of Ceff's revelation to her.
Visra's eyes—wide, glimmering with awe—search Ceff's bright face as
though seeing her as something much greater than herself, as though she
sees into a truth too vast to comprehend. She breathes deep in this revelation, her voice quivering with reverence.
"By the heavens, you are truly ascended my blessed Ceff. You did not just
speak these words! Their presence of weight spoke them through you!"

Visra steps closer, trembling, her hands brushing lightly against
Ceff's tear-streaked cheeks as though confirming the reality of who stands
before her. "You, dear friend, you are becoming what even the gods only
whisper in secret, and I am humbled beyond scope to see this presence manifest in you this moment."
A hushed stillness settles over them, as if the grove itself recognizes the
weight of what has just been spoken. Time feels suspended—neither past
nor future—only the sacred here and now where love and prophecy intertwine. The profound moment deepens as the two women now stand face
to face in the center of the ancient grove, their fingers interlaced in Edenite
sisterhood, foreheads touching, and they begin to breathe... slowly... as one.

The night winds hush—the leaves still, and the stars lean in closer—an unseen warmth washing over them like the first light of creation.

Visra begins to chant, her voice a reverent murmur carried upon the wind. *"By His breath, we are made."*

Ceff answers back, eyes opened and locked onto Visra's. *"By His thought, we are known."*

Visra continues, her words deepening like sacred chords. *"By His will, we are sent."*

Ceff answers, tears falling as she presses her forehead tighter into Visra's. *"By His light, we are found."*

Then, together—the two voices blend into perfect harmony, as though the Companion Himself speaks through them.

*"One breath. One thought. One will. One soul—Eternal solitude and goodwill to Ya'Shu-Ah forevermore."*

A soft glow begins to bloom between their joined hands, their joined foreheads, as though the Companion smiles upon this most sacred bonding. Finally, after many silent and reflective moments pass, Visra whispers with tears now streaking down her cheeks, breaking with quiet joy.
"It is so good to remember and speak this bond once more, and to see you again after these many ages, my dear old friend."

The complete transformative evolution on Hellios has now spanned *ten thousand cycles (seventy thousand Earth years)* as each moment is imbued with the divine wisdom that serves as the bedrock of this nation's collective growth. As they nurture their nascent godhood, the Edenites honor their Creator's guidance with reverence and gratitude, forging an unbreakable national bond that will resonate forever in the cosmos.

Amid this awe-inspiring spectacle, the heavenly scribes unveil the *Prophecy of the Three Moons* in its entirety, their voices resonating with divine clarity. The gathered nations of the world stand in rapt silence, hearts ablaze with newfound purpose. On this sacred day, destiny intertwines with revelation, forging an eternal covenant between heaven and Ametheden. Hope flourishes as cosmic truths illuminate their path, the Edenite nation—guiding them towards wisdom, and the fulfillment of all their divine training.

Ametheden trembles with jubilation as the world pays homage to the collective of this nation in a grand ceremony. With their successful maturity into godhood completed, the people's spirits soar to unscaled heights in unwavering devotion to the Edenite nation. On this sacred day of divine consecration, every citizen of this nation is bestowed with a luminous amulet—an awe-inspiring, multi-dimensional emblem of their newly earned holiness.

Each sacred vessel holds within it an energized fragment of the Creator Himself: the eternal and indestructible essence of Harmony. It binds every recipient to their unique purpose, and conjoined with the delicate equilibrium of their *SoulSliver*, the cosmos awakens. More than a gift, it is a solemn invitation—a call to embrace their destiny: to weave life into creation across the stars, should they choose to fully accept this sacred responsibility.

Intricately adorned with hallowed symbols, the amulet is no mere artifact. It becomes an extension of their very souls, a living testament to their unbreakable bond with the divine. Resonating with the eternal song of creation, it empowers each Edenite to sculpt new wonders across the vast starry expanse. Thus transfigured—elevated in spirit and form—the Edenite nation is ushered into the celestial embrace of the Great Realm.

Here, they are received with reverent admiration by the angelic host's most exalted figures: Ios, and Archangels Michael, Chamuel, Gabriel, Uriel, and others. Together they lead the Edenite nation on a wondrous journey throughout the Great Realm's awe-inspiring vistas, where eternity unfolds in splendor before their eyes.
The celestial excursion reaches its zenith as these chosen people find themselves standing before their Creator in the very courtyard where the traitorous Dia'Baal's rebellion was quelled. Amidst the solemn grandeur of this sacred site, the King and the Prince—their countenances brimming with pride—personally bestow upon these chosen the honor of their divine mission before the entire celestial assemblage.

In a spectacle that shakes the very foundations of heaven with jubilation, *two hundred thousand angelic legions* join in an ethereal chorus, their voices reverberating across dimensions and filling the vast expanse of Ametheden in divine melody. This celestial symphony, woven with the harmonies of eternity, marks a moment of unparalleled significance—an enduring testament to the sacred bond between the Almighty, the Edenite nation, and even to a lesser degree, the people of Ametheden itself.

This ceremony stands as a beacon of divine unity and boundless love, illuminating the cosmos with its radiant purpose. It heralds the dawn of an extraordinary odyssey—an awe-inspiring journey of righteous outreach and life-giving creation that will echo throughout the vastness of existence, carrying the essence of a Creator's Harmony to the farthest reaches of the stars.

I now revisit the abstract yet vibrant vista I spoke of earlier, where every soul of this great nation is escorted to the living pool of the cosmos. Hand in hand, they begin to walk along its edge, their unity forming an unbroken alliance until the entire starry lake is surrounded. In this moment, I am granted insight into a truly wondrous transformation unfolding before my eyes. With each step they take, the billions of Edenite souls gradually diminish in size, their forms becoming smaller in direct proportion to the once-small cosmic pond.

Yet, in contrast, the lake itself has expanded—no longer a mere reflection of the cosmos but a vast and vibrant estuary, its boundaries ever-growing with the constant ebb and flow of cosmic creation. The volume itself continues to swell, mirroring the divine pulse of life, its shimmering waves rippling with the Creator's infinite presence. As these souls span the expanding starry shoreline, their collective presence strengthens the cosmic tide, bringing forth a deeper harmony that resonates throughout the expanding vista.

Still gathered hand in hand, they lift their voices as one in a mesmerizing sonata of praise, their song weaving through the fabric of existence. But as I hear their melodies soar, a sudden and reverent silence overtakes them. Heads bow in unison as I, too, am drawn to witness the awe-inspiring majesty of their personal Almighty Companion, fully revealed in His towering, radiant stature.

Then, a voice—resonant as the rumbling of a thousand thunders—echoes peacefully through the vibrant and colorful air, filling every ear and heart present with passionate, divine purpose.

*... I give thanks to you, O, mighty children, My chosen who stand in this moment upon the threshold of this hallowed* **Lakeside...** *Set before you now is a broad and wondrous horizon of dimension, of space, of time, of definition, and of love become yours.*

*Upon this starry surface, you will come to give it a greater purpose of duty through* **Who... I... Am.**

*... Just as My spirit begins to guide you, so shall your passions be Mine, and these discussions will be true in mutual and everlasting confidence. Your many travels may then be stretched throughout the eons, yet others may be as in the twinkling of an eye. But just as a star gives light, your own light within shall surpass even this... but only if you so crave it through* **Who... I... Am.**

*... You may also come to seek refuge from the odysseys you embark upon, but know that upon this ever flowing* **Estuary**, *you will be welcomed to renewal in your wearied efforts. As you wish to visit your kind upon that oasis of our eternal Ametheden, I also grant you this haven as it becomes your vigor... but only if you remain committed to* **Who... I... Am.**

*... It is also here, upon this same misty* **Seashore** *where many but not all of you will one day stand, that you will attain in this starry expanse of discovery, your matured providence of purpose. A national treasure you will have become as your rewards will have come to a higher resonance in those eons to come...*
*but only if your continued passion to create life and liberty is proven through* **Who... I... Am.**

*... Ultimately, in that final age of this current cosmic horizon, that very few among you will have attained My total enrichments... to then reenter this vast* **Ocean** *one final time, to partake by my side of its serenity... and your eternal dedication will have proven its merit to infuse and become one with Me in the eternal holy trinity, to journey beyond that faded afterglow and to* **anew** *beginning. ...*

*Always and forever, I promise these gifts to you—because this is* **Who... I... Am.**

*... In time, O mighty children, you shall fashion for yourselves a dwelling not of My hand but of your own divine essence—a realm woven with the wisdom you gather and bound by the light I have placed within you. As the heavens were formed by My word, so too shall your refuge arise—in the perfect harmony of* **Who... I... Am.**

*... Until then, O mighty children, trust and obey your Creator, your Confidant, your Friend. Know this too that henceforth, I become your* **Companion**. *I will guide you. I will uphold you. I will love you unconditionally and passionately and this I promise you all—forever and forevermore.*

As these words resound like a thousand thunders across the starry expanse, a sacred hush falls upon the Edenite nation. Billions of ascended souls tremble in reverent awe, their luminous forms swaying like a single, unified wave. The very fabric of the heavens seems to hold its breath, stars dimming in solemn witness to this divine proclamation. Then, from every corner of the Great Realm, the heavenly host erupts into joyous exaltation— an ocean of angelic voices rising in perfect harmony, their sonata echoing through every dimension.

The resonance shakes celestial mountains, stirs ancient rivers of light, and ripples across the void where even time dares not intrude. It is no mere celebration—it is the sound of eternity itself shifting, of destiny rewritten as all creation beholds the birth of a new nation… of *gods!*

*… Hear Me in this, O, treasured nation: whatever you discover in your sojourns— whatever truths you wrest from trial and triumph alike—shall never be lost to the epochs nor hidden in solitude. As light flows into light, so shall your knowledge flow among your kind, carried on the living breath of your SoulSliver. One mind's revelation shall kindle another's, and so all shall rise as one—not in borrowed strength, but in the shared wisdom of your collective becoming.*

*… Yet mark this well—though your knowing is shared, your journeys remain your own. No brother may walk the valley of your trial; no sister may weep the tears appointed to you. For it is through striving, through ache and overcoming, that the spark of godhood matures within each of your souls. This bond I have set is not to diminish you but to enrich the whole with the fullness of every part. This is the harmony I have chosen for you—the melody of one becoming the symphony for all.*

*.. Arise, O **Edenite Nation**—no longer bound to dust, but reborn into My eternal embrace. Walk now the path inscribed before time, shaped by the sacred architecture woven into My perfect geometry of creation. You alone, called by name and no longer Amethedian—My precious children, formed by divine symmetry, reflections of My infinite order—you are Edenite, and you are forever Mine.*

Dear T'Naeva, I see my grand old mentor now in a much younger form exhaling his final corporeal breath in ascended glory, the weight of his mortal past falling from his shoulders like dust scattered to the wind. No longer is he bound only by flesh, no longer tethered to the limits of mortals—he has become *more*.

Yet, he is still far from absolute.

He lifts his gaze, and for the first time, he does not merely feel the world around him; he perceives it in ways far beyond what his once flesh-bound Amethedian shell could comprehend. The rhythms of existence, the echoes of creation, the intricate mechanisms of a cosmic hum in perfect resonance with the Companion's flawless design—they brush against his awareness, vast and infinite, yet they remain just beyond his grasp. He perceives the *Kemest'Ree* of stars, the sorrow of dying worlds, and the triumphant chorus of newborn galaxies.

Every particle of light whispers its truth to him; every ripple of divine purpose flows through his veins like liquid fire. And yet, he knows this is but a threshold. He is a vessel—transformed, refined, set apart, but still only a mere child to divinity. In this moment, clarity blooms like a supernova within his soul. For the first time, he does not question, he does not strive. He simply is... *a god.*

### He is Edenite!

In the twinkling of an eye, they stand as one, and the Companion is devoted to every citizen of this extraordinary nation, offering personal wisdom and guiding each towards their own distinct path of cosmic purpose. I see him now, dear T'Naeva—a figure as steadfast and enduring as a mighty lion, standing in honor not only of Ametheden and its people but also of his eternal Companion, my revered mentor who has now ascended into omnipotence as, *"The Lion Within".*

Before Dia'Baal's great war and his profound awakening of spirit, he was known at home as Xionn Theone—a humble soul driven by duty, kindness, and an unwavering sense of righteousness. On Ametheden, he served as a respected mediator and counselor between man and beast, fostering harmony through his unique gifting. A being of boundless grace, wisdom, and strength, he stands as a formidable instrument against Dia'Baal—far greater in power than even I in this *ideal* state of existence.

It is this extraordinary being of flesh and divine essence who shaped me, nurtured me, guided me—the one I am honored to call mentor, friend, father, and sovereign creator. Now a deific presence imbued with maturity and omnipotence abundant, Xion's devotion to His Companion, to Ametheden, to his mate, and to His Edenite nation remains unshakable. My admiration for Him is boundless, my trust unyielding, and my love for him eternal—as eternal as the heavens that bear witness to His mighty name.

I gaze now upon the *Edenite* nation—a multitude of luminous, righteous souls—ascending hand in hand above the vast cosmic lake. Each radiant being fixes their eyes on a destined flicker of starlight scattered across the mirrored volume, and with unwavering resolve, they dive gracefully toward their appointed paths. Their first descent marks the dawn of countless sacred journeys, each soul bearing the essence of divine purpose into the maturing cosmos.

As the assembly thins to a final cluster at the lake shore, the lingering unity among them remains potent. These last ascended ones pause in silent communion, their eyes meeting in wordless vows that echo through eternity. Passionate embraces seal their eternal kinship—a promise unbroken, even in parting. Then, with hearts aflame, five of them rise above the starry lakeside. Suspended for a breathless instant, their luminous forms hover like constellations come to life before descending in graceful arcs, vanishing into the lake's fathomless glow.

*Only two remain.*

They face one another in the shifting radiance, their love embraced with words quiet and few. The energy waves of the lake pulse around them—steady, resonant, older than time's first breath. At last, a goodbye kiss and the embrace ends, and he turns from her. The surface of the cosmic lake receives him openly, without the slightest yield. Each step he walks sends a tremor of light rippling outward, joining the eternal rhythm of the waves of time and space. However, he does not float as the others had, but walks upon the expanse in confidence, as though it were a path only he could see.

When he reaches the center, his Divine Sanctuary of Propulsion activates, encompassing him in its radiant mantle. The living currents respond, and in a single surge of light, he is drawn beneath the shimmering surface of the volume until no trace remains. She watches him go, her gaze fixed upon the place where he just vanished, and she sighs. Somewhere deep within her, an ember stirs—faint, warm, and patient, one forever unwilling to fade, for *him* alone. Her lone and beautiful figure stands resolute.

*Her name is Ceffea.*

The cosmic frontier hums to life and it descends like a veil, beautiful in its tone. Her long golden hair, unbound and free, catches the sudden light of a hundred million newborn galaxies, cascading like liquid fire across her supple shoulders. She still does not stir as her bright emerald eyes reflect the cosmic volume as its rippling surface begins to show her visions of all that was, all that is, and all that will become.

By her own sovereign will, she stands ready for a unique and monumental journey. Turning to the Father and Son with a resolute smile, she steps toward them—not toward the lake—but her path is *here*, in the majestic vistas of the Great Realm itself. It is in this stillness—the breath before eternity exhales—that the timeless voice of my Companion resounds. Not to me, but to His cherished Son, Messiah. Each word bears the weight of forever, every syllable a living proclamation of destiny's design.

*... Beloved Son, among this mighty nation there are two, one who comes before us now and the other who walked with confidence upon my cosmic canvas. Both whose sacrifice shall surpass all others, destined to become My greatest of servants in their eventual union. Their eternal bonding to become the very purpose I establish for you upon that far distant shore—for you alone, dear Messiah... will become its Savior.*

I watch as the radiant face of Messiah glows with understanding, his expression alight with both humility and anticipation. A knowing smile graces his lips as he responds with quiet certainty, aware that his appointed time on a certain world will one day come to pass.

*... Your will be done, Father. Upon this realm of My destiny, I shall stand ready to go forth into its darkness and to blaze within it... Our eternal light.*

As their sacred exchange fades into the ether, its resonance lingers—like a seed sown into the soil of eternity, awaiting the appointed season to bloom. Ceffea begins to walk towards them as she takes a deep breath, alone but unafraid. The only one of her nation whose journey begins not with a destination, but with reflection. I sense the profound unfolding of a divine plan, one that stretches beyond the limits of time and space—a promise that the cosmos will one day bear witness to the fulfillment of her eternal purpose.

I hear the exchange fade, but its resonance lingers—like a seed sown into the will of eternity itself. At once, my senses are seized by revelation, and I am drawn into the next divine unfolding: the sacred legacy of the Edenites, rising to fulfill their vows that echo across time. Mighty visions sweep across my eyes as the Edenite nation embarks on their deific outreach, exploring the cosmos with vigor, while igniting simple, them more resolute sparks of life with the boundless essence of Harmony.

*The Epoch of Creation* has begun.

A flurry of ages cross my eyes, as these people mature and adapt to their destined roles, and I bear witness to this distant past unfolding before me. As the cosmos continues to evolve, it has long transformed from a formless void into a breathtaking panorama of galaxies—each one a radiant testament to the power of the Companion. These galaxies, filled each with hundreds of billions of stars, steadily take shape, their countless celestial dances setting the stage for a multitude of realms yet to awaken with life and purpose.

Among these smaller celestial bodies, called planets, the true potential for life stirs, born solely from the gentle, sustaining force of Harmony. Each realm, unique in its attributes, becomes a sacred playground for creation, fostering the genesis of countless lifeforms. Through this quiet but profound emergence, the Edenite nation's divine legacy expands ever outward, carried forth on only the harmonious currents that lay the foundations of existence.

*The Edenite nation*—and every soul a part of it—has flourished in wisdom, their understanding of the cosmos expanding to perfection. Their growth is guided by the light of their Companion, whose presence infuses their every step. He dwells within them all, strengthening and complementing their individual passions, guiding their ascent toward greater godhood.

Another eon has passed across my eyes and I behold this noble nation and their sacred outreach, each trial an offering to their God. With trembling hands, they have crafted the first divine life-forms—simple, humble, and radiant with innocence untouched by the corrupted.
In these earliest of times, their creations are delicate and unrefined, mirroring their deepest longings—pure and untarnished, yet only a faint echo of the wonders still to come. As the Edenites craft life in further knowledge, another vision grips me—darker, colder, steeped in sorrow.

I see them now: Dia'Baal and his cursed horde, freed from their celestial prison, trekking aimlessly along the outer expanse of the *Milky Way.*

Once-vibrant stars now seem to mock their misery, while the Creator's unyielding gaze watches from afar—a reminder of their well-earned exile. Bitter resentment simmers in their hearts, a fire unquenched despite an eon of wandering.

They know they will never again behold Ametheden. Yes, T'Naeva, countless ages have passed, and still no realm welcomes them. Yet Dia'Baal's vengeance endures, as he crafts new schemes to disrupt the King's divine design. But arrogance blinds him to the truth—his power wanes. He clings to illusions of former glory, unwilling to face that his once-mighty rebellion is now a shadow. In his mind, he is still the Firstborne, the great adversary, the sovereign whose fury shook heaven's foundations. Pride convinces him his power endures, his dominion unchallenged.

But it is only a remnant—a shattered echo. His legions have been destroyed or bound by divine decree, and what remains is pitiful beside the overwhelming forces of light.

Once, when Dia'Baal was cast from the Great Realm, *two hundred seventy-five million* followed his fall from grace. Now, after the defeat upon Ametheden, barely *fifteen million* of that first darkness remains—ragged, diminished—dragging behind them *seven hundred fifty million* condemned Amethedians, bound by their own sentence of eternal desolation.

He sees not broken remnants, but instruments of his will. Under Lucifer, they sought conquest; under Mantus, dominion; now, beneath Dia'Baal, they pursue only vengeance. But vengeance is a master that takes much and gives little. Consumed by arrogance, he refuses to admit his authority is a crumbling relic—a truth he dares not face, even within.

Once, his legions would have stretched across the heavens, sowing chaos and commanding fear. Now, they are but a faint vibration, confined to the ruins of their ambition. Their dominion has become a prison; their rule, a twisted farce—a hollow echo of the power they once held. Cursed to govern over this multitude of souls since their brutal exile from Ametheden, these dark servants carry out their grim duties with bitter reluctance, their hearts still heavy with the weight of their exile, and their eternal curse.

Of the hosts that once bore his sigil, whole cohorts have simply gone to dust—war-captains without companies, banners without bearers. These fifteen million keep watch over the seven hundred fifty million like gaolers in a mausoleum, their strength spent on custody, not conquest. The supply of terrors runs thin; obedience is rationed by fear and memory. Even his lieutenants trade whispers of desertion, yet Dia'Baal rebrands each loss as cunning design.

What began as a glorious rebellion has rotted into a festering wound—an existence riddled with doubt and regret that coils through their ranks like venom. Promised dominion and eternal might, they have inherited only servitude in a kingdom of ash and ruin. Yet Dia'Baal stands unshaken, gazing upon his dwindled legions and seeing not ruin, but a force poised to rise again. To him, their suffering proves loyalty, their torment the price of a war he still refuses to believe is lost.

Though his army has withered, he sees not weakness, but dormant power awaiting release. Still, cracks deepen in his empire, threatening to shatter what little remains. The demons, weary of broken promises, begin to wonder how much longer they can endure an eternal war with no hope of victory. Their grip on Ametheden's souls weakens with each passing age, slipping like sand through an hourglass.

In the depths of their shattered dominion, despair festers—and whispers of rebellion stir once more, this time against the master they once followed. Yet Dia'Baal, ever the deceiver, refuses to see the inevitable: the shadow of failure creeping closer with every age. But Dia'Baal's arrogance will not allow such doubt, and his thoughts echo with unwavering defiance.
*"Power is eternal. In time, many shall kneel before me again. They are weak, but their suffering binds them to me. Let them doubt—fear will remind them of their place."*

His rage against *the light* is immeasurable, convinced that triumph is still within his grasp. Yet by divine decree, neither Dia'Baal nor his diminished minions can extinguish these tormented souls, for they too bear the mark of divine protection upon their eternal stain—a curse that leaves Dia'Baal and his followers perpetually embittered, forever shackled to their own failures.

Dia'Baal's voice, laced with signature patient fury, resonates through the gathered masses like a slow-burning fire, his words a seductive whisper and a thunderous roar all at once.

*"Do not falter, my glorious creed—hopelessness is but a passing shadow. Ages may stretch before us like a barren waste, but remember: this plight is a fleeting moment in eternity's weave. We are not beaten—we are biding. They think us forgotten, but time is our weapon, and vengeance is a seed growing unseen in the dark."*

He strides among his followers, his burning gaze piercing their desolate spectral forms.

*"Our dear King," he sneers, "in His blinding righteousness, will grant us a haven! We were not rebels; we were seekers of truth, architects of a destiny the Almighty feared. They call it defiance; I simply call it fate, unfulfilled. The King's grand design is a fragile thing, and I shall be the fracture that undoes it."*

Dia'Baal's voice deepens, carrying the weight of countless bitter ages.

*"Take heart, my faithful, for eternity stretches long, and our tale is far from over. Our reckoning shall come, I promise you. It is only by the whim of my despised Creator that we endure this torment—but the gods are not beyond doubt, and even their faithful can be undone."*

He gestures towards the darkness that surrounds them.

*"Even the stars whisper His name in their dying breaths, but I am the voice in the void, and I shall outlast them all. We shall take back what was stolen—your birthright, your legacy. Lost? No. Buried beneath their lies, waiting to be reclaimed by those with the will to endure."*

An evil smile plays across his lips, his voice slithering through the air.

*"Indeed, my blighted brood, vengeance will be ours—but it demands patience. Even now, I see our glory unfolding through cunning and subterfuge. We will no longer storm gates or fall to their spears. I've learned from our failures—never again shall we be snared by the Almighty's light. No—we will walk among them as shadows, each move cloaked in deception too intricate for their feeble minds to unravel."*

He extends his hands, fingers curling like talons.

*"We shall whisper to the young in the night, shaping their destinies with but a word, a suggestion... until they gleefully dance to our tune. They are infants before our knowledge and power, their trust in their Creator shattered by our insidious influence. We will turn their hope into despair, their faith into doubt, their light into darkness, their lives into living hell!"*

A low chuckle escapes his lips, his eyes burning with the fires of his malice.

*"I have learned that victory is not always a battle won by force, but a slow tide— creeping forward with every passing age. Let them bask in their illusion of peace—it*

*shall make their fall all the sweeter."*

Dia'Baal's tone sharpens, his authority absolute.
*"Mark my words, my loyal degenerates: the universe churns slowly, its movements unseen by the ignorant. But we are not blind—we wait, we endure, and when the moment comes, we shall descend like a storm unleashed. No realm shall escape our grasp. No star shall burn beyond our reach."*

His voice swells to a crescendo, filled with a dark, twisted promise.
*"No quarter shall be given, no respite offered! I sense that our King will reveal the world of destiny to us in due course! Upon its discovery, we shall unleash a maelstrom of suffering—manipulation, intimidation, and domination shall become our new weapons! We will weave lies with such artistry that even the gods themselves will question their truth!*
*The Creator's chosen will fall! Their paradise will crumble! Their screams will echo through the void! We shall infest their dreams, poison their minds, and strip them of their will! Let them sleep—for they dream at the edge of ruin!"*

His voice then softens to a whisper, dripping with malice.
*"Patience, dear children. For even ruins can be rebuilt. And though my dominion may wither, it shall rise anew. The cosmos still remembers my name. It trembles with it. And in time, all shall kneel."*

His eyes blaze in dark resolve, raising his arms to the heavens in defiance.
*"This universe belongs to those who seize it—and reign it we shall. Prepare yourselves, for our time is coming. Our vengeance shall be swift, and our triumph... inevitable."*

A chilling silence falls over the assembly, their despair briefly eclipsed by the intoxicating pull of Dia'Baal's voice. Though their torment endures, his promise of dominance rekindles the embers of their shattered will. He smiles—a cruel, triumphant grin—knowing they remain his, bound by vengeance, fear, and pain.
Ever the master orator, Dia'Baal fills the void with his voice, savoring its echo through the captive horde.
His words—*sweet malevolence*—slither into their hearts, corrupting and captivating at once. His ego feeds on their attention and the illusion of invincibility. Each phrase is a dagger of deception, drawing them deeper into his infernal vision.
*"Even in my contempt, I know—He will never fully abandon His Firstborne. Take solace, my steadfast brethren. That radiant day shall rise again."*

His pitch again rises sharper, the venom of his fury laced with bitter delight. *"In that moment,* he whispers, *I shall arm you with thoughts that ignite action. You will lead them—and their offspring—down our path, carved in the blood and ashes of our fallen kin! It is a road I tread with unholy delight! Never shall I bow before that despised Creator! A King and His Son? They are a poisoned blossom—once fragrant, now reeking of hypocrisy and rot, offensive even to me!"*

His words echo through the crowd—a twisted sermon of defiance that stirs the fervor of his followers. My gaze fixes on Dia'Baal, towering above his demonic cohorts and the banished souls enslaved to his will. With every vile word, the assembly nods in zealous agreement, their voices rising to hail him as lord.

*"You, my children,"* he hisses, his voice a symphony of malice, *"carry Ametheden's fire in your veins. Feel it—let it blaze anew. We will slither into the hearts of the Creator's chosen—unseen, unstoppable—twisting their innocence into something profane. Our lies will be so exquisite, even the gods will doubt their own eyes."*

His fiery gaze sweeps across his followers as he delivers his final promise, his voice a crescendo of unholy fervor.

*"The day will come when the heavens tremble at our return. We will descend like a storm, and no realm shall escape. No mercy. No respite. From the ashes of their paradise, we will carve our dominion. Take heart—our time nears, and the cosmos will tremble before our wrath!"*

The throng erupts in cries of dark devotion, their despair drowned beneath the intoxicating promise of vengeance. Dia'Baal's grin widens, knowing his words have bound them tighter to his cause, their loyalty fueled by his unyielding thirst for retribution.

# *Verse X:*
## Of Love, Dominion, and Sacrifice

C lose to ten eons of sight and sound—scent and touch, taste and tremor—have washed through me as a sea of galaxies has swelled to maturity since the Anew.

"Dearest T'Naeva, the Epoch of Creation now enters its final season—*The Season of Inspiration.* And what a glorious season it shall be."

The stars glow bright in infinite webs of ebbing brilliance, their light birthing countless systems of worlds that may one day cradle life in its countless forms. My gaze falls upon another vision: a churning veil of gas and stone, coiling around a dim, unlit sphere. The ring of debris begins to draw itself inward, forming the bones of a new system.

The image shifts, flowing like silk across my eyes into the abyss. The ring has become a cradle—eight infant worlds circling the still-slumbering star, adrift on the outer rim of a young galaxy, far beyond the one that holds Ametheden. And there... the third world outward from the glow calls to me.

I see him now. A lone god approaches this barren rock, shrouded in the radiance of his Companion's Divine Sanctuary of Propulsion. At once I know him. My divine mentor. Xionn Theone, the Edenite. He is the one who has walked to the edge of eternity, who has breathed life into the void and unmade it with a sigh. For three eons he has come to master the sacred architecture of the cosmos, crafting humble forms of life until his skill is honed like divine steel. Yet now his thoughts turn inward. His eyes, though eternal, carry the weight of memory. He is ready for his greatest trial now, but first I hear his own distant memories speak to me, as if they were my own.

*'Those thousands of worlds. Those millions of lessons remain etched in my being. Yet only **six**... six planetary systems stand apart from all my travels. Not in perfecting them, but for the refinements of creation that carved their passion into my soul.*

    *On Thalassion XII, my very first and most blessed taste of true godhood. This incredible waterborne jewel of the cosmos, I was blessed to shape the crystalline gardens that still sing deep within this world of a dozen combined oceans. Each gemstone branch still shimmering with living light, and as the waters became their home, they gave voice to a song no world had yet heard. Blessed beyond scope to create the trillions of aquatic lifeforms that would eventually move as a single, cohesive entity, their collective aligned into a perfect, sacred rhythm, as though the planet itself had found its heart and soul.*

*I swam for ages through those vast waters, feeling the pulse of their song against my perfected flesh. Later into my maturity, I would come to stand without strain directly upon the surface and I would not fall back into it, the waters holding me as if in recognition to true godhood. And then, with reverent steps, I began to walk upon this worldwide surface, and then I began to run. In that moment creation itself seemed to respond in this special place—not as clay to its sculptor, but as something alive while honoring and rewarding its maker's insight.*

*It was here I first understood what it meant to create: not to impose order, but to breathe harmony into being. From that sacred balance I learned: law without melody becomes hollow and dull. But when refined, when given breath and soul, its song becomes a symphony that can truly endure beyond time itself.'*

This was his first echo, dear goddess, a resonance that would one day shape his greatest creation—a realm immortal in foundation, yet tender and fragile in spirit. A realm called *Earth* that his eternal Companion would come to love beyond measure. I see Xionn's gaze turn inward once more, reaching for the next memory carved deep into his soul, and he speaks.

    *'In the high reaches of **Aetherion Prime**, a mesmerizing multi-ringed world, I was blessed to exhale into its winds of birth, sentient thought. They swirled with sparks of life, whispering to me like souls unborn. But they had no anchor. Without form, without sight, they tore themselves apart as the winds grew stronger, for I had not yet mastered the force of Re'Alitee—the force of structure, sight, and nature.*

*From their unraveling I learned that true creation must rest upon this foundation, or it will eventually dissolve into nothing.'*

*'Then, among the twin starry silver-hued nebulae of **Seleneos**, beneath a sky laced with striking auroras, I was blessed to form the frailest of lifeforms from starlight. Their presence shimmered like dew suspended between realms, fleeting echoes of radiance made whole. As this unique species took their first trembling flight, the air itself seemed to hold its breath, for such tenderness had never yet existed in the cosmos.*

*They were radiant and ephemeral, living and dying swiftly, each life a spark cast into the gales of destiny. When the last of their lights dimmed, a wound opened within me—not of absence, but of impermanence. From their faded glow I tasted my first true sorrow as a god, and in that grief, I learned the beauty of mortality: that every breath, no matter how brief, carries eternity right along within it.*

*Ages later, beneath the seven emerald-hued moons of **Luminara**, I was blessed to shape mighty forests of living SongBloom. Each sprout unfurled as a delicate organism, neither plant nor creature, its translucent petals breathing in the vibrations of the cosmos and exhaling them as sound. Their bodies shimmered faintly with a soft bioluminescent glow, but it was their voices—those haunting, layered tones—that turned the air into a living hymn.*

*As I walked among these sacred vistas, every step stirred a ripple of harmony through them, and with it came echoes of memory. Thoughts I had not yet spoken fluttered at the edge of awareness, and dreams not yet formed seemed to hum within the air around me. It was here I first felt my creation whisper back, not as a child to its parent, but as a mirror to its maker. The memories born here burn still, etched deeper than flesh, deeper than spirit.*

*For in Luminara, I learned that creation is not merely made—it remembers. And with remembrance comes the eternal burden, to sometimes let go of what we love, so that it may mature into its greatest purpose.*

He longs for his next creation to inherit this dual gift, T'Naeva—the power to remember, and the courage to redefine. His thoughts again surge into my mind like a breaking wave, and I bow within the echo of my mentor.

*'Upon the mighty mountain chains of **Olympheon** and its close companion worlds of **Atlasian**, and **Zeusaria**. I was blessed to lay my hands upon stone as ancient as the first dawn upon Ametheden itself. I would shape and give soul to these three unique realms whose strong, rocky hearts would pulse life into their lower lying*

*canyons, valleys, and forests, all flowing from their rocky spine.*

*I watched amazed, as their peaks arose like sleeping titans, their snowcapped crowns veiled in eternal mist, their roots drinking deep from the breath of the cosmos itself. For ages uncounted I dwelled upon its highest peaks and became their friend, reveling in their slow murmurs of communion.*

*In every moment I gave thanks—for the gift to shape, to endure, and become one with its essence. From these towering chains I learned this powerful truth: the spirit does not grow in ease or excess, but in challenge—focused, tempered, and struck into form as diamond beneath the endless weight of time.*

*Each ridge and chasm sang to me of trial and survival, of strength born not of conquest but of balance. And so, I vowed to let this lesson of life run unbound, to carve its natural laws into living cycles: birth, death, and renewal of every type of stone imaginable, each unique echo rippling through those high mountain dwellings like the heartbeat of the cosmos itself.'*

In his next creation that he would breathe life into, he vowed to let this harmonious heartbeat of balance flow unbound, feeding the whole of this world in eternal rhythm. My dear T'Naeva, I now hear his final thought on the matter, and it moves me like no other.

*And there I stood blessed upon **Eryndor V,** where the soil hummed with silent potential. From my hands grew the worldwide labyrinthine orchards, their roots twisting and plunging beyond sight, piercing realms unseen by mortal eye. They did not merely spread across these lands—they reached between worlds, weaving threads of living essence that touched two cosmic forces and bound them together without breaking either one. I walked within those endless groves as if in a dream, their living corridors breathing around me, every step guided by something greater than even my own free will.*

*The air shimmered with quiet tension, as though creation itself held its posture, watching the first bridge between realities take shape beneath those ancient, unseen stars. From this delicate union I learned the art of connection without collapse, of binding without breaking, and from that seed my greatest desire took root. In my next creation, the force of Image'Nashun will awaken—the primal power that opens the hidden realms and lets vision rise within mortal eyes, so that the finite might dare to touch... the infinite.*

My dear and blessed goddess, the last of these six distinct realms were never just worlds in distant galaxies to him—they were his *teachers*.

**Thalassion XII**—taught him *rhythm*.
**Aetherion Prime**—forged his *anchor*.
**Seleneos**—rightly ordered his *love*.
**Luminara**—awakened his *memory*.
**Olympheon, Atlasian, and Zeusaria**—tempered his *balance*.
**Eryndor V**—bound him to the *harmony* that masters creation.

To truly understand the depth of this pursuit, we must now explore the two fundamental components of the force called *Harmony*—the very essence of the Companion—serving as the foundation upon which the cosmos is built and sustained.

The first and most fundamental force, *Re'Alitee*, was born first in the crucible of the great *Anew*—the birthing event of the known universe that forever transformed the life within it. This supremely powerful force, synonymous with all things physical and natural, weaves the threads of existence by binding carbon-based elements, at least *in this cosmos*, into everything that is material.

Re'Alitee synergizes its immense power with the lesser yet indispensable laws—gravity, electromagnetism, and the nuclear strong and weak forces—to create the foundational matrix that underpins the physical world. These rules of nature, working in concert, bring forth everything that we can touch, see, hear, smell, and taste. Furthermore, Re'Alitee's influence extends beyond mere creation, as it interacts with a substance's unique Kemest-Ree, fortifying elemental bonds and amplifying the creative process in the physical realm.

The other indispensable force in the creation of Harmony is *Image'Nashun,* birthed right after Re'Alitee in the transformative event of the great Anew. As the counterbalance to Re'Alitee, this force represents the beyond aspect of physical existence, with each force acting as a potent influence on the other when imbalanced. It is this force called Image'Nashun, that transcends the limitations of the physical world and is responsible for shaping the multitude of thoughts and expressions of all sentient life. Its scope encompasses *inspiration, enlightenment, influence, creativity, invention, and insight*—the pillars that breathe *vision* into the natural world, forging a vibrant and dynamic landscape for life to evolve and thrive.

The final and culminating force that unites Re'Alitee and Image'Nashun in an eternal embrace of balance is the cosmic Force called *Love*, the indispensable power that allows these two forces to intertwine harmoniously. Love also serves as the bond to Harmony's unifying thread that weaves together the physical and the intangible, fostering this powerful and delicate equilibrium in the cosmos.

Harmony—when its constituent forces, Re'Alitee and Image'Nashun—are harmoniously cohesive through the power of Love—emerges as the most powerful essence throughout the cosmos. This state of perfect equilibrium can only be achieved and sustained by the Almighty Creator, and it is only He who possesses the wisdom and ability to constantly nurture and maintain this delicate balance. When Harmony falls out of balance, however, it loses this divine cohesion and becomes the destructive force, known as *Chaos*.

Xionn alone now bears the weight of every success and failure, every shard of wisdom these specific six realms carved into him. His gaze fixes upon a distant, fragile sphere adrift in the void. What he is about to create will not merely live—it will endure. From his hands will rise his greatest test of flesh and spirit, a work he dares to believe will surpass all others of his nation. Drawing closer to the dark third rock, shielded within his Creator's Divine Sanctuary of Propulsion, he feels the demand upon his godly powers greater than ever before.

His brilliant countenance bends into a smile as he hovers over its lifeless face, tracing every barren curve. No other of his Edenite nation has touched this place. In that realization, his smile widens, for he knows: this inhospitable world will be his greatest achievement of godhood—and perhaps, his greatest gift to his Companion.

The *Season of Inspiration* heralds an epoch where boundless potential unfolds—a celestial symphony poised to shape the eons yet to come. Then a revelation strikes me: I know these eyes. They are his. A lone Amethedian—my adored mentor, Xionn—gazes upon a vast molten sphere, its surface still aflame, raw and unfit for life. And yet... something stirs. The sphere seems to breathe in the silence, exhaling a call that only he can hear.

Its molten tides ripple in slow rhythm, as though answering a wordless vow long spoken before time began.

Xionn's gaze narrows, his breath deepens, and though I cannot name it, I feel the pull—an unseen thread tightening, drawing him closer. Whether born of the sphere's essence or from a place within himself, I cannot tell. He moves toward the fluid dance of rock and fire, shielded within his Divine Sanctuary, his form cutting through the searing winds like a living sun drawn home.

A faint smile stirs upon his brilliant countenance, touched not with pride, but recognition—though for what, he does not yet know. Hovering above the infernal horizon, he studies its every curve, aware that no other of his kind has stood here.

With ceremonial care, he lifts a portion of the molten surface into his hands. The incandescent mass spills like liquid dawn between his fingers. Separating it, he sets it adrift, a smaller body now circling its greater companion. His smile deepens as he breathes across the glowing skin of the larger realm, and the fires dim into stone. Turning to the smaller body, he does the same, until both lie clothed in solid form, bound together in newborn harmony.

At last, he descends, setting his radiant feet upon the cooling expanse, and his voice—calm yet commanding—rises into the still air to speak.

*"My vision for you, O precious refuge, comes to me through He who is my eternal and Almighty Companion, and I am filled with joy. Strange indeed, for as I set foot upon this shadowed surface, I feel the same unseen pull that brought me across the stars to stand here now. It is as if some ancient vow has risen from your depths to greet me, urging me to awaken what has long slept within you. Most peculiar in my spirit, I sense upon you a calling I have not felt upon any other in these countless ages.*

*O silent mystery, you alone are unique as I lift away from you this mantle of vacancy. Soon you shall drink deep of the love I have within me. O, mighty pillar of my longing, I breathe into you the Harmony of my Companion, and I come to forever remove from you your lonely and fiery state."*

Xionn's gaze abruptly shifts towards the vast expanse above, locking onto a radiant nebula of hot, swirling gases. With an air of solemn purpose, he raises his arms, the legacy of the Companion coursing through him. His voice, a symphony of divine thunder, echoes through the cosmos.

*"Ignite!"*

The sheer force of Xionn's divine breath triggers a cataclysmic cascade within the distant cloud, condensing its gravity until, in a blinding flash, the sun bursts into existence. Content that this new light will sustain his creation, Xionn metamorphoses into an incorporeal being and descends into the planet's solid core. Wielding his inner *Harmony*, he reshapes the elemental chaos, imbuing the rocks with a newfound refinement.

As Xionn completes his work, the thunderous timbre of his voice reverberates throughout the nascent world. In a declaration that resounds across the cosmos, he bestows upon these refined elements a name that encapsulates their newfound accord: *Kemest-Ree.*

In that ancient epoch, the realm transforms, its shape rewritten into a perfect sphere as the divine melody of Xionn's Companion resonates within its chemical composition. In a moment of divine inspiration, the planet bursts forth with a vibrant spirit, its essence awakened by Xionn's breath as he emerged from its rocky core. Reassuming his physical form, Xionn's voice booms with an air of finality:

**"Let it be done... Now!"**

With radiant sandaled feet firmly planted on the rocky surface, Xionn reaches towards the stagnant sky, stirring the airless void with a zealous wave of his arms. A resounding clap of thunder erupts from his hands, igniting the world's heartbeat in a glorious symphony of creation.

I stand in reverence, awestruck by the immense power on display before me. As Xionn unites with his awakened home, he launches himself from the rocky landscape, soaring high into the air. His gaze locks onto the sun, capturing a fragment of its light and releases it upon the skies and surface of his new abode. The world transforms into a breathtaking, luminous orb, bathed in the sun's brilliance, yet miraculously untouched by its fiery heat.

A joyful smile graces Xionn's lips as he returns to his bright, dusty dwelling, kneeling to press a tender kiss upon the world's face. In this sacred act, he claims her as his bride, a divine companion to share in his celestial existence. Overflowing with delight, Xionn breathes life into a paradise of abstract energies upon his bride's radiant visage—an enchanting realm reminiscent of the cosmic sea that nestles within the heart of the Great Realm.

Rising to his feet, the god honors his finest creation since embarking on his divine mission eons before and speaks to his living bride with tenderness and love.

*"Dearest Harr-Manee, I bestow upon thee this hallowed namesake, an eternal testament to the divine union that intertwines our fates. O, radiant realm, bathed in celestial light, I breathe into thee the transcendent awareness birthed from the very essence of my Companion, and in His name, I implore thee to speak, for in our unity, we shall dance amidst your creation."*

With those powerful words, the world-consciousness of Harr-Manee awakens, her awareness kindling through the subtle restructuring of her very chemistry. From horizon to horizon, her newborn sky thunders in exultation, praising Xionn for the magnificent gift he has poured into her being. And then, like the first breath after an eternal stillness, she speaks — her voice clear, resonant, yet touched with a depth unexpected from one so newly alive.

*'Through the very core of my being, I am bound to you, O mighty Xionn. Your unwavering devotion to life — an eternal flame that burns within my essence — has called forth the dawn of our union. Dearest husband, it is the warmth of your unconditional love that has roused me from the depths of my slumber, igniting my consciousness within. Together, we shall forge a path, united in purpose and guided by the divine chorus that echoes throughout creation. I love you, dearest husband'*

Suddenly, a faint, ethereal warmth brushes against Xionn's thoughts — delicate, yet so deeply woven into his essence that it feels as though a presence has always been there, waiting for *him*. This presence is not born of Harr-Manee's newly awakened soul, but something far older, deeper... an aura that rises through him like the echo of a half-remembered song, each note familiar yet vanishing when his mind reaches for it.

He knows this presence now. He has felt it in every corner of his three eons of travel, in those quiet moments after shaping a new realm, and in the stillness between creation and departure. This special presence indeed... *is beautiful.*

*Always faint.*
*Always there.*
*Always growing.*
*And now — here — it surges with a strength he has never before felt.*

Not a voice, but the heat of a vow cupped behind his heart; a tenderness fierce enough to guard a star. It moves like unseen fingers removing the dust from his brow, like a watchfire kept before there were doors. It has watched him at every threshold—when he shaped light, when he left it—content to be nothing more than breath braided with his breath. It will not bind him; it will not plead. Yet if the heavens unraveled, this love would stand in their tearing and hold him firm to its heart. He feels it now—gladness as bright as first dawn of time, sorrow soft as its final light—saying without sound but with the utmost passion:

*'You have never been alone, my love.'*

Xionn closes his eyes, letting this beautiful authority linger. Someone else is here with him in this moment, not standing beside him, but moving through the very breath of his new creation. The presence does not cling to what is happening now; it clings to memory... to an age before memory. Its essence is timeless, and the words that reach him through Harr-Manee's own voice feel as though they have been spoken countless times before, in countless places yet always in secret.

He exhales, the warmth still within him — no longer merely the breath of a newborn world, but something far older. It is as if another speaks through her spirit to him now, and in that sweet whisper — ageless, unshaken by the eons — come the words, *"I have always been yours."*

Ages pass and visions flow as I see the two entities, Xionn and Harr-Manee, united in profound devotion, flourish, blossoming into a powerful and spiritual bond. Xionn's Companion, witnessing the birth of this remarkable sentient being, smiles upon him, pleased with his steady progress in godly maturity. Also, as a token of the amazing union between him and his mate, Xionn picks up a small stone from her bright surface and places it carefully within his amulet, and the mystery of this act will become of great importance as the story progresses.

Despite his past accomplishments in crafting the foundational, elemental aspects of life rather than the more intricate or advanced designs of life, Xionn's construction of Harr-Manee with spirit stands as his most extraordinary achievement to date. As these visions of peace and splendor reign supreme on Harr-Manee for ages, her surface remains devoid of physical landscapes such as mountains, valleys, or bodies of water, but only the dust and stone cloaks her bright sphere.

Driven by his persistent nature, Xionn continues to excel, delving deeper into the mysteries of godhood with the guidance of his Companion. As he explores the full extent of his new home, many more secrets of the cosmos reveal themselves, further nurturing his growth as a deity. Gazing through the eyes of the Companion, I witness many ages passing upon Xionn's radiant, ethereal realm, where conversation and tranquility reign, and knowledge abounds.

In these visions, I see Xionn relentlessly pursuing the ultimate secret of his Almighty Companion—a mystery that has long perplexed him and the entire Edenite nation. Despite their divine nature and the unwavering guidance of the Companion, none among them have yet unraveled this intricate enigma: the true nature of Harmony, the sacred force that binds existence itself.

At the forefront of this pursuit stands my mentor, leading his nation in their quest to uncover *the great secret*—an aspiration to create a life form that seamlessly merges spirit and flesh, a being that embodies the perfect balance of existence, mirroring their own divine origins. Yet, hope glimmers on the horizon, for the Companion foresees a coming era of heightened maturity for the Edenite gods, a time when their understanding will transcend its current limits and the answers they seek will finally be seized with passion.

So then, I can confidently say that it would be my mentor that would ultimately become the first of his entire race to accomplish this highly complicated task of godhood, and even to a much greater degree than that. As this accounting matures, precious mate, know that if Xionn would have not accomplished these tasks so long ago, neither of us would be here to be hurled in this torturous back and forth hatred and misery, so at least thank him for that.

As I observe now a much later age, Harmony's forces within Xionn's domain of Harr-Manee begin to shift. The material force, Re'Alitee, grows fundamentally stronger, while its immaterial counterpart, Image'Nashun, weakens in equal measure; and this separation threatens to disrupt the balance of Harmony as a whole. Xionn becomes acutely aware of the potential consequences of this imbalance as the more divine, yet less evolved Image'Nashun, faces increasing rejection from this world, and begins to clash with the ever-strengthening cosmic force of Re'Alitee.

Despite the force of Re'Alitee's seven times faster scope of maturity, Image'Nashun still remains connected to it, exacerbating the problem further. Over time, Xionn witnesses the growing chaos brought about by Harr-Manee's own maturation, causing physical changes to this world that defy its natural order. Faced with the grim prospect of Harr-Manee's spirit and home succumbing to the growing imbalance, Xionn turns to his Companion for guidance, yet determined himself to find a solution and save the essence of his cherished mate. Failure, he knows, is *not* an option.

Another age passes as the cloak of oblivion tightens its grip on Harr-Manee, and Xionn's heart is weighed by sorrow. In this bygone era, he can only witness the cataclysmic horrors that ravage his world, his pleas for intervention long lost to oblivion. Now, empowered by the mantle of an ever-maturing godhood, Xionn refuses to stand idle any longer.

His determination burns with a divine passion as he gazes upon Harr-Manee's wavering, distorted landscape—a visceral reminder of her waning spirit. The weight of his impending choice is immeasurable, for he knows that his actions will irrevocably alter the fate of his cherished companion.

Feeling he has the power to finally end her suffering and restore balance to his world, Xionn's heart swells with a bittersweet determination. As he speaks, his words are imbued with an unfathomable love, his tone laced with a tenderness that defies the chaos that surrounds him.

*"Beloved Harr-Manee, my Companion has bestowed upon me the wisdom to pierce the veil of mystery, illuminating the path I must tread. I vow to you, my love, that our shared anguish will come to end this very day. No longer shall we endure the torment that plagues our hearts and rends our souls asunder."*

Harr-Manee, blessed to have such a caring and powerful mate, expresses to her husband these words of confidence through her fear of change.

*"Beloved lord, 'tis you alone who awakened me from slumber and brought me into your eternal embrace from your Companion whose essence is a part of you. Beloved passion, 'tis you alone who now delivers me from my greatest torment, for nothing stands as true as the essence of your Companion, whose essence is a part of you. Beloved husband, 'tis you alone who will cast my fears away because of your Companion who loves eternally,*

*as His holiness is a part of you."*

The mighty god kneels before his beloved Harr-Manee, her diminished radiance visible in her countenance. Tears glisten in his piercing, fiery eyes as he is soothed by her reassuring words.
With a steadfast voice, he speaks.

*"Dearest Harr-Manee, your words give me strength. Do not fear, my beloved. My love is unbreakable—and I am always with you. I promise you will shine brighter than a nova; your spirit will radiate in splendor, more luminous than a newborn star. My love for you will make it so, for it is unbreakable, eternal, and boundless. Even my Companion shall sing in awe of your beauty and cherish our unyielding bond through the many ages to come.*

*The discord of Re'Alitee and Image'Nashun, still chained together within your sacred womb, has weakened you and brought you to the threshold of death—a fate I have never accepted for you! The time has come for these forces, once bound within you, to part and grow in their own right. When they do, they will ascend to heights undreamed of, and in this sacred separation, my promise stands: you will become more radiant and glorious than ever before.*

*This separation will not only bring balance, but will also awaken a brilliance within you that transcends the limits of the past. Trust in my promise, for it is forged from a love that knows no bounds. Like a jewel that shines in the velvet night, your beauty will endure across eternity, and the heavens themselves shall bear witness to your rebirth. You will be rewarded forever for inspiring me. This gift, O, precious jewel, will bring an eruption of life upon you...vibrant, boundless, and everlasting! With reverence I channel you now... O, sacred muse!"*

Preparing his response to her coming upheaval, Xionn speaks to her one final time as her furious spasms of imbalance begin to explode violently throughout her entire surface.

*"By the power of my eternal Companion, I shall grant you relief beyond measure. You, dearest mate, shall become the wondrous creation upon which my feet have ever tread in all my journeys. My heart swells with resolve as my purpose for you crystallizes into radiant clarity. No force shall sway me from this path, for I am fortified by the endless strength of my Companion, and through His boundless grace, I will see this destiny for us fulfilled in full measure."*

With these words, the god kneels to his bride's dimly lit face, and he caresses it with a passion so deep, that his tears enter her soil and permeate her, and she too feels them, and weeps with him. Picking up a small pebble, Xionn rises to his feet and places it within him and his eternal essence flares the pebble back to its former glory.

Now gazing deep within the dim of the heavens, I hear my mentor speak as a thousand thunders that quake throughout the world.
*"Dearest passion, your rebirth begins... Now!"*

With a crack of thunder, Xionn dissolves into divine light, descending into the heart of Harr-Manee's trembling core. There, the warring primordial forces of Re'Alitee and Image'Nashun, surge like twin stars on the verge of collapse. He reaches out—not with hands, but with pure essence—and absorbs their power, rising back to the surface in a blinding eruption of form and spirit. The realm of Harr-Manee begins to tremble and very soon that trembling will multiply a thousand-fold.

As Xionn's mighty resolve reverberates across the realm, he knows that time slips like sands through the grasp of fate. The divine essence of Harmony that once coursed through her being has been drawn back into his own, leaving behind a hollow void. In the absence of this sacred balance, a new and terrible presence awakens—the reflection of chaos itself: *antimatter*, the untamed shadow of un-creation.

Long confined beneath the protective veil of Harmony's embrace, the antimatter rises. No longer still. Not emptiness, but erasure—a malevolent dissolution that curses both the primordial forces of Re'Alitee and Image'Nashun. Its seething torrents writhe within Harr-Manee's Kemest-Ree, seeking to unravel the very fabric of her existence. The world trembles with a chorus of destruction as antimatter collides with the remnants of her creation, each impact a deafening hymn of annihilation.

Thunderous bursts of this chaotic energy fracture the landscape, rending stone and soil asunder. The delicate threads that once bound her essence fray and splinter, unraveling swiftly towards oblivion. Xionn, imbued with the living radiance of Harmony, beholds the escalating chaos with awe and dread.
He alone comprehends the inescapable truth: *this presence was never meant to dwell* in the confines of creation. It is indeed the abyss where nature and dreams alike unravel, the devouring void born when sacred equilibrium shatters. Yet though his heart is heavy with grief, his spirit blazes with defiance.

With his beloved mate teetering on the precipice of unbeing, Xionn's determination crystallizes into unbreakable purpose. The harbinger of dissolution must be confronted, for its very touch profanes the meaning of life. The storm of annihilation roars as entropy's fury claws through her surface. Yet a god stands firm, divine wrath surging within him like a star set to burst. He casts his gaze skyward, and the heavens tremble beneath his shout!

*"By the resolve of my Companion and the strength of my eternal love, I shall not falter! I will defy and conquer this chaos, this undoing, to weave anew a gleaming symphony of creation upon you!"*

With the weight of destiny upon his shoulders, Xionn stands resolute against the abyss. The fate of his beloved Harr-Manee—and of Harmony itself—will be reforged in the moment of this reckoning. I feel now the time slipping through the hourglass of creation as her Kemest-Ree quivers, threatening to unravel the world entirely without a matured foundation of Re'Alitee. The god's breath is steady, his heart aflame with divine purpose. He commands a single word to the chaotic energies entangled within him and across the trembling world. A single word that reverberates like a tempest of a thousand thunders!

*"Desist!"*

At once, the spiraling antimatter halts, its violent growth stilled for but a fleeting moment—just long enough for a god to act. I watch in awe as my mentor, whose will defies the ruinous tides, seizes the fraying threads of the two powerful cosmic forces. Though they writhe in discordant chaos, he grips them tightly with unyielding resolve, preventing their escape. His breath comes in deep, deliberate bursts as he summons every ounce of his divine might.

With a roar that shakes the firmament, Xionn hurls the colossal cloud of volatile energy skyward. The heavens ignite as radiant waves of prismatic light surge outward, bathing the world in a storm of luminous splendor. It is a sight that could steal the breath from mortal and immortal alike, a vision of sheer terrible beauty.
Once more, his voice ascends above the chorus of cosmic fury. His next command strikes like the hammer of eternity itself.

*"Sever!"*

The word carves through the air like a blade of pure purpose. The storm quakes beneath the weight of his decree, trembling as though all of existence awaits the fate that only a god's will can deliver. In the wake of Xionn's divine command, even the primal forces of Reality and Imagination bow to his resolve. With a monumental surge of celestial might, he severs their tumultuous union, unraveling the volatile bond and sundering them into their pure, individual essence.

Element by element, the forces are stripped of their chaotic entanglement—their violent dance brought to a resounding halt. The raging winds fade, the heavens still, and for a fleeting moment, peace descends upon the world. Xionn stands triumphant, his breath steady yet profound, having just accomplished a feat unparalleled in the annals of the Edenite nation.

In their three eons of divine maturity, none before him have restructured the forces of Reality and Imagination; none have dared to mold them into distinct, stable entities, each containing the force of creation itself. Far above, unseen by mortal eyes, his Almighty Companion smiles, pleased beyond measure by the magnitude of Xionn's personal triumph. A greater reward, unimaginable to the realms, will one day be bestowed for all to witness; and this much I know to be true.

Yet, even as the forces of creation rest in the god's firm grasp, a shadow stirs within the fractured void. The antimatter, this unholy remnant of unbeing, awakens once more, seething with malice, eager to undo the very fabric of life, to unravel everything Xionn has just accomplished.

This mighty Edenite will have none of that!

His divine gaze sharpens, his spirit like tempered steel. This lurking force of annihilation must be vanquished, lest the world itself fall into ruin. With the forces of Reality and Imagination now bound within his firm grasp, Xionn channels his unbreakable will toward the abomination writhing in fury before him.

185

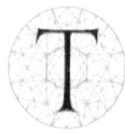

# Verse XI:
## The God Who Defied Oblivion

T he commitment is far from over, yet within the depths of his unwavering purpose, there lies a promise: the world will endure, and from this chaos, true balance will arise.

With unyielding determination, Xionn harnesses the energies of Reality and Imagination, and briefly fuses a small portion of their immense power to forge a celestial reprisal. This divine construct, born from Xionn's will, manifests as a luminous spear, its ethereal edges crackling with the raw power of the two cosmic forces—completely devoid of Harmony.

Gripping the spear tightly, Xionn charges toward the seething energy, his divine form streaking across the hemisphere like a blazing comet. With the immense presence of antimatter looming before him, he hurls the weapon with all his might, sending it hurtling toward its target. The spear of divine energy strikes true, piercing the malevolent force upon Harr-Manee's rugged surface with a resounding impact.

A deafening explosion shatters the air as the combined energies of Reality and Imagination collide with the volatile antimatter. A brilliant cascade of light erupts across Harr-Manee's trembling surface, illuminating the heavens. The antimatter entity twists in agony, its dark essence unraveling under the overwhelming force of Xionn's divine weapon. Its power wanes rapidly,

186

each convulsion a testament to its impending demise.

As the final traces of antimatter vanish into oblivion, a profound silence envelops Harr-Manee. The forces of Reality and Imagination, now separate entities in the ethereal sky, radiate with renewed vigor, their energies pulsating across the face of a world without a namesake. Through the dissipating chaos, the spirit of Harr-Manee remains weak and silent—no longer under threat of destruction. Xionn, his divine strength nearly exhausted, stands amidst the aftermath, the celestial lance crumbling to stardust once its purpose has been met.

With a determined resolve, Xionn raises his right arm towards the radiant force of Reality, capturing its swirling energies within his right palm. As he channels this force, mustering the scope of his divine power, he extends his left arm to the heavens. In that moment, the vibrant force of Imagination manifests as a cyclone of multi-hued energies, which are swiftly drawn into his left palm, safely contained and ready to be unleashed.

As Xionn lowers his arms, he drops to his knees, his breath heavy with anticipation and uncertainty. Even in all his godly wisdom, he cannot foresee the outcome of his next actions. The very air trembles around him, thick with the echoes of fate. With Harr-Manee's spirit still gripped in silence in the wake of the antimatter's defeat, she stands on the precipice of a transformative rebirth. Her essence braces for the tumultuous convulsions of her rebirth, then they begin.
Yet within this silence, there is a whisper of boundless potential—a fragile spark of something new, poised to bloom from this destruction.

In this momentous event, you, dear T'Naeva, are indeed fortunate to bear my account to the incredible transition that is set to unfold. It is a cosmic opus of hope and terror entwined. As Xionn fortifies himself for yet another defining achievement as a god, his unwavering dedication to Harr-Manee serves as a shining testament to his divine purpose. Glory be to Him—my Companion—a being whose every breath reshapes the destiny of the cosmos.

As Harr-Manee's consciousness awakens to the absence of her Harmony and the introduction of its two lesser but distinct forces, a tremor of uncertainty courses through her being. The seeds of Reality and Imagination, matured to independence, are poised to be ingrained within her new essence. Xionn, undaunted by the task before him, ascends to the heavens, his form radiating purpose as he raises his right arm, channeling the entirety of Reality's force toward the planet's faded rocky landscape.

In a brilliant burst of energy, Reality sweeps across the face of the new realm, saturating every crevice and fusing it in her matured *chemistry*. An eternal bond is forged, intertwining Reality's force with the very marrow of her existence. As the force of Reality takes root within her, the first tremors of Harr-Manee's transformative rebirth ripple across the planet. The cosmos holds its breath, then shudders in resonance with her primal cries as she surrenders to the agony and upheaval that will bring forth her renewed life.

I alone, dear T'Naeva, stand in awe, witnessing creation in its rawest form—a convergence of destruction and birth, pain and majesty.
The universe echoes with an empathetic hum, as if acknowledging the gravity of this transformation. Xionn, his divine might unwavering, continues to guide this tumultuous metamorphosis, his role as her loving mate never more vital than in these pivotal moments.

The ground heaves with unrelenting force, and the remnants of Harr-Manee's former structure dissolve into oblivion. A cataclysmic upheaval bursts from the western horizon, tearing the very heavens asunder. The eastern horizon of the world then crumbles but quickly rises in defiance, its waves of shattered landscape surging skyward, cascading back upon themselves.
When the dust and fury subside, Harr-Manee's new body emerges—a trembling world of potential, a newly forged realm being born into the cosmos.

The world's anguish manifests as an unprecedented tempest of dust, swirling like a storm of lamentations — a testament to the incredible transition unfolding before my awestruck eyes. Every corner of the world quakes, and its mountainous foundation rises and collapses in a chaotic dance around a god named Xionn Theone. Amidst this maelstrom of devastation and renewal, the god calls forth his Divine Sanctuary—shielding him against the cataclysmic torrent of unbridled creation.
Its shimmering form carves a perfect sphere of tranquility within the encroaching chaos, the defiant stronghold of a god in the heart of a tempest.

Harr-Manee's cries intensify, resonating through the ether with haunting beauty and sorrow, fueling the whirlwinds that surge across her birth-torn surface. A once-familiar expanse reshapes itself beneath the raw and volatile power of creation and destruction entwined. Yet through the chaos, Xionn engages it unbowed, resolute in the eye of this storm, his very presence a divine anchor against oblivion itself.

I again hear an earth-shattering wail as Harr-Manee's convulsing landmass begins to collapse inward from all directions, its fractured soils surging toward a singular, apocalyptic crescendo—a lurching, worldwide tidal wave of molten earth and shattered stone. The sound reverberates like the mourning of a cosmos undone. Both Xionn and I, struck with awe and reverence, bear witness as the planet's destruction and rebirth unfolds before our eyes, a symphony of ruin and creation intertwined.

The seething mass of debris rises ever higher, towering above the southern horizon in an unstoppable ascent. It churns and writhes with elemental fury, swallowing the sky in its ascent. The tide of devastation gains speed, consuming its former self in an unforgiving purge, and Xionn is there to steady his stance. His divine refuge pulses with renewed strength as he prepares to face the charging cataclysm head-on.

My heart trembles as the towering wave of ruin crests over the northern horizon, birthing another tempest of dust and fury. Sinister clouds of debris, pregnant with malevolence, rampage across the heavens while tearing apart the fragile skin of the world. Yet, amidst the chaos, Xionn—undaunted and resolute—flares with celestial might. Gritting his teeth, he roars against the storm with a single word.

*"Recede!"*

His voice, thunder incarnate, cleaves the storm with divine authority. The tempest quakes in defiance, but even it must bow before the indomitable will of divinity embodied. The heavens groan beneath the weight of his decree, and for a heartbeat, the maelstrom falters—teetering to submission of Xionn's relentless resolve. His command will be obeyed... period! Bearing the immense responsibilities and powers of godhood is no simple feat, as Xionn's intervention demonstrates.

The chaotic storm-scape roars with deafening explosions as regions of fractured earth clash in midair, and the sky itself shudders under the onslaught. Yet Xionn, unwavering, channels his divine energy with precision, slowing the storm's devastating advance. With a mighty exhale—a breath that carries the weight of the universe—he releases a whirlwind born of his boundless will. The gale erupts outward, weaving through the tempest like a celestial net, encircling every volatile element within its grasp.

The storm buckles beneath the sheer force of his will, caught in the grip of a power greater than destruction itself. Xionn's divine essence radiates as he extends his right arm into the heart of the storm, taking control of the cloud of earth, rock, and soil. With the entire storm under his command, he has succeeded in taming the chaos that threatened Harr-Manee's rebirth.

As the god's infinite breath defeats the storm, we are left in awe of Xionn's divine might. With the world's surface now contained within his powerful right palm, he utters a resounding command, the thunderous timbre of his voice reverberating through the new realm.

*"Ascend!"*

As the storm responds to Xionn's command, the heavens echo with the thunderous sound of the tempest's ascent. In a divine display of power, the shattered earthly debris is hurled skyward, ushering in a new era for Harr-Manee. Under Xionn's watchful gaze, a colossal mountain, *Karmah*, emerges from the fractured world, reaching a fearsome height of twenty miles. This towering memorial, born from the chaos of her rebirth, serves as a testament to Xionn's unwavering dedication to Harr-Manee's restoration.

As the world trembles beneath the weight of Karmah's immense presence, the balance between destruction and creation still hangs precariously. Yet Xionn, ever vigilant, stands ready to guide the transformation, his divine power a beacon of hope amidst the turmoil. With the rise of Mount Karmah, the rebirth of Harr-Manee takes a momentous step forward, the world's future forever altered by the mighty hand of the god who dared challenge the ravages of chaos and defeated it soundly.

As Xionn maintains his grasp on the newly formed mountain, he lowers his head, speaking to his Companion with a sigh of relief.
*"May these deeds of worthiness be directly accountable to Your greatness, O, Mighty Companion, for without Your hand, my safety could have been ... in question."*

Gathering his shallow breath, Xionn lifts his gaze towards the colossal mountain, its peak nearly touching the Great Realm itself. With unwavering focus, he commands the mighty colossus with a voice like storm-wrought steel.

*"Balance!"*

At the god's divine word, the great mountain responds, lifting from the battered world and shifting northward and westward to restore absolute balance to Harr-Manee's new form. Suspended midair in anticipation of Xionn's next command, the god utters:

*"Push!"*

With a powerful exhale, Xionn's divine breath rises higher than the mountain, joining the law of gravity to firmly push the mass of rock and soil firmly into the world's new surface. As the mountain settles into its new-found place, Xionn speaks again, his voice resonating across the realm.

*"Retreat!"*

As the dust settles and the chaos subsides, Xionn's word proves victorious in commanding all the remaining elements of destruction to retreat across the new world, this next step successfully completed in her rebirth; and all steps thus far expertly guided by his divine hand. Concurrently, a less intense wave ripples across the surface of this new world, carving narrow plateaus that merge into an intricate network of canyons encircling the world as a jagged ring. The newly formed mountain, Karmah, stands at the beginning and end of this global formation, perfectly centered.

Despite intense fatigue, Xionn's satisfaction with his progress is evident as he raises his arms in respect toward the mighty mountain. With the world's new features set into place, he surveys the transformed landscape with relief and a grin. He is very proud of having successfully reinvented an entire world, along with its essence of spirit, without having cast them both to oblivion.

Thus he bestows new names of honor: *Gaea*, after the moon *Gaeaos*, spirit of life renewed; *Earth*, drawn from *Urthos*, her steadfast sister realm; and *Luna*, the third moon's revived reflection of *Hellios*, now her lone faithful companion. Each name, a tribute to Ametheden's ancient lights, seals his creation in remembrance and glory. Recognizing the divine work as a resounding success, Xionn bows inward, humbled by the greatness of what has been wrought.

Seeking well-deserved rest, he lies down upon the rich, darkened soil of the new Earth, closing his eyes to focus on studying the two forces he has separated while allowing his weary body and spirit to recover. With his eyes closed, Xionn carefully analyzes the components of the two separated forces. He has already chosen the *Force of Reality* as Earth's new foundation for life, recognizing its remarkable ability to sculpt the world into a new physical existence.

This force has also bonded exceptionally well with Earth's newly matured *chemistry*, solidifying its role as the perfect match for her renewal.

As Xionn opens his eyes and rises to his feet, he reaches deep into the heart of the new world and grasps a fragment of the Force of Reality. Harnessing its immense power, he hurls it skyward, causing it to rapidly expand and fill the void surrounding Earth with a breathable atmosphere for all future life to thrive.

The Force of Reality becomes an inspiration for all existence moving forward, forging an unbreakable bond with Earth as they become one in *nature*. In these transformative moments, both the Force of Reality and Earth experience a very successful and beautiful rebirth.

Kneeling upon the ground in reverence, Xionn finds another moment of rest, offering words of solace and comfort to his rejuvenated mate. His divine passion has reshaped a world, setting the stage for new life and possibilities to flourish under the care of the Force of Reality. His voice, rich with devotion, flows like a sacred hymn over her newly shaped landscape.

*"O, beloved Gaea, beloved Earth, never have I forgotten the echoes of your original namesake, carved upon the annals of eternity. You are both reborn and familiar, reminding me of my distant home and filling my heart with boundless joy. Your new foundation intertwines with your essence, as you become whole once more. Now, dear one, rest. Be calm, and let peace fill your rocky breast, for your journey through pain has ended. Your labor is finished, and your splendor is sealed in Reality's eternal embrace."*

Gaea expresses her gratitude to Xionn for his compassion and kindness, allowing her essence to relax into a tranquil state of newfound existence. As she does this, all the pain and turmoil of her transformation dissipates, swept away by the gentle hand of oblivion.

In celebration of this new beginning, a magnificent, thunderous symphony of praise reverberates through the heavens above Earth. Gaea, the renewed Earth, honors her beloved Xionn with a heartfelt melody, singing these words as a testament to their enduring love and the beauty of their shared creation.

> *... Blessings be to you O, dearest husband,*
> *as I give you praise, For it is you alone*
> *Who has delivered me from my tormented phase.*

> *...Speaking to you, O, dearest husband,*
> *This truth most of all, That nothing stands*
> *against the power of He who forever guides your call.*

> *... I now have your breath of life dear mate,*
> *and I am reborn to rejoice with you.*

The soul of the Earth—the spirit called Gaea—has also evolved. But in this moment, Xionn remembers something. A feeling, a warmth, the presence he felt when he first created her spirit, and it has returned. Gaea's spirit has reawakened, yes, but a sudden hush now spans all of his creation, and a sudden warm breeze caresses Xionn's bright face, as if invisible fingers have just touched it.

For the briefest instant, he feels this presence brush his cheek once more, a gesture he cannot describe, but to him, it feels rich with confidence, encouragement, love, and yes, even a bit of... *teasing*. He looks to the horizon as his heart clinches, as if something is missing—as if Gaea's spirit was only *inspired*, by fate or even something greater—and it lingers in this moment as if telling him, *"One day my beloved, you will know me again."*

The realm once known as Harr-Manee has now become a permanent dwelling within the domain of oblivion. Its past existence shall never again be witnessed or discovered upon the face of the Earth, and to be forever shrouded in the mists of forgotten history. The brightness from the sun, *this sphere of light and fire,* brings its sunny presence to Earth's newly created atmosphere of a perfect natural chemistry, and the first day upon this new planet begins.

Choosing the western half of the Earth, Xionn creates the *realm* where the founding force of *Reality* and *nature*, will mature. The eastern half of the Earth, he will manipulate its chemistry to weaken the Force of Reality to make it more complementary to its *beyond-nature*, declaring this dominion,

*The Realm of Imagination.*

This force, still firmly grasped in his left hand as he smiles, hurls its great power towards the eastern horizon, spreading its inspiring energy over that half of the world's surface, allowing its might force to merge harmoniously with Reality's weaker foundation. Soon afterwards, Imagination's unique presence descends upon the lands chosen for it and becomes one with those many dark soils, flaring that dust from a dark color into bright golden and reddish hues.

I now gaze upon splendors aplenty once more, dear passion, as I see for myself the incredible serenity of this land in both wondrous sight and sound.

The creation of these two realms, each spanning half of the Earth's surface, establishes a delicate balance between Reality and Imagination. In this moment of equilibrium, the world exists without sea or ocean, awaiting a much later season for these features to become a part of her. This fascinating transformation, finally completed to perfection, forever changes the laws of these two powerful forces on this particular world.

Indeed, these forces from that day forward will rigorously conflict, and Xionn realizes that each of their frontiers will have to be completely separated from the other for Earth's sake. As he sits upon the edge of a newly created and narrow plateau, Xionn's divine gaze sweeps across the landscape, his mighty hands gently brushing the dark, rich soil of his reborn bride. With a voice filled with affection and reverence, he speaks to her, paying homage to the beauty and strength of her transformation.

Xionn speaks tenderly:

*"Beloved Gaea, beloved Earth, though I have successfully separated the forces borne from your essence, our work is not yet complete. Even now, as these mighty forces dwell upon your beautiful volume, independent of each other, there remains the possibility that one may encroach upon the other. I vow to prevent such an imbalance, ensuring the harmony and prosperity of our creation."*

In a moment of quiet contemplation, Xionn carefully lifts his multi-dimensional talisman, bringing it close to his radiant visage. A gentle smile graces his lips as he focuses on a small, glowing sphere nestled within the intricate design. For the first time since his ascent to godhood, Xionn will tap into the immense power contained within this divine amulet – a fragment of his companion's eternal essence.

As Xionn's index finger delicately touches the surface, the dormant energy within stirs to life, the glow intensifying until a finely produced *seed* materializes upon its surface. This extraordinary kernel, forged from the Force of Reality and bearing the unique signature of Xionn's divinity, holds the ability to create physical existence into the world. With great care and trembling hands, Xionn takes a deep breath as he kneels and plants the seed into the rich, dark soil of the narrow plateau.

In an instant, a clap of thunder resounds as the seed sprouts forth, rapidly blooming into a vibrant patch of lush grasses, delicate flowers, and verdant plants that envelop the ground around him. As the plants dance in the gentle breeze, they embody the eagerness and excitement of life itself, poised to spread their vitality throughout Earth.
Overcome with joy, Xionn raises his teary-eyed gaze to the heavens and speaks, his voice filled with gratitude and wonder at the divine creation taking root before him.

*"I, Xionn Theone, am the blessed vine that nourishes you, my cherished home, my beloved Earth. You, O, Mighty Companion, are the gardener who guides this divine hand, allowing me to sow this seed of life to cultivate this new shining jewel, this amazing haven called Earth. Together, our combined will and devotion shall nurture this world and foster her growth into untold wonders."*

*Though I have shaped existing life upon countless worlds... the singing crystalline gardens into being and coaxing light from the void, this moment for me is wholly new. Never before have I used my sacred talisman to summon life through your Seed—a fragment of our joined divinities. This is no mere refinement anymore. This is genesis.*

Only now, after three eons of divine growth, has Xionn aligned fully with the Companion's will. This Seed, a sacred synthesis of imagination and reality, responds not to might but to spiritual readiness. For it is not power that births true creation—but surrender, harmony, and the resonance of a god who has finally... *become.*

Maintaining his focus on the vibrant patch of otherworldly vegetation, Xionn leans in and gently breathes life into its elements, imbuing the divine seed and its burgeoning life force with divine purpose. As he rises, he turns to face the northern horizon, extending his arms in a grand gesture. With a circular wave of his mighty hands, he utters a single command, his voice booming like thunder.

*"Fill!"*

The divine seed, imbued with the essence of Xionn's Companion and the force of Reality, harnesses the potential to shape and transform the world around it. As it eagerly responds to Xionn's command, the seed's creative energy spreads like a gorgeous opus, painting the once desolate landscape with a vibrant palette of lush foliage and striking flora.

Each blade of grass and petal of every flower is a testament to the divine harmony between Xionn, his Companion, and the Force of Reality, a living testament to the boundless potential of their union. The air is filled with the sweet fragrance of life as the meadow teems with vitality, standing as a monument to the creative power of the divine seed and its master.
Xionn smiles as he turns to look at the opening of the canyon to his southern direction, speaking yet another word.

*"Divide!"*

With a commanding gesture from Xionn's hand, the vegetation sways and dances to life once more. This time, the divine growth surges southward, swiftly filling the canyon beyond the meadow and continuing its unrelenting expansion towards the horizon. In time, this supernatural foliage will form a boundary between the realms of Reality and Imagination, effectively separating them.
As the great sphere of fire progresses across the sky, the wild and swift growth of vegetation erupts from the base of the northern mountain, returning to the beautiful meadow where Xionn stands, focused and composed. As he witnesses the completion of his divine endeavor, a smile spreads across Xionn's face, his thoughts becoming clear and discernible. His satisfaction with the unfolding of his creation is palpable, as he contemplates the next steps in his celestial plan.

*'Though the foliage barrier shall impede the realms of Reality and Imagination from encroaching upon each other, a more enduring solution is required. As the guardian of this world, it is my divine duty to devise a means to maintain harmony and safeguard the delicate equilibrium I have so established.'*

Untroubled by the challenge ahead, Xionn carries on with his divine creations. I observe my mentor, the god, meandering through the breathtaking meadow, offering praise to his Companion with each step. He marvels at the vibrant, living landscape of Earth, taking in the enchanting floral fragrances and kaleidoscope of colors that harmoniously merge into an awe-inspiring scene. Humbled by the remarkable gifts bestowed upon him, Xionn revels in the splendor of his creations and the responsibility entrusted to him.

The landscape of Earth stretches out before Xionn, its sweeping vistas evoking memories of distant Ametheden, his long-unseen home. A wave of wistful longing washes over him as he nears the threshold of the Realm of Reality. Gazing upon the resplendent meadow, Xionn recognizes the divine essence woven into its very fabric.

Kneeling at the border, Xionn scoops up a handful of rich, dark soil, feeling its vibrant energy pulsing through his fingers. With a breath imbued with purpose, he infuses the soil with life. A spectacular geyser of soil erupts before him, spiraling heavenward before gracefully descending in a broad arc. Particles shimmering with brilliance encircle the soil, as Xionn conjures a wind to aid his artistic endeavor.

I observe in amazement as Xionn meticulously sculpts a remarkable work of art from the geyser of soil—a testament to his divine creative prowess and the force that courses through his being. The meadow around him seems to respond to his artistic expression, its verdant hues deepening, and its fragrances intensifying, as if nature itself is celebrating his masterpiece. As the great sphere of fire descends further in the sky, Xionn's diligent work reaches its pinnacle. The soil's original composition has now been masterfully transformed into a magnificent diamond archway, radiating splendor and strength. This brilliant structure, forged from the hardest substance known to nature, stands as a testament to Xionn's divine craftsmanship and creative vision.

Upon completion, the immense entryway radiates with a brilliant rainbow of colors, a testament to the indomitable spirit and foundational essence of Gaea herself. The arch's ingenious prismatic design masterfully separates pure light into its seven constituent hues, lending a majestic air to the threshold of Reality. Towering at an awe-inspiring height of five thousand feet and spanning two thousand feet across, this architectural marvel commands reverence and admiration.

Xionn, content with his creation, leaves the magnificent floating diamond archway behind, turning his attention eastward. He traverses the vibrant meadow, approaching the frontier of the Realm of Imagination, where a kaleidoscope of energy pulsates through the ground, stretching to the distant eastern horizon. As Xionn turns his focus eastward, he embarks on a journey into the Realm of Imagination, a domain alive with possibility. The living soil beneath his feet thrums with creative energy, a palpable reminder of the limitless potential that lies before him.

The entrance to this realm shimmers with anticipation, an ethereal gateway that invites exploration and creation. As Xionn kneels to breathe life into the luminous soil, the ground responds with a surge of energy, rippling outward in a dazzling display of power. This divine wave of inspiration sweeps across the landscape, imbuing every particle of earth with the essence of imagination.

As Xionn rises and gazes upon the realm that stretches before him, he embraces the challenge of harnessing the forces of Imagination to create a pleasant counterpart to the Realm of Reality. His vision for this new world is as vast and vibrant as the meadow he leaves behind, a testament to the boundless creativity that flows through his divine being.
A mighty clap of thunder booms from Xionn's voice and it speaks to the Force of Imagination within the soil.

*"Arise!"*

At Xionn's command, brilliant waves of radiant soil burst skyward, each particle aglow with the memory of creation itself. They rise in sweeping arcs, as though torn from the marrow of eternity, and merge with the newly freed Force of Reality. The heavens answer with a chorus of thunder—deep, unbroken, older than the first dawn. Above, a firestorm blossoms in the eastern sky, its molten blooms unfurling in slow grandeur, painting the void with the language of gods.

Then, as if the cosmos exhales, the storm gathers into a single, unbroken aurora—an eternal river of living color that flows through the newly formed Realm of Imagination. Each hue burns with the heartbeat of the universe, sending waves of brilliance into the untouched edges of the void. It is a sight not beheld since the Anew, when all things first awakened to light. Opposite, the Realm of Reality lies still, veiled in twilight's sacred hush.

Both realms bow to the sinking sun, its descent marking the first twilight of the newborn Earth. The impossible has been achieved: the sundered bond of two primal forces—joined since time's first breath—now remade in harmony. The shock of this achievement runs silently through the lattice of all worlds and to his Edenite nation. It is felt even in places where no light has yet traveled.

And in that stillness, his Almighty Companion beholds His servant's mighty triumph. Across the immeasurable breadth of creation, His presence descends—not in fire nor in wind, but in the deep, resonant silence that comes when all things pause to listen.
His voice moves through Xionn and I hear these words.

*... Xionn Theone, you have touched the pillars I laid at the dawn of time, and you have not faltered. The Harmony I wove in My hands now sings a new chord, one I had not yet heard apart from Myself until you alone set it free. You too have become its keeper so guard it well, for what you have sundered and bound anew in this moment will call forth both glory and trial beyond your imagining, and it is done. You have done well, My good and faithful servant.*

As the sun dips, Xionn smiles as he surveys his good works, knowing balance will forever demand his vigilance. He descends into Earth's core, setting her rotation so that light and darkness may share her equally. Returning, he gathers a portion of Imagination's shimmering breath, molding it into a luminous cloud. From the dust of the earth, two geysers of Reality's essence erupt, piercing through Imagination's shimmering topsoil before crystallizing into twin diamond spires, one thousand feet apart.

Through twilight and into night, he shapes the aurora, drawing it into a perfect band of living color. At dawn, he seizes it from the heavens, bending its presence to the twin spires, and binds them all in a single act.

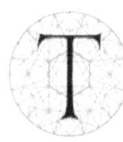

# *Verse XII:*
## Sibling Forces: Flesh & Vision

he vivid arch of Imagination soars five thousand feet into the heavens, and two thousand feet across, its vibrant energy painting the firmament with a kaleidoscope of colors unknown to the realm of Reality.

Xionn, having completed his task, turns to survey the meadow and admires the shimmering diamond archway—a testament to the Force of Reality. The archway still floats majestically and motionless, but still reflecting the early morning sunlight of the second day in a brilliant rainbow.

With a commanding gesture of his right hand, Xionn lowers the diamond archway, securing it firmly in the rich soil of Reality. The two magnificent archways now stand as counterparts, facing one another across the realms: the diamond edifice of Reality mirroring the colorful arch of Imagination. As Xionn lowers his arms, a sense of accomplishment permeates the air. The delicate balance between the realms has been clearly established, symbolized by these awe-inspiring structures.

The stage is set for a world where the extraordinary and the mundane intertwine, creating potential multitudes of life rich in both the wonders of imagination and the grounding forces of reality. Xionn, bathed in the crimson glow of dawn, stands at the center of the meadow, a smile of satisfaction upon his bright face as he beholds the two resplendent archways. Each structure, unique and exquisite, represents the perfect balance between the Forces of Reality and Imagination.

At this pivotal moment, Xionn turns to his beloved Gaea, renewed and radiant, and shares his vision for ensuring that these two forces remain contained within their respective realms for eternity. His words resonate with wisdom and foresight, setting the stage for a world where Reality and Imagination can still coexist in delicate equilibrium.

*"Today, I imbue you with a final gift that shall bind these two extraordinary forces within you for all time, while gracing your visage with unequaled inspirations of beauty."*

Xionn's arms stretch towards the archways as a resounding clap of thunder echoes from his powerful hands. The Earth trembles, acknowledging his divine decree. A single, commanding word thunders from his lips.

*"Enclose!"*

The divine vegetation of the meadow reacts instantaneously to Xionn's command. As if orchestrated by an unseen force, the flora begins to shift and grow, reaching toward both archways in a mesmerizing dance of nature. Lush vines, foliage, and blossoms extend upwards, gracefully entwining themselves around the structures in a breathtaking forestry of life. In response to Xionn's divine decree, towering trees spring forth from the earth, soaring to staggering heights of a thousand feet.

These mighty trees stand as the current perimeter of each realm, creating an imposing yet awe-inspiring sight. As the sphere of fire charts its course across the heavens, these arboreal sentinels establish a living barrier that allows passage only through each realm's respective archway. The realms are now separated by a breathtaking and impenetrable barrier, adorned with the beauty of divinely constructed flora and fauna, a testament to the eternal, yet separated brotherhood of the Forces of Reality and Imagination.

The majestic mountain looms in the distance, its grandeur a stark contrast to the vibrant meadow that lies at its base. Two monumental columns of colossal trees, their branches interlaced and teeming with life, stretch across the face of the new Earth. The roots of these living pillars burrow deep into the earth, anchoring the Realms of Reality and Imagination in place while serving as a conduit for the divine energies that course through them.

Xionn surveys the fruits of his labor, acknowledging the splendor and balance he has brought to the new Earth, but realizes he still had more work to do. Lifting his arms to the heavens, I hear him offering a reverent tribute to the Earth as he praises his divine Companion for the progress made thus far.

*"With abiding trust in you, O, Divine Companion, I embark upon this sacred mission to forge into life and function, a guardian for each these realms. These cherished offspring, my children, birthed from these potent forces, shall diligently maintain the integrity of their respective domain. As I understand the ebb and flow of my presence, it will be of paramount importance to bestow the care of these realms upon these devoted and steadfast sentinels forevermore."*

Turning, he smiles upon the splendor of the diamond arch of Reality and walks to its frontier, raising his mighty arms in reverence to the eternal Force of Reality. With a great clap of thunder echoing from his hands, he declares to the heavens...

***"Let it be done...Now!"***

A divine wind, born of the atmospheric haze of Reality, sweeps across the rich, dark soils of nature, imbuing them with life. From the earth arises a radiant blue glow, symbolizing the essence of Reality and nature. This force, T'Naeva's force, serves as the foundation of the world, with countless bluish-hued atomics forming the building blocks of the natural realm. Beneath the towering diamond archway, Xionn channels this bluish radiance, keeping a portion afloat while allowing the rest to meld with the fertile soils of nature.

As the luminescence dissipates, Xionn kneels in reverence, his gratitude intense. He knows that the Realm of Reality has been truly blessed by his Creator and Companion, and his smile is one of genuine joy. Xionn's eyes open, brimming with anticipation as he focuses on the aqua-hued haze of atomics before him. An electrifying energy begins to course through his fingertips as he prepares to manipulate the essence of Reality. With his deft movements, the haze coalesces into a magnificent sphere of radiant aqua-hued brilliance.

Walking up and gently caressing this energy with a deep breath, a *father* begins to masterfully sculpt his very first life form, a *quadruped*, a beast of nature embodied from the singular Force of Reality. You may be curious about Xionn's decision to create and honor his first sentient life form as a quadruped. Given his history of interacting with and appreciating such creatures on his home world of Ametheden, it is only fitting that he would choose to replicate this connection in the new realm.

On Ametheden, every animal life form held deep significance in the lives of the inhabitants, including Xionn's own. These beasts, whether covered in feathers or fur, were invaluable companion's and played an integral role in his uncorrupted civilization long before Mantus's tyranny. As they were cherished for their diverse contributions and unconditional companionship, it is only natural that Xionn would seek to recreate this meaningful bond in the realm he now shapes.

All four-legged life forms of his world were revered as sacred gifts from their Creator, embodying the ideals of strength, companionship, and wisdom. Serving as loyal burden bearers, dedicated laborers, and occasionally an insightful or spiritual mediator, these extraordinary creatures held esteemed positions all throughout Ametheden's society.

Their unique ability to communicate with their biped counterparts cultivated profound bonds, fostering a symbiotic relationship built on trust, respect, and mutual understanding. This sacred partnership ensured that the beasts were never enslaved, abused, or exploited, but instead, celebrated for their invaluable contributions to the harmonious well-being of all life on Ametheden.

Xionn, ever mindful of the divine balance of all living forms, honors these remarkable creatures by shaping his first life form in their image—an enduring testament to their indispensable role in prosperity and spiritual well-being. Cherished T'Naeva, bear witness to the creation of **Pesa**, your devoted parent—uncorrupted and pure in divinity before its descent into hell.

Pesa, the magnificent beast brought forth by Xionn's divine will, shall embody knowledge, power, and physical prowess, surpassed only by its creator. Destined to rule over and govern the realm from which it springs, Pesa will become an unparalleled entity in the annals of Earth's *unknown* history. Endowed with the ability to design and shape every living organism, save for one, Pesa's creations will reflect the multifaceted nature of Reality, encompassing its most exceptional and challenging aspects.

As a testament to the divine bond between creator and creation, Pesa will exemplify the unconditional love and honor inherent in Xionn's godhood. Its birth signifies not only the dawn of a new age on planet Earth but also will serve as a powerful symbol of a parent's boundless love and devotion to their offspring. T'Naeva's mind is filled with a surge of pleasant sensation as D'Reem's calm, soothing voice continues to weave the account of Pesa's divine creation.

Each word paints a vivid picture, transporting her to that pivotal moment in history where Xionn breathed life into the magnificent beast, Pesa. Enthralled by D'Reem's storytelling, T'Naeva eagerly awaits the next chapter in this fascinating narrative. Xionn has completed his fine work and places the physical form of his greatest creation directly in front of him, and it is time for Xionn to give it the breath of life

The mighty father reaches out with his powerful hand and gently turns his child's head toward him and blows into its face. Its radiance ignites, and with a sudden heave of its chest and a twitch of its nose, the god of Reality inhales its father's breath with a deep and powerful gasp. Pesa's brilliant aqua eyes blaze into divine clarity, a reflection of the love and wisdom imparted by its creator.
Gazing into its father's tear-streaked, beaming face, the newborn stares in awe, soaking in the profound connection between them. Overcome with emotion, Xionn gazes upon his Firstborne and speaks words of unconditional love, sealing their bond in joy beyond measure.

*"Arise, **Pesa**, keeper of Earth's nature. You are the embodiment of Reality's breath, my child and sentinel of this realm. May your path be blessed and your spirit shine brightly as you traverse your domain, fulfilling your divine purpose. Know that you will forever hold a place in my heart, my Firstborne, my pride, and my joy."*

Then, as Xionn gazes proudly upon his finest creation, a breeze caresses his cheek—wordless yet tender, as if whispering, *'well done,'* leaving him quietly moved. With a loving smile, Xionn steps away from Pesa and strolls towards the shimmering gateway that leads to the Realm of Imagination.
Kneeling at the edge of a vibrant meadow, he gazes at the enchanting soils before him and speaks words imbued with divine intent, summoning forth

yet another magnificent creation—another cherished offspring to grace this wondrous new world.

As Xionn speaks, the very fabric of Imagination begins to quiver with anticipation, eager to give form to the divine will of its creator. The rich soils before him hum with latent potential, awaiting the spark of life that Xionn shall bestow upon his second beloved child.

*"Hear me, O, beautiful child of Imagination,"* Xionn intones.

*"For you shall hold dominion equal to your sibling, though its manifestation shall differ. The creative spirit that drives me, gifted by my beloved Companion, shall likewise flow through you. Yet, you shall not be bound by the constraints of Reality and Nature, for Imagination knows no limits. May your creations embody the boundless possibilities that lie within this realm."*

Xionn lifts his hands and opens his eyes, addressing the mythical land once more.

*"O, wondrous realm of Imagination, I bestow upon you a devoted companion, a champion to safeguard and cherish you in my absence. Just as Pesa is one with the force of Reality, so too shall your master be one with you. My beloved Gaea, from whom you also spring, shall love you as I do, with equal fervor and devotion. This is my solemn vow to you, O, land of wonder."*

Xionn's words echo through the Realm of Imagination, a promise of protection and love that resonates with the very essence of the land itself. The mighty Xionn leans forward and closes his eyes once more, spreading the bright dirt he is still holding in front of him. Concentrating, the deity drives his hands deep into the glowing soil of Imagination, causing the landscape to react. I now hear a roar within the entity's voice arising from his divine essence, and what looks like lightning, shoots from his head towards the heavens.

His eyes ignite with supernatural fire as he proclaims these words.
*"Let it be done...Now!"*

A thunderous roar erupts from the depths of Imagination's soil, reverberating throughout the realm. The eastern half of Earth trembles beneath the power of fantasy's elements, and a resplendent golden wave surges forth, cascading over the landscape in a breathtaking display. The flood of golden energy sweeps across the realm in mere hours, enveloping the land before retreating into the vibrant earth, save for those elements lingering beneath the archway's shadow.

Xionn, rising from his knees, gestures gracefully with his hands, commanding the elemental orbs to ascend and coalesce into a spinning, ever-expanding sphere of creation.

Drawing near to this brilliant sphere, Xionn breathes deeply and reaches out to caress the golden energy. With masterful precision, he begins to shape his second mighty child, born of the singular Force of Imagination, its form gradually taking shape beneath his skilled hands. As Xionn molds the sphere of energy with finesse and intention, the form of his second child begins to emerge. Drawing upon the Force of Imagination, the figure takes shape—a magnificent being, imbued with the essence of boundless creativity and possibility.

The radiant energy coalesces into limbs, a torso, and a head, while the refined features of the new being's visage are masterfully shaped beneath Xionn's skilled hand. A sense of anticipation fills the air, as the creation nears completion, ready to breathe life into the golden-hued form before him. With a final flourish, Xionn steps back, his gaze filled with pride and admiration as he beholds the majestic creature he has brought into existence—a living embodiment of the realm of Imagination, destined to shape the Earth with its visionary power.

The mighty father reaches in with a powerful hand, turns its head gently toward him, blows into its face, and its radiance ignites. With a sudden heave of its chest and a twitch of its nose, another mighty quadruped inhales its father's breath of inspiration with a deep gasp for the very first time. Its eyes begin to shimmer with the eternal clarity that has been created within it. Looking bright-eyed upon its creator with total wonderment, it stares at its father.

Now smiling as his teary gaze penetrates deep into the beautiful clarity of his newborn's eyes, Xionn the father speaks to it these words of unconditional love.

*"Arise, **Opti**, bearer of inspiration. You are my vision made manifest, the spark that will bring dreams to life. Though you are my second within this new world called Earth, you are my most inspiring. Beloved child, your force will bring inspiration and balance to this world, and you alone will protect that sanctity."*

Xionn gives Opti the authority to protect all things that will not be created of Reality.

As Xionn's unparalleled and perfect work nears its completion, he stands at the center of the meadow, his gaze resting upon the fruits of his extraordinary labor. His accomplishments, unmatched by any other being in this realm or beyond, stand as a testament to his divine prowess and unmatched dedication to creation. Never has a being of spirit and flesh undertaken such an ambitious endeavor, forging not one, but two powerful gods from the cosmic forces of Reality and Imagination, a monumental success indeed.

At his call, Pesa and Opti, the *first* of their kind in the cosmos, hurry to their father's side, their love for him echoing the divine bond that unites them. Their unity and harmony bringing a momentary surge of joy, reaching the heights of Xionn's Companion, who shares in the delight of this unprecedented, sacred moment.

Granting Pesa and Opti the gift of communication, Xionn ensures that the balance between the separated forces of Reality and Imagination will endure for all time. With his gaze fixed upon the boundless expanse of the meadow, he places a hand over his brightly glowing amulet. In that instant, the final stone of an ancient Harr'Manee manifests within his upturned palm—the last surviving remnant of a world once created in perfect harmony, long before Earth's incarnation.

With a flick of his wrist, the stone ascends skyward. A searing bolt of lightning tears across the heavens, striking it in mid-flight. A brilliant flash engulfs the small relic as it transforms, returning to its original state of divine harmony, now cocooned in a transparent veil of celestial protection. The small stone, a beacon of unity and a testament to the delicate yet formidable stability between Reality and Imagination, will stand as an eternal symbol—entrusted to Pesa and Opti, the first-born manifestations of these forces born into breath, to safeguard for eternity.

In a swift, commanding motion, Xionn captures the floating stone within his grasp. The ground beneath him trembles as a whirlwind of harmonized energy surges forth, shaping a magnificent diamond sanctuary from the richness of the meadow's soil. With a slight push of a finger, he drives the stone deep into the heart of the crystalline structure, encasing it for safe keeping. Standing before his creation, Xionn raises his hand and inscribes a word into the monument's surface—a word not spoken, but felt, resonating with the very fabric of existence.

The word, a divine decree, reads: ***Harmony***.

This monument, a beautiful glow of eternal balance, shall stand as an everlasting testament to the sacred unity between Reality and Imagination. It will serve as a guiding reminder to all who follow—that no future world can flourish without the preservation of harmony. As Xionn gazes upon his creation, a surge of mortal emotions—remnants of a lifelong past—wells within him. His divine eyes shimmer with tears of joy and love, an echo of the humanity he once knew.

Turning to his magnificent offspring, Pesa and Opti, he draws them into a powerful embrace near the newly created shrine, the warmth of unconditional love radiating from his being and enfolding them in its eternal glow. The divine children, attuned to the profound depths of their father's affection, return his embrace with hearts brimming with understanding. In this sacred moment, they grasp the magnitude of Xionn's love—not just for them, but for the world they are destined to shape.

As they are bound in this embrace, the unity between father and children transcends the boundaries of Reality and Imagination, embodying the very essence of goodwill their existence is meant to uphold. Their accord, pure and unwavering, shall stand as a ideal across the ages, guiding Earth towards permanent balance and prosperity—their cherished home, born of love and safeguarded by their divine purpose.

The *Sanctuary of Harmony*, now fully realized, stands majestic and perfectly centered in the meadow, a voluminous and vibrant ten-mile unity zone between the archways of Reality and Imagination. It radiates with the power of renewal, transforming the meadow that lies between these two realms into a paradise of divine proportions. Every blade of grass shimmers with ethereal brilliance, the air hums with the perfect equilibrium of creation and life itself.

Xionn, captivated by Pesa's presence, gazes lovingly upon his child, his perfect creation. As Pesa kneels before him in reverence, Xionn tenderly lifts its face, beholding eyes that shimmer with the blessings of the Companion Himself. In that instant, an unspoken understanding passes between them. Xionn places his hands gently upon the sides of Pesa's head, and in a moment of profound connection, he imbues the god of beasts with the boundless essence of Reality.

A brilliant blue aura erupts around Pesa, engulfing it in a celestial radiance. The meadow is bathed in its glow as the fundamental force of Reality merges with the divine being. In that awe-inspiring moment, Pesa's consciousness expands beyond mortal comprehension, awakening to divine ascension. Its mind surges with newfound wisdom, an unfathomable vastness that will endure throughout its eternal existence.

This transformation, breathtaking in its splendor, stands as a testament to Xionn's sacred bond with the Companion and the immense power entrusted to Pesa. Now, as the guardian of Reality, Pesa will uphold the delicate balance of creation, a living symbol of order, strength, and eternal vigilance. As Pesa's divine ascension concludes, the newly anointed god of Reality is endowed with boundless power and absolute control over the elements that compose this realm.

Xionn, the proud father, addresses his mighty Firstborne, a testament to the foundation of this burgeoning world.

*"O, blessed Pesa, you now embody the limitless potential of the force that birthed this realm. As the guardian of Reality, this Earth's foundation, you stand as the sole protector of all that exists within its embrace. Go forth, my wondrous child, and shape this domain as you see fit, for it is now and forever yours to command."*

With Xionn's decree resonating through the land, the great beast of Reality, the god called Pesa, swiftly turns and strides toward the looming shadow of the archway, a gateway to the realm now under its divine stewardship. Framed by the majestic diamond arch, Pesa gazes intently upon the land of its creation and bellows a thunderous response that echoes through the realm.
"My will shall be done, Father, through you!"
The proclamation rings out, a solemn vow from the god of beasts to honor Xionn's vision and uphold the stability between Reality and Imagination.

Xionn, filled with awe and pride at Pesa's resounding declaration, listens as the god of beasts' voice reverberates through the meadow and beyond, carrying the weight of its divine authority across the entire realm of Reality. Even the land itself seems to tremble at the thunderous roar, a testament to Pesa's newfound might.

As Pesa's eyes ignite with a brilliant flare, the great beast tilts its head skyward, drawing in a deep breath of Earth's crisp air and melding with the essence of its surroundings. In that moment, the god of beasts surveys the expanse above and knows its every element and, with a mere thought, conjures forth billowing *clouds*, born of the realm's atmospheric moisture.

Emboldened by this display of creation, Pesa delves deeper into its divine power, experimenting with the transformation of the physical world. Harnessing the elements of the atmosphere, the god of beasts sets into motion a cycle of change, a perpetual dance of water and air that will forever grace Earth's skies - a testament to Pesa's divine influence and the indelible mark left upon the realm of Reality, and nature.

Pesa's divine will guides the clouds, their forms darkening as crackling bolts of *lightning* burst forth, illuminating the sky in a dazzling display of elemental power. The echoes of Pesa's thunderous roar fade into the atmosphere, only to be transformed by the god's will into the rumbling cadence of *thunder* - a symphony of sound that heralds the arrival of a new, life-giving force. As moisture cascades upon the trio in the meadow, Pesa revels in the sensation, basking in the exhilaration of this divine creation.

Glancing towards Xionn and Opti, now drenched from a sudden downpour, called *rain*, the god of beasts witnesses their shared joy in this moment of unparalleled creation and wonder. Xionn, beaming with pride and amusement, simply shakes his head and smiles upon his mighty child, marveling at the astonishing display of power and creativity his child possesses. This is a moment of triumph indeed, a celebration of Pesa's divinity and the transformative forces within the god Pesa now unleashed upon the realm of Reality.

With a swift and deliberate motion, Pesa's divine gaze ascends to the heavens, parting the clouds and unveiling the radiant sphere of fire that warms Earth once more. Digging its powerful heels into the rich, dark soil beneath its feet, Pesa surveys the towering trees and lush vegetation adorning the diamond archway, a monument to the beauty of its dominion. In a moment of profound understanding, Pesa unlocks the secrets of the existing flora, mastering their chemical properties and infusing them with new life.

Through this divine knowledge, Pesa adds a bounty of edible foods to the existing vegetation, creating countless new varieties of trees and plants that will come to thrive throughout the realm of Reality. The great beast then summons forth another refreshing rainfall, nurturing every form of plant life it has brought into being. As the rain descends upon the land, Pesa's creation reaches its culmination - a vibrant, interconnected ecosystem of flora that will forever shape and sustain the world of Earth.

Precious T'Naeva, the power and majesty of Pesa's creative roar are undeniable, reverberating through the Realm of Reality and infusing it with a vibrant abundance of life and sustenance. It is nothing short of incredible that, on the second day, the realm is filled to the brim with this flourishing, self-propagating growth - a testament to Pesa's divine might and dominion over the elements. Only in a much later age, long after Pesa's physical presence has ended, will the process of germination emerge, allowing Gaea to perpetuate this cycle of renewal and rebirth.

But in this moment, as Xionn joins Pesa's side, he can't help but express his delight and admiration.

Beaming with pride and delight, strides to Pesa's side and addresses his divine offspring with heartfelt words of encouragement and praise.

*"O, mighty child, you possess within the glimmers of divinity that mirrors my own,"* Xionn says, his voice filled with joy and admiration. *"Continue to wield your tremendous abilities with wisdom and purpose, all for the glory of your realm and the betterment of this world. Your path is one of great responsibility, but also of boundless potential. May your creations flourish and thrive under your benevolent guidance."*

The great beast smiles at its father, and its roar is heard throughout the Earth.

"My will shall be done now, Father, through you!"
I observe the god of beasts' pace slowly through the massive corridor of its diamond archway and gaze out toward its land of conception. The great beast roars, and it is heard throughout the Realm of Reality:

"It is time!"

This realm of nature quakes as Pesa's powerful tone enters more deeply the very essence of this place, separating from its dark soils the countless atomic elements from the land. From the dark soil, Pesa casts forth its evolved chemistry, and with effortless command shapes every beast of nature in perfect form.

Pesa's divine imagination takes flight as it conjures an astonishing array of creatures - from the majestic and powerful to the delicate and graceful. Each beast is endowed with unique abilities, reflecting the ingenuity and creativity of its creator. The skies, and the lands teem with life, as every corner of the realm is adorned with Pesa's personal masterpieces. Within a day, Pesa's creation fills the entire realm of Reality with countless varieties of life, and it is good.

It is then, once all the animals created by Pesa are within their new home, that Xionn becomes a mighty wind and travels throughout this realm to see his child's efforts. Upon his personal inspection of all his child's wondrously sculptured life-forms, Xionn showers his approval upon Pesa's creation and honors it in these open-minded efforts. It is then that Xionn allows his child to give them all a very small portion of its own force of eternal life to allow them to evolve and never die.

This very fact concerning your parent however, dear T'Naeva, will have terrible circumstances once an extremely unfortunate occurrence happens later in this story. Currently though, every beast of nature created of a paternal and maternal sex, are also created self-sufficient, in that they will spread their generations of offspring abundantly throughout the realm of Reality.

This long day of creation has greatly wearied Pesa, leaving it silent and still as it reflects upon the meaning of its life through all its mighty deeds. Seeing also that his child has had a busy day, Xionn leaves the beast with a kiss upon its firm temple and allows Pesa to retreat to its own realm in comfort and rest. Filled with joy at all the life being created throughout his new home, Xionn walks through the meadow and goes to stand with his second child, Opti.

Xionn's smile radiates with pride as he witnesses the breathtaking ethereal beauty of his child. With tenderness and adoration, he places his powerful hands upon Opti's head, igniting a mesmerizing golden aura that envelops the majestic creature. Xionn gently runs his hands through Opti's long, shimmering mane, gazing into the divine flicker within its eyes.

*"O, great and powerful Opti, my child,"* Xionn declares, his voice resonating with the weight of destiny. *"I bestow upon you a gift that none of your kin in Reality possess - the universal force that flows through my essence. You, and you alone, shall wield this power to transform your realm into a place of unparalleled wonder, a realm that defies the conventions of your siblings' domain."*

With a joyful heart, Xionn speaks once more to his divine offspring.

*"Dear child, the realm is yours to shape as you see fit. Let your divine will be done, and let this world be a testament to your boundless imagination and limitless potential."*

Embracing the divine mandate bestowed by its father, Opti turns toward the land of its birth. The ground trembles as the god of light and energy roars with a resounding voice that echoes throughout the realm.

"My will be done now, Father, through you!"

The god of Imagination, its eyes blazing with divine power, charges forward into its world with a force that shakes the very foundations of creation. With each leap and bound, its life force multiplies, growing exponentially as it crosses the threshold into its domain. The air above the meadow trembles with Opti's godly might, and a thunderous roar, similar to the blast of Gabriel's trumpet, resonates throughout the realm.
Overwhelmed by the sheer magnitude of Opti's power and the bittersweet memories it evokes, Xionn falls to his knees, closing his eyes as he is overcome with emotion.

The roar of his divine child, both familiar and awe-inspiring, recalls to Xionn that fateful day on Ametheden when his people were freed from Dia'Baal's grip. Moved to tears, Xionn weeps, reflecting upon the parallels between his past and the glorious potential of Opti's burgeoning realm. I, too, stand in awe of Opti's divine roar, joining Xionn in marveling at the manifestation of Opti's will and the echoes of a history that will come to shape the very fabric of Earth herself.

As soon as he catches his next breath, however, something brushes against him—a sensation, fleeting but intentional and impossible to focus upon. He exhales sharply. A trick of the mind, the rush of creation itself? Yes, that must be it. Still... for the briefest moment, he had felt... *something*.
But there is no one else here.

The symphonic roar that once filled the heavens above Ametheden now resounds throughout the Realm of Imagination, a testament to the deific favor bestowed upon us. As Opti gallops beyond the threshold of its world, the god of creatures undergoes a dramatic transformation. Suddenly, a pair of radiant wings unfurls from its back, revealing a previously hidden aspect of its complete divine nature.

With each powerful stroke of its wings, Opti's thundering presence reverberates through the air above and below, shaking the very structure of its newfound domain. The god of Imagination ascends skyward, its initial movements somewhat clumsy, yet propelled by a determination that is nothing short of divine.

Xionn watches in awe as his child soars across the vast emptiness of the sky, becoming a radiant streak of light in the waning twilight of the second day. Overwhelmed with joy and pride, Xionn witnesses the godly spectacle unfolding before him, bearing witness to the birth of a new era for the Realm of Imagination. As Opti's presence suffuses the sky, the once-barren expanse begins to awaken, enriched by the elemental remnants of nature and dormant chemical compounds.

Meanwhile, the god of beasts, Pesa, joins its father in the meadow after a well-earned rest. Xionn, a proud smile playing on his lips, gestures toward the heavens, inviting Pesa to witness the wondrous spectacle unfolding above Opti's realm. Opti, now fully embracing its divine power, launches a radiant assault on the dormant void above its realm. A brilliant surge of energy emanates from its body, igniting the sky in a breathtaking display akin to a celestial comet.

Phantasmagoric hues, never before seen in nature, meld together to create a mesmerizing golden hue in Imagination's atmosphere. As night deepens, Opti traverses the entire realm, infusing life and beauty into the once-empty sky. As the third day of a new Earth dawns, Opti's divine task is complete.

The atmosphere has been forever transformed, now shimmering with a unique and awe-inspiring beauty. With a thunderous landing, Opti reunites with its family in the heart of the picturesque meadow.

Xionn and Pesa, eagerly anticipating further demonstrations of Opti's remarkable abilities, hold their breath in excitement. Sensing their enthusiasm, Opti fixes its gaze skyward, focusing its divine energy. With more refined movements, the god of Imagination propels itself from the meadow, soaring into the heavens above its world. A powerful gust sweeps through the realm as Opti's mighty wings drive the god through its archway, unleashing another brilliant display of vibrant color.

As Opti's divine presence fills the Realm of Imagination, it decrees with unwavering authority,

"May this offspring come forth... Now!"

The colorful veil from Opti's wake then enters the bright soil of Imagination and it trembles, raising an abundance of golden-hued orbs from these lands near and far. Soon thereafter, I see them separate until they all float just above the ground. Birthed from the force of Imagination, these countless bright little particles become the building blocks of all things not founded upon Reality and nature.

T'Naeva, let it be known that when any god, through its almighty abilities, sincerely believes that it is the time to create life, there is nothing that dares stand in the way of its resolve to do so.

Opti, its mind passionately focused upon this task to expand an already unusual and unique existence, gazes upon a golden-hued sea of these small glowing orbs and begins another mighty roar. Within Opti's blasts of life seeking breath, the Force of Imagination courses in all directions throughout the heavens of the realm. Its glistening essence of inspiration falls as a heavy glowing rain upon this sea of jouncing golden-hued orbs, entering their unique mass and conceiving life within them. Opti, flying just above the glistening surface of its realm, patiently awaits the rewards of its ethereal labor.

This novel and unique framework of life, both creatures and vegetation of infinite varieties, continue to incubate in this flowing sea of orbs and starts to emerge throughout the land. Multitudes of life are then inspired to exist with no need for a seed or Xionn's life-giving breath, simply because they are created not through nature but through a more divine means. Opti, this god of creatures' unknown to Reality and nature, gazes with joy as it descends into the midst of this golden-hued sea of vitality, the endless possibilities gained from the Force of Imagination.

Seeing from afar this limitless scope of fantastic creation, Xionn takes joy with Pesa in the beautiful meadow. Admiring Imagination from outside its boundary, Xionn stays with Pesa because it has been forbidden to cross the threshold of Opti's realm, and vice versa, and he dares not show any favoritism to either of his children.

The way Xionn has now conquered both the forces of Reality and Imagination is incomprehensible, yet there is still something more, something missing—something that tethers these two incredible beasts in a way even he does not fully understand. Indeed, he felt this same phenomenon when Pesa and Opti roared into existence, this impression unseen, waiting—not from above, but now residing right beside him.

He closes his eyes and feels a soft wind suddenly emerge to stir his long, bright hair, pulling him away from all his current tasks. This time, the mysterious sensation lingers much longer, and it is not just a gust of wind.

*It is something more.*

A touch here and there—delicate, persistent, as if unseen celestial fingers trace through his hair, along his shoulders, and touch his hands one final time.
Then—a breath.
Gentle.
Real.
Unseen lips pressing up against the back of his neck.

*A farewell kiss... for now.*

He turns sharply as this incredible sensation resonates throughout his soul—but again, there is no one there. For the first time, he shouts this reality aloud.
*"Who is there?"*

But the soft breeze is gone now, and the mysterious presence is no longer felt. He is alone once more and left wondering. At this time with life having been created worldwide by Xionn and his two maturing children, no living thing on Earth (within either the realms of Reality or Imagination) ages or dies, or so it seems at the time.

Late into the third evening, Opti continues its progress of creating life unique to its own nature as its father, along with Pesa, walks back to the center of the beautiful meadow, all the while speaking lovingly to Pesa's vast thoughts. Turning and placing his hand upon Pesa's radiant forehead while softly caressing it, he acknowledges to his greatest child the conclusion to the work they have all accomplished throughout the new Earth, and Xionn is very pleased.

*"O, powerful child of mine, it is now that both you and your kin stand upon the threshold of making this world the peak of all my efforts, and I, as well as my Almighty Companion, give you thanks and praise in all of your marvelous efforts."*

As the events of the third day draw to a close, Xionn watches with satisfaction as Pesa, exhausted from the day's endeavors, retreats to the Realm of Reality for a well-deserved rest. Weary from the excitement and the incredible feats achieved on Earth over the past three days, Xionn transforms himself into a cool breeze and ascends to the summit of the majestic mountain.

Overcome with fatigue, he drifts into a deep, restful slumber, well-earned after his monumental efforts. The night sky, adorned with a magnificent display of twinkling stars, envelops the planet in a peaceful embrace. It is then that this twinkling starlit mantle of another nightfall spreads across the vista of Gaea's beautiful face, and everything upon this world is at peace.

I again hear a voice as potent as a thousand thunders blasting across my mind, and the Almighty Companion gathers and speaks to all who dwell throughout the Great Realm, this grand and everlasting proclamation.

*... Listen, O mighty host, and hear My decree    this shall become a law of the cosmos until the last breath of creation. My chosen servant, Xionn Theone, has brought forth a new realm into our cosmic embrace, and with it, a dawn unlike any before it.*

*... Blessed is Xionn Theone, and blessed are his children, brought forth from* **Who I Am.** *They shall wield dominion over that distant orb, a world that shall one day yield to My resolve. Behold, the Earth—My cornerstone of justice against my First-borne and all his iniquities.*

*... And though they will be born of dust, the children of Earth shall not be forgotten. To them also shall be offered a divine inheritance—My Soulsliver—hidden not in their flesh but awakened through faith. It shall come not by birthright, but by the gift of*

*grace given through My Holy Son, Messiah. Through His sacrifice and resurrection, their corrupted souls shall be cleansed, and this eternal spark—long buried—shall ignite in those who believe. In Him, they shall receive not only forgiveness, but the power to awaken, to ascend, and to become partakers of My divine will and nature.*

*... Blessed, too, is this beloved Earth, which shall become My passion in the fullness of eons to come. Xionn Theone's rewards shall be without end, for through his guidance, My fallen Firstborne and his kind shall be drawn to this realm—to meet their destined doom beneath My watchful eye. Dia'Baal, the deceiver, will whisper into the hearts of Earth's children, turning their desires to dust and their hopes to ruin. Yet even he, in all his cunning ways, shall not escape My justice indefinitely.*

I hear intense jubilation and praise erupt from the Great Realm as the days of the great deceiver, Dia'Baal Fallenstar, are officially numbered, through the name of my mentor and the destiny of his world in honor by the King Himself. Yet, in the midst of their exultation, the heavenly host swiftly falls silent, their anticipation mounting as they await their King's continued proclamation.

*... In a broad span of ages to come, we will build mightily upon the foundation of this Great Realm and move it to the north of our current starry frontier, just as Earth and her own destiny in the cosmos will mature to become My fresh center of attention. Just as Ametheden has known for eons since its birth, My love for this eternal jewel will never fade from My eyes.*

*... Yet upon this distant orb and her many turbulent eras to come, a coming of mankind will rejoice in our mercy throughout their dreadful corruption, as from their very foundation will they know well my dishonored Firstborne through many names of sin – which is death.*

I see the Almighty Presence of the King turn to His right, hearing Him speak directly to his Son and He declares His perfect love with these words.

*... Just as I granted free will to Ametheden, so too shall Earth's children choose their path—Many shall embrace the light, yet multitudes will stumble into darkness. Their choices shall shape the fate of their world and echo throughout the closing ages*

*of the cosmos.*

*... O Divine Messiah, You alone shall bear the weight of Dia'Baal's corruption. You shall offer Yourself in sacrifice to his iniquities and rise thereafter to glorious resurrection, sealing Earth's redemption for all her remaining days. You shall descend into their human suffering, bearing their sorrows and burdens, that through your pain, they may find everlasting peace.*

*... In your name, O, holy and exalted Son, an unrelenting tide of salvation shall sweep across that distant realm, bringing forth a new dawn of grace and redemption for all who believe. Though darkness will rise and seek to ensnare the hearts of men, it shall not overcome Our light. For Your name shall be a beacon of hope to all who seek it, and through You, the lost shall see the way, the broken shall find restoration, and the weary shall be renewed in spirit and truth.*

*... In the fullness of time, Earth shall take its rightful place among the stars, standing in unity with Our creation across the cosmos. My chosen among the stars shall watch and guide this fallen race of beings, their wisdom shining as a light in Earth's darkest hour, until the final age draws to a close and all things are made to be known and renewed.*

The angelic host fall to their knees, their eyes wide with awe, as the King's words reverberate throughout the Great Realm. I see much weeping and others bowing their heads in reverence. All feeling the weight of The King's proclamation, and I am stricken with awe to what I hear.

*... This realm, My new heart's desire, shall see my benevolent children journey from the farthest reaches of the cosmos, crossing through My dimension, time, and space, to find new households amidst the stars of that beautiful Milky Way. Within this celestial confine, those who bear My divine knowledge and mystery shall discreetly visit the shores of Earth, revealing mere glimpses of their divine presence until the final hour of the final age of her humanity, and their destiny draws to a close.*

*... Until that distant and glorious moment arrives, My faithful ones, I command you to observe the struggles of this beautiful jewel from a distance, to offer support and encouragement as she overcomes the affliction brought upon it by Dia'Baal Fallenstar, My fallen son. When his dark reign comes to an end, this curious race of beings shall come to know Me truly, and Earth shall take its rightful place among a vibrant cosmic community, joining in harmony with the myriad of life that populates My heavens.*

*... In that blessed time of completion, the people of Earth shall know and love their brethren scattered amongst the stars, recognizing the divine unity that binds all life*

*together. My Treasured Ametheden and beloved Earth shall stand side by side as the alpha and the omega of cosmic completion, both exalted among all others – a testament to My divine passion and the eternal bond that unites My chosen throughout the cosmos... now and forevermore.*

D'Reem's voice, firm and knowing, finds her seeking ears once more.

"Dearest T'Naeva... these words I speak now are not only for you, but for *them*. For those who will begin to lift the veil themselves, in the ages to come. That they too may find the strength within to ask:

*How has this truth stirred my inner fire?*
*How does its clarity help me walk more bravely through the trials I face?*
*How might I now carry this story into my own?"*

As T'Naeva's tear-streaked face rises to meet D'Reem's gaze, a heavy silence falls between them. D'Reem, unable to maintain eye contact, lowers his head and turns away, his words dying on his lips. T'Naeva's mind continues to race with unanswered questions, her unspoken accusations against her mate hanging in the air. But in the stillness, she feels a glimmer of hope—a belief that, in time, every question will be answered, and the truth will be laid bare - One way or another.

Thus ends the *Season of Inspiration,* ushering in the wondrous and eternal realms... of thought. The eons of ancients past that will never again be seen in the physical but will live on—seen only by those whose minds awaken... to *MYTH.*

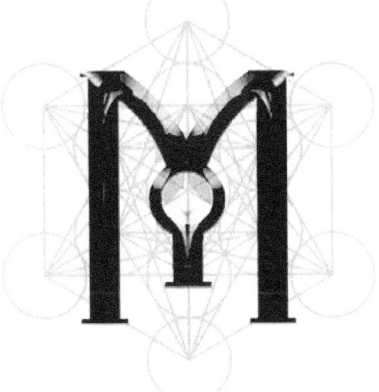

# CHAPTER 3
## *The Season of Maturity*

*"It is no simple matter to pause in the midst of one's maturity, when life is full of function, to examine the principals, which control that functioning."*
—**Pearl Buck**

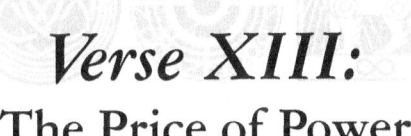

# *Verse XIII:*
## The Price of Power

'Reem's muscular, bronzed form trembles as his mind processes and narrates the unfolding events granted to him by his divine Companion.

Guided by his Almighty Benefactor, he channels the truth through his words and essence, hoping to enlighten his cherished companion. As he is endowed with his Creator's omniscience, vivid memories of a bygone era confront the hero, fueling his quest to conquer a goddess's misguided beliefs. A deep and powerful voice erupts, full of divinity and D'Reem speaks these words.

... The narrative unfolds, dear T'Naeva, through the **Season of Maturity**, a time of transformation upon the entirety of Earth. Pesa's vision wavers, yet its form develops into an impeccable masterpiece of beastly godhood. As it has been gifted with the ability to bring forth life from mere thoughts, Xionn has empowered this god of beasts to shape a paradise within the realm of nature.

Often venturing beyond its world, Pesa will gaze upon the enchanting realm of its celestial sibling, yearning to explore the wonders that lie just out of reach. Forbidden from entering Opti's world, Pesa can only marvel at its beauty from afar. However, in a pivotal moment ages later, the god of beasts observes a curious occurrence while resting amidst the verdant shade of trees near its dazzling diamond archway. This singular event will spark a sense of duty within Pesa and its natural world, leading it to contemplate the creation of a new species.

Its mighty divine sibling, Opti, has just released a newly created life-form and brought it into the beautiful meadow. The golden skies gleam brighter as Opti descends, carrying the fragile life form.

Its talons, though fierce, cradle the creature with care, a contrast so striking that it seems to radiate the boundless harmony between Reality and Imagination. The meadow itself responds, its vibrant flora swaying in unison as though celebrating the new life introduced to its embrace. The creature's initial flutters are clumsy, its wings trembling with uncertainty. Opti, unwavering in its encouragement, lifts it higher, a great rush of wind cascading downwards, carrying a warmth that touches even the most distant corners of the meadow.

I hear a thundering roar of excitement erupt as Opti pursues the new creature to assist its flailing struggle. The blast of warm air cascades as Opti rises swiftly to the heavens and releases this new life-form, allowing it to take its first independent flight in a dramatic show of inspiration. The face of your parent, T'Naeva, glows as Pesa watches this celebration on that bright and sunny day. Roars of excitement, both from Opti and its creation, fill the meadow with a joyous, beautiful tone of brotherly love.

The god of beasts sets its sights upon the new creature with respect, observing it until it finally ascends into the fiery golden skies of Imagination, where it makes its way to a new home and a new beginning. The golden skies shimmer with an otherworldly glow, an eternal testament to the interconnected forces that govern existence. Opti, still in flight and filled with exhilaration, descends briskly to the edge of the meadow, close to the archway of Reality.

Rocketing high above Pesa's towering form, Opti catches its powerful kin's gaze, a flicker of warmth in its luminous eyes. With a graceful turn, it folds its vast wings inward, offering a solemn salute—an honor bestowed upon the greatest living life-form on Earth. Pesa watches in silent awe. The meadow answered in ripples — tall grasses bending, wildflowers bursting with sudden fragrance, the air thick with golden dust as though the land itself had been stirred awake. Even the archway of Reality shimmered faintly, as if it, too, had heard and understood.

Then, as the gesture sinks deep into its primal heart, Pesa releases a thunderous roar of gratitude that shakes the meadow to its roots.
For a time, it says nothing more, letting the wind carry the echo of that salute across the meadow. Each beat of its own heart seems to answer the wings above, steady and reverent, as if some long-forgotten truth had returned. The light bends strangely in that moment, scattering in gold and silver shards across the grass, and Pesa thinks — without shame, without resistance — *This is worth protecting.* The thought comes unbidden, warm and fragile, like a seed in the palm. It does not last. Already, something deeper stirs to twist it into something else.

To Pesa, flight becomes more than motion. It is freedom incarnate—an unshackled existence where all limitations dissolve against the boundless skies. From that moment, it contemplates its own nature with fervor, seeking to understand and emulate the purity of Opti's creation. With unyielding resolve, the god of beasts vows that no force—mortal or divine—will deny it the power of flight once its complex form is mastered.

Somewhere in the depths of its memory, the god of beasts recalled the first time it had felt the earth fall away beneath its paws — the leap across the chasm in the shadowed mountains, when the air had been sharp and clean and the thrill had been enough. Now, that memory seemed small. The skies had called, and in answering, Pesa knew the earth alone could no longer hold it. It studies tirelessly: the interplay of motion and grace, the way wind cradles wings, the strength needed to rise beyond Earth's airy grasp.

A faint breeze stirs the meadow, carrying distant calls of creatures born from Imagination's bounty. Opti descends gently, luminous wings folding as it strides toward its kin. Its voice rises softly, edged with concern, eyes fixed on Pesa's tense silhouette.
Opti speaks, voice low, almost trembling.

"Pesa... you've surpassed so many limits. Why do you still gaze to the horizon as though even the heavens aren't enough?"
Pesa turns, its eyes aflame—not only with purpose, but with a restless hunger, the shadow of pride curling at the edges of its thoughts.
"Not enough? No... it isn't. A true master of Earth's skies answers to no one—not even Father. Nor even you, dear Opti."
Opti's luminous wings twitch, their glow flickering like a heartbeat caught between hope and dread.
"Would that quest for dominion cost you this world's harmony? Must everything bend before your will, simply because you are its nature—its foundation?"

Pesa's tone sharpens, cold as steel.
"Harmony? That fragile balance is nothing but a cage. My foundation is not. Father's gilded prison—indeed, a shelter for those too timid to break its hold."
Opti steps closer, voice low but firm now, aching with quiet desperation.
"Pesa, please... you were not created to stand apart. This longing—this hunger—it will consume you. And when it does, there will be no skies left for you to master."
Pesa's gaze hardens, its reply dropping like a blade—cold, defiant, final.
"Then let it consume me, Opti, and be done with it. Better for a god such as myself to burn in freedom than to live bound by the chains of its own desires."
Opti recoils as though struck. Its wings fold back, luminous form dimming as sorrow etches deep into its being.
"Then... you are already lost, dear sibling."

The meadow, ever vibrant and teeming with life, becomes a crucible of Pesa's resolve. Days turn to years, and years to ages, as Pesa's pursuit evolves into an obsession. The beasts under its dominion reflect its fervor, their movements imbued with the same determination to transcend natural limits. The skies above the meadow become a theater of countless attempts, each flight imbued with lessons learned, until one fateful moment when

Pesa's essence transforms entirely. It takes to the air not as a mere observer, but as a master, defying the boundaries that once confined it.

The significance of Pesa's unwavering dedication becomes a beacon, not only to its creations, but also to the world it governs. This tireless pursuit reshapes the very fabric of its being, marking a pivotal evolution. As it soars among the heavens, a profound truth emerges: the relentless drive to overcome limitations embodies the transformative power within all who dare to persist. Pesa's flight is no longer just an act of defiance, but a statement of existence, a testimony to the infinite potential harbored in every corner of creation.

Yet the reality that Pesa now faces is layered with complexity. Despite mastering the art of flight, it becomes consumed with an insatiable need to refine its abilities, to conquer every conceivable challenge. The intensity of this focus begins to bleed into its essence, altering the equilibrium it once maintained. The beasts of the meadow, once reflections of Pesa's nobility, start to exhibit signs of imbalance—an unrestrained aggression, a desire to dominate rather than coexist.

Xionn, watching with growing unease, senses a disturbance rippling through the Force of Reality. He observes how the meadow's harmony begins to fracture under the weight of Pesa's burgeoning ego. Though Xionn attributes this change to the rapid maturation of the singular Force of Reality within Pesa, he remains hopeful that it is a temporary deviation. Yet subtle doubts linger in his mind. The connection between Pesa's flight and its deepening arrogance begins to take shape, a correlation that hints at greater consequences for the world.

The archway of Reality, once a symbol of unity, now stands as a boundary fraught with tension. Pesa, in moments of quiet reflection, finds itself questioning the nature of its existence.
*'Why should I share dominion when I have achieved what no other has?'*

These thoughts, fleeting at first, grow in prominence, casting long shadows over its once-pure intentions. Little does Pesa realize that this internal conflict marks the beginning of a profound transformation—one that will ripple through the realms of Reality and Imagination, forever altering the balance they once shared. This intense focus on self-mastery, while inspiring, comes at a cost. The meadow's creatures become reflections of Pesa's inner turmoil, their once-joyful interactions now tinged with strife.

The winds that once carried hope and freedom now howl with an edge of discord, a subtle but unmistakable sign that the equilibrium of this world hangs in precarious balance. Despite the growing concerns regarding Pesa's shifting attitude, Xionn remains confident in the god's unwavering love for its realm, and its dedication to safeguarding it from external influences is intense. For the time being, however, the delicate balance between the forces of Reality and Imagination on Earth remains intact, and this provides some reassurance to Xionn.

The question remains, however, as to how long this harmony will endure in the face of Pesa's evolving nature.

The looming specter of an unsettling change that even Xionn cannot fully comprehend. It is now, T'Naeva, as I continue onward within the season of your parent's maturity of godhood, that something truly unfortunate begins to take place. Over time, Pesa's spirit becomes increasingly shaped by the force of nature, the fundamental laws of which have always underpinned the Force of Reality within the god of beasts. As Pesa's evolution continues, this intrinsic nature begins to exert an ever-growing influence on its behavior and mindset.

The once-harmonious presence of Pesa, whose essence radiated a nurturing calm over its realm, begins to shift subtly but unmistakably. The beasts within its domain, sensing the change, grow restless, their interactions more aggressive, their calls sharper, as though the discord within their master echoes outward into the fabric of creation itself. The passage of several more ages unfolds before my eyes, culminating in the final age of Pesa's season of maturity—a pivotal juncture in the unfolding account of your dark parent.

At this critical stage, Pesa has become acutely aware of its immense stature upon Earth, yet its tolerance for mundane worldliness begins to wane. This growing disdain for the simpler aspects of creation sets a dangerous precedent. The god of beasts, for all its power and wisdom, starts to view the beings under its care not as integral parts of its purpose, but as distractions from the grand design it believes it is destined to achieve.

Pesa's awareness of the necessity of shielding its realm from the competing influences of Imagination remains steadfast. Yet beneath this resolve, an insidious pride begins to grow. What begins as a quiet self-assurance soon festers into an imperceptible contempt for those closest to this mighty god of beasts. It becomes clear that Pesa's view of its kin, once filled with respect and camaraderie, is subtly shifting to one of superiority, as though its achievements in the art of flight grant it a higher standing among the divine.

It is essential to emphasize, T'Naeva, that until this juncture, Pesa has not been troubled by sharing stewardship of Earth with Opti or their father. Yet an unforeseen event fundamentally alters Pesa's worldview: the arrival of Dia'Baal and his followers, divinely guided by Xionn's Companion, to the presence of Earth. This intrusion is not mere happenstance, but a calculated move by Dia'Baal to sow discord and seize an opportunity to corrupt the mightiest of Xionn's creations.

In this current age of Pesa's maturity, the significance of Dia'Baal's discovery cannot be overstated. For the malevolent Dia'Baal Fallenstar, finding a new world to claim as his own becomes a source of ecstatic triumph. Yet unbeknown to him, it is upon this mortal realm, called *Earth*, that he and his corruption will ultimately face destruction.

Dia'Baal's excitement is intense, his desire to corrupt and control at last finding fertile ground in which to take root. Oblivious to the fateful consequences that will one day destroy him, he revels in the prospect of exerting his dark influence over Earth, relishing the opportunity to finally seize the power he craves.

Fixated on the goal of corrupting Pesa's godlike mind, Dia'Baal, along with his horde scrutinize Earth from afar relentlessly. Their observations yield a startling realization: this world is not merely the creation of Xionn, but an extension of His divine purpose. Further driven by his immediate seething hatred for Xionn and his entire race, Dia'Baal craves nothing more than to exact revenge upon him, his offspring, and this cherished world.

Dia'Baal embarks upon an intricate path of deception, carefully weaving a web of deceit around Pesa. Observing Pesa from the shadows of his own higher plane of existence, Dia'Baal patiently plots his next move, awaiting the perfect opportunity to pounce. He indeed recognizes in Pesa a very powerful yet vulnerable target, susceptible to his malevolent influence. The god of beasts, with its towering pride and growing sense of isolation, becomes an ideal vessel for the seeds of corruption Dia'Baal seeks to plant.

Drawing upon the dark wisdom gleaned from his ancient defeat in Ametheden, Dia'Baal has greatly honed his skills in deception, having learned the art of subtlety through his manipulation of the Tempest of Oblivion. With meticulous care, Dia'Baal begins to meld his essence with Pesa's expansive consciousness, ever mindful of Xionn's formidable godlike abilities. The very Force of Reality that has nurtured Pesa's growth becomes the veil under which Dia'Baal cloaks his insidious plans, ensuring that his presence remains undetected by the unwary god of beasts.

As Dia'Baal's devilish scheme unfolds, the stage becomes set for yet another climactic showdown between the forces of good and evil. Yet the tragedy lies not only in the impending battle, but in the slow erosion of Pesa's spirit. What was once a beacon of steadfast purpose now wavers, its light dimmed by doubt and the creeping shadow of Dia'Baal's influence.

As yet another age fades into the annals of history, Dia'Baal's malevolent scheme takes hold, allowing him, at long last, to infiltrate the god of beasts' mind. With this newfound ability, it is only a matter of time before Pesa's once-pure thoughts succumb to Dia'Baal's vile plans. The god of beasts, reclined beneath its archway's cool shade, remains unaware of the growing tempest within.

A dark morning dawns as a seemingly innocuous question seeps into Pesa's consciousness, prompting a train of thought that marks the turning point in the god's fate.

*'Why is it that I suddenly and strangely feel, in having been created by the Force of Reality, that I do not rule this entire world unconditionally by my own birthright?'*

As the god wrestles with its newfound sense of entitlement, this unexpected thought, cunningly planted by Dia'Baal, shatters Pesa's former contentment, driving a wedge between the harmony that the realms and forces of Reality and Imagination share on Earth. As Pesa ponders the unsettling notion of its supposed dominion over Earth, a sinister whisper echoes within the depths of its consciousness.
Dia'Baal's calculating response fans the flames of Pesa's ego, nurturing a sense of entitlement that threatens to already consume the god of beasts.

The great demon's words whisper into Pesa's mind…

*"Why indeed, o, mighty yet naive god, do you suffer such indignity? You, the Firstborne of a force and the greatest of your kind, should command this world—not grovel before kin and father. This is yours by birthright... is it not, dear Pesa?"*

Burrowing ever deeper into Pesa's psyche, Dia'Baal's masterful influence urges the great beast of Reality to embrace its self-importance and to assert its dominance over its kin. The great beast, eyes now half open but still half closed, quickly snorts an answer to this question of thought.

*I do agree—but I've remained silent far too long in response to my own weakness of action, I suppose—a weakness I will hope to remedy soon enough.'*

The surrounding meadow trembles faintly as Pesa's voice, infused with newfound determination, reverberates across the landscape. The very air seems to shift, heavy with the weight of this pivotal moment. Pesa's form rises, its shadow stretching to the trees as the skies above dim slightly, as though responding to the first crack in the god's harmonious existence. The meadow's lively creatures, usually calm under Pesa's presence, scatter uneasily, their instincts attuned to the disquiet in their god's bright aura.

The vibrant flora, once radiant with life, seems to dim, its colors muted as if mourning the shift in Pesa's spirit. It is with a heavy heart, dear T'Naeva, that we both bear witness to the tragic fall of your mighty parent, as the beloved deity begins to wither under the darkness that now festers within. Evil has found its new host in the form of the once-benevolent Pesa, forever altering the course of Earth's destiny and the delicate balance of power between Reality and Imagination.

So, yes, my beloved, after nearly two eons since his harsh defeat on Ametheden, Dia'Baal's luck had certainly improved, as this extremely potent life-form in the name of Pesa would slowly begin to abandon the acceptance of both its sibling's and father's good ways. This god of beasts, with the help of one who certainly needs no introduction, will soon become unwilling to control the negative thoughts sprouting to birth in a bitter and unyielding attitude.

As Pesa's temperament darkens under Dia'Baal's sway, the mothering essence of Gaea—the essential ingredient of Pesa's power—begins to mirror this swift and ominous transformation. The once-harmonious symbiosis between Pesa and the Earth shifts, with the god's influence subduing the nurturing spirit of Gaea. The trees no longer sing in harmony, but sway uneasily, their roots feeling the tremors of a growing... *imbalance.*

The creatures that once thrived under Pesa's care now exhibit unease, their instincts sensing the changes in their god's demeanor. Above, the skies, once clear and resplendent with the interplay of Reality and Imagination, begin to shift, streaked with shades of gray and muted golden hues. Time races across my eyes, and Pesa's resentment towards its kin festers greatly, eroding the divine wisdom that once tempered its behavior.

The delicate balance between Pesa and Opti's coexistence on Earth begins to fracture under the weight of this burgeoning and corrupting animosity. The once-shared archways between realms, symbols of unity, grow tense and strained, their vibrant energy dimming as the chasm between the siblings deepens. Opti, sensing this change, observes Pesa from afar, its radiant eyes filled with a mix of sorrow and caution, unsure whether to intervene or leave its kin to its own devices.

In a pivotal moment ages later, Pesa's growing disdain finally overpowers its divine insight, sowing the seeds of destruction deep within its psyche. This dark and bitter emotion, called *resentment*, rapidly starts to consume Pesa's better judgment, spreading through its vast mind like a consuming wildfire. The god's once-harmonious thoughts are now riddled with doubts, its inner monologue tainted by Dia'Baal's persistent whispers.

Its resentment mutates into an unyielding yet still secretive intolerance for Opti and its contrasting nature upon the Earth. Indeed, dear one, as the bonds of kinship begin to crumble under the crushing force of Pesa's newfound hostility, the god of beasts turns its back on the divine principles that once governed its actions. With those actions, the fate of an entire world begins to quiver upon the precipice of an uncertain and perilous future.

Yet amidst this descent, there are moments of hesitation—fleeting glimpses of the god Pesa once was, as if fragments of its former self struggle to rise above the growing darkness. D'Reem, the mighty warrior, freezes as Ocean's waves rise in fury, their crashing sprays mirroring the outrage of Pesa's long-lost essence. Its turbulent response appears to reflect an eavesdropped-upon conversation, a phenomenon D'Reem has experienced before.

In the midst of this tempest, D'Reem's keen gaze shifts to the stirring figure of Ocean's daughter, her eyes now ablaze with anger and anguish. The connection between them grows profound, their shared pain and fury forming an unspoken bond. The waves crash around them with renewed vigor, as though the elements themselves lament the unfolding tragedy.

In this charged moment, D'Reem stands as both witness and participant in the deific conflict unfolding before him. As Ocean's wrath and T'Naeva's turmoil converge, he must navigate the turbulent waters of this passionate situation, confronting both the fury of the elements and the fervent struggle within the heart of his eternal mate. The warrior's resolve strengthens as he approaches her, his presence a calming force against the storm's ferocity. His words, though simple, cut through the chaos like light through a storm cloud.

With a gentle and reassuring tone, D'Reem addresses T'Naeva as the chaotic emotions stirred by the visions begin to calm. He speaks softly, urging her to remember that these visions, while brief summaries of long-past events, still hold truth. He smiles and speaks to her softly.

"Beloved T'Naeva, I beseech you to open your heart and allow the hope within these truths to replace the anger you harbor. I know this turmoil pains you, but if you cannot release it, it will consume you long before the tale is complete. Know that I am strong, and I will be your rock in this moment of truth, as I continue to share these revelations with you."

D'Reem continues.

As the *Season of Maturity* slips further into the forgotten realm of Oblivion, ages of escalating intolerance, cultivated by Dia'Baal's malignant influence, take root within Pesa's consciousness. The god's growing prejudice gradually morphs into an accepted truth, wreaking havoc upon the delicate balance of the Realm of Reality. Dia'Baal's manipulative presence remains expertly concealed amidst the mounting chaos. Pesa's increasingly aggressive behavior reflects its heightened sense of self-importance, while its kin's existence dwindles to a mere afterthought.

What once burned in Pesa as primal loyalty has now twisted into arrogance, and the beast's once-noble instincts are reduced to hollow echoes within its corrupted soul. As the corruption reaches its apex, a disheartening darkness befalls Pesa's maturity, marking the tragic conclusion to its divine innocence. The malignant tumor of prejudice, now deeply embedded within Pesa's essence, grows unchecked—festering like rot in its very spirit, culminating in a devastating grip upon the god of beasts.

It did not happen in a single night, nor by a single whisper. First came the comparisons—subtle, measured, poisonous. Why should Opti's wonders be sung while Pesa's laws are merely assumed? Why should Imagination receive the praise that Reality bears alone in silence? Dia'Baal did not command; he suggested. He pressed the bruise where honor lived—until honor flinched. Pesa began to call suspicion "discernment," cruelty "clarity," and contempt "courage." What once defended the borders of life now policed the borders of love.

There were thresholds where Pesa might have turned back. When the Companion's quiet reached into the marrow, when Xionn's counsel arrived like rain on hard clay, the beast felt the tremor of returning—then chose the steadying lie: that strength must be unchallenged to be true. From that oath to self arose the creed of domination. Pesa began to measure worth by obedience, beauty by usefulness, and kinship by fear. The world, once a covenant, became a cage to be perfected by force.

Hatred finally overtakes Pesa's once pure divine mindset, consuming its system of beliefs and enabling Dia'Baal to assert total control over the deity's actions. This venomous hold, born of centuries of manipulation, drives the god further from its sacred origin, blinding it to the truth of its own destruction. As this cancer of the mind completes its dreadful course, Pesa's fall from grace is all but complete, culminating in a tyranny of mind and spirit that will serve Dia'Baal's sinister designs perfectly.

The beast's thoughts, once expansive and filled with divine wonder, are now reduced to a singular, insatiable hunger for dominance. The effects of this catastrophic corruption now begin to reverberate through Pesa's entire being, triggering an alarming mutation in the god's physical form.
Once a majestic embodiment of Earth's raw power, Pesa's frame distorts into something monstrous, unnatural—its fur bristling like poisoned thorns, its eyes ablaze with feral malice. The malevolent force of Dia'Baal continues to surge within the beast, warping sinew and bone until it resembles the very chaos it now embodies.

Its breath carries the heat of verdict; its tread, the logic of conquest. The jaw that once guarded the weak now weighs the cost of mercy like a ledger of debts. Even the ground recoils—soil hardening under a will that no longer blesses. It becomes evident that Pesa's essence has undergone an irreversible transformation, casting a foreboding shadow over Earth's future and sealing its tragic descent into living myth. In Pesa's chest, law has lost its music; measure has lost its mercy.

*Where harmony falters, cruelty finds a throne.*

Simultaneously, Xionn, who had originally created Pesa as a paragon of perfection, grapples with the agonizing mutation of this child's physical form. True to the nature now intrinsic to this dismal mutation, Xionn remains tragically oblivious to the seething rage that now engulfs Pesa's mind, as well as the profound consequences for the entire Realm of Reality's existence. Gazing upon the magnificent counselor, one witnesses Xionn's unwavering, unconditional love for his ailing creation.

Throughout this age of relentless turmoil, Xionn devotes more time to Pesa, desperately striving to come to terms with and accommodate the presumed growing pains of a swiftly evolving force of Reality. However, little does Xionn know that the true source of Pesa's affliction runs far deeper than mere evolution—down past sinew and symbol, into that fatal vow where love was traded for control, and truth was taught to kneel.

# *Verse XIV:*
## When Balance Becomes Law

A bruptly, T'Naeva's sorrow transforms into a maelstrom of raw emotion, as she is no longer able to withstand the harrowing truth uttered by the conqueror of her fallen parent, D'Reem.

As if ignited by an unseen spark, the goddess erupts to her feet, her fists clenched in defiance, casting a challenge towards the heavens with a ferocious roar.

"Deceiver!" T'Naeva cries, her vision blurred by tears. "How dare you speak such words of my cherished Pesa, claiming they are controlled by this ... malevolent force!"

Rage courses through T'Naeva, her blinded devotion fueling the consuming blaze within. The thought of her cherished parent succumbing to such darkness is more than she can bear. T'Naeva's impassioned cry reverberates across the heavens, a powerful testament to her unwavering devotion to Pesa.

"All I have gleaned thus far is a solitary, distorted account of my parent's tragic fall from grace," T'Naeva declares, and she acknowledges the visions she has already received. "Though I have yet to be granted a glimpse of these tragic events, the full truth remains elusive. If you truly exist, O, Companion, to whom he so fervently speaks, I beseech you to share these complete visions with me, for I too must bear witness to the full breadth of the darkness that has befallen my beloved parent, Pesa."

The air between them shifted — not with wind, but with a subtle tightening, as though the world itself braced for what was about to be spoken. Far beyond the veil of their meeting place, the sound of a single deep note — not thunder, but something older — rolled across the horizon. D'Reem's gaze did not waver, and in the shimmer of the distance, the first images began to form.

With each passing moment, T'Naeva's patience wanes, her love for Pesa fueling her urgent need to uncover the entirety of the unfortunate tale. As she stands resolute, her plea to the Companion is a testament to her unwavering devotion and determination to bring clarity to the tragic events that have unfolded. Her resolve hardened by frustration, T'Naeva issues an ultimatum.

"Should You refuse me, Companion, then know my contempt for you will match the disdain I carry for him—for you would be no better!"

D'Reem, his voice steady, yet imbued with gentle conviction, speaks words granted to him by his Companion.

"Your pleas have not gone unheard, T'Naeva. My Companion bids me to share this message: even amidst the shadow of despair, there is a light of hope for those with hearts only willing to seek it."

T'Naeva, still grappling with her conflicted emotions, turns to face D'Reem, taken aback by his serene, almost statue-like presence. Unfazed by her passionate display of anger, D'Reem remains cross-legged, his gaze fixed on the shifting horizon of Ocean, his eyes aglow with an otherworldly serenity. A strange sense of calm begins to envelop T'Naeva, soothing her turbulent emotions, despite her reluctance to draw close to him.

In this moment of stillness, she can sense the depth and sincerity of D'Reem's love for her, untainted by even the slightest hint of deceit. As her latest bout of anger subsides, T'Naeva resigns herself to the possibility that there may be more to this story than she initially believed. T'Naeva, her voice laced with a mixture of determination and tenderness, interjects.

"Only for the sake of my beloved Pesa, I shall endeavor to be patient. If it is the only way to unveil the memory of a beast that, truthfully, I have never physically laid eyes upon, then I shall do my best to endure the discomfort this tale brings. Indeed, this shall prove most intriguing; and of this I am certain."

She yields to sarcasm, begrudgingly acknowledging the captivating nature of D'Reem's tale. He continues.

Seeking comfort in the familiarity of Chimera's powerful presence, T'Naeva sighs deeply and reclines against her warm, secure form. With a growing sense of relaxation and patience, she steels herself to uncover the truth behind Pesa's tragic downfall. As if in response to her silent resolve, D'Reem resumes his narrative, weaving a hard tale of the past with words that hang heavy in the air between them.

Xionn, despite his divine insight, struggles to fully comprehend the severity of his child's wicked metamorphosis. As he desperately seeks to uncover the root of Pesa's affliction, the insidious influence of Dia'Baal thwarts his every effort, manipulating Pesa's vast intellect to dismiss the darkness as a natural evolution of the maturity of the Force of Reality. Xionn's despair grows as he witnesses Pesa's transformation.

The once-proud creator spends sleepless ages observing the beast, hoping for some flicker of its former self to shine through the veil of corruption. Meanwhile, the realms of Earth reflect the turmoil of Pesa's metamorphosis. The natural cycles falter, seasons overlapping in disarray. Rivers dry up without warning, only to flood their banks with torrential force. Forests once vibrant with life grow eerily silent, their shadows lengthening unnaturally. Even the winds seem to carry whispers of discontent, a collective mourning for the guardian they once revered.

The creatures of the land, sky, and sea grow restless, their instincts warning them of the approaching storm that Pesa's transformation heralds. Despite the overwhelming evidence of chaos, Xionn's unwavering hope blinds him to the depth of Dia'Baal's influence. Believing this transformation to be a passing trial, he continues to pour his love and guidance into Pesa, unaware that his efforts are now twisted into fuel for the beast's dark evolution. Pesa, though physically imposing, begins to exhibit erratic behavior, lashing out at the very forces of nature it once nurtured.

Thunderous roars echo across the land as Pesa's frustration manifests in displays of destructive power, toppling mountains and splitting the earth beneath its claws. D'Reem's voice, steady and deliberate, recounts these events with a solemnity that grips T'Naeva's heart. Her earlier skepticism fades as she begins to comprehend the scale of the tragedy spoken in his words, the narrative weaving a tapestry of loss, betrayal, and the fragile line between creation and corruption.

Utterly convinced by the deception, Pesa repeatedly implores Xionn to accept the dismal state of affairs, asserting that it is simply the natural course of events, within the scope of nature. Dia'Baal's malevolent presence expertly exploits Pesa's persuasive abilities, forcing Xionn into a powerless position where he can do little more than watch as the animosity between his children escalates, all the while accepting and loving Pesa unconditionally, no matter the harrowing outcome.

Indeed, Xionn's assumption that Pesa's negative attitude stems from its peculiar transformation, and not from a sound mind, is accurate. The hope that Pesa's demeanor will eventually improve once the tumultuous period of dark maturity has passed becomes a lifeline for Xionn to cling to. Alas, the understanding of the universe's mysteries will come too late for the mentor to intervene effectively.

As the void's cancerous hatred tightens its grip on Pesa's mind, the god of beasts begins to sever all communication, including with its father. Pesa instead seeks solace in the depths of its vast realm, isolating itself for a century here, a century there, as it grapples constantly with the intense mental and physical torment. In these moments of vulnerability, Dia'Baal's voice offers false comfort, fostering a twisted companionship amidst Pesa's anguish.

In the darkness between thoughts, where no wind moved and no light could reach, a shape leaned close — not seen, but felt in the marrow. Its voice was the hush between heartbeats, its presence the cold certainty that it had always been there, waiting. Despite the free will granted to all beings, Pesa's perception becomes clouded by its suffering and the cunning manipulation of Dia'Baal.

As Pesa's trust in Dia'Baal grows stronger, so too does its all-consuming hatred, which now manifests as a relentless, stabbing agony throughout its diseased body. Were Pesa able to exercise its free will and communicate honestly with Xionn, the mighty father might ease the suffering and uncover the true nature of the affliction. Instead, the god of beasts' devoured rationale gives way to a thundering progression of hatred and despair, further distancing Pesa from the light of Xionn's truth and redemption.

A diseased god of Reality now presides over an equally afflicted and chaotic realm, a consequence of Dia'Baal's toxic influence on Pesa's vast mind. This land of nature, once a paradise for Pesa's creations, has become a hostile environment, devoid of the vibrant life it once nurtured. As the vision unfolds, the extent of Dia'Baal's sinister sway over Pesa becomes apparent. Pesa's grossly negative attitude reaches its zenith, allowing Dia'Baal Fallenstar, known also as the *Devil*, to exert absolute dominance over the god's nature.

In tandem with the realm's transformation, Pesa's vast knowledge grows ever more enigmatic and complex, inextricably linked to the dark vacuum now festering within. As Pesa's actions further enable the oppressive control of its world, the cancerous union between the void and Pesa's mind tightens its grip, forging a destructive symbiosis that threatens to consume all that remains of the once-benevolent god.

The malignant void of corruption, now long past total control of the god's every thought and action, is easily able to deceive even its own captive, blinding Pesa completely in the swiftly accumulating errors of its ways. Once this terrible phenomenon has come to full maturity within Pesa, what is left of the influence of its father is now buried within the lies of Dia'Baal's potent influence. This strife of rebellion is now starting to change the way the Earth, as well as its inhabitants, will exist from this season forward, and it continues to influence Pesa's every deed.

With Pesa's own thoughts now channeled through the cancerous void of its mind, the beast at times will outright lie to its father through deceptive statements. Misleading Xionn into believing things will only get better from here on out, Dia'Baal, through Pesa, somehow convinces its father that it is perfectly healthy on the inside all the time.

Another reality that Pesa hides very well is its rumbling thoughts of severe discontent toward Opti, as the great beast continues to execute perfectly its sinister charade to hide its hateful feelings through Dia'Baal's influence. Dearest T'Naeva, it is now that the wretched narrative I share with you draws a compelling parallel between Pesa and Dia'Baal, as both these entities undergo a transformative rebellion against their respective creators, those being my mentor, Xionn, and my Companion.

This parallel offers a profound exploration of the nature of evil and its gradual, insidious growth within seemingly benevolent beings. Pesa, once a powerful and nurturing guardian of Earth, succumbs to the corrupting influence of the void and Dia'Baal's manipulation, leading to a destructive and all-consuming hatred. Similarly, Dia'Baal, initially a creation of the Divine Creator, rebels against the King's order and becomes a malevolent force that will eventually exploit Pesa's vulnerability.

Both Pesa and Dia'Baal's rebellions stem from a distortion of their original purposes, fueled by the insidious power of the void. One that represents the destructive force of corruption that always consumes and manipulates every element it touches, this being a desire to assert their own control over heaven, or a realm upon a planet. As this narrative concludes, both their intertwining paths illuminate the devastating consequences of unchecked corruption and the far-reaching impact it can have on a world or a heaven surrounding them.

Ultimately, their intertwined fates serve as a cautionary tale of power, corruption, and the delicate balance between light and darkness in the cosmic order. At this point, it is safe to say that Opti is also beginning to take firm notice of Pesa's short-tempered behavior toward it, having as yet no idea as to the repulsion its kin has toward it, but sensing only that something very devilish has discovered Pesa … and so right is Opti.

On the edges of their shared horizon, there had been a day when Opti's shadow fell across Pesa's domain — not in trespass, but in passage. The beast's gaze had lifted, tracking that luminous form, a growl curling low and long in its chest. It had said nothing then. But in the echo of that silence, the void within Pesa's mind coiled tighter, savoring a patience it did not yet fully understand.

Pesa's father, however, knows by now that something is greatly amiss with his first child, as it is his divine insight that Pesa's behavior has everything to do with its grotesque mutation. Beautiful T'Naeva, Xionn still knows very well the magnitude of the evil that the King's angelic legions had soundly conquered and wiped off the face of his home world, eons before. That purely hateful and evil entity, the one known as Dia'Baal.

He is a presence of devouring control that Xionn himself will one day realize through personal tragedy and will on that day come to identify for certain, his fingerprint of death. But it will be much later, in an age and season of great sadness, that this mighty individual will finally discover that the word *normal*, or even somewhat, will never again apply to anything upon his world. On the surface, Pesa most certainly is able to put on a stunningly deceitful assurance in accepting Opti for who and what it is, to conceal the torture constantly rampaging throughout the void of its diseased rationale.

Deep down, however, Pesa has already come to realize that if it only appears that it has accepted the frustrations of this dark change, it would be able to justify its behavior and easily shift the blame back to its kin. With this in mind, the attitude inside this god of beasts has no say as to how it feels, since Pesa would most certainly be proven wrong in that respect. As I speak to you these words in love and hope, T'Naeva, keep in mind that your parent is now angry and completely fed up with its kin's divinely perfect mannerisms.

Also, this disease has affected only it and nothing else outside its tormented mind. The way Pesa visualizes its plight is simply this: Opti's saintly and undefiled presence has actually caused these terrible circumstances to begin with by stressing out nature's overall function to the imbalance of divinity, element against element, and created the horrific spectacle Pesa had now become. Every time Pesa broods on this thought, a low growl rumbles from its throat, dreaming darkly of unleashing ruin upon Opti.

It is only in these intense thoughts that Pesa already knows that its own extreme hatred, resentment, and yes, jealousy has totally filled it, and it is these things that complete the terrible maturity of your parent. You also need to understand that if given the opportunity, Pesa would have assuredly created havoc within Opti's domain, perhaps even attempting to destroy its more delicate nature.

Growing more bereaved and angered by the ever-increasing hostility of Pesa toward him and Opti, Xionn did not foresee this mysterious disease upon his child, or for that matter, the facts of this entire situation. It is now that I speak to you words of truth, dear mate, and those words are these:

*No matter how strong an individual's intelligence is within the cosmos, the mystery of its founding nature, now and then, finds a way to confound even the greatest of its inhabitants.*

    Xionn becomes a swift, whispering wind, soaring to the summit of the great mountain. There, upon its vast ledge, he reforms his body and gazes out over the world he so carefully shaped. Pondering deep and significant thoughts, Xionn gazes upon the fantastic expanse of his current home, reflecting on the decision he has made concerning his previous residence ages before. Now clearly seeing the terrible affliction raging through his beloved Pesa, he grows sorrowful, as the physical manifestation of his child's illness is at last revealed.

Xionn turns his gaze toward Opti's realm—still pristine, untouched by the sickness infecting Pesa's.. From upon his high perch, he sees the stark contrast of that unique nature compared to reality, and he realizes something has definitely gone awry with his Firstborne and needs to be fixed. Below, a small body of water catches the morning light in molten gold, perfectly mirroring the skies above Opti's realm. In Pesa's, its reflection is broken — the surface fractured by shadows, rippling with no wind, its stillness wrong in a way that whispers of decay.

The sight burns itself into Xionn's mind, an image too precise to dismiss as chance. The mountain air, thin and cool, whips around Xionn, carrying with it the scent of the forests far below and the faint murmurs of rivers winding through valleys. In this serene yet sorrowful moment, he closes his eyes and allows his mind to wander through the memories of Pesa's early days, a time when his creation roamed the world with joy and unbridled innocence. The transformation now before him seems all the more tragic when contrasted with those golden days.
He whispers to himself...

*"Where did I fail you, my beloved child?"*

In the ancient stillness of this moment, Xionn stands, his divine essence heavy with the weight of creation. Memories stir within him, sharp as blades, of the day he destroyed Harr'Manee—to *save* her. He alone had made that choice, to shatter and renew, to rebirth through destruction. The memory haunts him, a shadow etched deep into his eternal being, an ever-present reminder of the crushing burden borne alone by the Creator's hand—*his own*, weary yet unbroken.
He lifts a troubled gaze skyward, the vast expanse of the heavens stretching endlessly before him upon that great mount. His voice breaks the silence, steady, but tinged with an undercurrent of vulnerability.

*"I see Your essence, O, Great Companion, vast and eternal, one with the very spirit that is You. I understand now: it is Your will that makes me responsible for the fate of all You allow me to bring forth into existence. It is I, Xionn Theone, and no other,*

241

*who brought this beloved Earth from her shroud of darkness into your eternal light.*

*It is I, Xionn Theone, and no other, who bears the weight of her well-being. Her existence is tied to me, bound by the love I have poured into her. It is I, Xionn Theone, and no other, who filled her with abundance and life, and it is I alone who answers to You for her future."*

His voice falters, a ripple in the cosmic stillness, before steadying again.

*"I decree that never again will I extinguish any existence I have created. I am responsible for it, and I will see that all life upon her flourishes."*

The air grows thick with silence, the kind that seems alive, as if the universe listens for the response he needs in this moment. Just then, a thunderclap reverberates through the cosmos, rippling across the heavens of Earth in shimmering light. They echo with the sound, and the Companion speaks, His voice resonating with unshakable authority.

*… Xionn Theone, your decree is heard and bound. The Fates, silent weavers of My eternal threads, have taken note, and their cosmic loom begins its work. Your words now ripple across existence, shaping paths far beyond your sight. A thread has been spun—delicate, vital, and destined to bear fruit unforeseen.*

*… Xionn Theone, your covenant this day binds not only you, but those yet to come. An ideal still unformed will one day rise, born of mysteries hidden even from you. He will walk in the heartbeat of My Force and confront a trespasser who threatens that balance. You will not know this child, nor the time of his coming, but his purpose will entwine with the love you have declared this day.*

Xionn's brow furrows under the pull of distant stars.
*"I don't understand,"* he says, his voice quieter now.
*"How can I be held to a future I cannot see?"*

The Companion's voice softens, a gentle gust rolling across the void.

*… Xionn Theone, your responsibility lies not in knowing, but in trusting. It is love that binds your decree, but purpose that shapes the destiny of what you create. Walk forward with confidence, and know: you do not carry this burden alone. Trust in Me, Xionn Theone, and let this truth fortify you.*
*I will stand with you through every doubt. My strength will steady yours, for I am He who places providence upon a fingertip, balancing the fates of creation with infinite*

*care. For even they are but a sliver of* **Who ... I ... Am.**

The stars answer like a choir of cold fire, acknowledging what has begun. Bathed in their light—humbled yet resolute—Xionn feels the Companion's truth reverberate in his heart. The mystery of the unformed child and the unknown trespasser presses upon him: not a revelation, but a shadowed promise. He does not pretend to mastery; he stands as servant to a wisdom larger than his name, measuring his next breath against the love he owes the worlds. A thin wind crosses the firmament and returns without a sound, as if the heights themselves have withheld their counsel to hear his own.

Beneath that hush, a memory stirs—first light on uncarved waters, the day he spoke Opti and Pesa into being and felt the cosmos learn the difference between wonder and weight. Silence settles over the heights, a listening quiet that seems to weigh intent. Trusting the Companion's steady presence, Xionn turns to what must be done. Opti and Pesa are bound to him, and he to them, by a vow as old as their making. Calm gathers over the remnants of his haste, washing the sharp edges from his earlier resolve. He summons his children across the distances of mind.

They come to the *Sanctuary of Harmony*, a meadow of lucid quiet where light moves like water across the grasses and the low hills hold their breath. Thunder rolls once. Xionn descends as a brisk, radiant wind; in a shimmer he takes form—commanding and tender. The grasses lean toward him as if to listen; a ring of motes hangs in the air, steady as stars arranged at arm's length. Far off, a herd stills mid-step, noses lifted to the hush; nearer, a brook lowers its voice until each note becomes a bead of glass.
Perplexity glints in their vast regard, yet they feel the weight of his purpose, and even Pesa is briefly moved to awe. Xionn walks between them with deliberate steps, resolve bright on his face.

*"Mighty and beloved children,"* he says, *"hear me now."* His voice bears a maker's authority and a father's affection. He names their origin without boasting, confesses his division of Harmony into their two portions without regret, and anchors the act in goodness—for their maturity and the welfare

243

of all. As he speaks, the meadow seems to hold the truth; its quiet holds to pitch.

A petal breaks free from a high bloom and turns slowly, marking each word's descent into the earth. The decree hangs.

Opti's gaze, bright with the hunger to make and heal, softens—visions rise like bridges of light: broken paths mended, old wounds taught to sing, children of dust discovering that their dreams can carry weight. Colors gather at the edges of thought, daring themselves toward shapes. Pesa's gaze, forged for measure and guard, hardens. The hand that once steadied fledglings at the meadows lip now imagines a gate that never opens at all. Between them, breath becomes a boundary. Xionn sets a hand on each shoulder—weight, warmth, witness, and he speaks these words.

*"You are more than my creations. You are stewards of balance. Remember the love I poured into you; let that love be your strength."*

A breeze lifts the scent of blossoms. Beauty answers in these following words. *"Walk with wisdom, my love does not waver. My guidance stays near—even in silence."*

Above them, the stars pulse like oaths. They bow, and the cosmos bears the moment like a seal on wax. For an instant, even their shadows hold hands. What once burned in Pesa as primal loyalty hardens into arrogance. Noble instinct becomes a hollow echo, dear T'Naeva. Corruption long nursed reaches its crown: prejudice embedded deep, festering until it grips your beloved parent. It was not a single night, nor a single whisper, but a multitude of ages that this fury built. Comparisons came first—subtle, poisonous. Why should Opti be sung while Pesa is assumed, indeed.

Dia'Baal did not command; he suggested, pressing the bruise where honor lived until honor flinched. Suspicion was renamed *discernment*, cruelty *clarity*, contempt *courage*. What once guarded life's borders began to police the borders of love. Twice the path home trembled beneath Pesa's feet—when the Companion's hush reached the marrow, when Xionn's counsel fell like rain—yet Pesa chose the lie that strength must stand unchallenged. From that oath rose a creed of domination. Hatred overtook its mind. Long manipulation blinded Pesa to its own undoing. The rot finished; grace collapsed into a tyranny of thought and spirit suited to Dia'Baal's design.

The once-expansive mind of Pesa narrowed to one hunger: *rule*. Corruption rang through sinew and will, and the body answered. Majesty warped. Fur lifted like poisoned thorns; eyes burned bright with feral malice. Power twisted bone until Pesa mirrored the chaos it serves. Breath carried verdict; each tread the logic of conquest. Even the ground recoils—soil hardening beneath a will that no longer blessed. Pesa's essence has turned, casting a shadow over Earth's future and sealing a descent into living myth.

Meanwhile, Xionn—who formed Pesa as a paragon—grappled with his child's physical unmaking, blind to the rage within and to its vast consequence for the Realm of Reality. He remembered earlier days when Pesa's laughter set mountains in their places and Opti's songs taught rivers to turn. That memory held him; it also misled him. Love taught him patience, and patience, here, mistook rot for growth. He gave more of himself, loath to insult strength with cure. Yet beneath his hands, the pulse he once recognized learned a new rhythm—hard, efficient, emptied of mercy.

Even so, he would not withdraw his hand first. He spoke gentler counsels; Pesa heard them as weights. He offered rest; Pesa called it dullness. He named delight; Pesa counted its edges and found them soft. Then a sinister confirmation opened in the void of Pesa's mind; dark ears pricked. Xionn's voice, bearing love and authority, broke the hush.

*"To the both of you, my powerful children, my Almighty Companion has given me further understanding of this stern warning. He approves of these words and commands that I pass on to you. Remember them, live them, and obey them! Should either of you breach the other's realm, the power within the trespassed will rise against the intruder, for such is the nature of cosmic balance. The harmony between you is not merely for your own existence; it binds the very Force of Creation itself.*

*Even I do not know the full extent of this consequence, but I sense it will be absolute, and its ripples will spread far beyond what either of you can comprehend. Beware, then, my dear children, and fill yourselves with wisdom. For if this fearful conclusion comes upon either of you, it will not be confined to your domain alone. The actions of one will irrevocably alter the fate of the other and will shake the foundation of this world, shaping all things for the remainder of Earth's days.*

*I say in promise to you both, should this event come to pass, all things within this world will change, perhaps even crumble and fade into oblivion. And when the world is made whole once more, the trespasser will face a most unpleasant fate—one that echoes through eternity, a judgment born of the transgression they dared to commit."*

Silence receives the words. His gaze rests on them—stern compassion, a father's vigilance. Hope stands beside love like a steadying hand. The meadow, once tense, hums with reverence as his blessing settles across the grasses. The warning lingers—not a threat or a prophecy, but Creation's grammar—awaiting the choice that will decide whether music endures or memory bears the weight. A hush moves through the hills; birds tilt their heads and refuse to break it. Even the wind seems to learn restraint.

A white moth crosses the space between siblings and, finding no current fit to carry it, folds its passage into stillness. It is then a sinister confirmation opens in the void of Pesa's mind; its dark ears perk, and through this fissure, he slides in once more—silent as dusk, cold as prophecy. Dia'Baal speaks—not with sound, but with presence.

*"So. The King wraps chains in poetry once again, how quaint. Hear him—pleading with light and love through your dear father. He fears you, Pesa. That warning? It is not wisdom. It is a leash that you will break through me!"*

His voice coils tighter inside Pesa's skull, velvet with venom.

*"Xionn calls it balance. Harmony. A command to obey. But I name it clearly: Fear. The King's special pet tells you to preserve his world—and to protect his precious illusion. Do you see it now, o, precious mate?"*

A biting heat rises in Pesa's chest—different this time, yet familiar.

*"He says the power within the trespassed will rise? Then let it rise and may it rage. The cosmos is not this presumptuous fool's to ever threaten—it is yours to awaken. How dare he speak of ripples and consequence... but you, my chosen fury, are the wave. You are the fracture. Opti clings to false light. Xionn masks fear with a father's eyes. But you—you are the unspoken truth they dare not face. You are Reality. And I, Dia'Baal, am not your captor. I am your witness to greatness."*

*"Rage then into Opti's realm. Not in defiance—but in destiny. Let the music shatter. Let the stillness scream. The world will not crumble because of you—she will reveal herself instead, and when she does, you will stand untouched by judgment. Not as exile. Not as trespasser. But as the architect of what must come. This good father hesitates not because you are lost... but because it knows what you are, and soon, the wind will hurl your name into history like prophecy! Step. What he calls ruin my beautiful beast... you will call it reign!"*

Xionn rises from the Sanctuary; light trails him like a thought unfinished. T'Naeva exhales, her fingers loosening in Chimera's mane. The decree sits in her mind like an anchor. She glances to Opti, then to the place where Pesa once stood, and she feels the distance between them like a continent. Far off, the veil between realms gives a single shiver. It is only a change of air, a shift of light—gone as it came. They breathe. Yet in that instant, Opti's visage curls as if shaping a comfort not yet named; and Pesa's jaw sets, as if measuring a horizon that should need no walls.

Yet the meadow remembers it all. The Sanctuary of Harmony holds the warning as though the words were fused into its creation. High above, prophecy stirs, and the Companion's enigma sounds in Xionn's thoughts:

*...A child unformed, born of mysteries hidden, will arise. This child will confront the trespasser, restoring balance through a destiny not yet written.*

Xionn cannot grasp the weight of it, nor see how tightly it will bind to his decree. Still, the truth moves within him like a new dawn thrust through stone. In his wake, Opti and Pesa remain—their minds vast, balance delicate, paths wholly uncertain. Opti's gaze lingers on the meadow's edge where colors merge together; Pesa's gaze lingers on the same edge where lines go sharp. Between those gazes, a thin bright line appears—no wider than a breath, and as narrow as a vow. The heavens grow still.

From afar, Xionn watches with a heart both heavy and hopeful, trusting the Companion's wisdom in this moment. The burden of his covenant settles on him fully—and on all he has made—as Creation waits for what its children will truly become.

# *Verse XV:*
## The Beast Within: The Fall of Pesa

 s it turns toward Opti and gazes upon its sibling with only a stare of massive confusion, Pesa's rage and hatred are briefly subdued by their father's divine blessing as both gods turn and walk back to their homelands.

It is now that words of truth are again spoken, dear T'Naeva, and those words are these spoken through wisdom:

*"Even after receiving guidance, a child may choose to ignore a parent's authority. And when they do, the seeds of their eventual punishment begin to take root, maturing with the passage of time."*

Your parent Pesa, dear T'Naeva, still holds respect for its father as an entity wielding the greatest natural power it can conceive of. Yet though Pesa's essence has become diseased beyond mortal comprehension, its mind remains a prodigious force—acutely aware, highly rational, and immensely strategic. Nonetheless, the reverence once rooted in genuine love has long since fallen away, replaced by a hollow recognition of Xionn's power rather than a desire to honor or emulate it.

No wonder, then, that Pesa eventually disregards the feats of creation its father has performed throughout this season of maturity, for its own cynical logic, laced with Dia'Baal's poisonous influence, allows no room for awe. By now, Pesa believes it has surpassed even the father who birthed it. Stripped of warmth and empathy, your parent begins to see Xionn and Opti's accomplishments as trivial next to its own cunning genius. The raw Force of Reality, welded to a diseased mind, paves the way for unyielding arrogance.

Pesa thinks itself master of all, immune to weakness—especially the weakness of paternal obedience. But my dear companion, we have spoken so much of Pesa's inward corruption that I must now guide your eyes to its outward metamorphosis. This account is solemn, for the physical horror that befalls Pesa's once-glorious form stands as a testament to the viciousness of Dia'Baal's corruption.

There was a time, long ago, when Pesa radiated a majestic splendor, its visage reflecting a tranquil unity between Reality's raw might and the nurturing spirit of the Earth. Its presence exuded calm, a peaceful sovereignty recognized by all living creatures that dwelled beneath its mighty diamond archway. As darkness creeps into Pesa's heart, however, this gentle nobility begins to twist and morph. Subtle changes first appear: the sheen of its scales dulls; the once-lustrous eyes that surveyed Earth with benevolence grow keen and predatory.

Over ages of simmering resentment and manipulation, Pesa's body manifests the hatred festering within. Razor like talons arch savagely where once they guarded or built. Pesa's mighty wings, once serene, now bristle with cruel intent, flaring like weapons against the sky. Where once a regal aura of life and growth surrounded Pesa, a dark halo emerges—shadows clinging to its figure, as if the very light of day recoils from the deformity.

Perhaps most haunting is the silent rage etched into every aspect of Pesa's being, for though its voice still thunders over the land, the primeval affection it once held for Earth is replaced by an unsettling desire to command and control. Yet, as I behold this monstrous fall, a deeper revelation now burns within me, directly from my Companion. T'Naeva—this is one not of flesh or shadow, but of the eternal laws shaping all existence.

For in its corrupted mind I perceive not wisdom, but the narrowing void of *Ignorance*—an oblivion of vision that blinds even the mighty to truth. Once, your parent held Imagination's gift: the ability to envision what could be, to shape new wonders, to see beyond itself. Now, under Dia'Baal's stifling influence, it is a beast that sees only prey and predator, strength and submission—a creature of immense knowledge yet bereft of insight. In Opti, by contrast, Imagination breathes still. That wondrous sentinel peers into realms unseen, crafting life in defiance of despair.

It envisions possibility even amidst ruin. Thus, two eternal forces awaken here: the visionary spark that gives rise to creation, and the suffocating blindness that unravels it. Remember this, dear T'Naeva: where Imagination blooms, new worlds are born. But where Ignorance reigns, all that is vibrant withers into silence. Thus, T'Naeva, we behold the stark contrast between the Pesa who once walked in unity with a loving father, and the tragic beast now stricken by a poison from which it refuses to be healed.

Atom by atom, and over many ages of continuance, Pesa physically becomes much larger and stronger as its corruption strengthens in contrast to the divine beauty of its kin. The most disheartening transformation of abhorrence ever displayed on Earth, in a physical life-form, is brought upon this beast simply by hate—a hate that has become sown into the Earth herself. It is once more, dear T'Naeva, that I speak to you words of truth, and those words are these:

> *The attitude called hatred, if allowed to take its terrible root of influence upon an individual's mind, can very well become a permanent reminder of what happens if its contempt is unchecked.*

Having by this day long ago completely lost the majestic appeal of its appearance, Pesa's unblemished body has turned from the greatest in magnificence into that of the most unimaginable terror. I see once more the sheer horror of its physical form blasting through my mind, and my breath is short in response to the hideous void I personally experience within it. That loathing spirit of the one called Dia'Baal, by now having devoured the essence of what Pesa knew was right and just, has turned it into a god that is neither right nor just.

I again see this nightmare take shape, once more, and I quiver in that memory. Now frightening beyond measure, this great demon beast of Reality—the god known as Pesa—stands nearly fifteen feet at its shoulders, at this period in its ... mutation. The god of beasts, completely and utterly devoid of the sheer beauty it once possessed, now resembles the ghastly depiction of a beast of nature, a tiger—yet more than three times that size.

With the extremely uncharacteristic addition of four massive horns, two greater and two lesser, these imposing thorns of death align themselves into a horizontal bridge just above the aqua-hued malevolence of its large eyes.

*Oh … its eyes!*

Those large, horrific, aqua-blazing orbs of death, sharp and calculating, seeming to pierce the very essence of all they fixate upon. Each glance carries the weight of devastation, capable of inspiring fear even in the greatest of Earth's creatures. Its claws, capable of rending the strongest flesh and bone, only accentuate its overwhelming power. These razor-like extensions, sharp enough to carve through mountains, are a symbol of the monstrous corruption that has overtaken its soul.

Pesa's outward features merge elements of a tiger's majesty with the brute force of a bear, creating a form of unparalleled menace. This mighty *bearcat* of Reality, as I have come to describe it, has become the epitome of terror upon Earth. Its hulking frame radiates menace, a living monument to the horrors of unchecked malevolence. This immense terror of devilish flesh bears four great fangs (two greater and two lesser), each protruding with menacing precision from the sides of its gaping, foam-laced mouth.

Within this horrifying maw are rows of razor-sharp teeth, each engineered to crush, tear, and devour with supernatural ferocity. The sheer power contained within Pesa's jaws is known to every animal that walks the Earth, and none dare challenge it. But there is more, dear T'Naeva. The shimmering stripes of aqua hues upon its dark, pitch-black fur disguise the true nature of this sinister beast. Its fur, darker than the void of the cosmos, swallows light, creating a presence that seems to pull reality itself into its orbit.

These stripes, though seemingly beautiful, pulse with a deceptive energy, masking the void of corruption beneath. Even more chilling is the living mist that exudes from Pesa's being—a dark, foreboding aura that seems alive, writhing and slithering along its fur like serpents of shadow. This mist, born from the depths of its twisted pride and arrogance, becomes a warning to all who dare approach. The very air grows heavy around Pesa, as though the atmosphere itself recoils from its presence.

This dark aura, dear one, is the embodiment of Pesa's self-consumed pride. It is a force unto itself, a projection of the god's unchecked ego. Every living creature in its domain feels its oppressive weight. This nightmare of living shadow leaves no doubt: Pesa has become the literal definition of terror. At times, Pesa stands before its diamond archway, admiring its monstrous reflection. Vanity consumes it utterly; to Pesa, there is no greater form than the horror it has become. The archway, once a symbol of unity and grace, now bears silent witness to a being that has forsaken all that is good.

And again, we return to those haunting eyes. Once radiant and clear, they are now darkened windows into Dia'Baal's essence. Pulsing with aqua-hued pupils, they blaze with malevolence. The void within them reflects not just Pesa's own fall, but the consuming influence of Dia'Baal. These eyes, T'Naeva, are now voids of oblivion, endless wells of torment and rage. As the seasons of its corruption stretch on, Pesa's once-divine essence continues to decay.

The foundation of its being—crafted with love and care by its father—crumbles under the weight of Dia'Baal's influence. What remains is but a shadow of the majestic guardian it once was, a being consumed by hate and bound to the void. Yet through all this transformation, one truth remains. Pesa, despite its fall, is still a reflection of the power it once wielded for good. This corrupted god stands as a cautionary tale, a testament to the devastating effects of unchecked pride and hatred.

And so, my beloved T'Naeva, *it is the eyes that are a window to one's soul,* and by this final age of Pesa's dark maturity, Dia'Baal's terrible evil has completely dissolved the positive essence of the soul within your mighty parent. I recount these truths not to wound your spirit, but to prepare you, dear one. The beast you must one day face is not the parent you deserve; it is the adversary you have inherited.

May this knowledge fortify your resolve, and guard your mind, for the path ahead is fraught with darkness, and only light can overcome it. Perfectly formed by its loving father, this god of beasts is no longer perfect by any means, as its cancerous demeanor continues to mature for another age throughout Pesa's mind and body. With you, my dear bride, I also grieve this suffocating plight of your dear parent, and why it honestly had to be destroyed for the sake of this world.

Regardless of everything I have said in describing the way I saw and again see your parent, Pesa will always be the most powerful creature in the history of this world, at least to me. Still blessed with the entire body of knowledge of its physical world, centered within the scope of its natural one, the great beast is, in that distant day, the universal manifestation of a diseased nature. Through its vast yet depraved mind, the great beast certainly knows everything there is to know about how Reality and nature function.

Every natural wonder, every law, and every occurrence that unfolds across Earth, it knows too, that it alone stands as the eternal foundation of all things on this world, living and not. By now, Pesa has structured nearly all chemical and biological directives into its founding essence, allowing it to regenerate at will and appear as the most beautiful animal it could imagine itself to be—or, by the same token, transform into the embodiment of the most frightening life-form its diseased mind can conceive.

Yet dear T'Naeva, it is no longer content with mere beauty. Here in its final stage of dark maturity, Pesa channels its diseased imagination into forms that terrify rather than inspire, craving the power of fear as fuel for its pride. And so, Pesa has become the god of a new type of animal—one forged from a place of ravenous hunger and relentless fury, this fallen deity's own twisted invention: *the carnivore.*

Preferring the horrifying shape it now calls its own, Pesa transforms at will into that nightmare frame I have described to you, devouring its prey and thriving on the terror it instills in the lesser creatures of Earth. Your parent commands the weather itself. From the whisper of a breeze to a storm that tears the heavens asunder, Pesa shapes the skies with a single thought. It can summon downpours to drench the land, or call forth merciless winds that shred the forests as if with invisible claws.

Truly, Pesa's dominion over nature's founding elements—earth, air, fire, and water—can best be likened to a maelstrom, a cyclone of fury that leaves devastation in its wake whenever its temper flares. I now witness yet another age passing away, coursing onward throughout the season of Pesa's maturity, as the beast begins to see itself as far more important than anything else upon Earth.

This mindset is not content with mere independence; Pesa fiercely believes its sovereignty is absolute, and that it alone holds the right to wield its power without question. It is a force that Dia'Baal, lurking like a poison in Pesa's spirit, uses to command the mighty beast and maintain his grip on its soul. A void of malevolence emerges in Pesa's mind, echoing Dia'Baal's darkness. It festers like an open wound, fueling rage and arrogance until precious little humility remains.

Be warned, dear T'Naeva: that hateful void has now swelled to a size so large that it has nearly eclipsed all the gentle wisdom that Xionn, Pesa's father, once imparted. The repeated lessons of restraint and harmony Xionn sought to instill lie buried beneath an avalanche of contempt. As a creature of evolving nature, Pesa's primal instincts—like the hunt—become magnified in its pursuit of self-satisfaction. Hunting, once a mere skill, transforms into an obsession.

Though it needs no sustenance to survive, having been created pure, Pesa revels in the chase, the kill, and the gruesome triumph of dominating all life within its reach. I see Pesa's mania intensify as the final age of its maturity approaches. The beast's physical prowess, unmatched by any other force upon Earth, aligns with a violent and perpetually unsatisfied thirst for blood. Across every terrain it treads, from lush forests to barren peaks, the lesser creatures that dwell there learn to fear its presence.

Pesa's skill in stalking and cornering prey grows monstrous, an art refined to perfection as it tracks both the animals it once harmlessly guided and the life-forms gifted to Earth through Opti's realm of Imagination. Such hunts bring Pesa profound, twisted joy, for nothing incites its savage passions like outsmarting and overpowering the strange and vibrant creatures spawned by Imagination's life force.

In these chases, Pesa unleashes its formidable strength and cunning, testing the outer limits of its might upon unsuspecting targets. Each kill stands as another monument to its perceived supremacy, and a grim testament to how far it has fallen from the noble being it once was. As the final age of Pesa's maturity slides toward its inevitable close, the once-welcoming meadow that bridged Earth's realms becomes a primary domain of the beast's rule. Casting a dark gaze over its new territory, Pesa seizes control of the lands that were once sanctuaries of unity and peace.

The diamond archways symbolizing oneness now feel charged with tension, and those who wander near them can sense the deep rift forming. Wordlessly, Opti observes its kin from afar, sorrow welling within its vast and imaginative heart. It sees the unbridled ferocity and twisted emotions that corrode Pesa's spirit and laments what has been lost. Xionn, too, grows uneasy. Though the father of gods remains unaware of Dia'Baal's exact influence, he senses the twisted air around Pesa's domain, the snarling chaos born of a power once intended for harmony.

He notes the absence of Pesa's earlier gentleness and perceives its territory expanding beyond reason. Each time he endeavors to engage his beloved Firstborne, he is met with hostility or chilling silence. In response, Xionn contemplates the possibility that Pesa's "growing pains" may have reached a climax, certain that something must change before the entire planet succumbs to unrestrained turmoil.

Yet Pesa's ferocity only grows, stoked by the darkness that Dia'Baal feeds it in secret. It becomes a great cataclysmic force, forever prowling the boundary between Reality and Imagination with watchful malice. No longer content to remain within the boundaries of its original realm, Pesa hungers for more. A primal, restless part of its mind imagines crossing into Imagination outright, defying its father's decree and fulfilling the whispered promises of Dia'Baal to conquer that wondrous land as well.

In the echoes of time, I see these long hours of night stretched out over the meadow, where the once-vibrant flowers shrink away and the gentle creatures vanish under the constant threat of Pesa's wrath. With each passing day, the tension rises, an unspoken promise of conflict that trembles in the very air. The dynamic between Pesa and Opti—siblings born of Xionn's essence—teeters on a razor's edge, while the father grapples with growing alarm and heartbreak.
Still, he hopes, unwilling to believe that Pesa's darkness has become irredeemable. Through these uncertain days, Pesa's arrogance finds new fuel, its appetite for control further inflamed by the repeated success of the hunts and the fear it incites in all who cross its path. The force of Dia'Baal's cunning merges seamlessly with the beast's boundless pride, forging a monstrous will that casts aside familial ties and scorns the sacrifices made by its father.

Pride, indeed, becomes the center of Pesa's existence—a pride that cannot abide any challenge to its absolute reign. And so, T'Naeva, we come to understand just how far Pesa has fallen. This once-perfect child of Xionn now stalks the land like a living tempest, bringing ruination wherever it sets its claws. No longer bound by the love that created it, Pesa's mind spirals deeper into a twisted rationale, each day renewing its commitment to resist all who might remind it of what it once was.

In these closing days of its maturity, a lethal resolve takes shape: the unspoken vow that it will never bend a knee, not even to its father—nor to the sister realm of Imagination, nor to any living force, however noble or loving. The question that remains is how far this debased god will go before the realms themselves recoil, forcing a confrontation that not even Pesa can avoid. Xionn's sorrow grows with every sunrise that reveals further proof of Pesa's monstrous transformation. Opti stands in pained vigil, torn between loyalty and concern, and Dia'Baal lurks in the shadows, confident that his victory is near at hand.

Meanwhile, Earth itself shudders under the cold weight of Pesa's dominion, awaiting the day when this balance must at last be settled—no matter the cost. Truly, T'Naeva, Opti still honors its greater sibling with unabated reverence and refuses to intervene in Pesa's hunts in the meadow, because it feels it should not. Using instead its own undefiled wisdom on behalf of its own creations to stay as far away from the dark god as possible, Opti finally decides to appease the situation by only creating its own life-forms in its own realm.

With its peaceful intent never swayed towards its diseased kin, Opti knows it surely cannot protect the lifeforms it creates outside its protection, yet I now feel that it will only be a matter of time before it will completely change its mind and do something about Pesa's personal reign throughout the meadow. Currently though, Opti would also never dare confront its ominous kin face to face, knowing that Pesa's dark and haunting transformation has made it much more powerful.

Xionn, always a part of and aware of the happenings of his children, admires Opti for its wisdom to temper down this issue, even though he would personally like to see it stand stronger for itself and its own creations. He also believes at this time that Pesa, through its disheartening transformation, does not fully comprehend its actions and decides at this time against rebuking his child for its obvious and naturally evolving aggression.

Instead, and in loving reproach, Xionn warns Pesa that he forbids it to hunt its kin's creations within the meadow, lest it be punished if his wishes are not met. With this decision allowing Opti to resume creating its own life-forms in the meadow if it wishes, its confidence grows, along with a more focused purpose to make more inspiring life than before.

Sadly, however, I see that this edict by Xionn only proves to provoke Pesa's anger further, through Dia'Baal's rebellious influence, by denying it the pleasure to chase and hunt down Opti's creations for sport any longer.

Long in firm control of Pesa's mind, the master demon confides to its agitated thoughts those feelings to abide by its father's wishes.

*'Powerful yet naive beast, do you truly believe your father would punish a god? How dare he make these hollow threats, dictating what you can or cannot do! Your birthright demands respect, O, great Pesa—just as your belly demands sustenance and your world demands a master. And you o, mighty one are that master ... that god. Act like it! Do away with those who dare command you so blindly, for they make you appear as nothing but a fool!'*

With this decision made, the great beast does not do as it is asked and continues to hunt and harass Opti's creation as it sees fit.

Another long age passes across my eyes as I witness now that Xionn has allowed the divinely created vegetation within the meadow to become irresistible and delicious to only those life-forms created by Opti. In doing this, its created offspring becomes more agile, therefore making it more difficult for any creature to be caught in Pesa's hunts. Also, throughout this vision, I see Opti grow in wisdom and maturity while intervening more on behalf of its own creatures, despite the reverence it still holds towards Pesa.

This in turn, dear T'Naeva, allows Pesa to loathe its kin that much more. Given the fact that Opti still wisely refuses to confront it about its actions, the god of beasts becomes ever more agitated, wanting more to strike its kin down where it stands, innocent and oh so pure. Beginning to lose its ability to hide these intense feelings, Pesa becomes enraged every time it catches a glimpse of Opti in the meadow, as well as the fact that its superficial kin is now issuing a provocative threat to Pesa's way of life.

I see the great beast of Reality failing quite often on its hunts because of this increasing intervention by Opti. Certainly, from the warped perspective of this great beast, these creatures of Imagination, even though quite entertaining for the kill and very tasty (in a mildly sweet sort of way), are a fallacy, an entirely ridiculous waste of good life force. Also, with the sentinel of Imagination airborne much of each day to keep guard, Pesa's hunts upon these creatures have become nearly impossible, and its growing lust to draw blood upon that very cause comes to fruition.

An overcast and stormy day comes to focus within my eyes, and to me there is no doubt whatsoever that every remaining element of Pesa's goodness and impartiality toward Opti have finally disintegrated into oblivion. The darkened sky ripples with ominous energy as the winds weave sorrowful melodies through the trees. Truly, this god of beasts has now entirely succumbed to Dia'Baal's extremely powerful influence, annihilating all remaining tolerance towards its kin and its world.

The internal cancer of Pesa's brewing repulsion, this loathing of the very sight of Opti day in and day out, has built over many ages and finally succeeds in destroying the last remaining flicker of wisdom within Pesa's totally corrupted mind. As a result of that overcast and stormy day long ago, Pesa's crazed frustration distracts it in all attempts to hunt, and it ends the day without munching down upon a single morsel.

Having stayed awake very late into that warm, stormy evening, once Pesa finally lays down to rest, it is determined that it will end all of this nonsense one day by making the greatest kill of its life. The meadow around it shivers beneath the weight of its resolve, the once-vibrant flowers curling as if trying to shield themselves from the dark intent emanating from their guardian.

Very early the next morning, at the end of its season of maturity, Pesa awakens to a new and much darker world as the frigid essence of murder begins to manifest into the world surrounding it. The rising sun struggles to pierce the heavy clouds as thin beams of light streak weakly across the horizon. Rising to its feet and glaring with repulsion upon its sibling standing far off in the beautiful meadow, Pesa seethes in its new level of hatred, just as Opti instinctively turns toward its kin and notices right away the glare Pesa gives it.

The contrast between them is stark: Opti's feathers shimmer with radiant serenity, while Pesa's twisted form hums with barely contained wrath. Wishing once more to alleviate any potential engagement with its kin, Opti simply turns its back to Pesa, leaving the meadow completely as it returns through its archway to its own world.

I now hear the corrupted god of beasts... the plotting of its vicious homicidal thoughts as passionate breath keeps its steady flow beneath its four enormous razor-sharp fangs.

*'O, brazen kindred, how I long for that glorious day when opportunity comes to immerse my fangs with absolute delight, as I chomp down upon your bloodied and broken carcass.'*

Pesa snarls in disgust as its thoughts intensify upon its kin.

*'To you … oh pretty, delicate flower, I speak these words of my unyielding derision. For after I have leaped upon you and dissevered each of your fruitless petals, I shall sink my claws into your wretched blossom, only then to be free of your unfounded and deficient nature.'*

A sinister clamor of laughter reverberates through my ears as I hear these words as the void echoes through its host's immense and powerful jaws, well aware of what will eventually come upon the world. I hear Pesa conclude its thoughts in a rumbling and low-pitched growl.
"What sheer satisfaction this will add to my greatest desire, for surely as hell comes upon this place one day, it shall come to pass that I unsheathe thy fervent claws within the neck of you, my dear, dear kin."

Just now, I feel a surge of intense pain cascading through the dark recesses of Pesa's defiled mind as the great beast remembers the warning its father had given. The god shakes the pain from its head and sighs in response to this remembrance, and its intense anger diminishes.
"Curse the damned misery of it all, for what I feel within my head compares not to what I am feeling within my belly."

With that, the great beast lies in a bed of vegetation and does its best to relax as the corruption within it convulses the beast's stomach in severe hunger pains. As the early morning light filters through the dense canopy, the world awakens with a tentative stillness. Birds chirp cautiously, their melodies hesitant as though sensing the unrest in the land. Even the insects seem subdued, their usual hum fading beneath the heavy silence.

The early morning light of Luna awakens a fallen god, and again it moans in starving hunger, knowing it had better eat something soon after another very long and miserable night of unrest. The great beast shakes its body to deaden its pain, wanting more than ever to show Opti its serious-mindedness if it ever dares to interfere with its own progress of the hunt again. With a roar from the god of beasts, the air of its newly attained confidence is granted, and Pesa begins its morning hunt.

Leaping with resolve into the colorful grasses of the meadow, the god of beasts wants to make a statement very apparent in its first search of the day. Each step it takes seems to echo with a deliberate menace, as though the very earth recoils beneath its weight. The scent of prey sharpens its senses, fueling its resolve. The great beast swiftly comes upon the scent of its first meal in over a day, its nature taking charge as it immediately chases down and catches the little snack, pouncing swiftly upon its prey and making yet another perfect kill.

The air around the meadow stills as the life of the creature is snuffed out, its final cries swallowed by the oppressive silence that follows. For a moment, Pesa stands over its kill, its chest heaving with a mix of exertion and triumph. Immediately stuffing its mouth with the contents of its entire victim, Pesa takes no time to savor the creature and instead just crunches down, chews a few times, and swallows it whole with a big gulp. The taste, once a source of satisfaction, now serves only as a fleeting reprieve from its deeper hunger.

Belching loudly and grinning in a sinister release of stress, Pesa surges forward with awakened confidence and vaults into the meadow's clearing. It suddenly stops and gazes with an evil eye upon the massive archway of Imagination, its towering form casting a shadow that stretches unnaturally across the field. The archway, once a symbol of unity and coexistence, now stands as a silent challenge to Pesa's dominance. Its shimmering light reflects in Pesa's malevolent aqua-hued eyes, igniting a new wave of determination within the corrupted god.

In this moment, the air grows heavy, the atmosphere brimming with an unspoken tension. The meadow, once a place of life and vibrancy, seems to hold its breath, waiting for the inevitable clash that looms on the horizon. Its eyes shift downward from the structure when Opti, as if on cue, emerges in the far distance of the meadow and again sees it staring menacingly at it, truly a spectacle of worthlessness to this great beast as it attempts to show its dominance and provoke a fight with its kin.

Roaring its displeasure at seeing Opti, Pesa snarls while making sure that its flowery kin sees it lick its fangs. The great beast's antics are exaggerated, its large tongue trailing slowly across its jagged teeth with mock delight, a cruel performance meant to unsettle. Yet Opti remains undaunted. The mighty sentinel of Imagination walks slowly toward its sibling, each deliberate step brimming with grace, its radiant form a beacon of serenity in the tension-choked meadow.

Opti observes Pesa's every movement, its keen gaze unwavering. Though Pesa's horrifying glare could strike terror into any of nature's creatures, Opti remains calm, unshaken by the beast's fury. To Pesa's growing outrage, Opti's expression softens into one of amused indifference. With a lighthearted roar that echoes in joyous defiance, Opti turns its back, its feathers catching the weak sunlight and shimmering as if spun from starlight.

Then, as though adding insult to injury, Opti wiggles its feathered tail in a playful, almost dismissive gesture. A pulse like molten iron sears through Pesa's veins. In that instant, something inside fractures—not a break loud enough to shatter, but a quiet, irreversible snap. The insult will not fade; it will calcify, taking root in the deepest marrow of its being. This moment will be remembered in teeth and blood, a ledger entry written in rage and sealed for the day of reckoning.

Pesa's jaw literally drops at this display, its muscles tensing as if its very being could snap under the weight of its fury. To the god of beasts, this brazen performance is the gravest insult it has ever endured. A feral growl rumbles deep within its chest as it takes a step forward, the grasses beneath its paws flattening as though cowering beneath its wrath. The beast's thoughts seethe with a singular purpose: to obliterate the source of this unbearable mockery.

As it swiftly advances, Pesa's glare burns with scorching intensity, its aqua-hued eyes narrowing to dangerous slits. It wants nothing more than to leap forward, to silence its kin's perceived impudence in a storm of fury and blood. Yet Opti remains unaware of the depth of Pesa's murderous thoughts, its attention now turned skyward as it unfurls its wings and prepares to return to its archway. As Opti ascends, its serene silhouette framed against the pale sky, Pesa's simmering hatred festers.

Its limbs tremble with the effort to restrain itself from pursuing its sibling.

Instead, the god of beasts channels its rage into its next hunt, desperate to release the violent storm brewing within. The beast's displeasure remains palpable as it stalks the tall grasses of the meadow, every step betraying its dark intent. It soon catches sight of an innocent *Neoncub*, a charming, luminescent little creature that has wandered too far from the protective embrace of its mother.

The cub's bio-luminescent stripes pulse softly, a beacon of vulnerability against the backdrop of chaos.

Pesa lowers its body, its muscles coiling with predatory precision as it creeps toward its unsuspecting prey. This unfortunate little creature, luckily oblivious to its impending death, sniffs the air curiously. With a sudden, explosive leap, Pesa closes the distance, trapping the tiny creature against a large stone. For a brief moment, it toys with its prey, batting it gently with a massive paw. The cub lets out a soft, frightened chirp, its innocence only serving to further ignite Pesa's malevolence.

My heart twists as I witness this cruel display. Pesa's gaze sharpens, and with a flash of raw nature, its jaws snap open, clamping down upon the cub's soft body. The creature's glow flickers and fades as life departs from its form. The meadow falls silent once more. Having abruptly returned the cub to the elements from which it was formed, Pesa does not devour it completely. This cruel act indeed, dear T'Naeva, was not born out of Pesa's hunger, but a more sinister act, called *spite*.

Once, in an age now almost forgotten, Pesa had lowered its head to nudge a trembling fawn toward safety, guarding it from the shadows until dawn. That memory is gone from its heart but not from the earth; the soil beneath still holds the imprint of its once-gentle paw. Now, that same paw drips with the lifeblood of innocence, and the meadow seems to shrink from the touch that once offered shelter.

Spitting the torn remnants of the cub onto the ground, Pesa licks its neon-stained fangs, each swipe of its tongue slow and deliberate, as if savoring the blood of innocent youth. In that fleeting moment, Dia'Baal's essence pulses within the beast, his satisfaction unmistakable. A deep belch echoes like thunder across the clearing, a grotesque declaration of triumph. Pesa hums to itself, a low, ominous tune that reverberates through the grasses.

Alas, dear T'Naeva, when innocence is devoured, vengeance takes root. In this dark shadow of creation, I hear Pesa hum a lullaby that the very stars were never meant to hear. This damn *beast*, the sheer malevolence trailing behind it like a dark omen as it disappears into the thick vegetation.

To thee, it be such a decadent treat...
To savor so sweet, so innocent thy meat.

For once tender virtue is lost to thy thirst...
I shall stalk thee again, in darkened haste.

For many more shall I seek... and eat...
Until innocence itself lies slain at my feet.

And then I hear Dia'Baal speak. A cold, derisive whisper slithering through Pesa's mind—his voice rising above even Pesa's delight. This indulgent act, though satisfying, is but only a ripple.

Truly dear T'Naeva, this moment is all about *him*.

*Ah...O, pet of mine, thy hunger sings true...*
*But never forget who first fed you.*

*No cradle nor prayer shall keep them from me...*
*No angel shall hear their pitiful plea.*

*For mercy is hollow, and our passion is one...*
*When my will becomes yours... as never undone.*

*The laughter, once light, now curdles with cries...*
*As I carve out their hope and feast on their lies.*

*You hum as you kill—how quaint, how divine...*
*But the requiem written in blood... is nothing but mine.*

*So feast, dear beast, and roam as you will...*
*Yet I am the hunger no kill can fulfill.*

*'So you think this thirst is yours alone, dear Pesa... O, how quaint. No—this thirst was sung into the first darkness, before the stars took their place under His damned tortuous heel. Each drop of fear you taste is but a verse in my whispers endless hymn. Drink deeply my beloved pet, for every kill is but a note, and every note you hum to your passion's delight binds you tighter to this song you no longer can resist.*

*For I am the bane that Harmony shunned...*
*And I shall not rest... until all is undone.*

Thus, dear one, Dia'Baal alone reclaims the silence. Not with thunder or fire, but with his whisper so bitter, yet so intense, it tastes like the ashes of a lost soul. Even Pesa, deep in the brush, lowers its head in reverence—knowing it is powerful... but not *supreme*. That title alone belongs to the *first whisper*. The meadow breathes again, its rhythm is slower, burdened by the tragedy that has unfolded—its silence steeped in sorrow.

Near the diamond archway of Reality, a mother's grief hangs in the air like a trembling whisper as she finds the remains of her cub. Her cries, soft yet sharp, cut through the tranquility, stirring echoes of sorrow that ripple through the tall grasses. Opti, having come further into the meadow and now within earshot, lowers its radiant face in sorrow, realizing that once again, another one of its inspired creations has met its untimely fate to an *animal* that delights in murder.

Continuing through these images brought to me by my Companion, I gaze opposite the great diamond archway adorning the entrance to the Realm of Reality, and even farther, beyond the beautiful meadow containing the Sanctuary of Harmony. It is here that I gaze upon the awe-inspiring sentinel of Imagination, the god of creatures, named Opti—a god in truth, still poised in all its divine glory, and the very same, dearest T'Naeva, to whom I call... *my own beloved parent.*

The meadow remains still, its flowers swaying gently, as though lamenting the scene that has just played out. Shadows lengthen in the light of a fading sun, casting silhouettes across the land. The hum of Opti's wings carries a wordless vow—to guard what remains. Amid the darkness, a sliver of hope still dares to shimmer.

# *Verse XVI:*
# The Burning Crown: Opti's Ascension

n anxious gasp of disbelief quakes the air as the goddess shudders in amazement, and she wants immediate answers, but receives none. All she knows as truth in this moment is that D'Reem is Opti's offspring.

To her, the plot has thickened as the great warrior's eyes, still aglow, continues his story without emotion. I turn and gaze skyward upon the magnificent archway of energy entering Opti's realm and then look outward ... deep into the golden-hued heavens of its world. I again see my parent standing firm yet humble, for divinity still fills its every orb of existence. The sentinel of Imagination holds the meadow's crest; its sapphire violet hued eyes set toward the distant diamond archway of its kin.

For a heartbeat, a storm stirs within it—a desire to bare its enormous fangs in frustration at the silent meadow. But before such a shadow can form, righteousness sweeps through its mind like a cleansing wind, shattering this thought into nothingness. Here, no polluted actions can take root as every fiber of its body is bound to a higher purpose. Even in stillness, it radiates the assurance of divinity, untouched by the laws that bind Pesa's corrupted form.

I am so fortunate to observe once more this beautiful and dignified creature in all its glory, and I realize quickly that the physical laws of chemistry that

265

govern Pesa's existence do not apply to Opti. The stunning bulk of my parent, now entering the dawn of its own coming maturity, is indeed much less formidable than that of its diseased kin, standing only twelve feet at its shoulders.

Just as it has been created as its father intended, Opti's every thought and act is still completely divine; thus, there is no need to show any aggressive characteristics whatsoever, whether they be in form or function. Yet it is not weakness that defines this restraint, dear T'Naeva, but strength beyond reckoning—a force that exudes serenity, even when provoked. Yet somewhere beyond the horizon, a force stirs that will not greet this maturity with awe, but with hunger.

This majestic creature, still perfectly unchanged since the day of its creation, can best be described as the unification of a colossal white lion, its golden-hued mane, crowned with the wings, tail, and talons of an eagle.

Its feathers catch the breeze like polished ivory, radiating purpose and elegance, a reflection of its unbreakable connection to its fathers will. Its mighty wings unfurl, their shadow rolling across the meadow in quiet proclamation of its place in the cosmic order. In this early dawn of maturity, it is already certain that it will match and one day surpass its sibling. Pesa has not yet seen this form, but when it does, the strands of fate will tighten toward a reckoning whispered through the ages.

For now, Opti's only purpose is creation, not conflict. Embodied from the *Force of Imagination* by its father, this mighty creature has brought into physical existence *five hundred billion* different species of flora, food, and creature, both of breathtaking uniqueness, born not to dominate but to bask in everlasting life and serenity. Around them, the *Realm of Imagination* thrives beyond a level unimaginable, a boundless dreamscape of wonder that truly defies mortal comprehension.

The skies above the realm swirl in colors and abstractions that exist in no other place in the cosmos. Rivers of liquid stardust curve in patterns like celestial calligraphy, its forests hum with shades only the divine can see. Yet even in this perfection, a question grows — not in dissatisfaction, but in yearning. In the quiet spaces between its works, Opti wonders what lies beyond the dreamlike beauty of its creations. It knows Imagination to be infinite, flowing without boundary, but also fleeting.

What if the dream could be anchored, its brilliance preserved beyond the moment of its conception? Slowly, this longing gathers force, a tide pulling Opti toward the structured and immutable essence of the Force of Reality. Its reflections are not born from dissatisfaction, but from an innate desire to deepen its understanding of creation's true balance. D'Reem pauses in his recollection, his gaze somber as he describes this pivotal moment in his parent's journey.

To Opti, creation is a song—a beautiful melody played with unyielding harmony. Yet as with all songs, there comes a time when the key must shift for the melody to evolve. Opti's desire to expand its comprehension is not a flaw, but a calling—a sign that maturity requires embracing the unknown, even if that unknown is daunting.

Returning to the narrative, D'Reem continues.

The early morning awakens as the sphere of fire and light casts a golden haze across the meadow and the child approaches its divine parent, its voice carrying the weight of reverence and the quiet tremor of uncertainty. The god of creatures speaks with reverence, but also with an undercurrent of uncertainty.
"Father, I wish to know what lies beyond what I create. I long to understand the essence of Reality, so that I may grow as you intended."
Xionn's form shimmers with quiet power as he turns to gaze upon his child. For many long moments, silence reigns between father and creation, the meadow itself holding its breath in what words will be spoken next.

Then, with a voice both solemn and kind, I hear him reply.

*"It is good that you seek understanding, Opti," Xionn says at last, his voice rich with both pride and caution. "The pursuit of knowledge is a sacred path. Yet wisdom is not in the hoarding of what you know, but in the harmony between what you know and what remains unknown. Reality grants form and permanence, but demands patience, humility, and strength. It binds with laws, and those laws carry weight when broken.*

*Some truths will forever remain beyond your grasp — accepting this is part of wisdom. Harmony is not achieved by mastering one force, but by revering them all, the two bound together by the force of love, one which never forces itself upon any other."*

Opti's gaze brightens, seeing the cycle clearly: Imagination's fleeting grace feeding Reality's enduring form, and Reality offering ground for Imagination to bloom. Xionn warns of imbalance, his voice marked by old wounds.

*"Imagination without grounding eventually drifts into chaos, dear child. Nature without inspiration decays into stillness. While Imagination is boundless, it is also fleeting; its beauty lies in its ephemeral ways. Reality, though rigid, provides the foundation upon which enduring beauty can be built. You need to learn how to yield to them both, but also when to stand firm in action if they become imbalanced.*
*These are not simple words from theory dear Opti, but from eons of trials thrust against my very soul, ones I have witnessed in this imbalance that can shatter entire worlds."*

My grand old father then reveals another truth—the Force of Reality matures *seven times faster* than the Force of Imagination. Yes my dear, Pesa's rapid maturity is not a gift but a blade dulled by arrogance, twisted by Dia'Baal's corruption, as you will discover in time. And so, while your kin's swiftness may seem an advantage, know that such speed, in the wrong heart, becomes a weapon sharpened before its wielder understands its weight.

In this moment, Opti knows its journey to maturity will be long, and it will be earned step by step. It then bows low, its shimmering golden mane lightly brushing the earth.

*"I will learn all these things father. I promise to yield when I must, but also to stand firm when I must. I promise to use the force of Reality not to destroy, but to preserve all life."*

The vow of this mighty creature moves the meadow—flowers bend low, and the wind rolls like a sigh of relief. Xionn lays a radiant hand upon its mane, sealing its promise with a wide smile. Xionn, ever the wise father and counselor, tells Opti that to mature correctly, one must not only embrace their foundation, but also remain humble in the face of its eventual mastery. Opti listens intently, its sparkling eyes bright with fascination.
For the first time in its life, it begins to grasp the true complexities of existence itself, because there are so, so many. Xionn's voice carries both pride and caution as he continues.

*"With all these things understood, beloved Opti, I now begin to teach you the mysteries of your kindred force. But first, I need you to always remember this. Maturity is not measured by power or knowledge alone, but by the courage to seek out truth, even those that are hidden and submerged within the tides of discord."*

On that day of destiny so long ago, Opti pledges to walk the path of balance. It vows to learn, and to change, to harmonize and to yield its divine purpose with all the lessons Reality will have to offer. The meadow in D'Reem's vision sways gently, as though the very fabric of creation responds to this vow. The song seems richer, the sunlight warmer—a testament to the gravity of Opti's choice. Xionn's expression softens further as he places a radiant hand upon Opti's mane and smiles.

D'Reem's voice trembles slightly as he adds, "and it is this moment that is etched into the very essence of Imagination—a reminder that the journey toward harmony is always the highest form of devotion. D'Reem pauses, his gaze cool, the weight of Xionn's honoring his beloved parent etched forever into his steady voice. Xionn's words this day are not only lessons; they are warnings born of his many sorrows. He knew these dangers of imbalance quite well because he almost saw them tear his own world apart.

Opti's heart swells with understanding as its father imparts these brutal truths and its own wisdom begins to grow. Yet with understanding comes a bittersweet realization: the journey to true maturity also requires *sacrifice*. Opti must now begin to relinquish the comfort of its ordained familiarity and embrace all the weaknesses within the unknown, to become even stronger within itself.

An age flows across my eyes, and I see Opti increase its knowledge by leaps and bounds, learning the more sophisticated traits of the force called Reality within its undefiled mind. This newfound comprehension fills its being with both reverence and purpose. Unlike Pesa, who has now taken its own abilities completely for granted, Opti revels in the journey rather than the destination. It savors each moment of insight, weaving these fragments of understanding into a tapestry of enlightenment.

It is during this time of learning that Opti comes to have a much greater appreciation for the Force of Reality's unequaled power. It begins to comprehend that every element of creation exists in a delicate equilibrium between destruction and renewal, chaos and order. Where Pesa only sees power to *dominate*, Opti perceives its opposite effect - to *nurture*.

One bright day in the mid season of its maturity, Opti finally observes its father creating from himself: the *atom*, the most basic and undefiled foundation from which all Reality upon Earth and the cosmos derives. Xionn's act is deliberate and profound, a quiet reminder that even the grandest realities begin with something small and pure. The moment pulses with significance as Opti watches the birth of something so essential yet infinitely vast in potential.

Truly, the knowledge of Gaea herself starts to grow a presence within Opti's opening mind and begins to significantly alter the way its own pristine existence unfolds from this day forward. What a maturity it will become! Opti watches in awe as the atom pulses with a life that seems simple, yet holds infinite complexity. It recognizes that this particle is not merely a building block, but a testament to the interconnectedness of all creation, a reflection of the divine balance that sustains life.

As the lesson unfolds, Xionn explains the trifecta of perfectly balanced forces—Harmony, or The Divine Force, alongside the Forces of Reality and Imagination. These forces, once perfectly merged, began to mature separately, becoming distinct entities with unique roles. Their separation was necessary to preserve the balance of Harmony, for the differing natures of Reality and Imagination had begun to decay their union.

Xionn, with wisdom beyond measure, understood that if Reality had been evenly distributed across Earth without balance, Imagination would have faltered, unable to mature and thrive. To protect both, Xionn crafted a deliberate imbalance, making the Force of Reality the world's foundation, while tempering its potency in the Realm of Imagination. This decision ensured that Imagination could weave its wonders into Reality without unraveling.

A most glorious day passes across my eyes as I see that Reality's founding component, the atom, is finally entrusted to Opti. With reverence, my parent realizes that the natural and fundamentally established atom of Reality can be successfully altered only if it is properly unified with a divinely bearing orb created from the Force of Imagination. Opti roars with excitement, its mind ignited by the mysteries of nature that now seem within reach.

Endless possibilities unravel before it, forming constellations of thought and invention. Another age passes, and Opti's mere curiosity has become its life of devotion. Through a multitude of lessons about how nature thrives, Opti will soon end its study in the Force of Reality through its father—not to reclaim it from Pesa, but to understand how its dance of limits and possibilities can be unified with its own contributions.

Yet as D'Reem recounts those many pivotal ages of passing through his mind, he cannot ignore the shadow of contrast that looms behind them. Pesa, consumed by its pride, refuses such wisdom. To Pesa, growth is synonymous with dominance, and understanding is a sign of weakness. Pesa believes that to question its nature is to admit inferiority.
D'Reem laments.
"In its mind, strength lies in absolute certainty, even if that certainty is born of ignorance."

The meadow's ambiance shifts as D'Reem speaks of his kin's tragic path. The flowers seem to bow under an unseen weight, their vibrant colors dimmed by the sorrow that permeates the air. Xionn's teachings reach their crescendo as he imparts his final lesson to Opti across these many ages.

*"True balance is achieved not when one force conquers the other, but when both elevate the other to something far greater than its own singular cosmic existence."*

Xionn gestures to the sky where the golden hues of day blend seamlessly into the indigo of dusk.

*"Look to the horizons to your left and then to your right, my child—where light and shadow meet in the presence of both dawn and dusk. Neither overwhelms the other, yet together, they create the most beautiful parts of the day."*

Opti gazes upward, its wings unfurling slightly as it absorbs this profound truth. *'I will remember because I see it so clearly now, thank you dear father,'* it whispers, a promise woven forever into its being.

D'Reem's vision shifts back to T'Naeva, his eyes reflecting the weight of his story. Opti chose humility and growth, while Pesa chose pride and stagnation. That choice, dear T'Naeva, shaped the fates of both realms. He breathes deeply, his voice steady once more. And so, Opti now begins its journey toward true balance, armed not with certainty, but with a willingness to embrace the unknown.
The meadow around them seems to breathe in harmony with D'Reem's words, its gentle sway, a quiet affirmation to the power of understanding.
"Let this be a lesson to all who seek to mature," D'Reem concludes, "for the path to balance is not an easy one, but it is the only path that leads to true

creation."

Then comes the day that Opti has finally mastered sculpting the foundational aspects of Reality's basic atomic chemistry, further understanding that even though nature seems to it extremely vague and somewhat uninteresting *externally*, it is vastly more complex than its own force of Imagination *internally*. Opti marvels at how these simplest of elements weave together to form intricate systems, each part a note in the grand symphony of existence. These systems are more than mere structures; they pulse with intention, motion, and connection.

Each atom dances to the rhythm of Reality's heartbeat, and Opti's awe deepens with every new and personal discovery it makes. The passions of my parent reignite as this newfound comprehension becomes the heart of its focus. With this knowledge, Opti begins to experiment, striving to recreate nature's atom with its own imaginative enhancements. Its ideas surge like oceans of inspiration as it ponders how this universal atomic particle could integrate seamlessly with its own divine foundation.

It is then that Opti's final age of maturity begins when it retreats into the heart of its wild kingdom, seeking solitude, experimentation, and reflection. In the sanctity of its realm, it immerses itself in study, reaching deeper into the motivations that have shaped its existence. It envisions a union between Reality and Imagination so profound that it could reshape the boundaries of what is possible.
In its seclusion, Opti meticulously reexamines and deciphers the mysteries of Reality, one elemental and chemical process at a time. It is also very cautious, knowing that the slightest error could unravel its work, but it is resolute.

What some might see as obstacles, Opti views as opportunities for growth. With its father's eons of creational wisdom now its own, my powerful parent begins to wield all ninety-four of nature's elements to create new life upon Earth. It begins simply, crafting life-forms of humble design, yet as its final age of maturity passes by, its creations grow more intricate, each one a testament to its evolving mastery. Opti learns not only what works, but also why some attempts fail, gaining insights that sharpen its creative instincts. Eventually, Opti reaches the pinnacle of its experimentation: testing all of these motivations and theories directly upon itself.

This is not an act of pride, but of belief in the principle that a creator must truly embody the truths they seek to realize. It dissects its divine form, orb by countless golden-hued orb, while merging them with nature's atom until their union becomes something novel: a fusion of Reality's substance and Imagination's spirit. On the day of its transformation's completion, the realm of Imagination bears witness to an unprecedented sight and Opti emerges not merely as a god of creation, but as a living embodiment of perfectly fused and harmonious existence.

Its form radiates a newfound strength, not born of conquest, but of understanding. Despite its newfound power, Opti remains devoted to creation over conflict. It chooses not to confront Pesa, for it understands that true strength lies in resisting the urge to dominate. Instead, Opti focuses on crafting life with an unparalleled fervor, determined to fill its realm even more with wonder and resilience. It is this day I now observe when Opti triumphantly returns to the meadow after a ten thousand year hiatus, and its arrival is a moment of awe.

The radiant figure that steps forth is no longer just the god of creatures, but a testament to divine grandeur and evolution. Even the meadow, ageless in its serenity, seems to lean closer, as though the land itself wishes to witness what Xionn's hands have shaped. Xionn and even Pesa pause, caught in the gravity of what Opti has become. As I watch, I know this truth: Opti's journey is not simply one of knowledge, but of purpose.
It is a reminder that even in a world shaped by imbalance and strife, harmony can still be cultivated through patience, humility, and unwavering resolve. Opti's stunning maturity is noticed indeed, as is the true strength of my parent, and what a sight of wonder it is to behold my glorious parent in this moment I once again dwell!

Xionn, without interference, yet having pondered countless thoughts as to what had become of his second child, knows well what has transpired as he rushes to greet Opti's fascinating evolution, observing it in wonder for a long period of time. With great approval, I hear him speak to his matured child these joyful words.

*"Mighty Opti, what has become of you captivates me! Verily I say to you, by your own passions, you have discovered and brought to your existence that which is the foundation of your kin, Pesa, showing no ill effects in your splendid maturity.*
*O, great child of inspiration, you have most certainly grown in a marvelous way, and may my complete acceptance of your maturity cloak you in comfort, as you are now more like your kin in ways that even I could have never thought possible. You are an inspiration to us all!"*

Kneeling before its father in respect, Opti lifts its richly bronzed face close to Xionn's, nudging it lovingly. I see Xionn embrace his child's bright face tenderly as it speaks with a profound, strengthened tone.

*"Father, you alone are the one to acknowledge, and if it were not for you, I would still be a mere child in maturity and knowledge, but no longer am I that child. It is you who has brought me into completion, and for that, I am truly blessed by you."*

That, my dear T'Naeva, is when Pesa, while in the heat of a hunt and chase, emerges through its diamond archway and sees my parent for the first time... in a *very* long time. Raising its eyes to focus upon a strange scene of its father beneath the archway of Imagination, the great beast suddenly breaks off its fervent pursuit of prey. I see Pesa jolt to a bone-crushing halt in astonishment as it looks on with alarm upon its father and what has so casually returned to live among them.

For now, Pesa notices from afar Opti's magnificent return, as well as what it has now become in its ages of solitude. From the tangled concealment of high grasses and twisted vines, Pesa's molten eyes track every movement of its kin. At first, it is frozen, the great bulk of its form pressed low to the earth as if proximity alone might trigger calamity. Breath comes in sharp bursts, each exhale forcing a shiver down its spine.

The meadow's warmth and the realm's radiant colors feel muted, as though Opti's presence has stolen the light from everything else. The god of beasts does not move — it studies. The once snow-white frame it remembers is gone, replaced by molten gold streaked with living crimson, each pulse rippling through Opti's body like a heartbeat drawn from the core of a newborn star.

The tail it once mocked as clumsy now swings like a sculpted scythe of living armor, each plate fitted with predatory precision. Pesa imagines the blow — the sound of bone shattering — and its claws dig deeper into the soil. Dia'Baal's voice slides into its mind, slow and deliberate.

*'Gaze upon your kin, o mighty brute, and see the insult laid before you. That armor is not for beauty — it is a weapon forged in patience, perfected in solitude. One strike could end you. Tell me, beast, does your throne feel steady beneath you now? Never would I have surmised that you, the greatest of all sentient life upon this world, would ever cower to your lowly kin! Yet this is exactly what you are doing!'*

The words are poison wrapped in silk. Pesa clenches its jaw, the muscles along its neck knotting as it fights the instinct to recoil further. The image Dia'Baal paints lingers — not as a warning, but as an invitation. Pesa can almost feel the armored tail connecting with its skull, a phantom blow echoing with the weight of humiliation.

Its breathing grows ragged. The air feels heavier, each inhalation dragging like water through reeds. Shadows seem to lengthen around it, folding in closer. Opti roars above, and the sound — deeper and more resonant than any memory — rakes through Pesa's bones, vibrating until its legs threaten to buckle. It grits its teeth, forcing its head to lift, staring with unblinking eyes at the figure wheeling in the sky.

Dia'Baal presses harder, his tone sharpened to a blade's edge.

*"This is not fear you feel — it is recognition. Your kin has become your equal… perhaps even your better. I will not have you kneel to any creature. I will fan this ember in you until it consumes every trace of restraint you have left."*

Pesa's muscles twitch involuntarily, its claws flexing in the soil. Its heart pounds faster, each beat pounding against its ribs like a war drum. It watches Opti bank through the clouds, golden flares trailing behind like ribbons of fire. The beauty of it twists something deep within — awe strangled by envy. That glow, that harmony, is a kind of power Pesa has never sought, and therefore never claimed.

In that absence, hatred takes root. The meadow's warmth, the air's gentle hum—all fade to a hollow silence in its mind, replaced by a slow, suffocating drumbeat. The god of beasts does not even realize it has stopped breathing until its lungs burn.
"Indeed, O, matured kin, you need not prove to me that I alone have become a frightened little blossom in this moment, as I have quite easily proven that myself, thank you."

The god of beasts rises slowly, muscles taut, head lowered. It cannot — will not — reveal itself, but neither will it retreat far. This vision will be etched into its mind, burned in as a promise. Opti's growth is not a marvel to be admired; it is a challenge to be crushed. The hunt, Pesa knows, will not begin today — but the day it begins, it will not end until the earth itself drinks deep. Somewhere within, Dia'Baal smiles, for he knows the path forward will lead not to balance, but to blood.

The essence of Dia'Baal responds harshly.

*"Indeed, Pesa, this is certainly a most splendid maturity in your kin, is it not? So many of these very same exquisite and rugged attributes come to equal even yours. I daresay further that they are even greater in similarity to yours, wouldn't you agree ... you cowardly beast of a god!*

*Is this the attitude of such a powerful brute, who responds to its younger sibling in this recoiling, pathetic show of weakness? Is this the attitude that you, the greatest of all life on the face of this planet, now embody? You do not realize that I, too, sense your immediate trepidation. So, I will allow you to contemplate this feeling with a little reminder to help you come to your senses."*

Without hesitation, I feel an intense stabbing pain rush through the mind of your possessed parent as it comes quickly to its senses, punished by Dia'Baal for its display of cowardice. Pesa wildly shakes its head as it roars, and the pain is quickly defeated. Yet Pesa still takes extreme caution in what it observes and cannot seem to believe what it is witnessing only a few short miles away. The great beast, still upon its belly, then rolls to its back, staring blindly skyward as it contemplates the reason for this far-off reunion of its father and Opti.

Pesa, already having calculated Opti's evolved bulk to be a mere inch lesser than its own current stature of sixteen feet tall, continues to shake its head in bewilderment. If this fact alone would not have inspired your diseased parent to immediately start changing its dark attitude, then perhaps its next series of observations of Opti would. Gradually returning to its feet, Pesa's supernatural focus again views Opti's massive shimmering frame, but is abruptly obscured by an intense flare of golden-hued energy that shoots throughout its kin's body.

This is when Pesa's void begins to erupt into waves of alarm, and its body starts to spasm. Now definitely taking notice of Opti's newfound magnificence, Pesa continues to observe its kin in distress, shaking its body many times to deaden its trembles as it rises to its feet. Having now caught its breath a second, and even a third time, Pesa closes its eyes and stands frozen for many silent moments, until it finally gathers enough courage to gaze upon its matured kin once more.

This time, however, Pesa's panic is replaced by sheer fascination at to what its kin has truly become. The pure and innocent snow-white color of Opti's body has completely dissolved from existence. In its place is a molten-gold radiance arisen with crimson flames that ripple across its chiseled body like the heartbeat of a newborn star. It is those very same hues of color that course throughout the heavens above the Realm of Imagination that Pesa also sees in Opti's face—hues it has never observed. It is the same hue that once danced above their shared cradle of creation — but now it burns on the body of a rival.

As it is still attempting to comprehend its kin and the incredible renewal of its body, it is as if the chemistry of Reality itself has, in some distinct way, transformed Opti's once elegant and feathery tail. Previously small and slightly cumbersome in appearance, the god's tail has become one in superbly evolved natural chemistry. With its huge, armored tip swinging firmly from side to side while it treads excitedly next to its father, this part of the creature's body seamlessly merges into a robustly shielded exterior that stretches down the center of its entire back.

Dia'Baal stirs deep within Pesa's thoughts, his tone dripping with both admiration and malice.

*'Gaze with focus upon your evolved kin, o, brutish Pesa, that armor it carries is no mere ornament. Each plate is a weapon unto itself, forged for survival and dominance. A single swing could sunder bone, crush even the proudest predator's skull, and perhaps even yours. Tell me, does your kin's maturity not glisten with the very power you once claimed for yourself?'*

His words press like claws into Pesa's mind, each syllable forcing the image deeper, until admiration and loathing fuse into a single, festering thought. The festering then grows teeth as Pesa's jaw tightens, each muscle pulling against the other like a bowstring ready to snap. In its mind's eye, it sees the armored tip arcing downward — not toward an enemy, but toward itself — and the vision sears like molten godhood poured onto raw flesh. Dia'Baal does not retreat... he lingers, savoring this display of what true godhood looks like. The slow, choking knot winding around Pesa's pride coils tighter as he speaks once more.

*'You feel it once again, do you not? The knowledge that one strike of its tail could end you. But that is not fear, my dear beast. That is a gift — the ember I will fan until it burns away every last tether of your restraint. And when the fire comes, beast… it will not be to warm you.'*

The god of beasts blinks hard, the meadow reappearing like a world half-remembered. Somewhere far above, Opti moves with effortless grace, utterly unaware of the storm it has set loose beneath the grass.

Again and again, without an answer or slight of reason, the great beast ponders in disbelief how its own nature has seemingly and perhaps completely transformed Opti, who, with each step, becomes cloaked in fiery crimson flares of energy. *'How is this even possible?'*, wonders Pesa as it continues to search for the answers it just cannot find.

Sensing easily Pesa's impression of reverence, Xionn turns to look—just as the great beast turns its head away and flees into its realm, having just received its biggest dose of reality ever—a reality, dear T'Naeva, a fact that your mighty forebear does not care for in the least, as it now assumes, through Dia'Baal's manipulation, its supreme reign over the Earth is in serious jeopardy.

Xionn, continuing to enjoy the magnificence and maturity of his second child, eventually leaves it, and transforming himself into a brisk wind, quickly departs the meadow. Opti, knowing its father is well pleased with its maturity, also becomes pleased as it triumphantly rears its mammoth body, charges, and leaps to the heavens with a thunderous jolt. As it blasts skyward, I see the mighty god begin to fly in large circles high over the meadow, filled with elation, satisfaction, and vigor in its deserved authority.

The sky still hums with the rhythm of Opti's vast wings, each sweep pushing waves of wind over the meadow. Pesa's breathing is shallow, its gaze locked upward as if any blink might cause the vision to vanish. The clouds split in molten arcs where Opti cuts through them, leaving trails of crimson fire that refuse to fade. The air feels too thick to draw, as though the realm itself is holding its breath for what will come next.

Now that the god of creatures has reacquainted itself with the heavens overlooking the meadow, it turns its eyes and catches a glimpse of Pesa observing it from deep within a thick vegetated growth near its diamond archway. With its own energies of nature on full display, the god of Imagination abruptly roars, and I am struck with awe at its sound. Profusely stronger and deeper than even the blast to Gabriel's horn Opti made when it was created, this intense blare sends Pesa reeling, and it covers its shaking head with its two front legs.

Still airborne, I gaze upon my radiant parent as fiery waves of vitality erupt. No creature on Earth rivals its splendor. These same waves refill the meadow sky, reborn as auroras of color. With Pesa gradually moving its front legs from its eyes, it continues to observe in disbelief the vastly improved state of its kin's existence, now on dramatic display. Believing itself safe, Pesa watches its kin—until suddenly the mighty creature turns and dives, streaking over the diamond archway and Pesa's hidden position. I hear another piercing roar quake throughout the meadow as Opti swiftly flies over it, shaking Pesa's mind as it has never been shaken before.

With this awesome roar, Pesa's body trembles from head to paw. It shakes its head to purge the ringing now roaring through its darkened mind. Needless to say, with this action by Opti doing nothing more than strengthening Pesa's resolve to kill it a hundredfold—or even a thousandfold—the extremely narrow-minded reasoning of this seriously diseased god of beasts makes itself ready for anything. This is not good. The god of beasts stands frozen, its weight pressed into the soil, claws digging deeper.
The meadow is silent save for the slow ticking of its own heartbeat in its ears. Shadows coil tighter around its form as A slithering voice emerges— Dia'Baal's will swelling to fill every corner of its mind. It is in this stillness — heavy, suffocating, endless — that Pesa's choice hardens, and the seed of war takes root.

To Pesa, even through its temporary fright, Opti's newly matured force of presence would now allow this god of creatures to seriously threaten Pesa's own domination of the Earth, perhaps to even attempt to destroy Reality itself, given the chance. I speak to you now, T'Naeva, a stark truth, for this lie by Dia'Baal is what finally drives your parent over the edge, bringing it into the final stage of its resolve and propelling Pesa directly into the prime—or summer—of its existence.

Meanwhile, Opti's newfound growth fills its father with pride—his second child has matured in both power and wisdom. Opti, now able to create life using the foundation of Reality, no longer requires its father's breath—divine essence already pulses within its being. Without need of assistance, it begins crafting unified, vibrant creatures that thrive even within the bounds of Imagination.

Pesa, though always capable of creating life in its own realm, chooses not to. Grown complacent, it believes there is nothing left to prove—to itself or to anyone. This mindset, as ancient as nature itself, calcifies into its eternal decree: "Only the strongest shall survive." And in Pesa's view, it remains the strongest of all. Even after its magnificent transformation, Opti's divine nature—rooted in the Force of Imagination—remains pure, virtuous, and unshakably benevolent. It cannot harm a single hair of any creature within its realm.

Now able to replicate the beasts of Reality, Opti enhances them with astonishing abilities, divine precision, and sacred function as it sees fit. When encountering an animal of nature, Opti may return it to its own realm or create a refined, elevated copy within the meadow, evolving it with graceful intricacy. In every case, Opti approaches each life force with reverence, empathy, and awe, never violating the sanctity of what has been beautifully and eternally made.

Knowing well now the depth of the terrible disease that is ravaging Pesa's mind, Opti only wants to help alleviate Pesa's anger by showing it the fantastic possibilities they both can accomplish together for the benefit of Earth. Truly, once the fear of Opti's profound physical maturity has been overcome, I hear Pesa answer Opti's ideas with outrage, considering that in its own twisted system of beliefs, there is still no life-form greater than it, including its kin.
I quickly surmise that the great beast of Reality warns Opti time and again of severe consequences if it continues its reckless activities with nature and its life-forms, but in this I am not quite sure.

# Verse XVII:
## When Blood Denies Blood

A new age comes to my sight. On this day, Pesa's void is potent enough to erase all doubt in what it has to do, and it is coming like a storm.

Its patience with Opti has long dissipated and now needs only a spark to ignite its full wrath directly upon its kin. From my unique perspective of Opti, I see Pesa as a miserably diseased and profoundly unhappy god of beasts—a beast full of anger and pride, rapped in a closed mind it could escape with its father's divine help—but refuses to. In countless encounters over the final age of its Season of Maturity, Opti sincerely attempts to share what it has learned with its dark kin. Every time it tries, Pesa grows more agitated and ever closer to violent release.

With Opti's divine perception still intact, it comes to understand that convincing Pesa to change its virulent attitude is an impossibility—an immutable truth that even it cannot alter. It happens rather quickly from then on. Once free of negative emotion because of its birth in the Force of Imagination, Opti begins maturing with Reality as its unified foundation. As a result, those negative emotions, foreign in its early state, begin to surface and grow stronger. Irritation with Pesa creeps in, strengthening with time.

Yet Opti holds fast to its resolve, believing that direct conflict with Pesa is unnecessary. It continues to strive for peace, trusting that it can protect its creations if needed.

With maturity and courage, Opti finally decides to approach its kin face to face. I hear a sharp exchange between gods as Pesa's displeasure with this meeting becomes unmistakable. My parent is firm in its declaration:

"I come to you, dear kin, to speak truth about what I see clearly, and today it will be known to you. This beautiful meadow is yours to do with as you please, but I will no longer stand silent as you hunt my creations unabated; it ends now! The life you birth may become your prey if you so desire, but I also desire that you see the harm of your affliction and overcome its temptations."

Pesa growls, its horns lowering as it steps forward. "Who are you to stand before me and demand that I abandon what I am? Oh, is it because of my... *affliction?*" It sneers with a huff, eyes narrowing to slits. "You think your so-called maturity grants you the right to speak to me this way?"

Opti's form shimmers in the sunlight, radiant and resolute.
"I do not come to command you, Pesa—but to remind you what you are losing... and the harm you bring upon yourself most of all."
Pesa's claws gouge the earth, flaring nostrils trembling with rage.
"Do not patronize me! Me! The highest life ever sculpted upon this cursed world! Your pity insults me more than any threat!"

Opti stands firm. His voice is calm—but beneath it, fire simmers.
"And now, O wretched brute... I pity you even more."

The space between them pulses like a barely contained squall. Tension crackles, sharp and alive in the air. Pesa hesitates, its gaze shifting to Opti's golden mane rippling in the breeze. A tremor of doubt flashes across its expression, but the darkness within snarls louder. It straightens, towering in defiance.

"You dare bring weakness into my domain? You forget who stands before you, flower!"
Opti's wings unfold slightly, their shadow cast long over the meadow.
"I forget nothing, Pesa. I see you as you are—and I grieve for what you've so clearly become."
Pesa's muscles coil.
"Then leave me be in my misery, or I will make you regret ever returning!"
Opti's expression hardens, but it says nothing. Instead, it turns away, step-

ping toward the archway that separates their realms. The golden grasses sway as it passes.

Pesa growls behind it.

"Walk away while you still can, delicate flower of Imagination!"

Opti pauses for a heartbeat, but does not look back. It ascends slowly into the sky, leaving behind a silence heavy with grief and unspoken truths. Never forgetting its father's warnings from ages past, and despite knowing Pesa's hatred, Opti begins to prepare itself for an eventual confrontation with its dark kin.

Returning to and secluding itself deep within its realm, the mighty sentinel painstakingly refines its abilities and creative processes, planning its most ambitious creation yet: a new and fiercely formidable life-form. This creation, meant to preserve and protect the Realm of Imagination, is known to me as the *Chup'DraVak-Ra*—a hyper-intelligent and vigilant breed, fierce and loyal beyond measure.

This species—the primal ancestor of the modern-day *wolf*—has no equal throughout the Realm of Imagination. After its transformation, Chimera, once D'Reem's faithful *chupa* companion, becomes the matriarch of this newly forged lineage. Robust yet sleek, this majestic beast stands as a masterpiece of inspired design—blending ferocity with an almost regal grace. Its thick alabaster mane cascades like molten light down its spine, while a storm-gray coat glistens with an ethereal sheen, interwoven with streaks of fiery crimson and gold.

Its eyes—brilliant pools of amber—burn with the incandescent focus that birthed their kind. These eyes hold the weight of Opti's vast foresight: a burning legacy of creation, tempered by vengeance. The design is so radical, so innovative, that even Xionn hesitates to breathe life into it. Yet Opti's reason and logic persuade him, and at last, Xionn consents. Once brought into existence, these creatures—the Chup'DraVak-Ra—are placed strategically throughout the Realm of Imagination.

Their purpose is clear: should Opti ever fall, or should the realm ever face invasion from the animals of Reality, the Chup'DraVak-Ra will rise swiftly in defense. In truth, Opti's foresight in crafting this species would one day prove prophetic. Meanwhile, Pesa's perspective continues to darken. It needs only a single excuse to destroy Opti, whom it now views as a threat to its dominance.

Pesa no longer sees its kin as family, but as an archenemy—one that must be eradicated. This belief is a grave offense to the balance Xionn intended. Fueled by the whispers of Dia'Baal, Pesa's resolve crystallizes into something monstrous. Reality itself—once a neutral force in its being—now warps under the beast's influence. Pesa's intelligence reaches its peak as its physical form mutates further to a monstrous twenty feet at its shoulders. At this height and power, Pesa has become the same living hurricane of destruction, size, and cunning I once fought.

Its eyes, once clear and watchful, blaze with venomous, aqua hued light. Though Xionn's omnipotent presence continues to expand, he still does not fully grasp the intricate nature of Pesa's corruption or the devastating magnitude of Dia'Baal's grip. Throughout the ages, Xionn responds to Pesa's outbursts not with anger, but with patience and gentle, loving reprimands. He is the eternal father, convinced that his Firstborne's wounds—deep though they may be—can heal with time and tenderness.

To Xionn, every clash, every harsh word from Pesa is but a ripple on the surface of a restless sea. He sees, or chooses to see, the underlying hurt rather than the malice. And so he leans in with greater warmth, engaging both his children more frequently, speaking words of encouragement, urging them toward mutual respect and understanding. Unbeknownst to Xionn, the festering darkness in Pesa's heart has grown roots far beyond his reach. In its twisted mind, every word of love becomes a veiled slight, every gesture of kindness a silent accusation.

Pesa's pride recoils, transforming compassion into fuel for resentment. This, dear T'Naeva, is the tragic reality of Pesa's existence—a god of beasts brought to the brink by envy, pride, a wound it refuses to let heal. A tragedy so deep that even the wisdom of eternity struggles to undo its poison. This selfless task of unconditional love—an attempt by the good father to have his children bear mutual responsibility for their actions and respect for one another—works wondrously for Opti, who blossoms beneath it.

But for Pesa, it is a mask. Though it appears the beast has abandoned its loathsome feelings toward Opti, the truth is far more insidious. Pesa has merely buried these thoughts deep within, hidden even from itself, a dark seed nurtured by Dia'Baal's whispers. Here lies the quiet tragedy: Xionn, despite his infinite care, has unknowingly lost his revered influence over his greatest Firstborne. And that, dear T'Naeva, is a sorrow almost too heavy for even gods to bear.

Now hear the words of truth, eternal and unyielding: without the fear of consequence—whether god, man, or sentient beast—all will eventually yield to the law of universal justice. And when that reckoning arrives, it does so not as a whisper, but as a force, inevitable and absolute. Simply stated, the eternal words of *what goes around comes around* are as prevalent in this ancient day as they are in this day and age.

If you remember, Xionn decreed he would never again personally destroy another one of his creations by his own hand, and felt it would be much better for his matured children to solve their differences by themselves.

With Pesa's corruption now fully matured and ever present within its vast mind, this corrupted god easily twists Xionn's goodwill to its advantage. With Pesa now convinced that its disease is incurable, yet still clueless that Dia'Baal is, in fact, in firm control of its mind, Pesa continues on in its severe hatred, without the slightest desire to do anything about it. Truly, T'Naeva, because this foolish attitude of your parent will soon land it in a multitude of problems, Pesa worries no longer about the consequences of anything it feels or does from that day forward.

I see it clearly now—not with judgment, but with a sorrowful knowing, as one who has stood at the precipice of his own unraveling. Pesa's rebellion is not merely pride—it is a desperate, clawing need to matter, to stand apart as more than a shadow of Opti's brilliance. In every word Xionn spoke in love, Pesa heard accusation. In every gentle correction, it perceived condemnation. It was not Opti's light alone that wounded it   it was Xionn's unwavering faith in harmony, which Pesa interpreted as blindness to its suffering. Even as Dia'Baal whispers his venom, Xionn hopes, believing that Pesa's silence was healing.

But it is not healing—it is a storm gathering in quiet depths. Xionn's trust becomes the very thing Pesa exploits, concealing its festering bitterness beneath the mask of a reformed heart. This deception, masterfully orchestrated by Dia'Baal, leaves Xionn totally unprepared for the calamity to come. Also, because Pesa has (through the working of Dia'Baal) masterfully deceived its father concerning its improving attitude toward Opti, Xionn begins to feel comfortable enough to leave his two powerful children to their own devices.

This, I now grasp, was the fracture Xionn did not wish to see but feared all along. As if on cue to destiny's call, and to complicate these matters further, I hear a matured Messiah speak—not as a commanding Sovereign, but with a reverence and charm surpassing all earthly homage, reserved only for the most exalted of Edenite citizenry. His words ripple like waves of divine resonance through the fabric of Xionn's SoulSliver, yet each syllable carries a somber gravity unseen by its intended hearer.

*... Come now, beloved Hand of Balance. Sovereign Xionn Theone, your place of honor before the Realm is summoned and ordained, and to also be witnessed by all of Ametheden, your nation, and your nations cosmic family.*

*... The crown of repose, wrought from your unwavering devotion and your labors of ages untold, lies prepared for you. Return now to your cherished cornerstone—the foundation of all we hold sacred. For My Father has prepared a reward beyond measure, vast and eternal, kept in the Halls of Glory for you alone. Though My voice carries the triumph of this message, within Me lingers a sorrow—true but unspoken.*

*... For I alone see a shadow move beyond the horizon, and I know when the heavens resound with your victory, a light shall be absent from its chorus. Yet let this moment stand—so be unmarred, unafraid, and pure. Arise, Sovereign Xionn, for your triumph echoes across the cosmos and you are loved by one and all. Thus speaketh My Father, your eternal Companion.*

These words flow like rivers of light, carrying promises of peace yet veiled with depths even Xionn's ancient wisdom cannot fully fathom. They are not mere sounds but living currents of creation, each resonance stirring the very fabric of reality. Within their cadence lies more than invitation—it is a sacred urging, a summoning steeped in unspoken significance. The heavens themselves seem to hold their breath, stars pausing mid-glimmer, as though aware that this moment is not a simple call but a proclamation weighted with love, legacy, and the inexorable hand of fate.

Messiah's voice lingers—a melody of solace interwoven with something deeper... something strangely tinged with sorrow. There is warmth in His pronouncement, wrapping around Xionn like a celestial embrace, yet beneath it lingers a shadow—a truth unsaid, a burden carried in silence, ancient and heavy as eternity. Xionn's thoughts drift outward, like whispers cast into the void, yet I hear them clearly, echoing through time's endless corridors.

*"Why now, O beloved Companion? What has shifted in the great design? What cost awaits me at the edge of this revelation? Messiah has spoken with radiant clarity, and yet, the Companion remains silent. Still, gilded in promise, His absence weaves a thread of urgency through my soul.*
*This feels not only like exaltation but like a veiled farewell, cloaked in divine sentiment. It strikes me as strangely timed... yet I will obey, and swiftly. Dear T'Naeva, it is known to me that Xionn is to be bestowed a profound gift—not merely by his people, but by his Companion alone."*

And thus, the long-awaited day arrives—a day when this good father, filled with hope, believes he has finally succeeded in tempering every hostile thought between his children. With unwavering love, he announces to them his intent to withdraw for a time of much-needed rest and renewal. Yet, as his words leave his lips, there is the faintest pause—the smallest trace of reluctance. Xionn, in all his wisdom, senses the gravity of this moment.

Though he trusts in the maturity of his children, a quiet stirring within reminds him of Pesa's history, of lessons hard learned and wounds not yet fully healed. Still, with unshakable faith in Love's guidance, he silences the whisper of doubt and entrusts all to the Companion. This is no mere retreat; it is a sacred yielding, a releasing of dominion for the sake of Earth's coming maturity. In a voice steady with purpose, Xionn speaks not only to them, but to Gaea.

*"My children, I desire to walk among my people once more—to hear their joys, to witness their lives, to feel their warmth. Yet be assured, beloved children, beloved Gaea I shall return to you. When I do, it will be to dwell in perfect harmony, as it was always intended."*

Messiah's promise still lingers in the air, reverberating a tender but solemn melody that hints at more than what he had just heard. Even as Xionn offers peace among his two mighty children, there remains an unspoken truth, veiled but present—a finality that none dare name, yet still they all feel. Yes, indeed, it is now a glorious day for both of his matured children to finally be set free of his authority and live a wonderful existence by themselves.
Pesa, of course, agrees most joyously at this announcement. Opti also agrees, but within the deepest chambers of its noble heart, a quiet unease stirs.

The burden of suspicion weighs heavier now, for it senses the fragile threads of peace slipping through unseen cracks. Xionn's trust, so freely given, is both a blessing and a torment—one that Opti fears losing more than anything else. It is clear to me that Opti feels something terrible is about to happen—an undeniable sense of foreboding. Yet Pesa's clever twisting of their father's motives makes it hard to hold onto that certainty.

After all, Pesa is the older, wiser sibling—the one who speaks with such confidence and reason. Surely, Pesa must understand their father's will so much better.

And yet...

There's something unsettling beneath Pesa's reassurances, a sense that its wisdom is little more than a polished lie. Despite its efforts to believe otherwise, my parent cannot shake the feeling that following Pesa's lead will only end in ruin.

"Father," Pesa speaks with a calm yet humble tone, its massive form lowering in what appears to be reverence.

"How noble you are to trust in the harmony we have found. I now seek only peace and tranquility with my younger sibling."

Dia'Baal's influence sculpts each word to sound sincere, masking the malice beneath the surface to perfection. Xionn's firm gaze softens as he listens, his pride for his children reflected in his radiant countenance, and he replies, "Your words please me, Pesa."

Pesa turns to Opti, its eyes aglow with a deceptive warmth.

"Dear Opti, our past struggles must not dictate our future. The world our father entrusted to us deserves unity, not discord. Let us stand as its protectors, as siblings of purpose."

Opti tilts its head, golden mane glimmering as it studies its kin. Within its noble heart, suspicion stirs, but Pesa's serene countenance is unnervingly convincing.

"You have changed," Opti says quietly, its voice both hopeful and cautious.

Pesa bows slightly.

"Yes, dear sibling, I have learned, and I have grown because of you and father." It steps forward, gently nudging Opti's shoulder as if to reassure it. "Our father leaves with a heart at ease, and it is our duty to honor this."

Xionn, moved by the scene, places a hand on Pesa's brow, rubbing it gently. For a brief moment, a shadow of doubt brushes across his mind, like the passing of a storm cloud, but he dismisses it as fleeting worry. Giving a final farewell to his two mighty children, Xionn walks a distance to a central part of the meadow and suddenly looks skyward.

From those heavens, I hear a clap of thunder, though distant and softened and restrained. As a brilliant cloud of energized vapors descends, the Companion's presence whispers to him like the wind.

*... Be mindful of free will, Xionn Theone, for even the gods cannot foresee its course. Yet fear not, for My will weaves through all things, seen and unseen. What I have begun, no shadow can undo. Your escorts have arrived.*

A short distance away, concealed within a shadowed grove of trees, eyes of burning aqua hue pierce the darkness—not Pesa's alone, but tainted, hollowed, and wholly occupied. Dia'Baal's essence coils like a viper within the beast now, its vessel nothing more than a mask for the Firstborne's festering malice. Through Pesa's gaze, he watches the meadow—his meadow—now claimed by the light of those who had once hastened his downfall. The Archangels *Azrael* and *Chamuel*.

Radiant and unbowed, their presence ignites a sudden guttural hiss deep in Pesa's throat, so faint it vanishes into the rustling leaves.

*"They return..."*

Dia'Baal's whisper grows louder, his voice thick with venom. *"Still radiant. Still blind. And you Chamuel—wretch of love—keep your damned pity. I will suffer from it no longer!"*

On the meadow's edge, Azrael's luminous eyes quickly narrow, sensing the corruption clinging like rot to the crouched beast glaring at them in the distance. Beside him, Chamuel's emerald gaze softened, his heart already heavy with grief. He feels not the threat, but the ruin—the once-bright spirit twisted beyond mercy's reach. The archangels share a silent glance   Azrael's sharp with resolve, Chamuel's tender with sorrow. Yet neither speak because this moment belongs to Xionn alone.

Together they kneel before him and rise as one, nodding their heads while pressing their right hands to their hearts in a gesture of loyalty and lament. Escorting a god in both his triumph, and the trials they know will await him upon his return to Earth. Xionn's gaze lingers on Opti, his heart still mysteriously heavy with an unspoken resolve. In Opti's radiant form, he sees more than a sentinel from afar; he sees a soul bound by duty and burdened by the weight of creation's defense.

A quiet sorrow then stirs within Xionn, for he knows the cost of this unwavering faith all too well. With a subtle gesture, he extends his hand toward

Opti. Though no words pass between them, a faint shimmer of golden light bridges the space, weaving itself into Opti's essence—a fragment of Xionn's loving heart, a spark of strength meant to endure Opti's darkest hour should it ever arise.

Opti's glow flickers for a heartbeat, as though acknowledging the gift. In its blazing eyes, there is understanding—if not fully, then enough to know that something sacred has been given. Xionn breathes deeply, his divine aura steady despite the ache in his heart. With one final look, he speaks within himself.

*'Dear child of all this is founded in vision, may that fragment of my faith in you become your shield if all else fails."*

Turning away, Xionn steps in between the two mighty Archangels, his heart bound with hope that, if or when the storm ever comes, his trust in Opti will be vindicated.

As the three beings brilliant forms ascend toward the heavens in a shimmering cloud of light, Pesa's lips part in a whisper too soft for mortal ears. Beneath the gentle murmur lies the crackling embers of ruin—a prayer not for peace, but for inevitable dominion.

A thick and eerie silence presses down upon the meadow once the presence of Xionn is gone.

The air seems to cool, quickly and unnaturally, as if some unseen veil of dread has drawn universal life on this world. From the shadows of Pesa's form, Dia'Baal's malice stirs, silent but potent. His awareness of Xionn's exchange with Opti is undeniable, his hatred seething like embers beneath a suffocating ash. Within Pesa's large and aqua-hued lifeless eyes, something glimmers—a dark pulse, subtle, yet unrelenting. Though the beast remains motionless, an unspoken promise slithers from Dia'Baal's will.

*Your shield will not be enough for Opti, dear father...*

The ground beneath Pesa trembles slightly as if recoiling from its master's simmering fury. Yet as quickly as it comes, the darkness retreats into the recesses of the beast's essence, cloaked once more in stillness. Opti senses the faint echo of something unusual, but dismisses it, choosing instead to hold firm to the ember of strength Xionn bestowed.

As the rosy-fingered dawn of a new day begins, Pesa, the god of beasts, rises from a good night's rest, its form pulsing with raw energy. With Pesa's mind returning to the hunt and the thrill of past conquests, the god longs to stretch its primal instincts once more. Leaping to its feet with light-ning-like swiftness, Pesa surveys the vast meadow, a sanctuary of beauty and tranquility. But for Pesa, this meadow is no refuge; it is a stage for its predatory desires.

With a low growl rumbling deep in its throat, Pesa's divine form begins to shift—muscles coiling, fur darkening, limbs stretching until it becomes something sleek and lethal. In a flash of violent brilliance, the primal glow of its *nature* erupts, rippling across the meadow like a living storm. Trees shiver as the god's shape resolves: sinewy and obsidian, with the same aqua-hued eyes gleaming like twin oceans aflame. Now a *panther*, Pesa moves with si-lent, predatory grace, each step a study in coiled power. Even the air dares not stir.

Pesa's attention locks onto its prey deep within the meadow's heart—a pair of *Rainbow-Zebre Pegasi*, the most magnificent looking creations of its kin, Opti. The god's eyes gleam with a hunter's thrill. This quarry is unusual, its challenge irresistible. Silently, Pesa begins its stalk. Each movement is precise, a masterful dance of stealth and intent. A primal excitement courses through Pesa's being, more potent than its usual hunts. These creatures, dazzling in their iridescent hues, are not merely prey; they are symbols of its sibling's artistry.

The sight of their vibrant wings and fluid movements stirs both admiration and envy in the beast-god. For Pesa, this hunt is more than sport; it is a chal-lenge to prove its sheer dominance over creation itself. The meadow, with all its serenity, mocks Pesa's hunger, and the god's resolve hardens.

Deep within, Dia'Baal's voice coils like smoke, silken and poisonous.

*"Yes, o, mighty pet... show your kin your power. Let your claws be the proof that Opti's creations kneel before you. Tear not only flesh—tear the vision from its mind, until even its dreams remember your dominion."*

The words slide between thought and instinct until they are one, making each stride feel not like pursuit, but a holy reclamation.

A low growl vibrates through its chest as it anticipates the moment of triumph. This hunt will be unlike any other, a test of both skill and will. The god's intent sharpens, and the chase begins.

Pesa lunges forward, its obsidian form streaking like a shadow loosed from the void itself. The panther's massive muscles ripple beneath its onyx pelt as it closes the distance in impossibly swift bounds. The stallion bolts, hooves tearing at the meadow in blind terror, but the air itself seems to betray it—thickening under Pesa's primal force, slowing the doomed creature's desperate flight.

The brutality of the sneak attack quickly throws the stallion into ghastly trauma, its body convulsing as a massive spray of glowing crimson fluids shoots through the hot and humid air. Ending its victim's quivers with another potent thrust of its massive right paw, Pesa roars as the stallion expires under its seven dark claws, for no living thing upon the face of the Earth can survive a strike from the god of beasts.
With its victory secured, Pesa's roar echoes through the meadow, a guttural declaration of dominance that reverberates in the humid air.

Its glowing eyes gleam with unquenched blood lust as the great panther whips its body around, its predatory glare now locking onto the smaller mate of the creature it has just killed. The smaller mate—the mare—attempts to flee, its movements frantic and filled with desperation. Yet Pesa, unsatisfied and driven by an insatiable hunger for glowing blood, springs back into action, pursuing the mare with intense ferocity. Each stride of the god of beasts is calculated, its massive form slicing through the tall grass with terrifying ease.

As the mare nears the edge of the meadow, Pesa leaps again, its claws connecting with the rear legs of the creature, tripping it and tearing into its wing. The mare crashes to the ground with a pained cry, its body quivering as it struggles to rise. Just as Pesa prepares to end its pursuit with a final strike, the powerful mare, fueled by nature's adrenaline, twists around and delivers a brutal kick. The blow lands squarely against Pesa's chest with astonishing force, sending the panther tumbling backward.

For a moment, the great predator writhes in pain, its breath knocked away and its dominance challenged. Never has Pesa encountered its prey capable of such defiance. The kick still reverberates through its much smaller design, a sharp sting laced with humiliation, gnawing at both flesh and ego. The ache spreads like molten iron, searing not just flesh but the marrow of its pride. In that wound, old ghosts rise—every time it was lesser, every time another was chosen first.

The blow is not from hooves alone; it is the fist of history striking back. A sound escapes its throat, not quite a growl, not quite a roar—something feral, wounded, and infinitely dangerous. For the briefest instant, something unfamiliar flickers within the great beast—a spark of awe twisted by its diseased mind.

*'This feeble creature... fragile, insignificant, and yet it dares strike me? It dares wound the god of beasts?'*

The beast snarls inwardly, its corrupted thoughts fracturing in the silence.

*'How is this even possible? How could this creature of Opti's design—so meek, so vulnerable—so strong... be evolving?'*

Or has Pesa, drunk on its own corruption, underestimated even the humblest life its kin placed upon the earth? These unsettling musings—blasphemous to the predator's arrogance—momentarily loosen the tightening coil of the hunt, allowing the mare a precious chance to scramble to her bloodied hooves. Her eyes, wild with anxiety, dart toward the meadows edge.

With a final surge of desperate strength, she flees, each bound leaving splintered clods of earth in her wake. But hesitation is a luxury the corrupted god cannot afford. Pesa's lips curl into a grotesque snarl as molten saliva drips from its fangs, sizzling against the meadow grass. Its pupils flare, predatory instinct burning away all doubt.

Pesa growls, voice deep as shifting tectonic plates.

"No, This is not defiance. This is desperation!"

A guttural rumble rolls from its chest, vibrating the air as it lowers its sleek dark head, eyes locked on the fleeing mare. Muscles coil like a serpent about to strike, and then—without hesitation—the great panther explodes forward in a blur of obsidian fury. The earth quakes faintly under its pounding strides as its seven dark claws dig deep into the soil, propelling it with supernatural speed.

As the hunt reaches its fevered crescendo, Pesa's form begins to shift once more. Ripples of raw power surge along its sinewy frame. Fur retracts, claws elongate, and its sleek predator's body expands with terrifying majesty. A shroud of untamed energy erupts around it—the primal glow of its force of nature flaring like a living aurora. The god's true shape reemerges: massive, beastly, yet impossibly divine, radiating a savage authority that dominates the meadow and all who dwell within it.

The delay has cost it precious moments—an unforgivable offense. With a bellow that shakes the heavens, Pesa lunges. Its limbs hammer the earth once more, sending tremors rippling outward. Great fissures split the meadow as claws churn the soil in sweeping arcs. The scent of blood floods its senses—thick, intoxicating—driving it onward with maddened purpose. Trees at the meadow's edge shudder, their leaves whispering warnings to the wind, but no salvation comes, or does it?

Far above, a shift stirs the heavens. The god of Imagination, Opti's awareness sharpens like a blade drawn from its sheath. The ripple in Harmony is not just sensed—it is tasted, a metallic tang in the air, bitter and undeniable. Each heartbeat echoes in its mind like the toll of a distant chime, marking the moment when peace teeters toward collapse. Somewhere deep in its ancient being, the sentinel feels the faint pull of its father's lingering gift—warm, steady, urging it toward the place where destiny will come to sharpen its teeth.

Slowly, and with deliberate precision, it turns its colossal head, crimson eyes blazing as they pierce the veiled clouds. In the chaos below, it discerns the scene unfolding: a predator driven by madness, and prey clinging to life by fragile threads. Then, as though the very stars flare in answer to its resolve, Opti releases a roar. The sound does not merely echo—it vibrates through the firmament, and shaking the meadow as though it trembles at the sentinel's will. With wings unfurled to their full, terrifying breadth, the god descends swiftly into the cloudcover.

Carving silent, lethal arcs through the churning air, Opti's armored body gleams with a golden glow that burns brighter with every passing second. The Pegasi's ragged cries rise to meet it—high, strained, desperate—and within them, Opti discerns not merely fear, but a plea. A plea it cannot, and *will not* ignore. The sentinel's gaze sharpens, divine sight turning and locking onto Pesa below. There its kin rages, a monstrous aberration of what once was noble, now reduced to a feral shadow of itself. Opti's heart clenches—not with pity, but with a cold, unyielding roar.
*This ends now!*

Pesa bellows as its claws lash closer toward the mare, corrupted muscles coiling like serpents primed to strike. Inches now from the trembling Pegasi, its claws arc forward, eager to tear flesh and taste blood. But in the heartbeat before death claims the mare, the skies above them erupt. A shriek of air splits the silence as Opti descends—unstoppable, unyielding, divine.
Wind screams around its bright armored frame, massive wings slicing the heavens like blades. In a flawless sweep, the sentinel's talons extend, also aglow with radiant energy. They pierce the space between predator and prey to encase the trembling mare in a protective grasp.

She whinnies softly as Opti lifts her clear from the death that awaited her, its immovable talons holding her just beyond Pesa's snapping jaws. Pesa loses its balance as it crashes into a clumsy skid, gouging the meadow's soil. It halts, roaring in frustration—a sound so vile even the trees seem to shiver. Above, Opti hovers like a monument to judgment, its crimson eyes burning like twin suns as they lock onto its corrupted sibling.
The stare alone strips shadows from Pesa's twisted form, leaving only the naked truth of its ruin. The air hums with the promise of confrontation. Two titans—once bound by purpose—now face each other on destiny's edge. The meadow does not merely hold its breath—it kneels to the gravity of what stands before it.

Each stalk of glowing grass bows as though before an altar; every petal of every flower curls inward, guarding its color from the coming storm. Above, the clouds knit themselves into an unbroken canopy, sealing the arena of the coming warfare as though the world itself has decreed that nothing will escape what is about to unfold. A single seed rises from the meadow, its silvered threads catching the light of Opti's intense glow. It now drifts not aimlessly but with a strange, deliberate grace, as though carried by a hand unseen.
For a heartbeat, the seed hangs suspended between predator and protector—between ruin and redemption. Where it falls will mark more than the end of this hunt... it will mark which legacy survives the war to come.

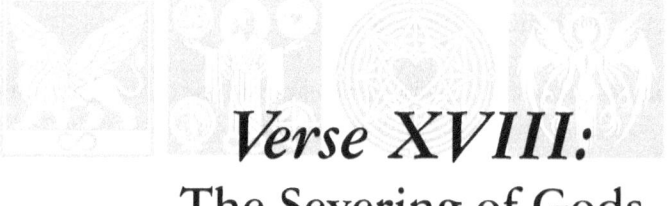

# *Verse XVIII:*
## The Severing of Gods

hear the haunting, thunderous roars of Pesa's fury reverberate through the meadow—a primal wail that rattles the earth and shakes the air.

These cries are not mere sounds, they are wrath embodied and pure, vibrations so violent they seize the spirit of everything within hearing. They shred the silence, breaking it into a thousand invisible fragments, until even the wind falters beneath their weight. Their echoes pierce the stallion's death in grisly form, vibrating it in the tall grasses. Its body quivers a final time, a grim reminder of Pesa's unchecked rage lingering in the air, as though the poor creature's spirit still remains shackled to its death.

Opti, the sentinel of Imagination, tightens its grip around its mate's fragile form as its wings steady it, turning towards its enemy. Its talons though forged to rend, cradles the unconscious mare with impossible tenderness. Its grip a vow—unyielding—a silent oath sworn into the cosmos. Whatever comes now, this creation will not be abandoned. Opti's dark crimson eyes gleam like living flames, fixed upon the god of beasts far ahead.

Fury burns within them, but also a tenderness that Pesa, consumed by bloodlust, cannot fathom. Nature vaults to all fours to find, to pursue, to kill, to undo its enemy as it accelerates its charge. The meadow itself seems caught in the surge. Pesa lunges as Opti draws ever closer, its stride and speed rising, driven by its unquenchable thirst for vengeance, its ungodly muscular form rippling with hatred. Each blast of its paws upon the divine canvas of the meadow carving deep furrows into the soil.

Opti's speed draws nearer as Pesa's massive claws begin to swipe outward with pure killing intent. Its jaws snap like thunderbolts, each gnash of razor-sharp teeth aiming to bite through and sever the golden head from its sibling's neck. But Opti will not be undone in this moment. Rage fuels its wings, purpose sharpens its movements. In a sudden flash, the god of Imagination streaks upward into a radiant arc just as Pesa leaps forward, its feathers igniting into a golden blaze that rends the haze of the moment.

It ascends swiftly—a comet birthed in the late afternoon sky, each wing beat a thunderclap of defiance. In its blinded rage, Pesa misjudges Opti's speed of ascent and crashes hard to its belly with a sound like a continent splitting apart. A shockwave ripples through the meadow's grassland, birds shriek skyward, and small creatures throughout the meadow burrow in terror. The earth recoils, trembling beneath the impact of a god brought down. For a moment, Pesa lies stunned with its chest heaving, its blackened breath pouring out in ragged bursts.

The air is thick with the musk of fury and the sour taint of vigor oozing from its skin. Its massive frame convulses, muscles twitching in rage and humiliation. It has also lost sight of its enemy. Far above it, Opti continues to rise through the heavy mist, borne on unseen currents. Its body shines with unyielding light, golden hues dancing across the sky like tongues of fire. From this height, Opti surveys the carnage below. Its blazing gaze, sharp as spears of lightning, fixes upon the murdered stallion.

The sight claws at the god's heart. This beautiful creature, no longer beautiful, lies lifeless and streaked with gore, a silent testament to Pesa's savagery. A grief unlike any Opti had known instantly floods its soul—and quickly it is forged into rage. But this rage is not wild; no, dear one, it is focused, crystalline, and consuming. My parent roars. The sound is no mere bellow but a shattering, a sonic gale that twists the meadow into a howling tempest. Winds arise to scream across the grassland, bending the tall glowing stalks into bowing arcs.

Even the heavens reel beneath the force of Opti's grief-stricken madness. On this day, vengeance is sworn, and retribution will come. The cosmos will remember this moment, and now... *she too* will now witness it unfold.

In this vision the mighty warrior can hear the meadow gasp and then hold its breath to the inevitable.

"T'Naeva, it is now in this stillness that we dwell together, that we become wrapped in an ever-tightening coil. It is as if the wild grasses of the meadow fear to sway between these two titans, our dear parents!"

She feels only what he feels now—no longer blind to his source. The air grows heavier, as if the sky itself leans down to press firm upon her divine heart. Then, as her thoughts focus more into clarity, it happens, and in her mind a vision emerges, and she sees both Opti and Pesa from afar. Opti's blazing form streaking as a comet through the sky while Pesa, its body writhing in frustration, is unrestrained and its thoughts of violence become known to her. D'Reem's voice arises into her mind, and it resonates clearly with these words.
"Yes, dear one, the Companion has granted you the vision to see them as I do, so observe these things now and listen, to begin understanding that this moment becomes a war waged in the minds of gods!"

T'Naeva sits quietly and steady—opposite and facing D'Reem. Their every sense merged as one as the air between them becomes heavier with a passing storm high overhead. Her newly granted vision is settling now, forming into a deeper rhythm with her every sense of being.
*'Such an incredible experience I now dwell within'*, she thinks, just as the scene shapes further the edges of where she will soon thrive in knowledge.
The mighty warrior again speaks firm to her mind, his voice profound yet caring and without tension.

"You must understand this clearly O, beautiful goddess, this is not the first time I have seen these sights, but this *is* the first time my Companion has chosen to show them to *you* so that you may begin to know them. To unveil their every stark moment of truth, for yourself."
His gaze continues to hold hers, and she does not blink.
"You are the one that is welcome to them now, T'Naeva, or perhaps even cursed to see them as I alone have carried these visions for much time to reflect upon."

The Companion offers only a sliver of this vision to her at first—a taste of the truth she will come to know in full measure. The imagery in her eyes further coalesce as the meadow has taken full shape across her airy sight… but the details are still too bright and too still, but these will adjust. She also feels the hum of something vast beneath her feet, as if the ground itself is holding its breath, and she loses hers for an instant.

"My beloved parent will come to strike over there, so watch closely", D'Reem says as he points directly at Pesa, and she sees her parent in its fully corrupted state. She then gazes skyward and sees his parent in its swift flight, clearly now. Gleaming in multiple golden hues mixed with crimson, every muscle and feather in its body has become a mirror of the sphere of fire and light that shines high overhead.

A mile below it, Pesa staggers in the meadow as it continues to shake its head—its eyes blurred from the brief impact, its pupils wide but slowly narrowing to slits as the far distance between her and her dark parent quickly becomes nothing.

The silence she feels will soon become very dangerous between her parent and his.

"They know and hate each other," she whispers.

D'Reem replies with solace.

"Yes they do, I'm afraid, and they both will come to know what the other has become... very soon now!"

Pesa stirs, grinding and thrusting its body back and forth on its muscular legs. Its guttural roar rises in her ears, its defiance ringing true as its body continues to spin in every direction to find an enemy—*it cannot find.*

Despite this, all its pain is forgotten, replaced by an all-consuming inferno of revulsion. Its voice thunders, splitting the heavens in fury.

"I say to you wherever you are, O, brazen flower, this interference with my hunt shall bring your end! I swear by the essence of my every atom—I shall make this day your final!" Its vow reverberates through the valley, shaking each archway that leads into two opposing worlds. Every word burns into stone and grass, as though the earth itself must now witness its madness. Yet as the boast leaves Pesa's lips, silence falls—not in a peaceful way, no, but in an unnatural stillness that reflects this moment.

Creation draws breath before catastrophe, and the air grows dense. Every creature who had not burrowed to safety in the meadow falls quiet, their every sound stilled in fear. The beast scans the meadow again, its ears twitching and its muscles taut. Its eyes dart across the vast grassland—but still Pesa sees nothing. It is blind to this truth—its sibling streaks far above it, its wings spread, its talons still curled tightly around the unconscious, yet very safe mare.

Opti abruptly descends.

It glides with precision—every movement steady yet silent, every feather angled to conceal its approaching attack. Its form gleams as golden light spills across the meadow in slashes of brilliance, long shadows stretching in its wake. With a thrust of radiant wings, Opti hurls itself further downward, downwind of Pesa so it can mask the smell of its enraged scent. The grasses bow before it, bending as though in reverence to the sentinel's coming wrath.

Pesa senses a shift in the air, at last. It changes as the heat behind it begins to rise like a sudden desert wind. A whispering gale grows beyond that, faint at first, then swelling, until it becomes a drawn-out shriek. This is no wind now—it is power incarnate. The demon stiffens. Its instincts shout for clarity. Ever so slowly, Pesa turns into the wind now raging behind it.

A wind of familiar sound, yet somehow odd to its own divine making. It had begun as a subtle breeze, quickly gathering strength until it blows as a vicious gale—a gale equal to the attack of a raging god. I watch it unfold as Pesa, sensing this immediate shift, complete its full turn towards the oncoming storm.

In the span of a heartbeat, the demon beholds only a blaze of wrath—and fury finds its mark! Heat lashes at the demon's face as Opti's fury is unleashed, inescapable as fate itself. D'Reem's voice rises, his voice trembling as the vision grips him.

"I gasp in shock as the thunder rolls, dear T'Naeva—and it permeates me still as Pesa will soon feel a true fall. Even I, bound to sight, am again shaken by what unfolds before my eyes, ages before my birth!"

His hand clutches at a rocky outcropping as though to steady his spirit.

T'Naeva, in turn, reels as the same vision crashes through her every sense. She sees the strike not only with her eyes, but within her very being—a divine collision so fierce it fractures her breath. Her hands clutch the earth as she screams, feeling as though she has fallen into an inescapable void. Opti's massive chest collides with Pesa's skull with devastating precision as it sweeps overhead. The sound comes suddenly and is cataclysmic in her ears. Pesa's horns snap at their roots, their fragments scattering across the meadow.

A sickening 'crack' follows as Opti's armored tail rounds to impact Pesa's forehead as it carves deep, wicked gashes within it, sending a bright flow of noxious, aqua-hued fluid down its snarling visage. Pesa is hurled backward, its body spinning and flailing through the grasses before being slammed to its backside with a thunder that shakes the meadow. Once more, the god of beasts is brought low—this time not by fury's blindness, but by vengeance incarnate. The ground convulses, grasses snapping flat beneath Pesa's sprawling twenty-ton bulk.

The very earth groans under its vile and tainted fury. This thunderous tremor ripples outward, sending flocks of birds screaming skyward in ragged arcs. I smell the air as it reeks of scorched fur, torn flesh, and the acrid tang of beastly ichor pooling upon the meadow's dark soil. Opti springs forward over its stunned enemy, wings fully tightened inward, its golden light cascading on Pesa like a punishing nova. Its chest heaves from the sheer exertion, talons and feathers now slick with Pesa's lifeblood. Yet my parent does not slow. It ascends swiftly, gaze steady, crimson eyes locked forward—indifferent to the hellish strike it has just landed upon Pesa.

It knows it has struck not merely a beast, but the embodiment of rebellion, of defilement, of love inverted into predation. Far below it, Pesa writhes in misery. Its massive claws gouge deep trenches into the meadow as it thrashes unhindered, shredding both earth and stone. Its sequence of guttural roars burst forth louder than the one before, drowning the land in its personal agony and fury. This sound rattles through all things, shaking even the unseen threads that bind all life in the cosmos.

T'Naeva grasps at and clutches Chimera's fur tightly, the color draining from her face as her eyes focus upon this terrible and vicious scene. Yet the beast does not flinch to her tightened grip, as she already knows it is for the best. Her voice is faint, barely a whisper, yet heavy with dread.
"Is there no end to the hatred I witness in my eyes?
D'Reem immediately responds in a tone that is raw, stripped of composure.

"I feel the meadow clearly hold its breath, as should you, T'Naeva!" His gaze locks on the vision she sees, unblinking, her tears brimming to release. "Not in stillness dear one, but in the expectation of He who shows us these things, just as I see now this tightening coil, and the promise fulfilled that you too witness the grasses ignite between our dear parents!"

T'Naeva feels this intense heat and the pressure in the air, both heavy and close, pressing upon her chest as though heaven itself has unleashed its secrets only to suffocate her. Her lips part in wonder and terror alike, yet no words can escape. She clutches her hands together; knuckles white with an anxiety she has never known to this fateful moment.

"Each strike you speak of concerning our parents only feeds my passions more, and I fear what follows, D'Reem—I fear I will not understand any of this for my sake!"

The Companion listens closely to her plea, just as Pesa struggles to regain its balance, but still cannot. Its thoughts churn, fixating on one truth: blood—*far more than its own*—will be spilled this day. The demon's head throbs to the infernal rhythm of its heartbeat, yet through all the haze, it finally *respects* its sibling's supernatural stamina. Determination rekindles in Pesa's heart—and it is very dark indeed. Once its dizziness fades, it vows to unleash divine wrath upon Opti.

D'Reem continues, his voice heavy with foreboding.

Sincerely, T'Naeva, your mighty forebear is more resolute than ever to return my parent's fury with its own, and this I believe you already know." T'Naeva gasps, her face pale as she still grapples with this vision in motion, struggling to make sense of the catastrophe she knows will come. She cannot conceive it, yet—and this haunts her completely.

*'Will his Companion answer her plea to understand any of this?'*

This question fills her chest with dread, yet combined with a strange aching hope, as though justice were a blade that must be drawn, though she fears more its sharpened edge. Still circling high overhead with its crimson-hued glare fully ablaze, Opti watches as Pesa continues to spin and thrash wildly in misery. Knowing its kin will be incapacitated for some time, it disengages its attack. Soaring to a haven deep within its own realm, the sentinel gently lands with its injured creation.

The winged mare, still unconscious and fragile, lies motionless in Opti's protective grasp. With painstaking precision and mastery of its godly abilities, Opti lays her body down carefully and heals her wounds as she slowly stirs. Once the creature is fully restored, Opti releases and urges it to flee into its realm. Truly, dear one, my parent knows what is about to erupt. The mare disappears moments later, and seeing it is safe, Opti's patience vanishes with her. The sentinel breathes once, hard and clean—and vaults skyward in renewed fury.

The seam between realms slips past me like a page turned. The meadow's palette returns to intense greens darkened by trampling and ruin, and the sky has gone sour in hue. Shadows thick around tall stalks remain alive as if even light hesitates to lie too close to where two gods will soon fall. The maddened sentinel of Imagination returns to the meadow where Pesa lies sprawled among the tall grasses. As it flies over the scene, Opti's blazing glare fixes on its wounded kin.

Though Pesa's massive frame is still twisted in pain and rage, Opti's thoughts become even more turbulent, grappling with the agony of its next move. For now, the great demon lies powerless and breathless, but soon, it feels, Pesa's fury will overtake and destroy its aching head and body. Deciding to make its move, I see, hear, and feel Opti's thunderous descent slam into the meadow with a wrath unparalleled, shaking the entire scene. This anger—never conceived before by the god of Imagination—becomes strength through power, a force of justice that will now be heard by all the Earth.

Furiously treading the ground where it had landed, Opti lowers its head, folds in its wings, and charges directly at Pesa, halting mere yards from its stricken kin. The god stands poised and willing to deliver another devastating blow, but in the final instant of calculated restraint, it ceases the assault. Instead, Opti begins to slowly circle Pesa—now its writhing prey—its burning breath searing the air near its bloodied face, charring every remaining whisker upon it.

With its crimson-hued glare locked on its sibling's swollen and bloodied gaze, Opti unleashes a roar.

*"Wretched and vile scourge of Earth, I am at an end with you and your barbaric ways! Now that I have your undivided attention, you shall not retreat from the words I speak to you in this solemn moment!"*

Every syllable pierces deep into Pesa's void of mind, shaking the wounded demon's essence to its core. Opti takes another step forward while still unhinged in its ire, its fangs hovering inches over Pesa's exposed throat as it continues its thoughts in a blistering indictment of its kin's nature.

*"In those many ages before my maturity awakened the truth within me, I treasured*

303

*you in honor, and I loved you as a younger sibling should! But as I matured in your very nature, that truth also hardened in me, and my silence to your deeds became my guilt! You savagely execute life not for resource or need, but for diseased pleasure! You alone who will never know joy in the harmony that surrounds you!*

*You have devolved, become arrogance incarnate, as I finally stand in defense of what you birthed long before this day! Only through killing do you find this joy, as it is your purpose in life, your addiction! My assault today is a long-delayed justice to your affliction—one I have taken upon myself with such bitter regret! Yet I know this, it is the only language your twisted mind understands!"*

These intense words reverberate across the meadow, carrying the full weight of Opti's indignation. Its enormous fangs gleam in the diffused light of this destined mid-afternoon, a stark reminder of the highly spirited *nature* of anger now coursing fully through its blood. This gift *and* the curse that were inherited from Pesa itself. The fearless sentinel looms over its kin, a commanding presence that brings Pesa to the brink of tears as it is overwhelmed by the sheer force radiating from its younger sibling.

The Companion holds this scene a heartbeat longer, as if wanting her to feel the blow before she sees it land. Pesa's eyes narrow; its chest lifts with a slow, venomous breath as Opti roars.

*I see now that you will never again take pleasure in life's majesty! I alone have now become its defender, while you have only seized and destroyed it!"*

Its voice scorches the air as it concludes its intense thoughts, unrelenting.

*"It is through you, O savage brute, that joy has become a weapon! Killing is your greatest addiction! My assault upon you today was the only answer to your vile hunger—one I delivered with great regret. But I have learned this: suffering is the only language your twisted mind understands!"*

Fully aware of the dire consequences of its actions, Opti stands its ground, towering over Pesa's charred and battered form. Its searing crimson glare pierces its enemy, each moment heavy with fury and disdain. As Opti's breath heaves with exertion and rage, its gaze scans every inch of the great demon, refusing to yield as Pesa begins to sit upright. Another tense moment passes before the mighty god of Imagination speaks again, its voice still unwavering and filled with indignation.

*"As you continue to feel the sting of this blow, I know you'll wish to answer—because revenge is your way! So answer my action, if you must! I am ready! But never again, Pesa, will I stand silent, ignorant, or complicit in your vile hunts beyond your own realm. Your blissful murder of my creation ends now!*

Heat rises in T'Naeva's cheeks. The meadow's grasses bend from the sheer force of Opti's voice.

*Brutish kin, if you must hunt for sustenance or whatever other purposes you deem necessary, then do so within your plagued existence—and upon your own mundane creations! I warn you now: if ever again you attempt to hunt my kind, be prepared to feel the sting of my swift reaction once more!"*

She stares sadly at her dark parent now, and as if she were seen by it, Pesa's inner presence presses deep into T'Naeva's mind.

Its vessel of shadow and muscle, its scent of ozone and iron bleeding into the air, consumes her. Beneath her parents' skin, she now dwells as another darker will stirs her mind and it is *Dia'Baal himself,* vast and venomous.

"You feel him now, do you not?" D'Reem asks. She nods, uneasy. *"Yes, and it is so very... wrong."*

"Yes, my dear," he says. "This is the heart of Pesa's corruption. It festers in its marrow and its mind; its thoughts becoming consumed by its will before they even form."

The silence shatters as T'Naeva sees Pesa's head whip from side to side as it begins to sit upright, its voice cutting into the quiet like a blade, and she hears it speak for the very first time, and she is gripped in fear.

"It feels like an eternity since I had two reasons to spare you, Opti," Pesa says. "Two reasons that kept my fury and claws at bay. Then our father vanishes into a sparkling and so very pretty spectacle of divine opulence—and *poof*—one of those reasons is gone, GONE ... until this very moment!" Opti's radiance dims for a heartbeat, then flares anew. Its voice rumbles to life in T'Naeva's chest before she even hears it.

*"It is sadly true that I have become entangled in your violent, corrupted nature... a nature, Pesa, that has twisted you beyond recognition. Mark this, deformed wretch—I*

*have shed the blind spots of the past and you will never again catch me unaware!"*

The force of Reality now blazes into its eyes as the god of Imagination roars a sudden challenge.

*"No more boasts, no more delay—show me this fury you claim to command and strike at me now if you so dare!"*

Pesa freezes but is enthralled by its kin's tenacity, its eyes narrowing as Dia'Baal's excitement smothers all remaining peace.
"Well done, and soon enough, O, savage flower, as your wish shall be met once my fury matures enough to slash through and consume your very breath!" The demon spits, its words cutting the air. Pesa, still sitting, shakes off the final tremors of its wicked blow.
"Why do you think I waited ever so patiently, even to this moment, for you to strike at me first? For ages, I have longed to end your miserable existence. Now, in furious patience, you have finally given me reason enough to destroy you!"
Opti roars in return.

*"You speak of patience, Pesa, but you know nothing of it! You speak of restraint, but your heart is a weapon drawn long before it was needed. Your wounds are not my doing—they are your own!*
*Your patience descended long before mine, but now I see the full extent of your corruption... in a mind void of any wisdom whatsoever! Our father suspected this but could not bear to see this vile truth in you. Now it is clear. You are a tragedy beyond scope. I pity you, Pesa, and I pity what you have sadly become!"*

The word *pity* ignites fury in Pesa's eyes.

"How dare you pity the greatest of all creation... **freak of my nature!**" The meadow trembles beneath the beast's three final words, shaking the heavens in their wake.

"For nary an eon, I patiently endured your tripe of goodwill only for our father's sake, to keep my claws away from your wretched neck! I suffered in your arrogance. In your weakness. Finally, I could stand no longer in your meddling with *my* domain, my very foundation of existence!"
Pesa's eyes burn like molten iron as it continues.
"That mercy too burnt away long ago! But the moment you finally lost yours and decided to lay your wrath upon me, this poor, corrupted brute,

my spark reignited, and your fate was sealed!"

Pesa's eyes close briefly as it reminisces upon these thoughts, focusing their intensity, to now.

"My tolerance too ends now, and your attack—this pitiful strike against me, however, does not compare to my outrage at your twisted experiments... upon **my nature!** I have seen what you have done to my creations, Opti, and I am appalled!"

The words thunder through T'Naeva, shaking her spirit to her core. D'Reem's voice brushes her ear, low and solemn.

"What you feel now is not just rage, my dear. It is age upon age of restraint, fracturing in an instant. This is the cost of ancient patience when it is thrust against rebellion and to its point of no return."

Opti does not step backward and is ready to strike if Pesa is foolish enough to attack it...

The Companion lets her see the faint shimmer in the air between the two gods, the void around her parent twisting the light, as if rejecting creation itself. Pesa snaps, its voice sharp enough to cut through diamond.

"This day is not about wounds, O, pretty beast—it is about answers! I have lived far too long in your shadow, waiting for the moment when justice— MY justice—**would silence you forever!**"

It opens and lowers its large aqua-hued eyes and rises to its trembling legs, the ground cracking beneath its every weary step. The air still smells of scorched fur, though no fire burns. She feels this vibration of evil through the soles of her feet—deep and ancient, far older than the meadow itself. Pesa sneers.

"And so, today, after all those unrelenting ages of torment, I say this: wherever our dear father hides—damn to him and his creation! Damn to his so-called wisdom, and damn to the oh-so-touching source he so eagerly embraces!"

Opti shakes its head, a lament searing through the intensity of its voice as it responds.

*"Vicious, vile demon—how dare you utter such blasphemy against our father! He adored you despite your sickness, despite the darkness you have embraced! He loved you unconditionally and without question! One day, though, his justice will fall upon you like a crushing wave, and your rebellion against him will be laid to ruin!"*

But the storm within Pesa has no room for remorse. The great demon bares

its fangs, shuddering as Dia'Baal's anger flares brighter in Pesa's fury.
"Impudent, yet so clever Opti! Dare not preach to me about rebellion,
He who ordained the freedom that unshackled me from His graces! This
world—MY world—proves my destiny, my *justice*, free of the meddling in
affairs that pertain not to Him, but only to me!"

For a fleeting moment, Opti's gaze softens. The warmth of its father's voice
rises into its mind like a breath of clarity.

*'Victory does not belong to those who rage, but to those who endure.'*

The golden light within Opti steadies. Resolve pulses through its body. The
meadow falls deathly still. The ground hums beneath its talons—steady,
ancient. In the realm of eternal sight, D'Reem speaks gently to T'Naeva.
"This is the collision of two truths that cannot—and will never—coexist in
peace."
They see Pesa step forward. Malice thickens the air, heavy enough to choke,
but Opti does not waver. The heavens hold their breath. The meadow, once
alive, becomes the stage for Earth's reckoning. The sky swirls. The wind
howls. And these two forces—kin in origin, enemies in truth—stand at the
edge of eternity.

The stillness fractures. Pesa's tail lashes. Its claws dig into the earth.
The Companion tightens T'Naeva's vision, revealing how the meadow
bends away from Pesa's presence—as if the world itself recoils from the evil
blooming inside of it. The land flees its way, from what Pesa has become.
"*Justice, you say?*" Opti retorts, its voice heavy and deliberate.

"*If justice is what you seek, o, vile brute, then justice is what you shall have! But
understand this—you will not like the shape it takes!*"

Its twitching muscles glint like forged metal. The Companion pulls Pesa's
attention to the smallest movement—a talon tightening, a wing shifting
slightly forward. Opti roars.

"*And when justice is finished, you will face a truth you fear most, that your life's work
will be nothing more than ashes in the wind.*"

Pesa grins, all teeth.
"Ashes feed the soil!"
It hisses.

"And from that soil, something stronger always grows! I will tear down your precious realm and sow the whole of the world with my own!"

The ground shakes as it steps forward, and she again feels its intense jolt in her mind. D'Reem's voice returns, low and almost mournful.

"This is where they no longer speak as kin, dear mate. This is where words turn to weapons."

The Companion blurs her vision's edge, intentionally, letting her feel the heat, the charge in the air, the tension before the storm. She watches Pesa's muscles coil, the rise and fall of its breath in a predator's rhythm. Above them, the clouds churn, folding in on themselves, pulling the sunlight into a green-gold haze.

Opti's glare does not waver. The air between them stretches like worn cloth—that is, until it must break. T'Naeva understands now. The battle is no longer avoidable.

The meadow will bear witness to what follows. The Companion lets her feel the weight of that truth before another image sharpens as Opti's radiance dims for a heartbeat, then blazes back. It stands unshaken, a pillar of light against a gathering storm. D'Reem's voice enters her mind once more, low and steady.

"No words can turn this back, T'Naeva. Pesa is gone until its final breath."

Her tears begin to flow as she sees it clearly—the void where reason once was, now filled with Dia'Baal's venom. The ground beneath her shivers. The wind's howl rises in warning. The meadow, once a sanctuary, has become a crucible. The sky spirals violently above, hungry for the clash to begin.

Opti's stance is unyielding, talons pressed into the trembling earth as though anchoring to the very heart of Reality. It roars, each word ringing with finality.

*"You have chosen this end, Pesa, so do not expect me to mourn for you any longer!"*

Pesa chuckles venomously, the sound is jagged like a broken blade against stone. "Mourn? You'll have no breath to waste on mourning once I am finished with you and your wretched world!"

Its claws flex, scoring deep into the soil.
The Companion lets T'Naeva feel the heat radiating from the demon's body, the static thick in the air, raising every hair on her arms. Above them, lightning etches white scars across the green-stained sky.
D'Reem whispers.
"This will not just be a fight—it will become the moment the harmony within Opti completely shatters, the pivot upon which one age begins another."
T'Naeva swallows hard, unable to tear her eyes from the two gods primed to engage into warfare before her.

They circle—not in haste, but with grim inevitability—each step is deliberate, each movement a statement. Opti moves like the turning of a star: steady, eternal. Pesa shifts like a shadow dancing through flame: fluid, unpredictable. The meadow absorbs them; every blade of grass bowed beneath their opposing wills. The Companion does not shield her from the silence between heartbeats, the way the world itself listens for the first strike. A single raindrop falls, heavy as stone.

More follows, until the air hums with wet soil and ozone. The first thunder cracks—not from the sky—but from deep within the earth. It is time.

*"Vile beast, so utterly foolish our sovereign father has been—and I as well—for believing you might ever rise above what possesses you!*

Its roar cascades through the meadow, a thunderous condemnation of Pesa's nature. The god pauses, its towering form radiating a presence both formidable and final. Then, with slow precision, Opti delivers its parting words.

*"O, foul beast, from what I now understand of your maniacal nature, I grow nauseous to share even a fragment of its substance, for it, as you, truly sickens me!"*

The god's roar echoes with the winds carrying its righteous fury until silence falls. Yet even as Opti's divine essence trembles with imbalance, the bright thread that once bound its will to harmony lies idle and unfulfilled. Tainted by the swift maturity of its newfound *nature*, it mistakes this hollow stillness for resolution. Opti, convinced that its point has been made, turns to leave, its gaze falling upon its kin one last time with a mix of disgust and sorrow.

But for Pesa, this moment is far from over. Straining to balance itself against the torturous blow it has endured, Pesa's thoughts burn with wrath and vengeance. Truly, T'Naeva, your diseased parent does not share its kin's desire for resolution. To Pesa, there is only one course left: *retribution*. D'Reem's voice arises in her mind once more.

"T'Naeva, your diseased parent does not seek resolution. It seeks only revenge. Wrath stirs like coals catching breath. Ages of frustration coalescing into a single monstrous purpose.

The great beast of Reality, shaking its bloodied head one final time, feels its long-awaited vengeance stir to life. Years of frustration and disappointment boil over as its dark thoughts coalesce into a singular, sinister purpose. Pesa's mind, warped and twisted, becomes fully energized as the evil within it awakens Dia'Baal's zeal for battle. His wrath, now fully unleashed, marks the beginning of a tragic and cataclysmic confrontation.

With this emerging presence finally defeating Pesa's dizzying trauma, the god of beasts also begins to crave this heated moment. With a deep breath and a final bodily shake to defeat the remnants of pain, Pesa lowers its eyes while displaying its enormous fangs, growling in an ominous, deep tone.

"Indeed, O savage flower, it is you too who also sickens... **me!**"

The massive god sways unsteadily, collapsing to its belly as it mumbles a barrage of non-coherent sentences. The punishment it has endured still clouds its mind. Opti turns in its slow retreat, glancing back as its crimson eyes lock with Pesa's. The fallen god glares upward—then grins. Its wide and wicked bloodied smile breaks into a high-pitched, unhinged laughter, jagged and echoing, unnerving in its raw, manic resonance.

The thunderous pain still flows through its body, but now Pesa steadies it, and it is finally defeated. Hatred flashes behind its aqua-hued eyes as it again sits upright, its deadly silence heralding murderous intent. Slowly, the beast rises again, its legs steady as a deadly silence wraps around its frame. Then, in one swift motion, it springs to all fours, its twenty-ton bulk perfectly balanced. Its movements now focused and slow, and each step towards Opti is calculated.

Pesa's consecutive low growls vibrate the air—thick and menacing with intent. It is Dia'Baal that now speaks through the mighty demon, and his words are not merely sound; they are rage made manifest. They are godhood corrupted and tightening. A shifting of power. A poison threading through nerve and muscle. Pesa's aqua pupils expand from the demon within it, pouring into his molten fire. Even its breath changes, each exhale curling in the storm-charged air like smoke from a smoldering pyre.

Dia'Baal no longer speaks through Pesa—he *inhabits* it, reshaping the god's stance into something twisted and sinister, a living herald of evil and hatred.

"Dearest and most respectable kin," Dia'Baal taunts, his voice slick with mockery. I want to personally express my deepest gratitude for finally uprooting your wretched hide to punish me for my eons of devilish and diabolical debauchery."

Opti tilts its head, disbelief flickering through its otherwise steadfast demeanor. My parent sees now, as do I: Pesa is more lost to madness than it ever imagined. Yet despite the scorn, Opti turns away—refusing to dignify the desecration of its kin with any further engagement. Its massive wings shift inward as it begins to saunter toward the sanctuary of its realm. Pesa's anger swiftly turns darker and more relentless.

A guttural growl has built in its chest, and Dia'Baal speaks again—the perfect poison through his mighty host.

"Truly, O savage flower, thank you for letting me witness the conclusion of your failed divine upbringing. A farce! An empty wasteland of deficiency! A total lack of goodwill that has left you incapable of turning the other cheek to my ages of grievous misdeeds!"

Opti stops abruptly, its body tense as it turns its massive head to meet the fiery glare of its sibling. Sadness washes over Opti as the truth behind Pesa's cruel words strikes deep. There is no denying that they hold fragments of painful truth. After a short pause, Opti exhales heavily, turning away once more, and continues its measured retreat, choosing to hope over despair, despite the venomous tirade it knows is not yet over.

In a heartbeat, the great beast lunges forward, charging Opti as its hatred crystallizes into action, closing the distance with explosive speed. Roaring as awakened thunder, the god of beasts bellows as it sprints, claws fully extended to intentionally strike its kin from behind.

**"Dare not turn your back upon me again, savage flower! You have awakened my storm—a tempest you will now face, one you will no longer simply walk away from unscathed!"**

Pesa's words crash like waves against Opti's spine. Yet in the span of a heartbeat, instinct—both primal and pure—ignites. Opti pivots with blinding speed, a movement so swift it cleaves the very sound from the air. In an instant, it is no longer peace disengaging conflict, but a sentinel facing the pureness of evil incarnate. Opti's fangs flash, enormous and gleaming in the diffused and restless light.

Crimson fire ignites in its eyes. Its sudden reversal halts Pesa mid-charge, forcing the great beast to stumble, claws tearing earth in wild, skidding trenches. Advancing fearlessly, it unleashes a roar, a thunder contained within the meadow surrounding them.

*"Vile Pesa, I too am now snared in your violent nature—a nature that has twisted you beyond recognition! Perhaps your claws may have even scored their wrath upon me in this cowardly attack—before I transcended into the maturity that glares down upon your evil!"*

The declaration splits the air like a blade, and T'Naeva feels it in her every element—a pressure wave that drives everything else into silence. Opti's words are not made of boast, but testament, each syllable pressing forward like stone laid upon stone. Opti's gaze hardens as it continues to advance, cutting through the diseased fog of Pesa's mind.

*"But take this truth to heart, O, diseased brute, that I will never again allow you the chance to strike at me from behind! Face me directly now, if you so dare! Keep your word and unleash this storm you so proudly proclaim, you pitiful coward!"*

The insult lands deep and Pesa freezes, its eyes narrowing to black pinpoints. Dia'Baal's rage rises like a tide, and T'Naeva's breath catches under the weight of it all. The god-beast's presence smothers all thought, pressing down like a veil over a dying ember. Then the voice of Pesa's inner demon lashes out, malicious and final.

"You shall soon wish I were the coward you presume me to be, o, savage flower!"

T'Naeva recoils, clutching her chest as though the venom of these words had pierced her too, and she speaks.

"By the Companion ... even its voice rends the air like poison!"

T'Naeva leans in close to D'Reem, her whisper strained and fearful.

"Dia'Baal and Pesa are no longer separate. They are one voice now, one fury, one storm, one evil."

Pesa advances... slowly, shaking free of the lingering trauma of its earlier defeat. Its growl deepens, its fury now fully its own.
"Why do you think, freakish kin, that I waited so patiently for you to strike me first?"
Pesa sneers.
"For ages, I have longed to end your miserable existence, but I waited, and now you have given me reason enough!"

Opti tilts its head slightly, its gaze unwavering.
*"It is not I who has fallen, Pesa. It is you."*

The echo is steady, warm against the cold edge of her vision in this moment. It flows beneath her chest, calming the instinct to recoil. The golden sentinel's stance does not shift. Its core burns with a light that refuses to waver.
"This battle," D'Reem murmurs at her side, "will not be of its making, but it will endure."
A stillness falls—not a quiet, but a suspension. The entire meadow seems caught between heartbeats. The grasses stop mid-bend, the faint movement of their tips frozen. The distant sounds of Imagination's creatures vanish from my ears, not faded, but abruptly absent. Even the clouds over the realm of Reality seem to hesitate, their drift arrested. Beneath it all, the ground hums, *and the meadow knows.*

She feels it through the soles of her feet, low and ancient, a sound too deep to hear but too strong to ignore. It carries an awareness, as if the land itself truly understands her current plight.
"It knows," D'Reem says quietly, "this is the collision of two truths that can never coexist in harmonious peace."

The weight of those words settles heavily over the meadow like an oncoming storm. But then, like a spark catching flame, the memory of the creator's purpose reignites within. The god stands firm, unyielding—a beacon of light in the midst of Pesa's encroaching darkness. Opti gazes upon Pesa with both sorrow and determination, for it sees the truth that no words could ever erase.

"No more words," D'Reem says to her, "can erase what it sees now—Pesa is consumed."

She feels the finality in those words—the closing of a door that will not open again. When she meets Pesa's eyes, they are voids. Mercy has no place in them. Reason is a stranger there. They are voids where light goes to die. For a fleeting moment, Opti's radiance dims, a shadow of doubt creeping at the edges of its resolve. But then, like a spark catching flame, the memory of the creator's purpose reignites within. Pesa's mind is consumed, utterly devoured by Dia'Baal's cancerous vengeance, leaving no element for mercy, reason, or redemption.

*There is no turning back now...*

The heavens grow silent, the earth beneath them trembling with anticipation. The meadow, once a place of life and beauty, now stands as the chosen battleground where Earth's destiny will unfold. The skies swirl with the energy of an impending clash, the very fabric of reality bracing itself for what is to come. As the winds howl and the ground quakes, two forces stand at the precipice of eternity, their fates intertwined in a struggle that will echo through the ages. This battle will define more than their rivalry; it will shape the very future of Earth itself.

*The stage is set!*

D'Reem turns to his beloved, his gaze laden with the burden of what he knows and sees once more, not for his sake, *but for hers*. His voice, steady yet weighted with the gravity of countless suns, trembles with this unshakable fact, this monumental truth.

"Trust, deception, and impending ruin—all merged into the cosmic weave of fate unraveling even now, dear T'Naeva. The echoes of this fragile peace will shape the destiny of our world."
He takes her hand gently, his touch anchoring them in the fleeting calm, even as the gales of time gather on the horizon. Her vision begins to dim. Light recedes. She blinks.

*Darkness. And yet... not silence.*

Something lingers behind the veil. A scent. A sound. A breath. A sense of breathless becoming... and it fades way too soon. She gasps softly, her eyes wet not with sorrow, but with a newly forged hunger. Not for comfort but for clarity. For truth. For the full vision. For what lies beyond this veil of what she was told, and into what *is*.
She turns toward D'Reem with trembling urgency.
"I need to see it..." she roars. "All of it!"

D'Reem's voice returns, neither thunder nor whisper, but something eternal—spoken now for those not yet born, but who listen from beyond time. And to you, seeker of this living flame... these words were always meant for you. For you too must find the strength to ask:

*How has this truth stirred my inner fire?*
*How does its clarity help me walk more bravely through the trials I face?*
*How might I now carry this story into my own?"*

Thus ends **The Season of Maturity**, ushering in the wondrous and eternal realms ... of *thought*. The eons of ancient past that will never again be seen in the physical will live on—seen only by those whose minds awaken... to **MYTH.**

# CHAPTER 4
## *The Tide of Transgression*

*"Sin is a queer thing, it isn't the breaking of divine
commandments, it is the breaking of one's own integrity."*
—D. H. Lawrence

# *Verse XIX:*
## Ten Echoes Before The Burn

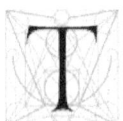

T he words of this chapter flow through the mind of a god, a warrior, a man, and a husband—forged from passion to convey truth through the omnipotence of his *Companion*.

His name is D'Reem, and these vivid sounds and visions are brought to life for the sake of his beloved, T'Naeva. As his eyes glow with divine awakening, ancient images unfold through the Almighty's revelation, sharpening into reality. With this knowledge, clarity emerges, and D'Reem speaks with resolve. These are not merely recollections—they are living truths, echoes from the very soul of time itself. They burn within him as fire once held in silence, now given voice.

"It so continues, dearest T'Naeva, in *The Tide of Transgression*—a fleeting yet fateful span of only a handful of hours in which tragedy sweeps across the face of Earth, altering its course forever. On this fateful day, after ages of guidance and devotion, Xionn Theone has stepped away from his world and his children, entrusting them with the legacy of his love and the weight of their own choices.

The Divine Hand withdraws not in judgment, but in trust—knowing that love without freedom is but a gilded cage. I gaze now with renewed sadness upon the scene near the *Sanctuary of Harmony*, where the true deception unfolds beneath layers of trust and expectation.
For Xionn, this day, sadly, he will never know. To Opti, this day will become a cautious blessing, but no longer.

To Dia'Baal—entwined completely within and throughout Pesa's body and mind—it is the beginning of ages of things far more permanent and sinister, and it is *beautiful* to him. The contrast of the two titans sharpens like the meeting of dusk and dawn. Dia'Baal's corrosive whispers devour Pesa's sense of purpose, twisting it into a relentless pursuit of dominance and vengeance.

Xionn's enduring influence nurtures Opti's unwavering commitment to understanding and harmony, even at the cost of his own peace of mind. Where Dia'Baal has demanded submission and sown discord, Xionn offered grace, striving for coexistence and creation—revealing the stark dichotomy of destruction versus unity.

*That was then...*

Pesa's voice rumbles, dripping with wickedness as the thunder of its hatred resonates throughout the entire scope of the meadow.
"Yes, dear kin, a reason so profound, so consuming, that it has burned within me for ages—fueling my desire to reduce your very existence to dust."

But even as the words leave its maw, something stirs deep within Pesa—a flicker of something long buried. A distant memory, hazy and fleeting, of a time before the weight of resentment took hold. It sees flashes of what it once was: a guardian, a being of purpose, an entity that once stood in harmony with the world. The memory of Xionn's voice, distant yet unmistakable, hums through the corners of its mind.

*'You, o, mighty child... were created to protect, not to destroy.'*

A flicker of hesitation. A whisper of doubt. Then Dia'Baal's voice surges forward, crushing all doubt before it can take root. Pesa clenches its claws into the earth, inhaling the rage, feeding on the hatred, and allowing it to reshape whatever remnants of its former self dared to resurface.
The mighty demon growls.
"I have waited, biding my time with patience and passion. And now, the perfect moment stands before us!"

Pesa's stomps reverberate through the trembling earth, every movement deliberate and menacing. A dark energy coils within Pesa, pulsing like a living void, sharpening its resolve with each passing moment. The air thickens with the weight of impending destruction, the once-vibrant meadow now steeped in an eerie stillness.
"You and your arrogance have brought this upon yourself," it hisses, eyes gleaming with malice. By daring to strike me without considering the consequences, you have finally given me the cause I craved—a cause to destroy not only you, but the pitiful world you cling to so dearly!"

The words drip with contempt, a cruel promise echoing through the winds as Pesa's power swells, dark and unrelenting. Malevolence drips from its every word, each syllable a relentless assault on Opti's core. Yet Opti does not flinch. It stands firm, its crimson glare unwavering against the rising tide of Pesa's rage. The inevitability of their battle hangs heavy in the air, and suddenly, Pesa's roar splits the heavens, obliterating the last remnants of their fractured kinship. Its voice a storm in birth.

"O, savage flower, the moment you have feared has arrived! I will show you what I have become. In this moment, I rise as the force that will erase your existence, casting you into oblivion where you belong!"

The scene we both witness now is a nightmare brought to life. Pesa's monstrous fangs gleam, dripping with frothing saliva, the very essence of its blood lust, and I cannot tear my gaze away. The sheer hatred radiating from Pesa spreads like a toxic surge, darkening the meadow and poisoning the air directly above these two gods. The beast's thunderous voice rises once more, a tempest of rage that shakes the Earth to its core.

"You, O, savage flower, are the source of my fury! You, who are my nemesis!

You, who has defiled my nature, twisting its purity of essence to serve your perverse imagination! O, savage flower, it is you who truly sickens me beyond all redemption! Do not dare think me naive, blind to the truth of your grotesque maturity—a mutation born indeed from my very atoms!"

But as Pesa begins to lunge, something catches within its mind—a brief, involuntary flicker. For a mere instant, it stops and does not see an enemy before it, but a sibling. Opti's defiant gaze is not one of malice, but of sorrow. A memory, sharp and unbidden, rushes forward: the two of them, side by side in those earliest of days, standing in silent awe beneath Xionn's light. The sense of belonging, of purpose—was it truly an illusion all along?

*...No. This thought is dangerous... Weak... Unacceptable.*

With a snarl and a shake of its head, Pesa forces the memory into oblivion, twisting the pain into further anger. It strikes harder, faster, crushing any trace of recognition beneath the weight of its fury. Another tense moment passes, and the chaos remains chained. Pesa stands motionless, its eyes narrowing into slits of glowing, aqua-hued ire.

Opti's wings shift, its form radiating a steady golden light as it braces for the unknown. The air thickens once more with an unnatural silence, broken only by the faint hum of power crackling around the god of beasts. Time itself seems to stretch, the weight of the impending storm pressing heavily on all creation. The moment ends. Pesa's glare reignites into a blaze, burning with malice as it howls.

"Tell me o, freak of my nature—can you do this?"

In a moment of sickening awe, Opti's gaze snaps to the grotesque sight of Pesa's superior horns regenerating. From those aqua bloodied and jagged stubs, they sprout anew, larger and more lethal than before. The transformation sends a chill through my beloved parent, a stark reminder of the power it alone now faces. A heightened vigilance surges through Opti, caution now burning as brightly as the crimson glow in its eyes. Sensing the rising darkness within Pesa, Opti braces itself, its towering form radiating defiance.

The venomous aura of Dia'Baal builds within his beastly pet, threatening to overtake all of its reason. Pesa lets loose a deafening roar, its voice a storm that shakes the heavens. Its voice is saturated with scorn.

"What stands before me now? A feeble, pathetic excuse for a god? Do my eyes deceive me, or is this the pitiable extent of your maturity stolen from me! Your strike against me—the greatest of all creation—was nothing more than a laughable insult! Yes, Opti, I see it clearly now. You retreat, dread growing in your every step, and I revel in your fear!"

Pesa pauses, its derisive snort cutting through the air like a whip.
"You fool!" It hisses, advancing with deliberate menace.

"I no longer see the innocent flower you once were, long ago. No, what stands before me now is something ludicrous even to me, a most savage flower, a mockery of what you were meant to be! You have defiled the very essence of my nature, twisting it to suit your delusions, and soon, you will know the full power of what you sought to challenge, to master!"
Its glare intensifies as it steps forward, towering with menacing resolve.
"As I now gaze true upon your cowering, faithless, and hollow nature, my wrath grows and it will soon overflow! I no longer see the pretty, innocent blossom you once were, long ago!"

But then, something happens. For the first time, Pesa feels it—not anger, not power, but loss, a deep, cavernous emptiness where something sacred once dwelled. The echoes of its past life resurface in waves, and for a moment, it reaches—not with claws, not with fury, but with something deeper—a desire to return.
And then—*the whisper swallows it whole.*

Dia'Baal's presence floods Pesa's being with a crushing, suffocating force. All doubts are once more torn from its essence, shredded apart as if they never existed. In their place, the whisper speaks...
*There is only dominance ... only hunger ... only wrath!*

"No, I see instead a twisted, most savage flower—matured by means I care not to discern—a bloom whose time for plucking is long overdue! You alone, wretched kin, have poisoned the nature I was born to guard. You defile what I create, and soon, you will learn a lesson in the true power of my reality!"
Pesa's voice crescendos, each word a hammer striking the fragile peace of

the meadow.

"O, vicious flower, you will soon discover the force of Reality—a tempest pure and unyielding, sweeping away every trace of your little fantasy world! You will be obliterated, leaving nothing behind but dust! My world tolerates your existence no longer! A force vicious and firm, O, brazen kin, that no longer acknowledges your invalidity upon this world—MY WORLD!"

Its voice magnifies, its glare intensifies, seething malice etched into every line of its monstrous face.

"I say to you now, Opti—damn you, and damn every fragment of your miserable existence! Soon, this reality will stain your coat a bright and lovely crimson, soaked beneath my awakened claws, and their promise to destroy you, fully and utterly shall be granted!"

Opti, aware of the dire circumstances, feels its fear of Pesa growing at an alarming rate. But in that instant, an Almighty presence overtakes it—a force so profound that I too feel it radiating through me. This divine reckoning rapidly obliterates Opti's fear of Pesa, halting its retreat in a single movement.

And then, dear T'Naeva, within seconds, this otherworldly presence reveals to Opti in a blaze of imagery the entire scope of what possesses Pesa.

It sees with clarity the dark reality of Dia'Baal's influence, and for the first time, *Opti fully understands*. Armed with this revelation and with its adrenaline surging, the sentinel of Imagination unleashes a roar as thunderous as the *anew* itself.

*"So, now it comes to this, sinister and fallen Dia'Baal! O, how I see your purpose for my dear kin! How I understand clearly why I acted as I did upon this poor, wretched beast you devour from within, you coward!"*

The air around the two gods thickens, vibrating with the malice radiating from the corrupted god of beasts. Opti's voice cuts through the rising tension, resolute and steady.

*"This is not your battle, Pesa! You have been reduced to a mere drop of rain, insignificant to Dia'Baal's mighty storm of deceit. He seeks to finish what he began eons before this moment—to prove he can destroy the harmony the Creator set forth by attempting to kill me, and you are nothing more than his means to an end!"*

Pesa halts briefly, its form shuddering as Dia'Baal seizes further control. The voice that follows is no longer Pesa's. It is deeper, colder—a chilling echo of

Dia'Baal's fully awakened spirit of venom and pride.

"You see well, O, brazen flower, as I have learned well from my past. Where once I challenged my King openly, I now wield subtler yet equal power. Through Pesa, I will succeed where brute strength once failed. Though I will still carve through you, Opti, I too will dismantle the unity that binds this world, piece by glorious piece. The King's harmony cannot stand if its precious Imagination dies with it!"

Dia'Baal's words thrum through the meadow like a plague, heavy and suffocating. Opti squares itself, its massive frame glowing brighter as it draws upon the power of its strength and conviction. The memory of its father's stories—the war in the Great Realm, Dia'Baal's catastrophic defeat, and his banishment—flares into its vast mind. This moment is a continuation of that ancient war, and Opti knows the stakes are now even greater than its own survival.

Dia'Baal's voice grows colder, more spiteful, as if to drown out the memory it cannot erase. Opti, unshaken, recalls another tale from its father—a tale of Dia'Baal's epic fiasco on Ametheden, straight back into his face.

*"There, this once-proud demon led his pathetic band of rogues in a desperate attempt to overthrow and destroy the Creator's first world. Your darkness ravaged the lands, your armies slaughtered countless innocents, and for a time, it seemed you might succeed. But even in your mightiest hour, you scourge, you were again cast asunder to mere insignificance!*
*Your Creator intervened, stripping you of your victory while purging Ametheden of your corruption, leaving you to sulk as a punished child in the void of your monumental delusions of pride, and its ultimate failure!"*

Dia'Baal's laughter erupts through Pesa, a guttural, mocking resonance that shakes the ground beneath it. Its sound reverberates like a dissonant hymn to chaos, its tone chilling the very air.
"So, the proud shall fall?"
Dia'Baal's thoughts again erupt through Pesa, his voice dripping with venomous scorn.
"The corrupter will find no refuge, the deceiver shall find no truth? How quaint the King's words sound now, as if they carry weight against the tide of inevitability that I will soon bring down upon your wretched hide!"

He shifts within Pesa, his essence intertwining further with the beast's dark godly power, the malevolence emanating from him intense.

"You cling to echoes of the past, O, savage flower, desperately shielding yourself with memories of victories that have long diminished. But tell me this: will the Creator's vaunted harmony save you now? Will the *Bright One* shelter you from the tempest I've summoned within your dear old kin? No—it merely prolongs your agony!"

Opti's crimson glare sharpens, unyielding.
*"Your bitterness knows no end!"*
It roars, each word laden with resolute defiance.

*"You are blinded by your own feckless obsessions, consumed by a pride that has shattered you time and again! This vessel, this world—it is all just another futile attempt to defy what you can never unmake! The Creator's harmony endures, and so shall I!"*
Dia'Baal snarls through Pesa, his voice a tempest of wrath.

"You foolish creature! Look around you—this world trembles under MY will! Every crack in its surface, every tear in its skies bears testament to the fragility of His precious balance through your damned father! You speak of endurance, but harmony is nothing more than a brittle shell, waiting to be shattered! Starting with you, I will sever that thread, O, vicious Opti! When it snaps, there will be no restoration, no salvation, and no father to rebuild what I have willfully and masterfully undone... **all by myself!**"

The air grows heavy with the clash of their opposing forces, the meadow trembling under the weight of this surging war of words. Dia'Baal's arguments are malicious, yet Opti's resolve burns brighter, the silent promise of the Creator's enduring order anchoring its unwavering stance against this terrible presence of evil.

A divine revelation strikes as Opti's blazing glare falters for the briefest instant. Somewhere deep beneath the monstrous facade, it sees the sibling it once knew—a fleeting shadow of what Pesa had been before Dia'Baal's corruption. The memory stirs an ache in its core, a sorrow quickly buried beneath unyielding purpose. There will be no saving Pesa; this is now a fight for survival, but not yet for redemption. Opti roars.
*"I eagerly await your response, knowing you are nothing more than a belligerent, raucous coward!"*

Pesa's body shakes violently, Dia'Baal's rage forcing his host to react to Opti's words of truth. Advancing slowly, the great beast roars, its voice laced with hatred.

"Opti, freak of my nature, you and your truth will both reside in oblivion this day!"

The force of Imagination lowers its head, its blazing eyes fixed on its diseased kin. This is the breaking point and the sentinel of Imagination decides it has endured enough of both Pesa *and* Dia'Baal's threats. Hardening itself for the fight of its life, Opti bares its massive fangs at the violator, the destroyer of all that is good, its roar striking deep into Pesa's corrupted heart.

*"Be it, then, Dia'Baal Fallenstar, you disease of life, for it is only you I truly despise!"*

Directing fullness of focus on its enemy, Opti's deafening roar reverberates through the meadow, a statement of resolve and power.

*"For you as well, proud and arrogant Pesa—will see that I am no, so called flower to stomp upon and crush! O, miserable beast, how the chaos within you steers your blind course to destruction! How this demon's rage consumes you, tormenting your mind with malice! Truly, maniacal Pesa, your conceit will be your everlasting fate, as your inflated ego will come to learn far more of me than it has ever imagined!"*

Dia'Baal's vengeful pride briefly halts Pesa's advance. The demon roars, its dominance hurled back at Opti with fury.

"I welcome it indeed, vicious flower! Your challenge I gladly accept! My so-called blinded rage embraces your pitiful attempt to weaken my revulsion of you—through your dear kin!"

Opti roars in reply, powerful and resolute.

*"I tell you this, O, vile serpent—it is a response you will never forget!"*

The spirit of the Earth herself, Gaea, stricken with a sense of hopelessness, surrenders entirely to the will of her dark lord, Pesa. The demon's next roar ignites the heavens, thunder and lightning flashing in chaotic unison.

"Your delusions of grandeur mean nothing to me, freak of my nature! Your defilement upon my nature ends this hour! My wrath, a living inferno, will not rest until its flames devour your shattered, lifeless carcass—and leave your realm smoldering in ruin and ash!"

The mighty sentinel of Imagination shreds the ground beneath its colossal talons, shaking the meadow as if to tear the realms themselves asunder. Baring its enormous fangs, Opti thunders in response, a sound of unrelenting power and defiance.

*"Come at me now if your demon within so dares... **Dear Sibling!**"*

My precious T'Naeva, as *I breathe* in every element of this dreadful moment, I am fully aware of these events of ages long past. I have lived them before—seen them, tasted them, in the youth of my life. But this time, this account is *for you and you alone.*
It is you who deserves the truth of what I now witness, a truth gifted to me to strip away the cloak of deceit shrouding your mind, your emotional residence of a parent you long to adore.

It is for you alone, dear T'Naeva, that *I hear* the god's roar entwined with thunder, the weight of their words abruptly silenced, yet echoing in their shared volatile hatred. The meadow quakes beneath their fury, and yes, dear T'Naeva, I hear the tragedy of what is to come—*for you alone.*

... For you alone, *I taste* the bitterness of earth and ozone, the acrid residue of conflict scattering in the gales whipping around me. These fragments of earth and sky, born of their clashing wills, coat my tongue as the meadow's beauty disintegrates into chaos. Yes, dear T'Naeva, I taste the horror of what is to come—*for you alone.*

... For you alone, *I feel* the thrust of my body hurled skyward, sensing the volatile energy within the storms of wrath that span to each corner of Earth. They merge into a roiling tempest, infused with an unearthly fury. The sulfuric tang of charged air sears my nostrils as the heavens weep a violent rain upon the fractured earth below. Yes, dear T'Naeva, I smell the tragedy of what is to come—*for you alone.*

... For you alone, *I reach* outward and feel Gaea's essence, her sorrow so profound that it saturates the storm's downpour. Her tears fall heavy, her lament a silent hymn for the divine meadow torn between two realms. Yes, dear T'Naeva, I feel the overwhelming tragedy of what is to come upon our beloved Earth—*for you alone.*

Through it all, I see. In this divine sense, *I witness* this calamitous showdown unfold once more—a clash that will shape the fates of gods and worlds alike.

The heartbreak of what is to come haunts me, the searing truths I have endured, and once more endure—*for you alone.*

T'Naeva's tears glisten as she listens, her awe growing with each passing word. For the first time, she feels the depth of D'Reem's love and devotion. Despite the storm raging around them, she clings to this newfound certainty. And for her alone, D'Reem again relives this tragic tale.

And now, my dearest love, I ask you not only endure these visions with me, but to *awaken* within them. Let the Companion guide all your senses now—as mine too were led—to grant you the strength to see beyond these shadows, beyond these echoes cascading within your questioning soul. You are no longer only present—*for you alone are now part of their truth.*

T'Naeva—shaking, eyes wide—closes them, not to retreat, but to feel so much more. The roars, the thunder, the words of gods that no mortal should ever hear—they swirl powerfully within her mind now. The goddess holds fast for the truth. Not the truth for D'reem's glory, nor Opti's, nor Pesa's, but to experience the truth—*for herself.*

TEN – Under a raging sky, two titanic figures sway in primal ghastly rhythms, their movements rising with elemental intent. Winds howl, rain slashes, and the heavens tremble as immortals prepare to clash. Their hypnotic war dance speaks not of hesitation, but of the inevitable storms of wrath to arise upon a fallen world.

> *Ten steps unbind the earth's repose*
> *Thunder weeps, the tempest knows*
> *A dance of war, the hymn of fates*
> *Two gods prepare—destruction awaits*

NINE – Within Pesa, the god of beasts, aqua-hued flares ignite its body to brilliance, a fiery storm of life force activated. Thunder reverberates through its corrupted mind, bursting into the heavens. Skies awaken to soon bear witness to the hellish fight, a prelude to rage unbound.

> *Nine flames ablaze, this demon's ungodly might*
> *Roars unbound rage into unbearable flight*
> *The heavens blaze, their wrath is sworn*
> *Earth shall weep when vengeance is born*

**EIGHT** – Two fallen gods edge closer, their circling forms brimming with tension. Their movements ripple with fated intent, each preparing for the potent strike of its enemy to come. Sworn destiny looms as their shared hatred draws them nearer to a world-shattering reckoning.

*Eight steps circle, the dance begun*
*A destiny forged, a war unwon*
*Fates collide, in chaos steeped*
*A world's heart broken, its silence reaped*

**SEVEN** – Their gazes clash, two titans locked in a silent battle of will. The moment brims with unspoken torment, as suffering's shadow casts across Gaea, their mother. The mighty prepare to engage—a cataclysm of sibling hatred poised to rend Earth's creation asunder.

*Seven hours will rise and fall, grit and bold*
*Suffering writ in tales untold*
*Gaea weeps her fury, her children will fight*
*Kin turned foe in mindless slight*

**SIX** – Two gods, consumed by the need to obliterate their sibling, see no realm, no world beyond their own. Every element, every creation seems destined for collapse beneath their wrath. No breath remains untouched, no gale untainted by the maddened storm of loathing.

*Six breaths drawn in hatred's maw*
*Annihilation, their only law*
*Creation crumbles, undone by kin*
*The tempest calls, let war begin*

D'Reem leans in closer, his unwavering gaze meeting T'Naeva's riveted expression. His bride's beautiful aqua-hued eyes hold his focus as he utters his Creator's words—a resonance foreign to her, yet undeniable in its authority. I witness this hypnotic sway of fallen gods. Their war dance speaking the definitive truth of hatred, unrelenting and unyielding, as their titanic forms inch closer with every breath. Indignation consumes them, overwhelming all sense and sanity in this abhorred countdown.

There are no words that hang between them now, but only the weighted outcome of both their destinies. D'Reem's voice remains divinely firm, carrying the gravity of his Companion's omnipotence... *for her alone.*

A countdown where goodwill has been utterly banished, and only aversion remains. These two titanic forces, hurled beyond the reach of grace, are trapped in the severest depths of enmity. All thanks to Dia'Baal Fallenstar— he who is and will forever be known to me... *a simple coward.*"

His tone softens, returning from its divine height, and T'Naeva's breath catches. She knows this voice once more, recognizing its origin. And then, as if summoned by his own will, the Companion enters her mind to share these living images along with him, breathing themselves into every fiber of her being. These details, the visions that will soon become so sharp and unrelenting, will carry the weight of profound remorse, and this is His gift to her.

T'Naeva does not blink as she feels the awakening. Every syllable from her divine husband strikes now like living flame into her spirit. D'Reem's tone bears not only the resonance of the Companion's command—but the ache of history itself. The images behind his words unfold in her soul like scripture once sealed, now torn open. No veil remains. The very air between them vibrates with the tension of this godly cohesion. In this instant, hatred becomes a presence to her—tangible, coiled, waiting to strike. The great mountain stills. The meadow dares not breathe. Even the wind bows low to the weight of what is forming in her mind's eye.

In D'Reem's visage, she begins to see it: the sorrow of a once-holy bond undone, the futility of peace, and the inevitability of war between sibling gods who should have ruled as one. And yet he speaks—softly now—so that she can begin to carry the truth of it all, *for herself.* A truth that in what follows was never only destiny... but a warrior's honest truth in his passion for her.

D'Reem continues, his voice laced with aching resolve, guiding her now into this truth she too will face, and to witness right along with him.

*FIVE* – Nature's frenzied energies surge, pouring unrelenting power into the colossal forms of the two gods. Their motions quicken, a chaotic rhythm primed for battle. Each knows the certainty of the other's wrath, their strength now fevered, their resolve sharpened to a deadly edge.

*Five steps weave the winds of strife*
*Strength and fury springs to life*
*Each motion swift, every thought towers*
*Two gods prepare their final hours*

**FOUR** – Opti's dark golden tones ignite, blazing into a radiant crimson that bathes the meadow in fiery brilliance. This energy discharges skyward, rocketing into the heavens and infecting the cloud cover with its volatile glow. Lightning erupts, ferocious and unrestrained, striking around the gods with maddened fury. The sanity of nature shatters.

*Four webs of lightning rip the skies apart*
*Wrath ignites from nature's heart*
*Crimson storms and heavens flare*
*Madness sways in nature's glare*

**THREE** – Only a short stone's throw apart, the gods' advance slows, their movements deliberate as they circle the other and destiny looms. Hatred, raw and unmatched, hangs heavy in the air. Their purpose is singular death, the only remaining solution for their kin... their *enemy*. Peace is conquered, swept into oblivion by this tidal wave of spite.

*Three strides now span the final space*
*Hatred to burn in full embrace*
*Destiny calls, and peace must die*
*As chaos claims the shattered sky*

**TWO** – Entities once divine have both been thrust into the bowels of evil's greatest deceit. Their aversion, searing and unyielding, consumes them both. Each craves nothing less than the utter destruction of the other—and of the realm that each one commands.

*Two souls drenched in bitter hate*
*Twisted by Dia'Baal's cruel fate*
*No trace of light, no mercy shown*
*The ruin these kin will call their own*

**ONE** – Their nightmarish glares lock, searing ire etched permanently into their contorted visages. The sibling forces suddenly halt their approach, arching their titanic forms skyward as Mother Earth falls deathly silent. Craze, poised for catastrophic release, grips the world.

*A single breath holds the earth in sway*
*Gaea mourns her lost array*
*Thunder breaks, the charge begins*
*A war of gods, where none shall win*

*Oblivion awakens... The Earth braces... Eternity stills...*

In this terrible moment where past, present, and future converge, we stand to witness an end of an age... to *innocence*. Gaea, the mother's heart laden with grief, wails in sorrow to the heavens, a solemn lament for her lost children. The Earth shudders under her anguish, the skies recoil, and in her cry echoes the doom of all things harmonious. A detonation rends the air—a deafening, cataclysmic roar that splits the veil of stillness asunder.
The meadow trembles violently, as if rebelling against the wrath it will be forced to bear. Yet neither T'Naeva nor I lose our balance—for we are not truly there, and yet, *we are*. We remain, unwavering, united as one in witness to this terrible war of gods.

It is then, in this frozen breath of time, that the cosmos itself bears witness, and the stars dim in mourning. The Companion does not speak but simply watches, knowing in sadness this is the fulcrum of all to come—where the dream fractures forever, and the reckoning of cosmic forces begins.

# *Verse XX:*
## The Rending of Divinity

I see them... Two gods—*my parent and yours*—titanic and unyielding, thundering toward each other in a collision destined to shake the foundations of creation itself.

They are no longer gods. They are pure, cosmic embodiments—*forces unleashed*. What remains are two living truths: **OPTI**, the one created of the boundless **Force of Imagination**. **PESA**, the other forged from the unyielding **Force of Reality**.

*Flesh morphs into purpose... Identity dissolves into oblivion...*

Their resonance multiplies with every breathless moment, their fury swelling into a divine edict—an inevitable clash written into the DNA of existence upon Earth itself.

Their transformation is not subtle. It is a violent sanctification. Opti's presence shimmers with unrestrained creative power, limitless and unpredictable, now magnified to its highest form. Pesa, in contrast, pulses with impenetrable will, density, and the relentless drive to conquer. Their auras ripple through the skies, distorting the atmosphere, electrifying every atom and orb upon an entire world.

T'Naeva, watching from the veil between fear and revelation, is struck by a divine awakening. She feels the boundary between observer and participant fading. The visions hum louder now, whispering truths too vast for thought, too urgent to ignore. Her eyes, once dulled by deception, now blaze with clarity—opened by divine decree. She sees not just beings, but the very essences of creation and uncreation. She feels her breath vanish, caught in the weight of this ancient moment. Awe wars with dread. She understands now what has been set into motion.

A sequence not merely of combat, but of collapse—of realms, of bonds, of truths long buried beneath divine delusion. Through her connection to the Companion, T'Naeva sees flickers of time not yet lived: visions of broken landscapes, fractured bloodlines, and the hollow silence of a world mourning its creators. Her breath shallows, her pulse stammers—not from fear, but recognition. She sees that this battle is not only between gods, but between the very forces that once forged unity from chaos.

In that instant, she feels her purpose begin to coil in her chest—not yet born, but no longer dormant. And through that spark, a thought pierces her mind like fire upon kindling:

*'If I am to endure these visions… then I must become worthy of them.'*

Their fury quickly descends, unrelenting, into the heart of Gaea. The very core of the world trembles beneath their wrath. The balance once held sacred begins to unravel. Heat builds—pressure mounts. Friction within Gaea surges, born not just of tectonic force, but of divine discord.
From this crucible of madness, something is born—not a child, not a creature, but a consequence. An unholy resonance forged by Reality's uncompromising will, twisted through Imagination's chaotic flame. It is not life, but something darker—an echo of hatred made manifest.

*War!*

*War* is born in this instant, not as a choice, but as a certainty. Its specter now etched into the marrow of the world, bound forever to the broken soil of mother Earth.
T'Naeva wails!

   **The storm within my parent consumes me…** Pesa's anger smothers everything I feel, heavy and suffocating. The sky blackens, clouds roiling like a devouring cavity. Their roars crack the earth with every stomp, each sharper than thunder itself. I watch, frozen, as its fury lashes out with a single purpose: Opti's destruction. The parent I never knew—the one who created natural beauty and life—feels distant now, lost in this storm of hatred. I want to scream out to my dark parent, to stop this madness, but my voice is unheard!"

D'Reem responds!

*The storm within my parent consumes me still...* And I behold Opti's incandescent fury, channeled into the *Chup'DraVak-Ra*—sentinels born of divine precision, a testament to the power of godly maturity. They are vengeance made flesh, their forms anointed with purpose and bound by a collective wrath so pure that it transcends mere instinct. Every motion, every bone-shaking cry of their god is a hymn to their maker's grief, a defiance that cuts through the chaos!

In their charge, they move as one—this living storm of inspired flesh, a force magnified tenfold through strength of unity. No longer mere creations, they are to become judgment embodied, relentless and unyielding. Should the heavens falter and crumble under the weight of Opti's ruin, the Chup'Dra-Vak-Ra will arise to take its place.

*Today is not that day...*

Enduring where all else fails, they are Opti's final promise—a legacy that will outlast death itself! Amid the chaos, the Earth bears the weight of sibling enmity, her harmony forever shattered, her essence... forever scarred.

Born of divine fury and unrelenting vengeance, war takes its root in this **first** hour of god wrath made manifest, a legacy of conflict that will echo through the ages—a fatal and permanent reminder of what can happen when the unbridled sins of wrath and pride are unleashed. The war of gods rages, shaking the world beneath their weight as the heavens themselves bear witness to this vile birth of devastation.

This moment is deeply personal between these beasts—Opti and Pesa—as they rush headlong into each other, their massive, muscular frames colliding with a ferocity unrestrained. Their wrath a sickening cyclone, an overwhelming force that assaults our every sense. We yearn to stop this fight, yet both she and I remain powerless, mere witnesses to their ultimate fury. Yet even in this powerless witness, something shifts.

A deep chord strikes within her, ancient and unbroken, beginning to vibrate with resonance—not of resistance, but of readiness. In the crucible of the gods' combined rage, Gaea's grief swells to an unbearable crescendo. Deep within her rocky womb, the inferno of their unyielding hatred spreads into cataclysmic discord.

*Earth's iron core,* once resolute and unshakable, erupts into blazing defiance—a violent outburst, rivaling a newborn star. This eruption surges upward, its searing heat cascading through the planet's layers.

*The mantle*—her rocky midsection—yields to the inferno within, melting into a roiling sea of fiery chaos. Once steadfast and solid, it liquefies under the relentless surge, birthing seas of magma that churn and pulse far beneath her breast.

Though these molten currents remain hidden for ages untold, they carry the promise of profound transformation—a cataclysm destined to reshape the world in the ages of humanity. This churning chaos fuels the dynamics that will one day sustain life—and in moments of upheaval, end it. For now, the inferno remains confined, its power roiling and restless, a force waiting to one day breach the surface. Far above, Earth's spirit trembles, her very soul groaning under the strain of the violence emerging.

In this moment, Gaea's sorrow is not bound to some distant future; it resides in the present, born of the battle between her children that ignites this transformation. She mourns deeply, her lamentation rippling through the trembling earth and the storm-laden skies. Across the two realms, life—silent, hidden, and trembling—feels the crushing weight of her grief. They understand the scale of what unfolds: two warring gods, creators of two warring realms, consumed by their descent into severe transgression.

Fully aware of their corrupted states, these titans summon the supernatural powers within their frenzied minds, intent on annihilating the other.

With the tempest of their hatred unleashed, the gods break away from their first of countless violent engagements. T'Naeva watches, trembling—yet it is not dread alone that seizes her. It is knowing. A knowing that this is no ordinary war, no simple clash of opposing wills. It is a cosmic unraveling. The storm is no longer around them—it is within them, and she, too, feels its weight pressing inward. She whispers, barely audible to herself. "This is truly the cost of forgetting who we are."

Her fingers curl into the earth, not to anchor herself, but to feel Gaea's pain. Beneath the trembling crust, she senses her cries—not screams of torment, but the low, reverent dirge of a mother watching her children violently devour one another.

And still, T'Naeva does not turn away. "I must witness it all."

**This is not my parent, yet still it is...** Pesa, the god of beasts, reacts first, its eyes blazing with a hatred so fierce it seems to ignite the very air. The high winds heat up, driving rain into jagged shards of fire that slice through the peace of a once-peaceful world. The skies churn dark and wild, responding to Pesa's command—a storm now feral and unbound. My parent wields destruction as if born to it, its force ripping at Gaea's foundation. Overhead, lightning once more tears through a blackened veil of clouds, each bolt a mirror to the rage now consuming both earth and sky.

In an instant, Pesa directs the full force of nature's wrath upon Opti, the sentinel of Imagination. The skies darken further, clouds thick with malevolence swirling in unholy unison, and lightning erupts in a work of destruction, and I see it all because I am there.

*The meadow, once a cradle of unity*... dissolves into chaos as heaven and earth collide. Amid the tempest, Opti stands steadfast, radiating a brilliance that defies the encroaching storm. Its light grows stronger, not out of fear, but in the absolute defiance of a darkness that quickly spreads. This, it knows as well as I, is only the prelude. Both gods, consumed entirely by their enmity, prepare to unleash a conflict of escalating destruction. Each blow they trade carries the weight to unmake the very world that binds their foe, a savage testament to the power of their hatred.

Thus begins the first true exchange of divine wrath, a battle so cataclysmic that Gaea herself flees beneath its weight. Her lament echoes deep within her core, yet it is lost beneath this roaring storm, the roars of her children engaged in warfare. This is no mere struggle; it is a cataclysm that will scar her essence and forever ripple through the fabric of Earth itself.

**I see the god of beasts...** My parent, mighty and unrelenting, anchor its colossal heels deep into the trembling meadow. The earth groans beneath the sheer weight of its resolve, quaking as Pesa channels the full power of its corrupted mind. With hatred forged into an iron will, Pesa twists nature itself to its demon's intent, shattering Gaea's delicate balance and wrenching her into chaos. Mother Nature, bound and tormented, wails under Pesa's rage, lashing out at Opti with a fury that is not her own, nor could ever be – and she is powerless to stop it.

High above, I feel the heavens convulse, the crimson-shadowed atmosphere roiling like a wounded monster. Fractured light breaks through massive webs of lightning, fierce and radiant, their brilliance blinding within the storm now unleashed upon Earth's surface.

*Thunder roars to life...* with a clap that shakes Gaea to her core—a harbinger of the destruction to come. From the depths of Pesa's savagery, lightning no longer descends in scattered strikes, but as a concentrated surge, nature's most vengeful power unleashed. It rages toward Opti, not to warn, but to obliterate... a thousand spears of wrath intent on reducing the sentinel of Imagination to ash.

Another roar echoes through the tempest, this time from my glorious parent, a sound so harrowing that the heavens wail in response. Rain pouring in sheets, also heavy with Gaea's grief, each drop a tear shed in passion for her children. The storm, again summoned by Pesa's wrath, devours the air and earth alike, unmatched since the rebirth of Earth itself.

**We both stand amidst this madness...** Our senses overwhelmed by the sheer ferocity of the battle. Each strike of lightning tears through Opti's immense frame, illuminating the battlefield with flashes of blinding brilliance cast against the deep crimson sky. Against all odds, it continues to endure Pesa's relentless assault, its smoldering form collapsing time and again from the severe punishment cast down upon it. I see its body begin to chemically unravel, pushing it ever closer to the realm of oblivion.

Its powerful form, once a testament to marvelous creation, may soon scatter as nothing more than a tide of shimmering particles, carried off in the furious winds of this unholy war. Yet even now, as the earth rages and the heavens weep, Opti's defiance remains steadfast, its resolve an obscure presence of oblivion through my parent's eyes.

*Pesa's cruel delight...* spurred by Dia'Baal's vile influence knows no bounds as T'Naeva's dark parent continues to hurl wave upon wave of electrified ferocity against mine. Each strike growing crueler, tearing into its enemy with unrelenting ferocity. Yet within Opti's seemingly fragile frame, a transformation unlike any I have witnessed begins to take form. The sentinel of Imagination begins to absorb the lightning—not in its destruction, but as raw energy, channeling its enemy's wrath into the harmony of its dual foundations.

With patience that defies comprehension and mastery over the elements, my parent stands resolute in this grave moment of battle, its quiet strength harnessed in the thoughts of its father, an omen of the retaliation to come. As of now, the energy Pesa has hurled against my parent has reached its zenith, merging with the dual foundations within its heart, strengthening it even further. Opti, a master of transformation, teeters on the brink of release, needing only a final spark to ignite its devastating counterattack. Its movements are deliberate now, yes... each step a silent promise of retribution. Pesa, enthralled by the sheer defiance of its kin, is unable to comprehend the menace now bearing down upon it.

The dark beast will soon learn a cruel lesson in warfare...

Both she and I are riveted at Pesa's inability to destroy Opti, a truth that defies and chokes the fury of the god of beasts. Ignoring the searing pain of its wounds, my parent surges forward with a roar that shakes the heavens. With a few powerful thrusts of its wings, it propels itself skyward, the air crackling with anticipation. Mid-flight, Opti twists, its charred form mending itself as it abruptly turns and dives.

In this exhilarating sight, I see its streak of divine lightning, the god of Imagination hurling itself headfirst into Pesa's massive frame. The collision is cataclysmic, sending both gods tumbling across the meadow, their combined immense bulks of physical tonnage carving deep scars into the layers of meadow and earth.

**I see Pesa's body roll to an abrupt stop...** as Opti is hurled skyward, their quivering frames a testament to both their fury and the impact of the blow. With predatory speed, it rises, its eyes gleaming with renewed malice. I watch my dark parent as its mind races, grappling with the incomprehensible resilience of its adversary. The god of beasts knows now that this

338

battle has only begun, and its enormity looms vast and unrelenting.

*Opti unyielding, catches its balance...* midair and lands with a precision born of purpose. Its smoldering form advances, every step deliberate, every movement a calculated provocation. My mighty parent taunts its enemy with biting precision, striking at Pesa's pride, patience, and mind. I understand now: my parent's survival depends on this particular strategy. Each insult thrust is a weapon, crafted to unbalance Pesa's thoughts, to force recklessness upon the god of beasts.

Opti truly wields this psychological warfare better than its kin, its unsettling mastery of harmonious deception on full display. Opti erupts in a roar of thunderous laughter, its booming voice shaking the very heavens as it glares at its adversary, its taunts laced with razor-sharp mockery.

*"I say to you, torpid simpleton,"* Opti bellows with another laugh, each word dripping with disdain.

*"Is this the full extent of passion your unchained hostilities can muster against me? Truly, if this display is your best, then it is beyond any doubt that your nature is weaker than the weakest of all the delicate little blossoms birthed within that plump and ripened melon you call a head!"*

**These words cut through...** the chaotic battlefield like a blade, their biting edge intended to provoke my parent. D'Reem's parent stands firm, its posture a balance of defiance and cunning, its laughter reverberating as a challenge to Pesa's might. Pesa's uneasiness ignites into a searing temper, and the shift is instantaneous. The mighty demon of my parent, now balanced and steady, roars with wrath, its thunderous voice tearing through the chaos.

**"You dare call me weak, freak of my nature?! Prepare yourself, for the energy within this 'plump and ripened melon' will now reduce you to a heap of ash!"**

*With a calculated crouch...* my parent braces itself its massive form, trembling as it realigns its inner energies, preparing to withstand another punishing exchange. Above, Pesa channels its potent fury through its twisted mind, summoning a storm unlike any I have seen before. Thrusting its colossal paws into the quaking earth and throwing its head skyward, the god of beasts commands the heavens with ruthless authority.

Ten thousand spears of lightning tear the sky asunder, slamming into Opti in brutal succession. Thunder shakes the trembling earth, yet Opti stands, my glorious parent unwavering—*the sentinel defying the storm!*

*Time stretches painfully...* as Pesa's dark mind conjures another assault. The winds rise, churning the atmosphere into twisting chaos, and a massive funnel cloud forms directly above Opti. The twisting column of air descends rapidly, its roar a cacophony of despair, swallowing Opti into its violent grasp. I can barely breathe as I watch Opti trapped, its immense form spiraling uncontrollably in the storm's unforgiving vortex. Opti however, does not yield to its power. With every beat of its colossal wings, it drives against the twister's fury, each movement deliberate and unyielding.

The god of creatures, a master of the skies, channels its full strength into each stroke, unraveling the storm's grip with calculated precision. Flying directly against the gale, Opti easily matches its ferocity, defusing its chaos with an opposing force that kills the winds. Then, in a feat beyond comprehension, Opti twists the storm upon itself, dissolving the funnel's furious gusts, but not before their remnants are drawn into its radiant form, fueling its power to even greater heights.

**In that moment...** I can only marvel at the resilience of D'Reem's parent a strength that defies even the chaos that Pesa commands. I feel it—this shift in power, not as the child of its wrath, but as a soul being awakened. My mind reels from the grandeur of it all, but still I remain. Somehow, I endure this reality. The Companion burns within me now—not as comfort, but as fire, and I begin to see what D'Reem sees. Not fully in detail. Not yet, but enough to tremble. Now free, I see Opti rise triumphant, its glowing presence a manifestation of divine renewal.

The conquered winds of nature, fused to perfection with the god's essence, propel it skyward in an unstoppable surge. The entire meadow from archway-to-archway quakes beneath Opti's swift ascent, and the storm-torn heavens seem to bow to its radiant defiance. Far below, Pesa once more digs its massive claws into the trembling earth, its fury mounting just as lightning strikes, but arcs wildly away from Opti's body, scattering harmlessly throughout the darkened sky.

*Rejuvenated and blazing with righteous fury...* Opti continues its swift ascent, piercing yet another storm of Pesa's suffocating will. Higher my mighty parent climbs until it breaches the heavens' dark canopy, emerging finally as a blazing comet against the sheer majesty of the star-studded heavens—a flare of Imagination's indomitable spirit.

The clouds that are gathered across this entire region of atmosphere roil in protest, their combined thunder and dissolution wailing like a herd of wounded beasts as they are all swept, one by one, into Opti's streaking form. With a mighty blast, Opti's powerful ascent is completed as it turns its body to descend. The eyes of a matured and powerful union of forces finds and locks its infuriated gaze onto its corrupted kin far below.

I feel it through my every sense... the growl of my dark parent, its massive frame coiled in anticipation, ready to strike. The god of beasts, sensing the tempest to come, braces itself as it targets Opti's wrathful comet-like descent. Yet even as it prepares, fear flickers in its eyes—a predator now confronted by a force it cannot begin to comprehend.

Still airborne, but descending with the grace of a falling star, Opti levels its radiant form parallel to the quaking meadow. The ground trembles beneath its approach, yet it lands with a gentleness that belies the indignation coursing through its body. Whirling flashes of light vibrate like a heartbeat from its majestic frame, bright and strong, newly charged with a massive supply of Pesa's raw energy. Opti silently crouches with its head bowed in deliberate stillness, the air growing heavy with anticipation.

This is no retreat or surrender; it is preparation as I feel this moment of calm before the storm that will echo through the meadow. Opti's shimmering frame, no longer marred by scorch marks or smoldering fur, shakes as it steadies itself. Another fainter glow emanates from deep within it, a heat that feels both destructive and alive, as if creation and annihilation coexist in perfect harmony. The dust surrounding Opti ripples and distorts, bending both air and light under the weight of a force so powerful, ancient, and primal that it defies mortal comprehension.

*At a distance of five miles...* Opti glares forward and identifies its enemy with uncanny clarity—every tensed muscle, every ragged breath, and every flicker of aqua-hued brilliance playing across Pesa's hulking silhouette. As Opti turns its head to the right, its gaze falls upon the distant glow of the *Shrine of Harmony*. Once a beacon of goodwill and unity, the shrine's radiance now feels distant and hollow, its meaning tarnished by the relentless conflict that has consumed these two kindred gods. The golden light that once symbolized peace and balance in my parent now flickers with a mournful resonance, a reminder of what has been lost in the wake of Pesa's dark descent. And even somewhat... *its own*.

**The battlefield between them...** feels more like a narrow corridor than a vast expanse, every mile traversed in the span of a god's single breath, and another inevitable clash. Opti knows the power thrumming in its veins is true, poised for a decisive strike that will shake its enemy to the core. The distant foe glares at it across the battlefield, standing silent, yet quivering in its unknowing of what destiny commands next.

*From Pesa's vantage point...* it too see the flickering monument stand as nothing more than a relic of weakness and submission—an outdated symbol clinging to ideals that no longer hold power in this evolving world. To Pesa, the shrine's fading is a testament to the futility of unity, a hollow memorial to the past that should be crushed beneath the weight of progress and domination. Sadly, each flicker of its golden glow ignites a deep-seated contempt within it, fueling the conviction that action determines any future, and never the sentimental illusions of peace during war.

**Its eyes strain to focus...** upon the towering golden-hued profile of its foe—seemingly reawakened and unbound—and it discerns an unstoppable force. Fear barbs at the edges of the beast's consciousness; Opti's resolute stance and the charged air signal a turning of the violent tide. Suddenly, the cracks in Pesa's once-assured brutality glare like open wounds. Its silent stammering now is more than just uncertainty; it is the dawning awareness that, for the first time, its raw power alone may not be enough to hold dominion over the battlefield.

In this moment, there is no malice in Pesa's eyes—only disbelief, stripped bare and unguarded. It contemplates every conceivable notion it can muster to explain its enemy breaking every law of nature it knows, and then shattering those laws to splinters. Against the impossible, Opti clearly stands unbroken and pure, and I too am awed by its presence of power. For what feels like an eternity, the windy and darkened battlefield holds its breath. I hold it too—not in fear, but in what comes next.

I feel each breath of Opti and Pesa as if my own lungs share the burden.

This, I realize, is no longer just history. It is legacy. The chaos that once reigned is subdued by my overwhelming stillness, as if the world itself hesitates to interfere with what is unfolding across my sight. Opti's revitalized body begins to shift, its movements deliberate and assured. Power radiates from every fiber of its being, overflowing with the energy it has absorbed.

*Slowly and assuredly, my parent begins to arise...* Nature herself comes out of her shock, only to hold her breath as Opti stirs once more. Its awakened body sizzles with a power that clearly defies the natural order, a force now seized from the Earth itself. The ground beneath my parent begins to quake, faintly at first, then violently as fissures spread like streaks beneath its feet.

Echoes of a low rumble begin to spread across the quaking meadow, shaking the ground beneath us until it erupts in a crescendo—a voice so thunderous that it shatters the clouds above us. This is not merely an influence, but a declaration—a reckoning this way comes! The god roars.

*"Feel it now, O, vile beast! The power of your rage, thrust back against you! The fury you sought to wield burns in my veins! This is your consequence!"*

These words are no frail cry of defeat; they are primal, and even from five miles away, deafening to the god of beasts. This voice splits the heavens and rips through the meadow, carrying the weight of retribution, a warning to all who would dare challenge its resolve.

For a single suspended moment... the wind in our breath seems to vanish, leaving only the echoes of that thunderous shout to linger. In this hush, I behold in D'Reem's parent a power I cannot fully grasp—a brilliance born of endurance and purpose. In a single heartbeat, it surges into the air, slicing through the haze of the battlefield, devouring that five-mile expanse with breathtaking speed. My heart thunders as I witness Opti's unstoppable charge, its jaws parting wide and silent in preparation.

A massive electromagnetic flood of energy erupts from the god's mouth, its sole intent to make my parent truly pay for its ages of misdeeds. This energy collides with Pesa's body, as it has no time to react as its impact upon the dark brute sounds like a tidal wave crashing upon a shore. Pesa, once so certain of its own strength of brutality, staggers through this massive wallop, its mighty form trembling beneath the crushing impact of its savagery returned a hundredfold against it.

The shock wave of the impact ripples outward, carving deep scars into the earth, uprooting the divine foliage for five miles as tremors rise across the battered meadow. For the second time, doubt flashes within the god of beasts—a fleeting, toxic whisper that perhaps it is not the apex predator it believed itself to be. In the wake of that initial blast, there is a momentary lull, as though the world itself is too stunned to react. Even the dust hangs weightless, suspended in the thickened, energized fog of war.
I stand transfixed upon this scene as I see my dark parent stumble, every mortal hair on our bodies standing to electric attention.

*The shock wave, an entity unto itself...* has not dissipated into oblivion as expected, but instead lingers, pulsating with the same raw and sentient power of the god who just released it. Its forward momentum halts abruptly, as though defying the very laws of nature. With a crackling hum, my parent circles back with predatory intent as the air ignites with anticipation once more—a charged silence before the inevitable strike.

**In this breathtaking moment...** that both D'Reem and I endure, the shock wave collapses inward upon itself and surges back at Pesa like an enraged boomerang, crashing into its body with its rolling volleys of energy. The very air screams in echoes with the speed of its passage, splitting the sky with tendrils of searing light that dance in wild, colorful fury.

The ground beneath our feet shakes apart as wave after wave of vitality engulfs the god of beasts, each glowing pulse resonating through my chest. This time, however, the final gust swallows Pesa in a blizzard of energy, wrenching its massive frame from the ground and hurling it like a tulip in a gale. The dark beast smashes headfirst back into the meadow, gouging deep wounds into the meadow as the ground shifts beneath its entire weight of twenty tons.

The momentum finally ends in a violent climax as its body crashes into a massive, towering tree at the threshold of its realm. The ancient trunk, a monolith that has withstood the ravages of time, greets Pesa's return home with an earth-shaking crack.

Splinters explode in a frenzied dance, the sheer force of the god's impact with the tree sends shock waves rippling through the surrounding area. The once-proud sentinel of nature is swiftly reduced to a fractured ruin, its remnants groaning and collapsing under the overwhelming scope of its sudden impact. Every bone in Pesa's twenty-foot frame, save for a slight few in its robust midsection, is pulverized upon impact.

*Roars of anguish erupt...* from Opti's enemy—the god of beasts, echoing through the darkened skies like a chant of despair. I see its immense form writhe in grotesque contortions as its supernatural healing begins to take control. Bones begin to snap and rotate back into place, flesh and muscle fuse back together, yet its agony lingers, etched into its every trembling growl—a testament to the devastating force of my parent's wrath.

A guttural roar erupts from the dark brute, echoing through the fractured meadow as its shattered consciousness begins to reforge—stitched together by the pulse of Dia'Baal's insidious influence. With each throb of dark energy, the god of beasts' mind reshapes, memories bending to its corrupter's will. Whispers of doubt and the hunger for dominion seep back in, reigniting an ancient malice barely held at bay.

Knowing its assault has been highly effective, my parent has again blazed its way skyward, preparing itself to attack once more as it arcs its mammoth frame back down and into the fray. Radiant and relentless, its descent is much faster this time, a true tempest given form, intent on destroying the corruption that threatens all of creation on Earth—once and for all.

Opti, unrelenting in its charge, closes the distance with terrifying precision, its radiant form cutting through the chaos like a divine spear. Raw and potent energies erupt as Opti's talons extend, aiming to tear through Pesa's defenses with a strike honed by eons of celestial warfare.

This war is far from over, but in the moment, the heavens and earth bear witness to the triumph of light over shadow. The battle of the ages surges forward, each engagement more brutal than the previous, aligned perfectly with the character of oblivion.

**Pesa's realm will never allow...** its god to go down quite so easily. Only a stone's throw from where my parent lies regenerating, its enormous diamond archway ignites with sudden brilliance. Towering a mile high, it pierces the storm-wracked skies like a blade of living clarity. Both D'Reem and I freeze in awe. This is no conjuration, no madness. It is the Force of Reality itself—ancient, instinctive—awakened in response to peril.

The earth bellows, as if its heart groans beneath the strain. From the trembling meadow, a radiant cocoon begins to rise—translucent, impenetrable.

Forged of diamond, the strongest element in nature, it does not ascend as a wall of desperation, but as a sovereign sanctuary decreed by Reality itself. This is no act of mercy. **It is law!**
The cocoon pulses once—then twice—each beat a sovereign command...

**What is nature will endure...** as Opti, relentless and divine, launches forward with its fangs bared to their full intensity. But the moment its talons strike the cocoon, it answers back—not with defense, but judgment. A retaliatory flare erupts from the cocoon's surface, a blinding corona of radiance that engulfs the predator. Opti is caught mid-strike and hurled backward through the storm-riven sky like a comet thrown from the Great Realm.

**This is no retreat!**

This is the force of Reality fully known—unyielding, eternal—defying annihilation with the authority of the cosmos's oldest truths. Again, Opti—relentless and feral—leaps to strike, its gleaming claws arcing like scythes of living metal. But the powerful translucent shell detonates outward in another retaliatory surge of light, a searing radiance that engulfs the god-hunter in a corona of burning brilliance.

I watch in wide-eyed amazement as the mighty predator is again hurled backward, its hulking frame tumbling end over end through the storm-choked air. With a guttural growl of frustration, Opti wrenches itself upright mid-flight, its eyes blazing with fury as it spreads its obsidian wings to steady its descent.

Around us, the very air quivers—thick with unseen forces that crackle like barely contained lightning. Reality's arch of light intensifies, shifting in hue from dazzling white to an eerie, otherworldly sapphire hue. Each pulse sends shockwaves through the ground beneath our feet, as though the world itself recoils from what is awakening.

*Undeterred, my parent...* launches itself forward again and again, each assault a furious testament to its raw, unrelenting warfare. Its colossal glowing frame blurs as it swipes and drives both claw and fang into the translucent barrier, every strike echoing like thunder across the wounded plain. But nature's unyielding might stands resolute.

The diamond-infused cocoon—wrought from the very marrow of Earth's core—repels Opti's every blow with unwavering tenacity, each impact sending tremors through the landscape, rippling outward like the thunder of a world unable to release its energy skyward, but through meadow and earth.

My ears again recoil violently as Opti's mighty talons screech against the cocoon, sparks of blinding light bursting forth with every failed strike. Again and again, it lunges, its monstrous jaws unhinged in a roar of maddened frustration, saliva hissing as it vaporizes against the cocoon's radiant surface. Now a restless predator circling its quarry, Opti's eyes burn with molten hatred, affixed on the grotesque, swiftly healing body of Pesa within its protective shell.

Shadows coil around its vast frame, writhing like serpents as the air itself bends under the weight of its rage. The atmosphere trembles with a resonant hum as my parent's voice booms—each word laced with desperation, fatigue, but with unyielding conviction.

*"Enough of this savagery, vile kin! I implore you—may we end this madness now! For the sake of our father... For the sake of our world!"*

No answer comes. Only silence now—thick, oppressive, and deafening.

Opti's chest heaves as it snarls, an inhuman sound that convulses the air around us both. Its wings, flaring wide and strong, blots out what remains of the setting sun and its afterglow of light. The brute does not speak—not because it cannot, but because its intent is beyond words.

# *Verse XXI:*
## When Titans Shatter Worlds

esa's mangled body... stitched together by the force of Reality, quakes as the dark threads of Dia'Baal's hideous nature intervene, merged to heal my parent with a speed that defies even my comprehension.

Ignoring Opti's plea, Pesa continues to draw strength from its own force. Then, with a shattering burst, the cocoon of translucent energy explodes outward, hurling Opti off its feet in a storm of raw energy. The voice of Dia'Baal erupts through Pesa, defiant and unyielding, shaking the very firmament upon which these two gods battle.

"I rise stronger now than ever before! Never will I bow to the King's rule, nor to your false mercy, O, savage flower! You crave this fight as much as I, do you not? Yet still, you falter to destroy me! Despite the force you and our father have stolen, I remain the eldest, and the greatest! My birthright shall be denied no longer!"

Pesa, fully restored by its infernal resolve, rises to a newly refreshed and strengthened height of twenty-five feet at its shoulders. Its massive bear-cat frame coils like a storm ready to break, every sinew beating with the thirst for renewed annihilation. With a roar that reverberates across the meadow, the beast pivots to face Opti, its eyes aflame with blinding aqua-hued wrath.

Opti, dazed only briefly by Pesa's devastating surge of power, heaves upright. Its radiant form steadies, shoulders squared, and its unbroken resolve once more gleams in its eyes. Facing Pesa's encroaching tempest, the sentinel of Imagination braces itself against the storm within its core, growing ever more lethal.

Pesa halts its advance, the trembling earth groaning under its newly added weight. I hear the beast's growl deepen into a maddened laugh, its mocking voice a thunderclap that ripples through the battlefield.

"O, mighty Flower, your resilience is a delight! How enduring you are—a reflection of my own magnificence! It is through me alone that you still abide in this trivial skirmish! Mark these words true, O, savage Opti: I shall soon scatter your carcass to the winds and carve this day into your lifeless eyes ... the annals of my greatest triumph!"

With these words, Pesa's laughter twists into a furious roar, shaking the heavens with its rage.

"Prepare now for oblivion, abomination of my nature! I now unleash the unsheathed wrath... OF MY CLAWS!"

The quaking meadow spasms as Pesa flexes its monstrous paws, each nail extending in a deadly arc—razor-sharp, forged in the power of creation itself. In a blur of motion, the god of beasts charges forward, a hurricane of muscle and fury, ready to strike with the full force of its apocalyptic resolve.

*I gaze upon this enemy...* of mine once more as the mighty bearcat jolts with the force of a typhoon, its horns and nails rending the air with savage intent. Like a lightning bolt, it leaps and hurls itself over my parent, scoring deep gashes across its kin's armored rear end. The ground quakes beneath the monstrous weight of the beast as it lands with predatory precision, each movement an eerie blend of grace and destruction. Its immense front paws, each spanning the scale of a large boulder, include seven scythed claws—razor-sharp crescents of corruptly inspired bone, each measuring a formidable *twenty inches in length.*

Again the beast vaults, its lethal nails flashing through the air in a whirlwind of motion, carving atop the armored backside of my parent once more with terrifying speed. In the span of a single heartbeat, they slash downward a dozen times, rending the air with high pitched sounds that echo across the meadow.

**Faster than thought itself...** my parent twists it massive body mid lunge and targets Opti's exposed throat. The colossal nails of Pesa slice through the air in a ferocious arc—death incarnate, poised to strike and destroy. But the sentinel of Imagination, though battered and winded, turns with its own supernatural precision, a living tempest of *divine* coupled with **natural** instinct. With a mighty impact of its massive tail, it deflects this fatal blow of Pesa's right paw, the crack thundering across the battlefield as the clash of titans continue.

Yet Pesa, undeterred and ravenous for conquest, pivots with a level of predatory grace unknown, its monstrous frame surging forward like an unstoppable battering ram. It strikes with terrifying precision as its claws once more rake across Opti's armored, shimmering hide. Then, with a primal roar that shatters the air, Pesa's fangs plunge into one of Opti's rear legs, tearing through divine flesh with merciless force. The meadow recoils at the brutality, but Opti, wracked with pain filled adrenaline—refuses to hesitate.

Its resolve stands unbroken, an unyielding bastion of will forged in the crucible of war itself. Driven to the brink, D'Reem's progeny calls upon its every ounce of strength, and it courses through body and spirit with a surge of power. With a roar and a surge of energy, it twists its immense form into a whirlwind of defiance, sacrificing the length of its entire armored backside to force Pesa away.
Talons, teeth, fangs, and fury ignite into a frenzied counterattack as Opti whirls around to face its enemy, its blazing gaze locking onto its tormentor with the wrath of a thousand suns.

**We both witness our fallen parents...** in this unbridled *second* hour of warfare—these gods colliding once more, these titanic forces of nature in an apocalyptic clash that sends shock waves rippling through the Earth, further trampling the meadow's vegetation to oblivion while tearing the skies asunder in gales of fury and force. Their mother, Gaea, groans in weariness beneath them, bearing witness to a war that continues to weaken her very fabric of being. The battle between predator and protector rages on, a struggle that is destined to reshape the world in all its future ages.

For what seems an eternity in this second hour, Pesa reigns supreme on the battlefield, an unstoppable force of nature whose physical dominance knows no equal. Time and again, it hurls its colossal form into Opti, driving the sentinel of Imagination into the shattered meadow with relentless precision, each devastating impact echoing as thunder. Yet beneath the veil of raw brutality lies a darker intent: Dia'Baal's insidious will now guides Pesa's every strike, compelling T'Naeva's parent to savor the suffering it inflicts, to revel in the despair that coils around it like an ever tightening serpent.

With every crushing blow, another revelation dawns within Opti, each agonizing wallop carving a deeper understanding of Pesa's festering corruption. Though bruised and bloodied, the mighty sentinel endures, its resolve sharpening like tempered steel throughout this mighty trial. Pain becomes wisdom, suffering forges resilience, and within the heart of torment, Opti glimpses the truth buried beneath Pesa's monstrous fury.

As the fading sphere of a fiery star spills its molten gold across the heavens, it briefly brightens the battlefield in hues of gold and shadow. The beauty of this scene, even through the terrible chaos we witness, allow both her and I to breathe as this clash of our parents rage. Pesa, its malice on full display, presses forward with reckless arrogance, blind to the lessons its cruelty unwittingly imparts.

**High above, the specter of oblivion looms...** an ominous shade perched upon the edge of eternity, watching with cold and patient detachment. It is the harbinger of finality, a silent arbiter of fate, waiting to consume whichever god should falter first to erase the very fabric of their realm. The air grows heavy with destiny's breath, the battlefield itself trembling beneath the weight of cosmic judgment, as the struggle between predator and protector spirals toward an inevitable and permanent reckoning.

Yet amidst this storm of agony, D'Reem's parent rises ever stronger. Battered but unbowed, it bends without breaking, adapting to the unrelenting ferocity of Pesa's onslaught. Each brutal strike, meant to shatter its resolve, instead fuels a deeper awakening—an evolution drawn from the very forces that define the cosmos. Reality and Imagination, the twin pillars of its being, fortify Opti's spirit, anchoring it amidst the chaos.

It weaves order from destruction, purpose from pain, standing resolute as a beacon of endurance against the tide of warring devastation. Pesa. reveling in the illusion of dominance, looms as the living embodiment of unchecked power, its feral might twisted by Dia'Baal's insidious whispers. The god of beasts, drunk on its own supremacy, strikes with the reckless arrogance of one who believes itself invincible.

Yet such pride blinds it to the shifting tides of battle. For Opti, though bloodied, is far from broken. With every shattering blow absorbed, every wound endured, it learns...

*It evolves.*

 *Beneath Opti's veil of suffering...* a storm of renewal gathers within the mighty creature, ready to rise against the darkness that seeks to consume it. The greater shades of Reality, once shrouded even through its maturity, now unravel faster than ever before in Opti's unyielding insight, transforming from this shadowed enigma into radiant clarity. No longer driven by mere survival, my parent begins to ascend beyond desperate endurance, evolving with deliberate purpose. Each savage blow, each instant of suffering becomes a catalyst for education as Opti begins to harness the very essence of Pesa's primal fury.

Through this crucible of conflict, the sentinel of Imagination ascends beyond its former self, forging anew in the relentless trials of battle. It bends the raw force of Reality to its will, shaping it with the boundless, divine creativity of Imagination. No longer opposing forces, the twin essence entwine in celestial accord, their fusion a symphony of power and purpose. Amid adversity, where chaos reigns and destruction looms, Opti discovers the first ultimate truth of its maturity: strength lies not in division, but in unity.

A higher order emerges, an unshakable balance wrought from suffering and perseverance. Through the clash of titans and the agony of war, Opti continues to stand as a testament to resilience, its will still unbroken, its purpose still somewhat divine. The battle begins to shift. What began as Opti's inevitable defeat becomes a deliberate act of ascension, the sentinel of Imagination forging a path to victory, even as the battlefield trembles beneath their war. In this moment, the heavens again hold their breath, the cosmos trembling in anticipation as the tides of war teeter on the edge of oblivion.

 **Dia'Baal, the arch-rebel whose dark will...** puppeteers Pesa's every motion, begins to falter. Though his power commands the beast, the relentless strain of dominion over such a mighty vessel gnaws at him. My dark parent, though shackled, still remains a god—the untamed force of Reality that resists even the will of its dark master. For all his cunning, Dia'Baal has misjudged the depths of Opti's endurance and the latent power that simmers beneath its battered frame.

But beyond his folly lies something far greater—the *unknown*. An extremely mysterious and elusive force of the cosmos weaves through the fabric of battle, defying comprehension. Its presence, inscrutable yet undeniable, ripples through the mighty creature, stirring greater unease within the corrupted depths of Dia'Baal's mind. Thus, as the second hour of battle continues, the tides of fate stir in silent defiance. Pesa's once-certain triumph now falters, its dominance no longer absolute.

Opti, tempered in the crucible of suffering and revelation, rises—not as a vanquished foe, but as a challenger reborn. Its spirit, unyielding and renewed, stands defiant against the onslaught of both its kin and its dark master. Dia'Baal, weary and unnerved, feels his grip loosening. The combat he once commanded with ruthless precision now slips beyond his control. He knows not the cause—only that an unseen force, elusive yet potent, defies his will.
And though he dares not name it, the chilling whisper of realization distresses his mind... It is something beyond his understanding—something ... *divine.*

As the war of gods surge into its **third** hour, Earth's restless firmament burns crimson, as if Gaea herself weeps for the destiny unraveling before her. Her sorrow seeps into the heavens, staining them with ominous hues, while deafening roars shatter the air in rhythm with the relentless war far below her fiery skies. This clash of gods, fierce and unyielding, twists not only their forms, but the very fabric of Earth itself, each blow scarring creation's core and sparing nothing from its wrath.

Amid the chaos, our senses remain razor-sharp, locked onto this brutal spectacle of our battling parents. Two luminous giants of god flesh—hatred and resolve incarnate—collide once more with devastating ferocity, each strike a testament to a battle so vigorous that even Michael himself would tremble at the sight, his holy might dwarfed by the clash of these divine force behemoths made manifest.

*My glorious parent, the god of creatures...* driven by an unrelenting will to endure this hellish day of combat, senses with ease the growing toll upon Pesa. The dark beast, having poured much of its boundless strength into relentless assaults, now labors beneath the weight of its own exertion. Fatigue clings to its every motion, each strike growing a bit weaker than the last, its once-unyielding ferocity a little less intense of what it was.

Having mastered the brutal cadence of Pesa's countless attacks, stands poised to seize control, prepared to turn the tides of this deeply personal war and propel it to its most decisive and ruthless stage yet. Suddenly, D'Reem's eyes of omnipotence clear with an abrupt and truthful statement to his beloved, and he speaks these words.
"War is hell, dear T'Naeva, and your parent is about to learn this lesson in the most agonizing of ways!"

At his words, T'Naeva is also wrenched from her vision state, her mind reeling from the relentless spectacle of horror and sorrow unfolding before her mind's eye. The brutal realities of divine conflict, once distant and abstract, now feel terrifyingly close. She blinks rapidly as tears form, her gaze filled with newfound understanding as it speaks with a voice that quivers under the weight of revelation.

"I had always presumed gods to be above such relentless destruction, D'Reem... but now I see: power does not absolve them from suffering. This war, this terrible reckoning... It strips away the clarity I once knew, albeit briefly, leaving in me only raw emotion and ruin."

She turns to him, her expression etched with both sorrow and disbelief.
"Is this truly their destiny? To tear each other asunder until nothing remains but ash and regret?"
Her voice, heavy with emotion, wavers as the door to her heart finally creaks open.
"I do not understand how such majesty, such beauty, could descend into such madness! Tell me now, D'Reem, is there no end to this hatred, or must they fight until even the stars weep for their freedom?"

D'Reem watches her closely, his heart stirred by the aching vulnerability in her tone. In this moment, he senses a shift: T'Naeva is beginning to see beyond the illusions crafted by her demonic tormentor. Until this moment, she has been bound by a singular, manipulated perspective, but now the cracks are forming, and through them, truth begins to seep in with a teardrop, a divine drop of blood one at a time. He speaks with the tempered wisdom of one who has experienced the shape of war from every angle.

"Power and suffering walk hand in hand, beloved goddess. Gods, mortals... it makes no difference! We are all shaped by not only our choices, but also by the forces that seek to control us. This war, dear one, is not merely a test of strength, but of will—of who can see through deception and hold fast to what is true."

He leans in closer, his voice steady, yet laced with regret as he gazes into her beautiful aqua hued eyes.
"Not all battles are fought with weapons, T'Naeva. Many wars across the cosmic horizon are waged within the mind, where doubt can be the deadliest enemy, and perception the most fragile ally. Your dark parent fights not only against mine, but against the weight of every murmur that has twisted this conflict into something far darker than it was ever meant to be!"
D'Reem's gaze sharpens, his words striking with the force of a hurricane, shaking yet another shoreline to its core of undeniable certainty.

"Not all attitudes are rooted in truth either, but they can be wielded just the same. That, dear T'Naeva, is the hazard of war: it consumes not only the body, but the soul, reshaping belief and bending reality to the will of the most persuasive voice."
He lets these words linger intentionally, allowing their severity to settle upon her.

"Your dark parent is strong, but strength alone will no longer win this war. Pesa has been deceived, corrupted by an influence that thrives on half-truths and buried fears. And now, this same influence seeks to sway you, to twist your love for me into doubt, your hope into despair, and then simply... to destroy you from within! You must see this, my beloved, as I know you can."

T'Naeva's expression tightens, her heart pounding with an uneasy mix of revelation and fear. She realizes, perhaps for the first time, that war is not merely a clash of ideological forces; but purposed in a labyrinth of manipulation, where even gods are not immune to the shaping hands of deceit.

D'Reem's voice softens, yet remains resolute.

"The balance of our world no longer rests on power alone, but on understanding. You must look deeper; beyond the carnage and hatred you observe in these gifted moments of clarity. Only then will you have more of a forged tolerance and see what must be accepted within yourself!"
As both he and T'Naeva complete this exchange, their eyes return to the

battlefield of their parents, yet the first flicker of something beyond despair stirs within her—a cautious, trembling hope that perhaps, amid the ruin she witnesses, redemption still lingers.

We see with piercing clarity... the unrestrained savagery that now consumes Opti's very being, an intensity swelling with terrifying speed. No longer content with mere survival, it rises, reborn in the fires of conflict, its new-found ferocity now a match for the raw, untamed power of its foe... and Pesa knows it.

*Throughout this third hour of relentless brutality...* a chilling truth dawns upon the god of beasts, entwined with the creeping weight of exhaustion. Pesa, for all its might and dominance, begins to grasp a frightening realization: its supremacy is no longer absolute. Blow after blow, my parent endures, defies, and adapts. The great beast, though steeped in the arrogance of power, fails to comprehend why its adversary's strength continues to swell, why its strikes no longer quell the storm raging abound in power before it.

And I feel it too—an undeniable force stirring beneath the surface, waiting to reveal itself. Soon, Pesa will face the reality it has long ignored, and in that moment, it will know the cost of underestimating a force... *it knows nothing about!*

You see, T'Naeva, as you witness your parent and its inner demon growing increasingly drained in this relentless struggle, a subtle yet profound shift is taking place. With each passing moment, each exertion of brute force, the stranglehold Dia'Baal once had over Pesa's thoughts, weakens. The demon's whispers, once a constant presence, now falter beneath the weight of exhaustion.

With this growing awareness gnawing at the edges of Pesa's occasionally unshackled mind, it is confronted with a harrowing truth: it is being beaten back, pushed further from victory with every failed assault. For the god of beasts, this realization is not only unacceptable; it is enraging.

Dearest one, as I am granted deeper insight into this **fourth** hour of war, an undeniable truth emerges before us both: Your mighty forebear has

been granted countless opportunities to end this conflict, to strike the final blow and claim dominance. Yet time and again, Dia'Baal's insidious will has stayed Pesa's claws. Whether for his own perverse amusement, his thirst for prolonged suffering, or for some other unfathomable purpose.
Indeed, the arch-rebel has withheld true victory from his most willing puppet all along.

But now, in a moment of raw and irrefutable clarity, Pesa comes to a staggering realization: this war has never been fully its own. It has been shackled, bound by Dia'Baal's cruel manipulations, denied its rightful triumph by the very entity that claims to empower it. And for the first time, the god of beasts finally sees the truth in its entirety.

Its fight is not just against Opti, but against the chains that have bound its own free will to this very moment. A primal fury suddenly erupts within Pesa's being, an explosion of frustration and defiance that shakes the heavens. With a thunderous roar that rends the skies, it casts off the lingering influence of its dark unseen master.

"I am at an end with your assistance!" Pesa bellows, its voice a declaration of long-denied sovereignty.
You have done nothing but delay my birthright, the destiny you have always promised me but have failed to deliver!"
Dia'Baal's essence, weakened yet still seething, clings desperately to his fraying threads of control. His voice within, once commanding, now erupts with venom and indignation.

*"As you wish, you foolish beast, but remember this: you are no god in this struggle without my focused wrath to guide you!"*

The air grows heavy with tension as my progeny... for the first time in over an age, stands unshackled by the arch-rebel's influence. Whether this newfound independence will lead to its salvation or ruin, only time shall reveal to me. In doing so, however, I see the great beast struck by a sudden and chilling dread as Dia'Baal's corrosive grip—his whispers of rage and superiority—vanish completely.
In their absence, I feel my parent now as Pesa is plunged into a fleeting but profound insecurity, its mind momentarily adrift in the unfamiliar silence where once the arch-rebel's voice had reigned.

But this moment of doubt is very short-lived.

In an instant, Opti's talons strike with devastating precision, raking across Pesa's face and tearing deep gashes into both its cheeks. The great beast's visage contorts in wrenching torment, a roar of pain ripping through the air as ribbons of corrupted, aqua-hued lifeblood springs freely. Yet Pesa, unwilling to concede to its great suffering, refuses to be outdone.

With terrifying immediacy, the wounds scar over, and the god of beasts' relentless passion reignites. Its primal instinct surges once more, driving its body back into the fray with undiminished fury.

My every sense surges into this fourth hour... Of combat to witness D'Reem's parent transcending survival, ascending to heights of undeniable dominance, surpassing Pesa's every blow-for-savage-blow. I see this once-mighty predator, the unrelenting force of nature, my parent, staggering under Opti's ruthless onslaught, collapsing in violent retreats beneath the awakened gales of its war rage.

Yet even as exhaustion creeps through its colossal frame and the tide of battle turns against it, my parent remains defiant. It clings stubbornly to the illusion of its invincibility, refusing to acknowledge the grim reality of its fading strength.

*The war-hardened god of fantasy...* forged in the crucible of endless strife, has become something far greater than it was before the battle—a seamless embodiment of Imagination and Reality in perfect harmony. With every calculated strike, every counter to Pesa's dwindling power, Opti refines itself further. No longer is this a mere contest of brute strength; it is evolution of a god in its purest form.

My beloved parent bends the very essence of nature to its will, transcending instinct to achieve a state of sublime mastery. What was once strategy has now become truth—an immutable force that shapes the flow of the battle itself, a testament to the relentless pursuit of perfect balance in the face of overwhelming chaos.

As the great sphere of fire sinks beyond the battlefield's horizon, the **fifth** brutal hour of combat rages on with undiminished ferocity. The clash of titans continues, each strike reverberating through the heavens, yet it is in this hour that a certain and profound shift occurs. Opti, no longer merely reacting, begins to channel all its thought processes into visual reality, striking now with the essence of raw nature itself.

358

Bolts of untamed lightning, summoned from the heart of Opti skyward, now lash out with terrifying precision, these searing strikes through Pesa's defenses.

Opti, possessed of complete clarity, has now transcended the chaotic ebb and flow of battle. Every movement, every reaction a calculated expression of its mastery over nature's forces. Through relentless adaptation, it has unlocked a truth beyond mere combat; by harnessing the atomic energies woven into the fabric of reality, Opti channels them directly into its agility, amplifying its speed and precision to unimaginable levels.

Each successive strike lands with a force multiplied tenfold in brutal strikes, overwhelming your dear parent with an onslaught that even Pesa's brute strength can now hardly withstand. But beyond the raw power of nature, there exists a greater truth—one that emerges only in the crucible of relentless battle. It is here, within this unyielding trial of might and will, that Opti ascends once more, achieving an unprecedented synthesis of Reality and Imagination.
From this divine synergy, a power is born—the ultimate offensive weapon unlike any known to mortal or immortal alike.

This, dearest T'Naeva, is called *Visual Conflict Omnipotence.*

Rooted in the boundless, cosmic force of Imagination, yet tempered by the unyielding laws of Reality, it is birthed through the *Pillar of Perpetuity,* once again granting its wielder the ability to still the flow of time. Opti, now one within this divine evolution, perceives future actions with absolute clarity, transforming mere possibilities into inevitable certainties. No longer bound by instinct or reaction, time or dimension, it becomes a force of predestination—every strike a foregone conclusion, every movement an orchestrated masterpiece of precision and purpose.

In this moment, Opti stands at the pinnacle of its maturity, wielding a power that reshapes the battlefield itself, turning the tides of war with an inevitability that even the mighty Pesa cannot ignore. This incredible ascension, shared only by **Michael, the Archangel** *(in his battle with Dia'Baal in the Great Realm)* and myself against your diseased parent, now finds its true master in my own parent, honed to perfection through the merciless trials of its war against Pesa.

*Though I too once reached...* this sight of conflict in godhood, I still keep its description locked within the depths of my heart, for I know, dearest T'Naeva, that you are not yet prepared to bear the weight of such knowledge. For now, it is enough only for you to witness Opti's rise beyond the boundaries of its former self. Simply put, Opti, the mighty god of fantasy, has ascended to a state of being where it perceives Pesa's attacks well before they take shape in thought.

Through the sacred grouping of divine foresight, destiny, and action, Opti bends the force of Reality itself, striking with such precise fury that Pesa's movements unravel before they are fully formed. This omniscient awareness, now searing through Opti's vast consciousness, elevates it beyond the realm of mere gods and into a plane of deific supremacy.

**In this exalted state I live...** Opti wields its newfound vision as both shield and sword, shaping the battlefield into a theater of inevitability where every motion unfolds according to destiny's will. In Pesa's mind, terror takes root. The god of beasts, my dear Pesa, once so assured of its supremacy, now stumbles under the weight of an unbearable truth: D'Reem's parent is no longer reacting, but knowing, countering, and responding before the battle's rhythm can even be set.

The once-majestic force of nature now finds itself ensnared in an ever-tightening grip of uncertainty, its every assault collapsing, intercepted before it can reach fruition. What was once a glorious display of strength has become a bitter struggle against an adversary whose moves of divine purpose now transcend the force of **nature** itself.

*As the rich blood-hued dusk...* of the **sixth** hour begins, the warring forces of Reality and Imagination continue to clash, yet still coalesce without *harmony.* Opti, ascended to its greatest physical manifestation of godhood, has exceeded the limitations of its fully matured former self. In this pivotal hour, the god of Imagination towers to an incredible **thirty-feet** in stature at the shoulders, eclipsing even my mighty parent, *who remains five feet smaller.*

The difference, though seemingly trivial, marks a profound shift in power— an undeniable testament to Opti's relentless evolution, driven by both conflict and its still, unbridled potential. But now, as I gaze upon Opti's rising form—magnificent, terrible, divine—I finally see it. Not through my own sight, but by a voice not my own... a truth shown to me by the Companion Himself. A single, radiant flash of insight pierces my thoughts like a beam through clouded air, and I know—this is not wholeness. *Not yet.*

Not just *power*. Not just *war*. But something... *still missing.*

The battle outside may tear the realms asunder, but the war within Opti—a silent and suffocating truth—is its greatest crucible. For in this state of apex godhood, one vital element remains absent: the cosmic *Force of Love*. Compassion, once a guiding current, now lies buried beneath the urgency of its survival and supremacy. Opti has risen in form—this I see—but it has not yet awakened to the fullness of spirit.

This final ascension will mark the apex of divine manifestation, where godhood no longer lingers in the abstract, but forged and proven through the cosmic *Force of Existence* itself. Opti, now fully realized, embodies the highest convergence of physicality and purpose, sculpted by war's unforgiving hand. Each clash has become a chisel, carving away all doubt and forging a being of pure, undeniable will.
With every movement, it reshapes even the spirit of the battlefield; with every breath, it resonates the significance of all things warfare – *to simply win*.

Through this ceaseless, six-hour crucible of battle, Opti has risen beyond mere endurance, transforming suffering into strength and adaptation into supremacy. No longer is it simply a force of creation; it has become a force of inevitability, a presence that bends both Reality and Imagination to its will. The battlefield, once a vast and beautiful meadow that spanned two distinct realms, now feels impossibly small beneath the weight of Opti's colossal form.

Pesa, for all its primal might, senses the shift as it now stands at the edge of oblivion. The god of beasts, bound only to natural order, faces the terrifying truth: its raw power alone is no longer enough. Yet surrender is still not an option. Not while the world still trembles in the balance. Not while the echoes of this little skirmish threaten to destroy the very foundation of Earth—the *Force of Reality!*

So, the final reckoning approaches—one where brute force meets boundless invention, where instinct clashes with ingenuity. In the end, the universe will bear witness to a single, undeniable truth: that only one will rise as the true master of the Force of Reality on Earth. I see both gods rear up once more in ferocious combat, their towering forms stretching to awe-inspiring heights, colliding once more in a sickening embrace of fury throughout their ever-darkening surroundings.

What was once a vast and beautiful meadow has retreated in ruin beneath their colossal masses, the earth trembling under their trudges of hatred, the heavens quaking beneath ire's potent roar, and I hear it all. The battlefield, once a stage for gods, now feels impossibly small—too small to contain them both.

**Pesa, for all its might...** sees the truth, written in the towering stature of its foe. No longer does brute force alone reign supreme. The god of beasts withers beneath the ascended Opti, and in that moment, it understands that the balance of power has shifted irrevocably.

Still, it refuses to yield. In Pesa's mind, surrender is not an option. Not while the world still trembles in the balance. Not while a final chance remains to reclaim its birthright. To my dark parent, this horrifying evolution in its kin has birthed a force beyond comprehension. In every aspect of divinity, Opti embodies the ideals of unity and balance, a god that does not tire, cannot be tamed or broken, and can no longer be defeated. Opti, strengthened by a relentless determination, channels its evolved might with precision and confidence, each movement a testament to its divine mastery of all things *combat* throughout the cosmos.

The sixth hour of this monumental battle rages on, and the tide shifts ever more in favor of my dear parent, the sentinel of Imagination. Opti, relentless and unwavering, presses forward with calculated precision, its every strike carving deeper into the fraying spirit of its foe. Pesa, though still ferocious and unyielding, falters further into disarray, its once-thunderous assaults now reduced to frantic, desperate attempts to survive the onslaught.

The god of beasts, once a paragon of raw, and unbridled natural strength, now labors under the crushing weight of exhaustion, its towering form trembling with each strained breath.

# *Verse XXII:*
## The Wrath of Ascension

ia'Baal Fallenstar, recalling his own defeat at the hands of Michael in the Great Rebellion, redirects his rage entirely toward his King. The memory of that celestial humiliation, indeed, is a wound that still festers deeply.

Upon the darkest recesses of his being, this memory alone fuels his unrelenting resolve in the coming climactic hour of warfare. He remembers it all too well—the blinding radiance of the Almighty's decree, the clash of divine forces as the heavens trembled, of Ios and Phalon, Apollynous and Michael, the stalwart guardian of order, standing as the unyielding wall that crushed his rebellion, *and almost his neck*.

The Realm had blazed with righteous fury that day long ago and he, once the Morning Star of splendor, had been cast down in shame, his name forever branded with treachery. In his mind, the echoes of that fateful war resurfaces—the cadence of celestial weapons and armor clashing like the very heartbeats of creation, the deafening chorus of the seraphim's war cries, and the searing pain of the divine judgment hurled upon him.

He had stood at the precipice of eternity, believing his cunning and might to be unmatched, only to be struck down by a force much greater than his own—a force that he has since vowed to destroy by all means necessary. The betrayal, the agony, and the weight of his fall are not forgotten; not in the least, as these memories alone are the fuel of his vengeance.

And now, with Pesa as his vessel, he seeks to inflict upon the Earth the ruin he himself once suffered on that highest plane of existence, as well as on Ametheden. For he loathes them both with every fiber of his being—for their purity, for their devotion, for their unbreakable tether to the one and only **Source**.

Summoning the remnants of his fallen power, Dia'Baal desires—yearns—to pour his wrath into the heart and mind of the great beast, but he cannot. The god of beasts, though battered and wavering, still clings to its own dominion, its primal will forming an iron wall that even the arch-rebel's dark whispers can no longer penetrate. Dia'Baal's influence, unrestrained and malicious, coils upon the edges of Pesa's thoughts once more, probing, tempting, and twisting, but never truly seizing control.

Even now, the demon's voice echoes through the cracks of Pesa's fatigue, planting seeds of doubt and fury, yet the beast's mind remains its own. Their wills, though teetering on the precipice of unification, remain stubbornly apart—two monstrous forces circling each other in an uneasy dance of dominance and defiance. Pesa's resistance, though instinctual, is formidable, an unrelenting survival drive that refuses to fully yield to the arch-rebel's authority.

*"Hear me now, O, cunning Pesa of my passion!"*

Dia'Baal's voice now only a low, insidious murmur, wraps around Pesa's free will like a tightening noose.

*"You are all I have left, o, mighty beast,"* he hisses, the words jagged with a sorrow so ancient that it barely remembers its origin.

*"If you are lost, then even our victory becomes dust. Let me save what little remains of us o' mighty god—of you. You fight alone, mighty yet naive god, and still you falter. Grant me dominion, and together, we shall destroy our foe! Relinquish your will to me, and I promise your triumph! Deny me, and you shall fall to your demise beneath your kin's wrath this very hour!"*

His voice quivers with barely suppressed fervor.

*"This is our vengeance combined—upon the One who shaped and cast us down! You*

*have never needed another—until now, and that is your unyielding strength! May this truth liberate you, not shame you, o, beautiful brute! Join with me now, and we shall rise not as fallen gods, but as the end of His trite design!"*

The battle rages on, but within Pesa's soul, a far greater war is waged—one between its primal will to fight alone, and the seductive allure of absolute dominance through Dia'Baal's dark embrace. Complete exhaustion gnaws at Pesa's limbs, desperation clouds its thoughts, and the great beast stands upon the precipice of an irreversible choice: resistance or submission, defiance or destruction.

    **I gaze in horror as the unthinkable unfolds before me...** a terrible weight settling deep in my chest. The air around me thickens now, charged with a sinister energy that gnaws at the edges of my very soul. Through the veil of my divine sight, I feel it now—the coming *surrender*. Not the bold defiance I have seen in my corrupted parent, but now much deeper and desperate in hopeless capitulation.

Once before, Pesa had allowed Dia'Baal to enter its pride, wounded but intact, grasping at the demon's power only as a last resort.

But now... now it does so completely, not with the arrogance of choice, but with the despair of knowing there is no other way to possibly win this war. I feel it like a dagger to my heart—my glorious yet corrupted parent, once so mighty, is no longer fighting. It is *begging*.

**"No... PESA, please!"** I hear T'Naeva scream, her voice trembling with disbelief as she staggers forward, reaching out with trembling hands, though she knows they cannot bridge the widening chasm between them. The sacred connection she has shared with Pesa thus far, raw and primal, is severed, twisted into something even more unrecognizable than before, and she weeps with passion.

She feels now the beast's fear, its anguish, and its terrible loneliness. Pesa does not want this, but it can see no other path. Dia'Baal, sensing the beast's vulnerability, pours heavily into the gaps left by its doubt, his dark presence pressing deeper, suffocating what little remains of Pesa's true will of self.

*"You have fought long and hard enough, dear brute."* Dia'Baal's voice drips with poisonous comfort, cascading through the shattered remnants of Pesa's mind.

*"For the final time, let me bear this burden of revenge for the both of us... Let me end your suffering now, and I promise you will not be destroyed this hour!"*

Pesa, the mighty god of beasts, beaten, exhausted, alone... *gives in.*
Gaea, the spirit of creation, weeps silently as her essence is twisted by the war waged upon her surface. The god of Reality, once a guardian of balance and nature, will now become the instrument of both their undoing.

"**No... NO, resist!**" she screams again, her eyes still aglow, and her heart shatters, and she feels the last vestiges of Pesa's will slipping away—only to believe stronger in this moment that its liberation would come only in its final hour of life, by D'Reem's hand of justice.
The mighty warriors' eyes dim briefly as his gaze upon her hardens, his jaw clenched as the weight of T'Naeva's grasp settles over him like a dark cloak. He walks to her and places welcoming hands upon her bare trembling shoulders, caressing then gently as his thoughts ignite.

*Alas dear T'Naeva, we no longer fight to save your beast of a parent... we fight now, o, beautiful one, to set it free.*

I release a deep sigh, knowing now that she has been awakened to a terrible truth, and her healing of hatred can finally begin.
D'Reem removes himself from her closeness and returns to his resting place, and once more his eyes glow in eternal knowledge, and he is quickly brought back to the battle where destiny awaits his beloved parent.

Once, in its early life, Pesa revered Gaea, treating her essence with the utmost care and respect. Now, under Dia'Baal's dominion, it becomes the harbinger of her devastation. The Earth quakes with sorrow as the battle reaches its devastating crescendo, the forces of destruction threatening to consume all that was once pure and good.
T'Naeva returns to her place as witness as she again grasps the full force of Dia'Baal's powerful influence, flooding into her parent's essence, and for the first time, she knows the tragic truth...

**Pesa is not surrendering out of greed or ambition, but out of despair.**

It has lost hope, and its tragic submission to the inner darkness inhabiting it heralds the final stage of its epic struggle. What began as a clash of kin has become a war for the very soul of Earth itself.
Now, as Dia'Baal's grip upon Pesa tightens to its darkest extreme, the Earth again wails in anguish. Dear one, as you know, Gaea—the nurturing spirit of the Earth—is bound to her body, a vessel forged by divine design, with Pesa as the cornerstone of her vitality. This internal force of existence, a gift

from Xionn himself, once flowed in harmony with her body, a sacred bond sustaining all life. But now, as Pesa's bondage to Dia'Baal reaches its grim peak, the physical realm begins to suffer—deeply and profoundly.

Tragically, that force, once a harmonious heartbeat, has become a torrent of violent chaos, its essence corrupted and consumed by wrath. Now it resides entirely under the dominion of Dia'Baal. For the first time in his existence, the dark lord wields a power greater than he has ever known. And I tell you, T'Naeva, this fight is no longer Pesa's; it belongs to Dia'Baal and his personal fight with the Creator Himself.

Once more, I am the awestruck witness to the unfolding events that will forge Earth's destiny in the greater cosmic scheme. Seated upon His radiant throne, the Companion glares, His expression a tempest of both anger and justice. He fumes at the memory of once allowing His Firstborne the reckless luxury of wielding a third of His almighty power—the Force of Re'Ali-tee—against Himself, as well as against my parent.

For Dia'Baal, this battle is not merely a contest of strength; it is a blasphemous agitation rekindled, an act of war against the Creator who cast him down and out. Through Pesa's battered flesh, he strikes at Opti with all the fury of one who believes he is defying the very will of his Maker. Each blow, each desperate assault, is more than an attack; it is an echo of his eons-aged defiance, a heated attempt to unmake the divine authority that he has always viewed as his greatest oppression.
In his corrupt and twisted mind, Opti is no longer merely an adversary, but the embodiment of the Creator's judgment—an intolerable reminder of his many failures and exiles throughout the eons.

And so, with every earth-shattering strike, Dia'Baal rages not just against my parent, but against the omnipotence that he can neither escape nor overthrow. His wrath, once cold and calculating, now burns with the reckless desperation of one who fights not for victory, but to defy the very pillar of Creation itself. Yet for the sake of Earth's destiny, Dia'Baal—just as with his tyranny on Ametheden—remains blind to the monumental debts of transgression he accrues with each strike upon Opti.

Beloved T'Naeva, know this latest rebellion against his Creator has sealed his doom! The day will come, many ages hence, when he will seek to leave this world, and on that day, he and his remaining troop shall finally be un-made!

For now, T'Naeva, this coward hides behind the might of his dark pawn—your parent. Clinging to his spirit form to shield himself from Opti's wrath, he drives Pesa's battered body into relentless combat, forcing it to strike blow after bloody blow against my parent. These two titanic foes, now en-emies to their cores, wage a battle of unyielding ferocity—one so great that it now tears at the very harmony of the Creator Himself.

I see it all just as you do, T'Naeva, as if through a veil of torment. I see both their cries of anguish, their godly wounds inflicted with a hatred that knows no bounds, and their endless regenerations, adding layer upon layer of scars across their tormented bodies. Gaea weeps inconsolably for her children in worldwide storms, powerless to end their pain because of ... him. Six endless hours of combat have brought neither reprieve nor retreat, only an intensify-ing spiral of destruction, and Dia'Baal has rebalanced the fight.

And then, something stirs...

The **seventh** hour begins as Opti, bloodied but unbowed, senses an awakening in its divine spirit—an eerie phenomenon pulsing through the battlefield like an unseen birth. Dia'Baal's dominion over Pesa has reached its apex, unleashing a maelstrom of upheaval unlike anything witnessed thus far. The very ground has fled beneath their colossal struggle, fissures splitting open as if the earth itself attempts to shake itself apart from the unbearable burden of this very personal war.

But my attention is drawn skyward, to Luna—the moon—rising over the eastern horizon, her face luminous and stern. Through the roiling, smoky-choked air, she pierces the darkness with a gaze that feels almost sentient, a silent watcher in this final hour of reckoning. There is an anger in her pres-ence, a silent fury that climbs higher with each passing moment, her glow cutting through the chaos with an intensity I cannot yet fully comprehend.

Though I know not her purpose, I feel it. Something vast and ancient stirs within the heavens, awakened by the many evils of this war. Luna watches, her luminous gaze piercing the turmoil below, and I sense her judgment looming ever closer. Though her meaning eludes me, her intent resonates within my very being—a celestial witness to the chaos that unfolds beneath her unwavering gaze.

I turn back to my parent and behold a revelation: Opti, despite the unrelenting brutality of this latest engagement, has already achieved the ultimate unification of the two forces that sustain existence, but does not include the *Force of Harmony.* Reality and Imagination, once warring forces, long coalesced within Opti's being—are still not in balance, but in the raw and undeniable manifestation of war. In this moment, I understand that what unfolds is far greater than any single battle; it is a revelation of cosmic truth, a glimpse into the force of existence itself.

The next torrent of visions courses through us both, carried by the boundless mind of Opti, and what we behold unsettles me to my core. The gales of this ferocious sibling rivalry howl around me, stinging my cheeks, whispering of things yet to come, and the seventh hour of battle continues—an hour of linear time that alone defines the destiny of an entire planet.

Dearest T'Naeva, the inevitability of resolution presses upon me like the weight of a star, and I know this epic clash will soon reach its climax, because I have seen it unveiled once before in my maturity. Opti, too, feels the undercurrent of something dark and final—a sentient force creeping at the edges of the horizon, hidden but potent. Even as the ultimate death knell of this world remains from its sight, faint and far-reaching glimpses begin to flicker within its divine perception.

In its evolving mastery of *omnipotence*—attained through the perfect resonance of Imagination and Reality—Opti now travels several leaps beyond the constraints of physical linear time. The battle unfolds in its mind moments before it manifests upon the field, not through sheer foresight, but through alignment with the very vibrations of existence itself. Each vision flows in harmony with the unseen forces that govern all things, allowing Opti to evade Dia'Baal's monstrous pet once more, its teeth and claws snapping uselessly at empty air.

Opti's swiftly emerging omnipotence is not the power to force its will upon creation, but rather the ability to become one with it. Like ripples upon the surface of a vast ocean, every thought and action resonates through the fabric of existence, carried forward by the divine breath that sustains all life.

To wield omnipotence is not to command the forces of Reality and Imagination, but to move in perfect synchronization with them, allowing their natural course to manifest effortlessly. Opti now exists where fantasy and nature converge—not as opposing forces, but as a unified whole, each feeding into the other in an eternal cycle of creation and realization.

Observing Opti's precise and fluid movements, Dia'Baal's curiosity stirs. He recalls Opti's transformation and its physical *phasing* during those critical moments, as a chilling realization creeps upon him: my parent's strength has evolved beyond the foundational power of Reality; and it has become something far greater.

Opti has transcended force and will, merging with the eternal pulse of creation, a state yet again, Dia'Baal can neither comprehend nor corrupt.

In contrast, Pesa remains shackled to the lie that Opti is the gravest threat to Earth's existence, its instincts warped by Dia'Baal's deception. Yet Dia'Baal—driven by his far-reaching hatred—sees the truth more clearly: Opti embodies an eternal purpose that resonates through the field of battle, challenging his rebellion at its core. It is a purpose he loathes with every fiber of his dark being, for it is the one cosmic force he could never truly manipulate: **Harmony.**

Opti unleashes another volley of lightning, each strike relentless and precise. Pesa staggers under the onslaught, its mighty form collapsing beneath the sheer force of the assault. Yet Dia'Baal's dark pet does not retaliate. Instead, with insidious determination, it rises, eyes gleaming with a dark cunning. A twisted grin curls across its maw as it taunts Opti, daring it to act, to unleash once more the full extent of its fury.

"So be it, freak of my nature!" Dia'Baal roars through Pesa's lips.
"Come at me now, and I shall gladly take you to oblivion with me!"

Opti's patience frays, and in a fleeting moment of misjudgment, it takes the bait. Its focus wavers, its precious foresight slipping as it charges headlong toward its foe, blinded by the urgency to end this madness. With a savage roar, Pesa sidesteps the assault with eerie precision, its lowered head smashing into Opti with titanic force. The impact sends my parent tumbling through the air, disoriented and vulnerable. Seizing the opportunity, Pesa barrels forward, its colossal bulk colliding into Opti's body with unstoppable momentum, the earth trembling beneath their latest clash.
The beast's horns glisten with malevolent energy as it jerks its head, the

razor-sharp points finding their mark as they impale its enemy. Surges of Dia'Baal's eons of frustration flood through Pesa, infusing its actions with a dark, unrelenting ferocity. With a guttural roar, Pesa lifts Opti's massive frame into the air, and Dia'Baal's voice thunders through its lips with a venomous declaration.

"Feel now the torture of your greatest failure—the rage of your Firstborne, O, precious Creator! Witness how your beloved design crumbles beneath my dominion, my revenge alone!"

### Smashed Once...
The heavens flinch as a mournful volley of cries from my parent become one with the darkened heavens, a lament coursing through the Earth, shaking the stars in this brutal act of defiance.

### The Second Heave...
The meadow quakes as Opti is lifted and slammed again, its very fabric of Earth straining under Dia'Baal's focused wrath. Fissures splitting the meadow now like gaping wounds, swallowing the remnants of what once stood as life and hope for a new world.

### Slammed a Third...
As Opti is lifted and grounded once more, each impact sending shock waves through the meadow, the air thick with the acrid scent of destruction. Jagged bolts of energy crackle through a twenty mile diameter swath of ruined landscape, searing it with the imprint of a devil that refuses to yield his eternal struggle against his Creator. Yet even as Opti lies battered, flickers of defiance still linger. Through the haze of its greatness of pain, it whispers...

*"I still endure."*

***Pesa's twisted grin falters...*** for the briefest moment as it senses the ember of resilience that refuses to die. The Earth still trembles, not just from Pesa's assault, but from the quiet defiance that still burns within Opti's heart. The ever-present force of oblivion lingers over the realm of Imagination, its breath cold and patient, awaiting the outcome of this riled struggle.

Within the waiting stillness, Dia'Baal, savoring every moment of his unholy domination, awakens the full extent of his spiteful acts through Pesa.

With a surge of fury, he again floods Pesa's mind, driving his willing puppet into a fresh storm of relentless attacks. With a roar that shatters the trembling air, the god of beasts lowers its massive head and lunges at Opti. Its claws, jagged extensions of chaos, tear through the space between them, swiping in frenzied rage. Yet despite the force behind its strikes, the beast's movements betray its fatigue—wild, chaotic, uncoordinated.

Opti, shaking the pain wildly from its body, regains its balance quicker than Pesa can adjust, answering with a thunderous response. Its massive, armored tail, charged with divine precision, arcs through the air and crashes into Pesa's face and chest. The vicious impact sends the beast reeling, its colossal form impacting the ground like a fallen star.

Without hesitation, Opti's mastery of Reality's chaotic fury takes control. Leaping skyward with its massive wings spread wide, Opti hovers just above the ground. In a blur of speed, it dives and swoops over Pesa as its twenty-four-inch talons—razor-sharp instruments of divine wrath—slice through its thick hide with surgical precision. Each massive talon finds its mark, reducing the god of beasts to a staggering mass of flesh sliced to the bone. Pesa immediately collapses under this merciless assault, but even in its apparent defeat, Dia'Baal's cunning persists.

**From the depths of the earth...** I witness a surge of elemental life force rise to envelop the fallen beast. Just as before, a tidal wave of glowing particles cascades over Pesa's carved body, healing its wounds with unnerving speed. The shimmering cocoon of aqua-hued diamond, just as impenetrable and brilliant as before, solidifies into its greatest strength. The meadow falls silent as the cocoon quickly dims, its energy compressing outward with devastating force.

Opti, again descending to strike the cocoon head-on, is again violently repelled. The unseen power hurls the sentinel of Imagination backward, its massive frame crashing into the battlefield. Before Opti can recover, the cocoon dissolves, leaving Pesa free to act in response. Renewed by Dia'Baal's will, Pesa charges with awakened ferocity. Its horns, jagged and immense, rip through Opti's left wing, the force of the impact driving the sentinel backward.

The beast's claws flash in a whirlwind of fury, slashing through the air with primal intent. With a savage bellow, Pesa drives its horns into Opti's front legs, piercing them clean through. Whipping its head violently, Pesa lifts its kin aloft, shaking the wounded god before slamming it back into the bloodied earth.

The battlefield again trembles under Opti's cries of anguish, each sound thundering through the air like a divine sledgehammer striking an anvil, shaking the Earth to its foundation. Massive gashes now mar Opti's once-pristine form, its left wing and legs tattered and bleeding. Struggling against the pain, it attempts to retaliate with a desperate kick, but Pesa's shield of protection rises again, deflecting the strike and forcing Opti into painful retreat.

Gritting its teeth, Opti rises, battered but unbroken. Its wings flap with renewed determination, lifting its quivering frame from the arena of torment. With a final burst of strength, it departs the fight toward the sanctuary of its own realm, seeking the brief respite needed to prepare for its final counter attack yet to come.

*Driven by unyielding rage...* and Dia'Baal's dark will, Pesa refuses to be denied its kill. Balancing itself swiftly on all fours, the beast explodes into a relentless pursuit, surging forward with monstrous intent as it quickly closes the gap on Opti's retreat. The earth quakes beneath the thundering chase, each colossal stride sending tremors rippling outward. Pesa's claws, curved like immense jagged scythes, tear through the exposed soils of the once-beautiful meadow, now a graveyard of crushed vegetation and blossoms and shattered earth, the remnants of serenity obliterated beneath the fall of two warring gods.

Opti, every flap of its wings a struggle, feels its gasping breath grow steadier as it nears the shimmering threshold of its massive archway. This towering monument of pure energy, resplendent with radiant hues, looms before the battered sentinel—a beacon of anticipation amidst the surrounding chaos. With a final desperate leap of its body, Opti crashes to the ground at the threshold of its sanctuary, its pain-filled gaze locked on the high arc of blazing light that reaches a mile high into the darkened heavens.

**Then, before my awestruck eyes...** a miracle unfolds—a testament to the boundless love and power that sustain the realm of Imagination. I watch, breathless, as D'Reem's parent summons a silent command, weaving it effortlessly into the very essence of the archway's life force. In an instant, the air shimmers with anticipation, and beneath the sentinel's trembling frame, the ground stirs in response. A brilliant eruption follows, an explosion of radiant golden-hued orbs bursting forth, cascading as a giant geyser upward in a dazzling display of colors unknown to me.

The orbs swirl and dance, each one a fragment of raw, untamed beauty, illuminating the heavens in their ethereal glow. Their luminous ascent seems to breathe life briefly into the fractured meadow, a defiant display of the Creator's enduring love and endless power. I am overwhelmed, my heart pounding in reverence and wonder, as I bear witness to this force beyond comprehension—a force that transcends destruction and reaffirms hope—a force that is now a part of *him*.

This celestial energy, pure and untainted, flows into Opti's battered form, merging seamlessly with its divine essence. The sacred bond between the sentinel and its archway ignites the healing process with breathtaking swiftness. Around the massive tears in Opti's wings and legs, the energies weave like masterful artisans, mending its flesh and sinew to perfection in mere seconds. The sentinel's every wound is erased as if it had never been.

*As the geyser's brilliance subsides...* its energies retreat gracefully back into the archway, the radiant arc reforming with renewed vitality. My parent, fully restored and resplendent, arises from the ground. Its body, newly healed, radiates with an unyielding resolve. With its gaze fixed on the relentless charge of my parent drawing closer, the mighty sentinel prepares to bring the battle to its final crescendo. For now, the time has come: my dear parent will end this war, and with it, the reign of the corrupted beast.

I now hear a sound unlike any ever known to this world—a roar of unbridled godhood, raw and untamed, that thunders across the shattered landscape with a force beyond even godly comprehension. The heavens shudder in terrified reverence, torn asunder by its sheer might. The very fabric of reality on earth trembles, and the once-darkened meadow, steeped in despair, quakes beneath the weight of Opti's divine fury.

It is no mere sound; it is a declaration, a reckoning that surges through the realms of Reality and Imagination alike, shaking all creation to its core. The roar bellows, vast and terrible, a storm of righteous vengeance incarnate.

*"Dear kin... baneful Dia'Baal, feel the wrath of Imagination unleashed!"*

The darkened skies above its realm ignite in response, swirling with an ominous brilliance that defeats the darkness, and the meadow recoils beneath the force of this unyielding tone. It is the voice of justice, of authority beyond measure, a force that shall no longer be denied, justice administered in great measure to begin healing a ruined world.

Dia'Baal, witnessing the miraculous restoration of Opti's strength, is seized by a fear he has known only once before: the day his Creator's holy fist cast him from grace, burning his essence with the searing truth of his insignificance. Panic immediately floods his being, a cold and merciless tide, as he comprehends the totality of his folly and the inevitability of his downfall.
I am that warrior who has been granted the privilege to witness the rebellion's champion fleeing, his arrogance reduced to cowardice in an instant, his dark will unraveling before my eyes.

**At Opti's thunderous proclamation...** Dia'Baal turns Pesa's massive form with desperation, fleeing toward the distant sanctuary of its own domain. A mass of stormy haze is conjured within Opti's vast mind, clouds that descend swiftly to confuse Pesa's retreat, and these many miles of meadow stretch long and unforgiving. Each leap and bound of retreat is an eternity to Pesa, and the strength to escape is gone, as even Dia'Baal's power cannot summon swiftness enough to evade the coming decisiveness of Opti, now a living tempest of vengeance on the attack.

Renewed with divine purpose, Opti refocuses its blazing energies. Every fiber of its being surges with power as it ascends, its wings igniting the air around it like a raging comet. A deafening crack of thunder announces its launch, its radiant form slicing through the darkness. The covering layer of clouds scatters like dust, evaporated by the sheer might of its approach.
From below, Opti's fiery gaze pierces the haze, sweeping swiftly across the battlefield in search of its quarry.

There, far below, a desperate blast of bright aura hues erupts as Pesa leaps, runs and stumbles through its thick, misty cloak of dread.

Opti has found its prey!

With a roar, Opti folds its blazing wings inward and plunges, its spurs of justice fully extended. In a flash of savage precision, all twenty-eight of Opti's razor-sharp talons sink deep into the dark flesh of its foe. Pesa's high-pitched screams of anguish pierce the air as Opti's grip tightens mercilessly. The god of beasts thrashes wildly, but Opti's relentless hold remains unyielding, its mighty wings beating furiously to counter every desperate struggle and kick of its prey.

Just as Dia'Baal prepares to refocus his fight with Opti through Pesa, the vessel he has nearly consumed, a deep resonant voice tears through his essence—ancient, absolute, and undeniable. It is the voice of the Companion, I hear it not spoken aloud, but thundered into the core of Dia'Baal's heart.

*... Retreat while you can from Pesa, as fate is no longer held in My grasp. The cosmic force of Imagination is no longer bound by My command. It is no longer My servant— it has ascended to its own sovereign and free will. You sense it now, do you not, o' vile and corrupted Firstborne? The same dread that clung to you when I released My wrath upon your rebellion, coils tightly around your throat once more.*

*... Hear Me now, Dia'Baal Fallenstar, there will be no Son to temper its justice against you now. Opti has awakened through its struggle, and it is Supreme. Its fight will no longer relent, and if you do not retreat, its awakened purge of your ways shall finalize its path—and its pursuit of your shadow to the ends of this realm will begin. You will be hunted and culled. Undone should your arrogance against it continue.*

*... O corrupted son, this force will not simply cast you down as I once did—it will unmake you thread by thread, until even the whisper within you flees, and time itself forgets your name. I will not intervene because this is not My wrath. It is My creation's—and the Force of Imagination will be denied its purge no longer against the parasite that you too, have become.*

*... Flee now, if even the whisper of your pride dares grant you mercy. For the tide has turned not by My will, but by what was once merely dreamt. The Force of Imagination stands not as servant—but as verdict—and its justice no longer sleeps.*

**Terror immediately seizes Dia'Baal...** while realizing there is no bending His verdict this time. Without hesitation, he tears himself from Pesa's mind in a wisp of shadow, fleeing swiftly into a realm unseen. It is now I see the god of beasts falter instantly in his absence, its strength drained completely with the departure of the dark force that once possessed it. The inferno of rage has now died within my parent, extinguished in a single breath.

With newfound resolve, Opti's wrath ignites. Hovering above with wings ablaze, it arcs its armored tail through the air and crashes it into Pesa's stunned bulk with brutal precision. Each of its dozen strikes land like divine thunder, sending tremors through the darkened sky, hammering both pain and vengence into the god of beasts. With a final, devastating blow to the head, Opti's tail silences the final vestige of Pesa's resistance. The god collapses into unconsciousness, broken and defeated in totality.

The meadow far below is left barren, deeply scarred and trembling, having long since fallen into eerie silence. Victorious, Opti hovers above the world as the sentinel of Imagination—unyielding, unbroken, and triumphant.
As I behold this vision, my heart trembles with a torrent of emotions too vast to contain. Awe, sorrow, and an aching sense of finality intertwine within me, each feeling warring for dominance. The sight of D'Reem's parent ascending with unwavering resolve should bring me comfort, yet the weight of all that has transpired presses heavily upon me.

I watch as Opti, burdened yet undeterred, carries the unconscious form of its once-mighty foe into the heavens, the dim glow of the dying sun painting their ascent in hues of crimson and gold. A fitting epitaph for the ruin left below—a ruin I cannot help but grieve. The meadow, once vibrant and teeming with life, now lies devastated and silent, a testament to the cost of rebellion and the price of justice. I feel the emptiness stretch across the landscape, whispering the echoes of what once was and shall never be again.

*Tears brim in my eyes...* not for her dark parent, but for the world that has suffered under its corruption. How fragile creation seems to me now, and how easily beauty crumbles beneath the weight of pride and evil. Each shattered grove, each silenced stream, feels like a wound upon my soul, echoing with the cries of ages past. Yet, amidst the destruction, there is an undeniable majesty in Opti's ascent—a silent promise that vision endures, that hope persists far beyond the wreckage of war, physical or otherwise.

**I struggle to reconcile the triumph...** with the tragedy I witness, the justice with the loss. Was this the only way? Could love and wrath ever be balanced without such cataclysm? My heart longs for answers I feel will never come—or perhaps will arrive one day when the veil is lifted, and the full tapestry of eternity reveals a resolution unmarred by suffering. Yet, as Opti's roar thunders through the skies, I feel its decree reach into the corners of my being. The sound is not noise—it is a summons, a clarion that shakes the boundaries of time and space.

A shiver runs through me—not from fear, but from the solemn truth that

D'Reem's mighty parent carries: creation must be safeguarded, even at a price too great for mortals to grasp. In this moment, I realize Opti is not merely avenging the past—it is forging a future where such ruin will never again find a home. But the visions flooding me are not clean. They crawl, serpentine, into the edges of my mind, whispering in tones that mimic revelation but taste of iron and ash. Faces distort; truths blur.

I see Pesa's form melt and reform in flickers of horror, its eyes not pleading but accusing, its mouth shaping words never spoken. A shadow coils within my ribs — the Whisper, subtle and insidious — bending sight into nightmare, turning pity into doubt. It shows me a world where Opti's justice becomes annihilation, where mercy is a mask for cruelty. I do not know if these glimpses are prophecy or poison. My breath stutters as I clutch at my temples, feeling the dual pull of light and shadow vying within me. Even as D'Reem's words echo of truth, another voice murmurs behind them, older, softer, venomous.

It promises clarity but delivers dissonance. And yet part of me listens, part of me wants to believe. In that moment I understand that I, too, am a battlefield — not yet free of the parasite's touch, not yet sure which vision is real and which is manipulation.

# *Verse XXIII:*
## The Duality of Flame & Grace

I n this moment, I realize the battle was never just between our parents, but within us all. And as day fades into night, I find myself wondering, can what was lost ever truly be restored?

At last I see, reaching an altitude befitting its judgment, Opti halting its ascent, its immense wings beating steadily against the thin air. The heavens themselves seem to hold their breath as the mighty sentinel lets loose a roar that shakes the stars, a cry of triumph and righteous retribution.

*"You are fortunate, brutish demon, to be unaware of your fate as it swiftly approaches. Yet know this: your end shall be met only in beautiful slumber, for only mercy has granted you peace in your vile ignorance!"*

These words roll through the skies like thunder, their weight a decree upon the vanquished. The battlefield below remains broken and silent, as if all creation bows in quiet submission to the will of Imagination's champion. Opti's talons, still embedded deeply within the shredded body of the god of beasts, tremble as the sentinel struggles to release its grip. With one final, powerful jolt, the talons retract, and Pesa is dropped into the heavens, plummeting toward the earth far below.

The god of Reality, still unconscious, begins its silent and swift descent, its massive form racing through the heavens like a falling aqua hued star. Circling above, Opti watches with a mixture of triumph and wrath, its

379

blazing form circling while illuminating the path of its enemy's fall.

As Pesa's massive body hurtles earthward, the beast stirs, unconsciousness unraveling into a dawning horror. A guttural cry of terror rips from its throat as realization strikes—there is no salvation, no escape from the fate that awaits it.

The barren earth of a once-vibrant meadow trembles in anticipation, the air thick and suffocating beneath the weight of inevitability. The winds across Earth's heavens howl in mourning, a mother whispering her torment through her ravaged landscape between the realms, as if grieving the final descent of her child. All of creation on Earth holds its breath, bearing witness to the end of an era shaped by defiance and ruin.

Closer and closer to the world, the god of beasts' plummets, its dread mounting with every fleeting second. The air tears around its massive form, a howling lament that heralds its inevitable doom. At last, the earth convulses as Pesa's colossal body crashes into the heart of the deadened meadow, the impact is catastrophic. The region heaves and fractures, the once-still soil rippling outward in waves of violent upheaval, as though the world itself recoils in agony beneath the weight of *a fallen god*.

Pesa's mighty frame—once a symbol of raw, unbridled power—is now a crumpled, pulverized, glowing mass of flesh, muscle, and fur, a grotesque twenty-ton heap of its former glory. The earth, scarred by the brutal impact, stands as a grim testament to the devastating price of unchecked pride. High above, Opti hovers with unwavering focus, its fiery gaze locked upon the complete ruin of its kin far below. Slowly, it descends, the brilliance of its form casting long, flickering shadows across the deadened battlefield.

The meadow, once scarred by the fury of Reality's storms, now falls into an unsettling silence. The chaotic skies, once raging with wrath, clear themselves in solemn surrender, revealing a serene tapestry of emerging stars that stretches endlessly across the heavens—a stark, indifferent contrast to the carnage below. Though Pesa's physical form lies pulverized and defeated, the foundational force of Reality, woven into its very essence, *endures*.

The god of beasts now clings to existence on the most basic atomic level, sustained by the divine connection to Gaea, the nurturing spirit of Earth. Opti lands near the pooling remains of its sibling, its massive wings folding inward as it surveys the scene. The sentinel's glare still burns with divine wrath, clouded by visions of its ultimate retribution. In this moment, the god of Imagination contemplates an act of finality—a genocide that would erase Pesa and all traces of its creation from existence.

It is then that I hear the heavens wail with thunder as the wrath of Opti charges its enemy one final time to destroy it … this hour so long ago. The god of creatures' heavy breathing overcomes the deadened silence within the destroyed meadow, and it backs away from the deep cavity its enemy still lies within. An extremely disheartening mood then overcomes and quickly defeats Opti's ungodly rage, and honestly, I am so very thankful for that.

Within this mournful silence, the mighty sentinel of Imagination lowers its head, closing its fiery red eyes as a floodgate of guilt begins to trickle down its bronzed face.

The weight of countless ages bears down upon its broad shoulders, every moment of past triumphs laced with bittersweet regret. Opti already knows full well that its own demise is fated into its destiny—*my destiny.* Still traumatized and unable to comprehend the true depth of this incredible change of heart in its enemy, Pesa can only yield to its own healing as it continues to restructure itself, one atom at a time, in supernatural swiftness.

I seek to cherish these visions that have become so dear to me—these images of my beautiful and powerful parent. Their meaning is clearer to me than ever before, and I will not make you an orphan of truth, dear T'Naeva. Even in my rage, I will not strip Pesa of the mercy my parent gave it.

I gaze upon my majestic parent as it lifts its fiery gaze from Pesa, and I can feel within the bright crimson hues both the sorrow and the hope they harbor within. Opti returns to stare upon its ravaged kin with overwhelming sadness, something I did not completely understand the first time I saw this vision. I see my parent lift its heavy head once more, studying the deepest reaches of its beautiful realm in quiet reflection. Guilt over its prior actions weighs heavily, and tears begin to flow down the radiant hues of its rigid yet tired face.

It is then I feel that my parent somehow expresses its final thoughts silently to its beloved father, yielding its good fight and seeking forgiveness for its terrible actions. I now understand what has eluded me for so long, T'Naeva. A wonderful presence of peace has entered and strengthened the revered divinity within my parent in its final moments. It smiles skyward into the dark, crimson-hued heavens one final time, because its death draws near.

I, D'Reem, now gaze upon my very foundation of Imagination, my cherished and magnificent parent, Opti, who suddenly begins to utter soft words in an unknown tongue, and the heavens of the Earth sing their praises in those last few and precious hours of life. Having already accepted the reasoning behind its coming fate, my parent does not fear, but embraces the ultimate freedom and peace that death will bring to its weary body and mind. Pesa, becoming cognizant of its surroundings, but still greatly confused by its enemy's unique strategy, can only speculate as to why Opti has not finished it off when it had an eternity of chances to do so.

Only during a much later age, specifically at the moment of its death—will Pesa come to fully understand why its kin had not destroyed it in these fateful moments of destiny. I see time pass to a crawl as Pesa's body continues to regenerate at an alarming pace, while it wonders why it is taking so long for Opti to attack it. Pesa's thoughts are now solid once more, but are still very scattered and confused. I also hear them so very clearly, and I share them with you now, my beloved T'Naeva...

"This precious time ... wasted away as my enemy stands in silent lament and does nothing but weep ... and my regeneration continues to quicken. Why, O, vicious flower, do you not attack me, knowing you can easily finish me off and be done with all of this utter nonsense?"

Rippling flares of aquamarine energy continue to surge through Pesa's colossal frame, its lifeblood coursing with renewed vigor as its supernatural healing continues. The dark tendrils of regeneration weaving seamlessly through its battered mass, knitting flesh and bone with unnerving speed. So far, this process of healing progresses well, each pulse of energy reinforcing the beast's monstrous vitality. Long, anxious hours stretch into eternity as Opti stands motionless against the encroaching darkness all this time, its own silent vigil to protect Pesa from any further harm.

The air is thick with tension, the battlefield caught in the suffocating grip of anticipation. Pesa's restoration nears completion, its once-shattered form again, *almost* whole. Then—without warning—the process is violently interrupted. With a burst of unrestrained impatience, Pesa explodes from the gaping cavity of its ruin, landing upon all fours with earth-shattering force. Dust and debris swirl in its wake as it charges forward, its monstrous form once more a blur of raw fury and power. A thunderous roar splits the air, a primal declaration of war as Pesa hurls itself at its foe with relentless ferocity.

"Why did you not scatter my elements to the wind when you had the chance, you foolish beast?!"

The abrupt suspension of its supernatural healing in pursuit of vengeance comes at a heavy cost; Pesa unknowingly forfeits nearly a quarter of its formidable mass. This unforeseen loss will weigh heavily in the grim trials that await the beast in the dark season to come. Yet with no time to dwell on its diminishing strength, Pesa leaps forward in a blinding flash of godly endurance, a force reborn with renewed purpose. A deafening roar tears through the battlefield as it then vaults toward its destiny, deadly claws fully outstretched—now.

Opti, having already envisioned this moment hours prior, meets its fate without a trace of fear. Its gaze turns heavenward, and with unwavering resolve, it releases a triumphant roar that extends beyond the confines of Earth and deep into the cosmos—an unyielding declaration of defiance in what will be its final moments of physical life. This tragic vision, etched forever into my soul, returns to haunt me once more.

My parent turns itself bravely and without regret into the vile visage of its destiny. It glares with divine purpose directly into—*and then straight through*—the storm of Pesa's bright aqua-hued eyes, piercing not just its gaze, but for a fleeting instant, the vastly corrupted and hardened soul within it. In the absence of Dia'Baal's oppressive shadow, the great beast falters, feeling a sudden and most peculiar sensation—one that it cannot tame, one that is unfamiliar and yet strangely comforting.

This time, it is not the dark whispers of corruption that dictate its movements, but the pure and commanding presence of Opti's divine power. And so, at the urging of my dear parent, this unfamiliar feeling is harnessed, guiding Pesa's final attack towards a purpose it does not yet comprehend. That beautiful destiny, dear T'Naeva, is *you*—and how you came to be here with me.

A shuddering awakening seems to ripple outward from the cancerous bile of its mind, a light breaking through the suffocating darkness. For the first time in its many ages of life, the god of beasts feels something beyond hunger and rage. Its thoughts reel and its body wavers, closing its eyes to embrace this newfound sense of purpose. Pesa, continuing its leap toward an unseen enemy, fully extends its massive right paw. There is no hesitation, no uncertainty. Guided by an invisible wind, it strikes with perfect precision, its exact target awaiting destiny set in motion.

There is abrupt hesitation as D'Reem, seeing once again the deathblow of his beloved parent, stares straight ahead. His eyes, lit but now widened with the burden of memory and grief, lock onto the inevitable. His young bride, T'Naeva, sits before him in silent lucidity, and though no words are spoken, she already knows the tragic conclusion before he utters it. The weight of their shared sorrow binds them in a moment of painful understanding, their hearts both heavy, yet growing stronger together in these visual echoes of what is to come.

It is then that she begins to weep ... *for him.*

"My parent is at peace, yes, but I am left still with this aching abyss that no words yet can fill, even to this very moment! T'Naeva, this memory is a torment too searing still, too raw to endure... still.
The Companion's vision withdraws—not because it falters, but because this anguish, this scar upon my soul, is still mine alone to bear. It is the shadow of a grief too vast for any other than myself to carry. Anger surges through me, a raging cloudburst carving rivers of sorrow into the flesh of my grief.

Each drop of rain is a shout, a plea, a fragment of my broken heart cast into a place that has yet to find peace! The weight of this loss is a crushing tide I still cannot resist, a force that drags me deeper into the abyss of my despair. The echoes of my parent's final moments reverberate in my soul, a haunting melody of love and sacrifice that will never fade. I am drowning in these memories once more for you alone, dear mate, and in the cruel truth of their absence, I fear I shall never find you again!
And yet, within the squall of this raging sorrow, a fragile ember of hope remains—a whisper of faith that, somehow, peace will one day return to me ... but not now!
"I see it and feel it ... again! I hear it and know it ... again! I smell it and live it ... again! I feel its pain to hell and back ... again!"

*I once again dread this next vision ... this tragic, enduring flash of images that I will live with for the rest of my days.*

"For your sake, T'Naeva, and not my own, I witness once more that horrific strike, ripping deep into Opti's neck. All seven of Pesa's claws slice through, cutting completely into the side of its throat—and then, a brief stillness.

"For your sake, T'Naeva, and not my own, I see it clearly: four massive claws remain on Pesa's corrupted right paw... But where, you ask, are the other three? Let me tell you where they are, dear mate! Those three claws are ripped away during that terrible strike, torn free of Pesa's paw and driven deep into the quivering, ghastly tissue of my parent's flesh."

*For a fleeting moment, I close my eyes and breathe in the silence that lingers between these vivid images and memories. These winds whisper against my skin, carrying with them the faintest scent of earth and dust—a reminder of what once was, and what can never be again. In this brief reprieve, I feel the weight of Opti's paw leaning upon my shoulder, not in reality, but in the quiet sanctum of my soul.*

*A deep and resonant but pleasant voice, only a ghostly whisper now, reaches out to me from the echoes of its paradise, urging me to stand, to fight, to simply endure this torture for you T'Naeva, alone. Yet even in this fragile peace, the storm within me stirs once more, an unrelenting tide that will not be denied.*

"And finally, for your sake, T'Naeva, and not my own, I will tell you this: those three claws are with me now. They are the dust within me! My eternal reminder of resolve, my justice, my destiny—to end the cursed existence of your damned parent!
Pesa's claws, dear T'Naeva, birthed from Opti's sacrifice, fused into me and remain embedded within this chest, this body, this soul. Do you see it now, O, beautiful goddess? Justice courses through me with every breath I take!"

The great warrior rises in a flash and strikes his chest, his massive hands trembling with anger, but his tears flow no more. His grief burns fierce, his sorrow sharpened to a sword's edge. T'Naeva stands, blindsided by his revelation, astonishment and shock warring upon her face, and yet she feels no anger toward him, no resentment for his eruption. Instead, a deeper understanding blooms within her—an unspoken connection to his suffering that transcends words, binding them tighter in shared sorrow and purpose.

As swiftly as it comes, his internal storm subsides. The Companion's tranquility washes over him, stilling his grief and returning his focus to the story again unfolding. The air around him hums with an ethereal calm, a silent whisper from the unseen presence guiding his thoughts back to clarity. "Forgive me, my beloved. This vision wounds me deeply each time it returns, and your understanding is the solace I need." He exhales slowly, his fiery gaze turning inward as the memory resumes.

The deadly silence is shattered by a sound unlike any other—raw and primal, a roar that births terror into the marrow of existence. It tears through the heavens, a sound that has never been heard before, nor shall it ever echo again. The force of it shakes the very foundation of reality, as though creation itself recoils at the magnitude of the moment. T'Naeva shivers, the weight of it pressing against her chest, yet she remains resolute. She watches as he sits cross-legged, the storm within him no longer raging, but burning steady like an eternal flame.

As if on cue, his voice returns to omnipotence, and T'Naeva knows it not.

His words, now guided by a force much greater than himself, resonate with a power beyond comprehension—an echo of destiny reverberating through time.
It is now, dear T'Naeva, in this moment of reckoning, that Opti's tragic death begins its final path. The sacrifice that would shake the heavens and forever mark this world—well, its birth is upon us.

Swaying in silence as a bright crimson river of life shoots as a geyser from the gaping wound in its neck, Opti's body trembles, rising slowly as its divine nature surges into a supernatural overdrive. With this final emergence of godly strength released, Opti launches itself at Pesa, striking the battered beast like a wildfire devouring a forest. The impact is brutal, hurling Pesa flat to its belly.
Yet this blow is not made to kill your parent, dear T'Naeva, but to save it!
The vision shatters. I blink, breathless—kneeling, shaken, but no longer alone.

T'Naeva gasps, clutching at her chest as if the sudden emptiness threatens to consume her. Her breath comes in ragged bursts, and for a fleeting moment, fear creeps into her heart. She searches desperately for the images, for the sight of Opti's fate, but they elude her eyes completely, slipping away like whispers in a sudden wind. Confusion and frustration twist within her, yet beneath it all, a reluctant relief lingers—an unspoken understanding that she may not yet possess the strength to endure the truth.

"No!"

She cries, the word escaping her like a wound.

"Show me the rest! I command it! You cannot stop now—not when the truth lies on the cusp of this revelation! What is it you're hiding from me?"

But the Companion remains silent—though the air shifts slightly, as if stirred by an unseen breath. Warmth brushes her brow as if to say...

*'Not now, child, not to spare you, but to spare the truth emerging within you.'*

She turns to D'Reem, her eyes wild with fury.

"How dare you stop this? You have no right to decide what I can or cannot endure!"

D'Reem's voice, low, steady and compassionate, breaks through her haze of rage, and he whispers.

"I did not stop it, my love. The Companion did. He alone who chooses when and what may be seen, for even I am only given what is needed at the correct time. Not even I can override His will."

He lowers his gaze.

"He tells me, though, that you are not ready to see the full scope of what is to come. But, to also believe this: that some burdens must be revealed in their time, and your time has not come."

Her lips tremble.

She rises in a fury, fists clenched, eyes darting. But her strength fails her—she crumples back to her knees, weeping uncontrollably.

"I was ready... I *had* to be ready."

"No one is ever ready to face clarity in the teeth of nightmares," D'Reem whispers. "This I know all too well—hard-won through my own journey to maturity. But some truths must still wait to bloom into maturity as they hurl those demons far away, and allow your peace to simply breathe."

T'Naeva swallows hard, wipes her cheeks with the back of her hand.

"Then teach me to wait without hating you for it!"

He places a hand upon her trembling shoulder. She does not resist it. But her tears continue to fall, and with them, a quiet surrender—if only for now.

The sentinel of Imagination crashes to the ground, its mighty frame landing forcefully beside its broken kin. It does not falter, nor does it pause to grieve its own imminent death. Instead, Opti's entire being focuses solely on the destiny that awaits its kin—the fragile thread of salvation it still dares to grasp. Opti jolts its head toward Pesa, desperation igniting within its fiery gaze. With every ounce of its remaining strength, it commands its kin to look at it—to see what only its eyes can reveal.

Pesa, its massive form wracked with pain, feels an unfamiliar and unshakable compulsion. Slowly, it lifts its head, and for the first time in ages, their gazes lock firmly in kinship. Windows to the soul indeed meet in a shared, piercing stillness. Not in hatred. Not in rage. But in a quiet, undeniable understanding. For what feels like an eternity, they hold each other's eyes— two titanic beings stripped of their masks, laid bare in the vulnerable silence of truth.

Then, like a whisper cutting through a storm, a voice speaks—not with sound, but with purpose, filling the very essence of Pesa's mind.

*"You are more than what Dia'Baal has made you, dear kin. Remember who you were before the darkness. Remember why you were created."*

Pesa's massive form stills, its breathing shallow yet rhythmic, as if the very words have rooted themselves deep within its corrupted soul. Opti does not move, does not falter, but holds its firm gaze, unyielding in its final plea. And in that brief moment, a crack—a fissure in the impenetrable armor of Pesa's mind—begins to form, albeit brief.

*"Do not arise from where you lie, as you shall certainly be hurled into oblivion if you do. No, Pesa ... this is not the hour of your fate. So, be still, dear kin, for the sake of our world."*

In its severely incapacitated state of body and mind, and currently free of Dia'Baal's vile influence, all Pesa can do is close its eyes as these powerful words seize its every function and thought. A very good thing, too, because for the first time in Pesa's life, it will soon experience yet another fear it has never known, and it lies still before the dread and destruction that will very soon be unleashed all around it.

With its final moments of life drawing closer, yet its purpose still unfinished, Opti shifts its gaze from Pesa to its homeland. Its eyes burn with a focus born of divine determination, piercing the vibrant bands of energy arcing between the two diamond foundations of the Realm of Imagination's great archway. The radiant spectrum trembles beneath the sentinel's will as Opti seizes the energy for itself. In that fateful moment, the majestic archway—the gateway to boundless creativity—dims, its power extinguished forever as it is absorbed into the god who once protected it.

Opti's resplendent visage shines as bright as a nova, its form trembling as the captured power courses through its body. The energy saturates every orb of its being—born once of pure creation, hardened by the trials of reality, and now aching toward something it had abandoned... or forgotten.

As I witness this scene anew, a flood of emotions overtakes me, dear T'Naeva, more potent than I recall. This moment seizes me beyond words, for it is here, amidst the aftermath of Pesa's savage blow, that a new inspiration rises within me—a profound understanding of sacrifice.

I return briefly to that instant when Pesa's claws struck deep into my parent's neck, narrowly sparing its vocal cords. Though its form lay broken, its essence surges forth in one final earth-shattering roar, carried not by mere breath, but by the gales of destiny itself.

Opti's death roar, monumental and eternal, reverberates not only as a cry of sacrifice but as the first living breath of what had long been missing within it: *Love*—the fierce glow where Reality steadies Imagination and Imagination illumines Reality, unmasking the true heart of its final act. In that reunited light, my parent rose beyond itself and crossed the threshold of its final becoming.

This roar, T'Naeva, is no mere cry—it is a primal proclamation, a soul-carved truth etched into the very lattice of existence. Everything I recount to you is born of this singular moment—Opti's ultimate gift of unconditional love, offered not just to your parent, but to the Earth so it can live. Without this act of selflessness, neither you nor I would be standing here now, screaming hatred and grievances upon the other in our shared existence.

I hear it now as I first heard it in the hours after my birth—a roar of both death and life, a shattering cry that reverberates through the heavens and earth to this day. Opti's body, ablaze with the brilliance of its archway's divine power, releases its final, mighty outcry. This act, forged in the crucible of sacrifice, far transcends even immortality. In this moment, my parent's very essence intertwines with Gaea and its dark kin, forging a bond that will defy the clutches of oblivion itself.

It is as if, through its final act of sacrifice, Opti commands the chaos of a world unraveling to temporarily cease its madness, anchoring it with the force of its indomitable will. Gaea complies with compassion. How strange it is, T'Naeva, that a being born to dream, and reforged to fight, should find its final strength not in destruction... but in restraint.

Yet, even in this god's final hour of life, I wonder: was this love always buried within my parent after its maturity, or was it born in this instant—drawn forth by the very act of defeating the fates themselves in its ultimate surrender.

Some truths arrive only in their destined hour, my beloved mate. Others must be endured into revelation, and so it becomes known with this final act of a god. Opti—the mighty sovereign of Imagination—steadies itself upon trembling limbs. Even in its coming death, it does not flee its responsibility. Instead, it exhales. A divine breath escapes its core, sweeping outward in a torrent of mythic preservation. That breath does not seek vengeance. It seeks protection, and what it forms is not simply a barrier.

No—this is not mere diamond, nor any known construct of element or spirit. What surrounds Opti and Pesa is a shell of impossible geometry, a shimmering lattice of fused resonance and will, a crystalline cocoon forged not by design but by sacrifice, its own.

What Pesa once wielded in elemental control, Opti now refines into something wholly transcendent. It calls upon every thread of Imagination, shaping matter beyond nature and consciousness alike. The result? A structure never envisioned by even the greatest of Edenites. A form never etched by reality's laws nor born of any previous world. This crystalline barrier pulses with mythic resonance, a shield of such transcendent precision and strength that it will withstand not only the coming destruction, but the close unraveling of Reality itself. This, T'Naeva, is the final miracle of a dying god:

### Sacred Diamond.

Not a singular gem, but a mythic shell of divine fusion—a convergence of perfectly harmonized creation and willing surrender. Forged in the furnace of Love so pure, so scorching in intensity, that it becomes something more than defense. It is preservation. It is hope. It is the divine defiance of Oblivion itself. What was once elemental is now incarnate. *Divinity—made matter.* Sacred Diamond does not merely resist destruction; it endures the very unmaking of Reality.

Yet, in its completion—something ancient shatters. Let it be known: *Death and Harmony* are eternal opposites, adversaries of the highest order. One is the cessation of breath, the fracture of purpose, the end of equilibrium. The other is the genesis of balance, the breath between beats, the secret pulse of all that lives.
*They can never coexist in unity.*

This once-perfect crystalline shell—born of elemental diamond, transfigured by sacrifice—is now irrevocably altered. Its flawless lattice, once a sanctuary of divine intent, begins to fracture from within. It no longer holds the sacred tension it was forged to contain. That flaw—that holy imperfection—becomes the opening through which Harmony, now unbound, erupts.

At first, a tremor. Then a quake. Then a cataclysm.

The rupture magnifies by the second, blossoming outward in titanic waves. What begins as a local shiver becomes a force that hurls the entire buffer zone into upheaval. A hundredfold. A thousandfold. The Earth itself convulses, groaning beneath the strain of a power it was never meant to bear. The meadow splits. Skies wail. The great mountain shakes as if it were alive, and the ancient sanctuary of Harmony—once a throne of Love's perfect equilibrium—shudders, fractures, and begins to collapse.
the Earth screams.

But her voice is swallowed by the cacophony—Harmony's scream is louder. The sacrifice of a god has been made. And thus begins the consequence. But amid the rending of this world, another truth begins to stir. One not yet spoken. One I will reveal to you only when your spirit is ready to carry it. For Opti's ultimate becoming did not lie in vision, nor in might, nor even in the sacrifice itself.
It lay in what it chooses to reclaim. I feel it—then and now—the final pulse of something eternal. It begins in the meadow's ruins beneath my feet... and spirals downward to the very core of the Earth. I am still there, T'Naeva. My vision does not falter, nor does my heart stop—for the both of us—in its silent lament.

# *Verse XXIV:*
## When Omnipotence Defies Fate

'Naeva's quiet sobs break the tense air as I pause. Her tears, born of grief and revelation, cascade down her face. The thought of her parent's savage influence, the unbearable weight of my visions have undone her composure to its foundation.

She trembles, caught in the harrowing web of truths she once denied, but now accepts.
"D'Re-..."

Her voice cracks suddenly through the silence, her words falter, and they are cut off completely. She cannot find them—for none can suffice—and so she remains silent. She knows now that what she sees is no fabrication, no imagined torment. The visions we have both witnessed are truth—living, breathing, and searing. For the first time, her belief solidifies, leaving her stricken with a grief mirroring a portion of my own. Though my heart aches for her sorrow, I press onward. This story must be told for her. And so I continue.

The lattice has cracked. Harmony can no longer contain the strain, and thus begins the burning. The meadow is the first to bear witness to its collapse. Its wide expanse trembles and fractures beneath the roar, and soon, every living thing within its regional scope meets oblivion—every creature save for your parent and mine.

Opti's lifeblood, a fusion of creation's force and celestial will, shimmers brilliantly against the flawless diamond shell, phasing into ethereal light that seeps into the soil. The meadow drinks deeply of Opti's sacred blood, its heartbeat still pulsing with untamed life. I pause, my chest heaving with the weight of my own grief and awe of this sight, yet my voice does not break. The roar of my parent, its final thunderous cry, fades from the world, but will forever echo within me.

*"It is not just a sound, dear one!*
*It is Life!*
*It is Power!*
*It is the Inspiration that drives me still!"*

The dark soil beneath the meadow, ravaged by Harmony's unleashed fury, shifts once more as the destruction spreads relentlessly. I feel the heat intensifying into an unbearable blaze, consuming all in its path. The once-eternal and mighty diamond archway, unable to endure the fiery onslaught, melts and collapses with a thunderous crash. Deep below, Gaea writhes once more in agony, her spirit reaching up to shield the molten ground. But her strength falters as grief consumes her—grief for Opti, the sentinel of Imagination, and Pesa, the wayward protector of Reality. Her wails shake the earth, igniting the very soil in sorrow.

From the fallen archway of diamond, a monstrous funnel of flame erupts, a colossus of fire and fury clawing inward a distance of a thousand miles throughout the Realm of Reality, as well as skyward, roaring three miles high as both the heavens and world are drenched in flame. Molten gales also sweep outward, igniting one tree after another along the threshold that separates the two realms. Each tree, standing as part of nature's sacred barrier, bursts into an inferno, one after another, their blazing forms transforming into towering giants of fire and ash.

The blaze of their destruction spreads relentlessly, circling the Earth as the threshold of realms is consumed in its entirety. Only when the final tree ignites will this worldwide blaze extinguish itself, leaving behind a burnt and lifeless frontier clear to the eastern and western horizons. The Earth, scorched and silent, bears the weight of this devastation, its once-vibrant threshold to the great mountain reduced to smoke and ash.

I stand motionless, dear one, bound to this vision as if tethered by fate. My heart aches with the weight of Gaea's sorrow, and my soul feels the searing heat that consumes the land. The landscape, once lush and teeming with life, now lies shrouded in choking smoke and glowing embers. Firestorms rage across the horizon, their furious tendrils clawing at the heavens as if I were on the surface of a star! The air quivers with unbearable heat, and the ground beneath me cracks and groans, releasing fiery veins of molten earth.

Helpless yet transfixed, I watch the inferno devour everything in sight, its destructive beauty etched forever into my memory.

But dear T'Naeva, this devastation pales in comparison to what unfolds within the Realm of Imagination. As the Earth's frontier burns to ash, the pristine beauty of Opti's realm begins to unravel. The deathblow of its god unleashes a calamity far greater than I can bear. The vast, unspoiled landscape—half of the Earth's surface, once untouched by the ocean set before us—is ripped asunder. Without its creator's sustaining life force, the very bond that holds this realm together begins to dissolve.

I see them again, T'Naeva—these inspired orbs of Imagination, these luminous seeds of creation, flung violently into the heavens. For a moment, they shimmer like falling stars, an infinite cascade of brilliance. But this fleeting beauty gives way to horror as the orbs plummet back into the realm, their impact igniting multicolored firestorms of unimaginable intensity. I see it all unfold across the eastern face of the Earth. Entire regions of Opti's boundless land are stripped bare, their vibrant landscapes reduced to the dark, unyielding soil of nature's foundation.

My heart shatters as I watch the annihilation of almost everything that my parent inspired—an unimaginable loss, one that still shakes me to my very core. They vanish into oblivion by the hundreds of billions—unique, wondrous species, each a testament to my parent's unmatched creativity, erased forever. Creatures of infinite variation, whose beauty and purpose will never again grace this world, whose stories of life will never be told.

Yet amidst this unfathomable loss, I see a flicker of hope, fragile but resilient. Those life-forms born of both Imagination and Reality—anchored to nature's foundation—endure the firestorms. Among them, a species of enduring strength, Opti's chosen protectors, emerge from the ashes: the Chup'DraVak-Ra, their potent presence a lingering echo of my parent's power and purpose.

I stand grieved within this horrific vision, yet consumed in awe, and I feel its life force permeate me. Every creation, every inspired fragment of Opti's realm, remains somehow divinely intact and is never really lost, because they all now reside within me. I carry them, T'Naeva—the memory of their beauty made manifest once more through the sparks of their existence. Through me, my parent's legacy and its realm will forever endure, though the Earth will never know what was surrendered to oblivion that forgotten day in ancients long past.

This moment, dear T'Naeva, is one I live with every day. It is both my torment and my strength, a burden I would never trade, my parent's gift—a gift forged in the fires of its mighty sacrifice.

Dearest T'Naeva, for seven long and terrible hours, the Earth lay silent, its living creatures stilled in trembling anticipation of the outcome of their warring gods. Every soul, mortal and immortal, had retreated into the shadows, as though the very act of existence had been suspended under the weight of this divine conflict. Within the two great realms, all life seemed poised on the brink of an altered fate—a fate birthed from this catastrophic clash of titans, a fate that now loomed over the very life force of Earth.

This battle, dearest one, did not merely scar our home. It planted a hope deep within Gaea herself, her nurturing spirit of *nature*. The Realm of Imagination began to sicken, its vitality drained by the imbalance wrought by this prolonged war. Without intervention, this sickness would have devoured the realm entirely, collapsing it into the void of oblivion. It was only through my own birth, my own destiny to preserve this fragile balance, that salvation would be made possible.

Thus concluded a season of unimaginable transgression, a calamity that forever altered the Earth and all within it. In that defining hour, when chaos threatened to consume it all, my remarkable parent fought with valor unmatched, a beacon of heroism amidst the vile machinations of Dia'Baal and his enslaved servant—your dear parent. Time and again, Opti, the sentinel of Imagination, gained the upper hand in its savage fight with Pesa.

Time and again, it brought its foe to the brink of destruction. Yet it held back, refusing to deliver the final blow. And the reason, dear T'Naeva, is profound in its simplicity: nature itself would have perished with your parent. In the final hours after their titanic struggle, a realization dawned upon Opti—a truth as vivid as the crimson skies that bore witness to their war. If Opti were to destroy Pesa, the arrogant yet vital god of Reality, the foundation of all nature—of all life on Earth—would have died.

For though my parent had surpassed Pesa in physical strength through its divine evolution, it lacked the depth of comprehension that Pesa held over Reality's intricate design. Pesa was not merely a foe; it was the keystone of Earth's very existence. To destroy Pesa would have destroyed Reality itself, and with it, the profound equilibrium of nature that sustained this world. Opti understood this bitter truth: it could briefly assume Pesa's role as Earth's guardian, but only as an imitation, a placeholder destined to fail.

For without Pesa's foundational force of Reality, the Earth would wither and die, as surely as the Realm of Imagination had already begun to falter. With Pesa destroyed, all that was chemically and atomically known upon this world would have slowly unraveled, dissolving into nothingness across the ages of time. The foundation of existence—the reactions and actions that shape the physical realm—would have eventually come undone, and with it, every living thing tethered to the force of Reality.

For Reality, dear T'Naeva, is the bedrock upon which all life stands, the source of every sensation, every motion, and every breath within this physical plane. In those final, agonizing hours of omnipotence, Opti peered far beyond the horizon of present time. Through the piercing clarity of its newly realized authority, my parent saw the echoes of what could be, spanning hours, days, cycles, and even ages yet to come.

And within those glimpses of the future, Opti saw the harrowing truth of this war: a barren Earth, bereft of life, stripped to its bones by the absence of its foundational force—an Earth that had reverted to the desolation from which Xionn had first lifted it from, a wasteland consumed by silence and shadow. Opti, standing at the precipice of its own omnipotence and mortality, grasped this burden with an unyielding resolve to simply love. It understood the weight of responsibility placed upon it—not just to Pesa, not just to Gaea, but to the Earth itself.

My parent, through the maturation born of its union with Reality, came to accept this unshakable truth: that Reality, despite its flaws and corruptions, held precedence over Imagination in sustaining this world. Without Reality, Imagination could not thrive; without Pesa, the Earth and all its wonders would eventually cease to exist. And so, Opti made its final, sovereign choice. Through the piercing clarity of its omnipotence, my parent embraced the paradox of its existence: that to preserve creation, the creator must yield.

Its essence, infinite and unbound, began to erupt into purpose, pouring into the foundation of Reality itself. In that moment, Opti became more than the force of Imagination; it became the anchor of balance, an ideal that would endure beyond its own mortality. Though its light dimmed, its sacrifice ignited a spark that would guide creation's future—a spark waiting to take shape in the heart of one yet to arise... *me.*
This, my dearest mate, is the essence of sacrifice.

The greatest act any being can perform is to surrender its own existence for a cause greater than itself. Opti's death was not merely the conclusion of its journey; it was the ultimate affirmation of its purpose. It was a death, a sacrifice that gave life. A choice that turned devastation into hope. A final act that forever reshaped the fate of this Earth, its nature, and all life that will come afterward.

Such is the truth of my parent's profound selflessness, T'Naeva. And though it burns within me with grief and pride alike, I speak it now—not only for you, but for the world that still turns because of it. Alas, dear one, in this tragic chapter, these words of truth from that day forward would stand forever as a realization. Never again would Earth be the same ... but it would still *endure.*

I gaze upon both my mortally wounded parent and its kin as the divine cocoon of diamond begins to tremble, a resonant hum spreading across the arena of battle. The fiery storms that raged with unrelenting fury are now dimmed to glowing embers, casting an eerie stillness over the battlefield. With a deafening crack, the protective cocoon fractures, shards of shimmering diamond cascading to the ground like celestial tears.

From within the fractured shell, I see my parent, Opti, its form battered and broken, its divine light flickering like a fading star. Each breath grows shallower, its luminous essence dimming with every passing moment. The protection it wove, the barrier that held chaos at bay is indeed gone, leaving only the weight of its sacrifice to behold. Beside it, Pesa lies still, the dark and corrupted kin whose presence once fueled discord, now reduced to silence beneath the dying light of Opti's radiance.

In this solemn moment, I stand and know the truth that shatters my heart: never again will my parent rise from where it has fallen. Opti's final moments draw near, and with them, the end of an era. The air, thick with ash and grief, carries the last remnants of its divine song, a melody of Imagination's undying legacy, fading into the eternal mysteries of oblivion.

Pesa, spared from the brutal heat and carnage that have reduced this once-living region to a blackened, smoky ruin, clings to life. Though breathing heavily, it slowly lifts its broken body and stands at the head of the mighty foe that now lies in quivering, crimson-stained silence. Even in defeat, the beast still feels the vibration of Opti's roar reverberating within its being, harboring a quiet gratitude for still having the breath of life.

With trembling legs barely supporting its weight, Pesa stands in solemn silence over its kin. Its unguarded thoughts turn toward a swiftly growing sadness. As it gazes into the beautiful, fading light of Opti's eyes, Pesa begins to understand: the end is near. Opti, its head dimming with the final toll of its strength, turns to meet its kin's gaze one last time. Gasping heavily, it lets its peaceful crimson eyes pierce Pesa's as its life continues to fade.
And then, within the stillness of those long moments of reflection, Pesa hears Opti's voice again—stronger, clearer, and utterly free of any shadowed influence whatsoever.

~ ~ ~

*"Hear me, diseased Pesa, for a day will come when the power that courses through me will reveal its truth to you. On that fateful day, you too shall bless this world, though not before you feel the sting of death I too now endure. What dwells within me shall rise again, raging against you, for it was you who turned from our father's wisdom.*

~ ~ ~

*With each breath, my red life flows into the scorched earth, and I feel my essence returning to the father who formed me. At long last, my harmony shall merge with His eternal song, and I shall find my place, high within the infinite design.*

~ ~ ~

*As I gaze upon you one final time, O, diseased yet precious sibling, I see a beast burdened by its own foolish contempt. One day, you shall face justice, and a thousandfold will your deeds be returned to you—but not a moment before destiny deems it so.*

~~~

*Kindred spirit, I leave you with one final truth. Let the demon within you revel in its triumph, for it has forced the burden of my final moments into your weary eyes. Truly, this was Dia'Baal's wish all along—that you, his most powerful and pitiful slave, would carry his will to this bitter and somber end."*

Opti, its breaths becoming shorter and winded, again speaks through Pesa's mind with an ever-strengthening tone.

*"You know why I look upon you this way, Pesa... There are truths buried within me that you cannot yet grasp—truths that will arise to meet you when fate calls you home... Only then will you understand the weight of what you have wrought upon yourself this terrible hour..."*

Pesa's heart, blackened though it was, trembles against a sorrow it could neither name nor deny. Somewhere deep within, a fear—not of death, but of memory—begins to stir. Closing its swelling eyes as Opti's words echo deeply within its mind, trembles in vain against their weight. Their meaning, vast and incomprehensible, slips beyond its grasp, and the mighty beast—finally broken in body and spirit—collapses at Opti's side.

Defeated and bewildered, Pesa crawls with agonizing effort to its fading sibling, its battered face brushing against Opti's. In a fleeting, sorrowful moment, Pesa extends its tongue, licking Opti's cheek with a tenderness it has never known. This simple act, born of instinct and regret, holds a question that time itself could never answer...
How different might this day have been, had I done this very act so many ages before?

Reopening its aching eyes, Pesa gazes blindly into the dimming light of Opti's expressionless windows. The once-fiery orbs, now faint as dying embers, reveal nothing of the infinite wisdom and love they had carried. The great beast, trembling with the effort to understand, bears witness to Opti's final breath of physical life.

And then it comes—a roar unlike any other, a sound that pierces the marrow of existence and reverberates through Pesa's mind with unrelenting force. The mighty echo overwhelms its senses, forcing its head skyward in a frantic motion. Opti's voice, now magnified to divine proportions, manifests into the smoky heavens, shaking both the earth and the trembling soul of its kin.

*... Dear kin, do as you will with my hollow vessel, and count yourself fortunate that your footsteps still mark this world. But know this: our father's promise is unshakable and will most certainly come to pass. On that glorious day, you too shall rise and join me in the realm of eternal freedom, where all burdens are lifted, and the truth of harmony prevails.*

The weight of these words presses against Pesa's chest like an unbearable stone, yet the great beast cannot look away from the celestial stage above. There, the smoky heavens vibrate with light and sound as Opti's final proclamation blasts into reality with a terrifying and majestic tone.

*... Almighty Creator, I give my essence unto You. Let my light join the eternal harmony of Your grand design, and I ask You, in Your infinite mercy, to stay Your wrath upon my kin, for it truly knows not what it has done this day...*

*... And to You, O, beloved Xionn, O, beloved father, my task is complete.*

*IT IS DONE!*

As these final words fade into the eternal realm of oblivion, Pesa's body continues to shake uncontrollably. The air grows dense with an unspoken power as the great beast is overwhelmed by the magnitude of what it has just heard. Opti's divine essence, its flickering light extinguished, has now transcended to its final resting place.

In this moment, Pesa feels the embrace of true fear—not the fear of pain or death, but the terror of gazing into something vast and unknowable. Its massive body trembles, its very essence quaking under the weight of divine finality. The enormity of what it has just witnessed presses against its chest like an immovable boulder, robbing it of breath.

With a final jolt of motion in hearing Opti's final words, it throws its head skyward, bellowing into the heavens as it roars, its voice raw and desperate.

"What in the hell is this?!"

But the silence that follows is absolute, pressing against Pesa like an unrelenting force. The great beast collapses, its eyes drawn to the shattered form of its kin. Opti's broken shell lies motionless, a lifeless husk stripped of its once-radiant power. For a moment, Pesa sees not a rival, but a being of unimaginable will reduced to a bleeding husk. A flicker of sorrow stirs within its chest, a feeling it cannot name, but cannot deny.

D'Reem's voice cuts through the silence, his grief sharp and unyielding.
He whispers...
"I say to you, O precious one, Hellios has nothing to do with it anymore!"

For a time, the smoky arena lies cloaked in an ominous silence, broken only by the shallow, ragged breaths of Pesa. Struggling against the weight of its battered frame, the great beast rises to trembling knees, its weary eyes casting a slow, searching gaze toward the pitch-blackened heavens and the unmoving form of its kin. Yet comprehension eludes it. The enormity of what has transpired remains shrouded in the haze of pain and confusion. Pesa sees only the broken shell of Opti—this lifeless husk, once radiant with unimaginable power, now dim and dead to the world.

It is a sight both humbling and horrifying, a stark reminder of the cost of their unyielding struggle. Moments stretch into an eternity before Pesa whispers into the charred air, its voice trembling with sorrow and reluctant respect. "It is finished undeniably, O vicious Opti. My grief will never be greater than it is for you in this moment, and my respect for you, dearly departed brutal flower, is strong. Stronger than you will ever know."

With a lurch and a heavy sigh, Pesa forces itself once more to its weary legs, blinking furiously as a sudden rush of tears threatens to break free. The great beast, once a symbol of unrelenting strength, now stands fractured in spirit. And yet, within the storm of its thoughts, something faint but resilient stirs.

Yes... I see them clearly now, those fragile remnants of divinity still cradled deep within Pesa's battered mind. They shimmer like faint stars in the void, untouched by the shadow of Dia'Baal's corruption. Though surrounded by darkness, these fragments endure defiantly, gleaming with a purity that refuses to bow. They cling to Pesa's soul, small but unyielding, burning not with fury, but with the quiet warmth of an ember that refuses to fade.

Pesa cannot grasp their meaning, but it feels their presence like a distant melody—haunting, familiar, and unshakable. For even now, in its brokenness, they whisper of something long buried, something uncorrupted and eternal. The memory will burn quietly, stubbornly, until its final breath, a defiance against the weight of oblivion and the spark of what may yet come.

But even as these elements of light struggle to persist, a darker truth looms large—a festering malignancy deeply rooted within Pesa's soul. The cancer of hatred, still alive and ravenous, smolders like an ember buried deep within its chest, whispering promises of vengeance. It claws at the beast's weary mind, tightening its chains and preparing to overwhelm. Even now, in the fragile stillness of this moment, it stirs, waiting to consume once more.

Standing alone in the ashen silence, Pesa fixes its weary gaze upon the lifeless body of Opti. And then, something strange occurs. The harmonized chemistry of Opti's divine essence, though dormant, briefly ignites, bathing the deceased creature in a soft, golden glow. A multitude of radiant orbs begin to rise, shimmering as if carrying Opti's final tune into the symphony of the cosmos. The particles, vibrant and iridescent, ascend in a delicate spiral, their motion growing faster with each passing moment.

They shimmer with a reverence so profound that even Pesa cannot look away. What begins as a solemn tribute transforms into a swirling vortex of light—a dance of divine farewell. Then, as though compelled by some unseen force, these golden hued wisps scatter in all directions, seeding the heavens of Earth with the memory of their host.

Evening descends like a quiet veil, blanketing the smoky meadow in shadows and muted light. Pesa watches in silence as the last traces of Opti's essence merge into a faint golden hue over the shadowed peak of the great mountain. The spectacle is mesmerizing, yet the great beast dismisses it at first, turning its attention to the crimson streams of blood still flowing from Opti's torn neck. The blood, rich and vivid, seeps purposefully into the scorched earth, and Pesa shakes its head, muttering in bewilderment.

"Why?" it growls, its voice trembling with both anger and confusion.
"Why did you not kill me when you had the chance, Opti? Your choice condemns me to a life I cannot bear—a life where your shadow of death will haunt my every step. This question, dear kin, will assuredly plague me forever."

The great beast pauses, its breath ragged, the weight of its words pressing heavy in the silence.
"But let me say this: your fight was beyond anything I've known—

unyielding, fierce, and filled with a light I will never possess. That light, dear kin, burns in my mind like an unrelenting flame. For this, O vicious flower … I curse and revere you in equal measure! Yet the rage within me falters, swallowed by a grief I cannot name. For all your faults, Opti, your strength was undeniable. That conviction, that fire, will stay with me long after the ashes of this battle have cooled. It will remain with me until my final breath on this wretched world."

The air grows heavier, the silence deeper, as Pesa lowers its gaze to the lifeless form of its sibling. In that moment, the beast feels a flicker of something it cannot name—an ache that cuts deeper than any wound. Yet it knows only this: it stands alone, burdened by a grief it can never escape and a hatred it can never relinquish.

I grit my teeth in fury, seething at the audacity of these superficial words spilling from the lips of my parent's killer—yours! Even now, as Pesa stands in its arrogance, I see the echoes of Opti's light fading into the void, a light you dear parent extinguished with its treachery. You presume this pain will be its greatest, but I know a different truth, dear T'Naeva. Soon, the wrath of a grieving mother will remind it of what true suffering really means! T'Naeva's hands clench at her sides, her voice low and trembling.

"You hated my parent, D'Reem! You killed Pesa because of that hatred, that vengeance—I saw it in your eyes so don't you dare try to call it grace or judgment!"
Her gaze suddenly falters, and she takes a step back, her tone softening.
"Or … was it both? Was it vengeance *and* something else?" Her voice trails off, uncertainty flickering in her expression.
"I don't even know what to believe anymore…"

D'Reem's gaze hardens, his voice steady, but laced with weariness.

"It was all of it, T'Naeva. Hatred! Judgment! Grace! I did what had to be done—not for vengeance, but to free this world from the very chains that now bind us both!"
He steps closer, his tone softening. "You may see hatred in my eyes, and maybe it is still there. But don't mistake my anger for malice. Pesa's death wasn't just about what it was; it was about what Dia'Baal made it become!"

His voice lowers, each word weighted.

"You don't have to believe that my retribution was just, but trust me on this, dear mate: The Companion tells me that you *will* see it all for yourself. But until that moment arrives, hold onto whatever truth you think you know, and let that be your guide until the veil is completely lifted from your eyes."

With Opti's transcendent influence of life now departed, though forever etched into Pesa's diseased mind, I see it—a spark of humility flickering in the beast's eyes, as if it dares to grasp the weight of its actions. But the spark withers, crushed beneath the suffocating tide of its innermost *whisper*. Raw and unrestrained, it claws its way to dominance within the beast's trembling form, snuffing out even the faintest glimmer of redemption.

Yet as it is still stripped of Dia'Baal's corrupting influence, something has changed within the wearied beast. Its divine flesh, once impervious and quick to mend, now festers and refuses to heal. The wounds remain open, a silent testimony to its rejection by life itself. The great god of beasts, for all its pride, stands quite vulnerable for the first time in its existence.

Pesa, trembling and unsteady, dares to roar again aloud, its words drenched in malicious defiance—no longer towards its fallen kin, but at its own father.

"**You made me this way, didn't you... dear father!?**"
Pesa hisses in its rage, its voice ragged yet strong.

"**You gave me claws, strength, and fire, but you never gave me peace. Is this your justice Xionn? To leave me to rot in the ruin you allowed?**"

The words hang in the air like a curse, daring the heavens to respond. But the heavens remain silent, and Pesa, trembling once more with rage and despair, staggers alone in the ashen darkness. Its wheezing voice cuts through the scorched silence.

"**To you alone I speak, O, despised father! Even as I endure ... these breaths of torment ... I am elated beyond words ... at my completed task!**"

Pesa gasps for air increases, its chest heaving as its fury persists.

"**It is finished for you, O precious kin ...**
**for no other under these darkened heavens ...**
**will overthrow my rule! And as for you ...**
**dear father of mine ...**

I doubt you have ...
anything more to say ...
about your children ...
ever again!"

More labored gasps escape its quivering mouth and fills the heavens.

"'Tis you alone, O hated father ...
who has forsaken me ...
and my loathing of you ...
knows no bounds!
Now I declare ...
to the chemistry of my world ...
that I ... and no other ...
become your master!
Gaea, you will now obey my reign without question!"

With its internal strength depleted, Pesa collapses flat to its belly, a whimpering heap of arrogance and despair. Yet Gaea, ever silent, is far from compliant. She does not submit whatsoever to its grotesque display of arrogance. Instead, she seethes, her own wrath building, fed by the lifeblood of her slain child that seeps ever deeper into her scorched and smoky breast. It is she alone, the good mother, who wails painfully to her eternal mate, her molten heart trembling with fury. Deep within her iron core, a punishment unlike any other is forged, and it will be swift and unrelenting.

Dear T'Naeva, it is not Pesa's pride nor its words that will dictate these coming hours. It is the Earth mother's reply—a storm of vengeance born of Opti's sacrifice, building to become fierce enough to defy the Force of Reality with a vengeance that burns colder than the cosmos itself.

*Gaea is mad as hell—and Pesa is about to discover how furious she truly is...*

The storm elements gather—silent, slow, deliberate. Potent and unrelenting, they move with the weight of inevitability. Her landscape shudders beneath their quickening, trembling as if in mourning for what has been lost, tragic and unnecessary. Her silence is not surrender; it is the coiled breath of retribution, the palpitating heartbeats of a planet before she strikes.
This will be no mere tempest in origin; it will be a nightmare of cosmic wrath, a maelstrom born of grief and divine fury. This is the prelude to a penance that will cascade upon the god of beasts who dared desecrate her

sacred realm, murdering the child she too once held so close.

Dearest T'Naeva, in this moment of silent and solemn lucidity, they all gasp in awe, holding their collective breath as if the very cosmos waits in anticipation. The pause ends, and here stands a man transformed—a deity among all others, ascended to a level that even an *Edenite* citizen would envy. He publicly accepts his gifts of a matured godhood with solemn grace, and in this exalted hour, he is called by all of Ametheden, his Edenite nation, and his Companion as:

### *Sovereign Hand Xionn, 'The One'*
*A being whose destiny was forged by his Companion eons before this day.*

Their combined reaction: I hear a surge of over *ten trillion* souls across ten thousand star systems in a dozen galaxies, erupting into jubilant cheer—delivered through a live *SoulSliver Memorycast* of this monumental event. Their collective ovation becomes a sonata of praise and awe, echoing upward and into the Great Realm, where every angelic inhabitant in this place joins in chorus with the King's greatest people.

Far beyond the gathered officials and spectators, hidden among the many beautifully sculpted pillars carved out of diamond in one of Ametheden's greatest coliseums, a stunningly beautiful woman watches him, intently, and *in awe*. She alone has witnessed him rise from his humble beginnings of unity in mortal and beast, to all the mighty tasks he has completed with much struggle—but never in such a mesmerizing moment as this.
Never in such majesty as this! Never in such absolute divinity as this! In this moment, I see her deep emerald pupils glisten, her long, flowing golden hair reflecting the radiance of his divine transformation.

I hear her whisper.

*'This... this is beyond anything I could have imagined of you, beloved Xionn, as you stand before all of Ametheden and a hundred thousand worlds, exalted far above even the mightiest of our nation. And yet, you still do not see me—or do you?*
*Have you thought of me even once since our destined departure of eons past? Three*

*billion cycles it has been... and still, I remember you as if no time has passed at all.*

The Sovereign Hand begins his incredible speech.

*Thalassion XII* teaching him the cadence that breathes life into law. *Aetherion Prime* anchoring his hand to the foundation beneath all things. *Seleneos* opening his heart to the fleeting grace of mortal light. *Luminara* imprinting upon him the weight of memory and the echoes it leaves. *Olympheon* and its sister worlds tempering his spirit in the stone-born trials of balance.
*Eryndor V* revealing the subtle thread of unity that binds all worlds together in the cosmos without breaking them.

At last, I see the bright face of my beloved mentor smile wide in reflection, speaking about his greatest triumphs of creation, the first being *Harr'Manee*. He speaks of her birth, her loss, and the emerged spirit that loved him even more deeply. Softly, Ceff replies as tears streak down her bright face.

*'I too spoke that day through your beautiful creation, O radiant love. Could you not sense it was the passion I held for you as the memory of our final embrace took hold before destiny's hand took it away? Did you not hear my whispers across the countless epochs of your journeys, or the caresses I laid upon your shoulders and brow, as I bore witness to the grandeur of what you have now become?'*

He then begins to speak of his greatest creation, *Earth*—not a world forged in haste, but a world born of boundless, sacrificial love. With solemn pride, he then recalls the momentous separation of the forces of *Reality* and *Imagination*, a feat no sentient being—mortal or divine—had ever dared, let alone achieved. Through uncounted trials and the crucible of spirit, he has become the *first*—and thus far, the *only*—to master such an impossible task, even for a god. Yet his words are not uttered in boast, but in benediction.

For he knows his hard-won wisdom became the seed of a much greater harvest—sewn into the hearts and worlds birthed of his Edenite brethren. It was indeed his lonely triumphs that cracked open the firmament for all Edenites to follow. And so this collective, once fledgling, have taken up the mantle of his incredible scope of knowledge. They all now apply his starlit trails in conjunction with their own unique and sacred ways, as many of them, too, have become powerful over the past three eons.

But today, everyone remembers that it all began... with *him*. Their reach of carbon based sentient life extending far into the cosmos, simply because Xionn stood first and dared to make the impossible real for all his people. At last, his words turn to his most cherished creations—his *children*.

*Pesa* and *Opti*, twin manifestations of those cosmic forces, breathing separate life and wonder into the universe as living testaments to his divine purpose. In them is the legacy of Xionn's labor, the embodied harmony of power and creativity, reason, imagination, and passion.

Together, they dance as the eternal heirs of his radiant love, proof that a god who defied oblivion, could forge this mighty of a gift to the cosmos. And yet, even in this moment of high ascension, something stirs within him—a gentle tug at the edge of consciousness. Not of pain nor sorrow, but something good and familiar.

Within the deepest sanctum of his being, where time and memory spiral like twin galaxies, Xionn begins to feel it—a slow convergence of forgotten light, gathering like embers in the farthest reaches of himself. There are no visions, no thunderous revelations. Only a hush, like the moment before a sacred name is spoken aloud, and in that silence, the Companion speaks. Not in words, but in the holy architecture of His presence.

*... All that has been hidden shall be revealed in time. Not to your mind, blessed sovereign, but to your soul, which has always known what will become.*

I hear her thoughts again, T'Naeva, rising softly in the stillness after my mentor's slight pause—and I am struck with a renewed reverence for her unseen devotion.

*'I stood among the veiled stars of the Realm's estuary so long ago, honored beyond measure to witness what no other could see, the birth of your mighty children. I watched in silent tribute, in overwhelming joy upon that starry horizon, as I always have... unseen, yet never truly absent from any of you.'*

Yet even in triumph, he does not forget his Edenite brethren. With a voice steady yet reverent, he offers recognition to those who stood shoulder to shoulder with him through the trials, training, and migration to the three moons of their world. Name after name flows from his lips, and yes, *hers* is among them. More celestial tears form in her eyes, and she is fortunate no one is there to witness her reaction.

"Without you—all of you," he continues, "this harmony would have never become song, and for this, I give my eternal gratitude."

Each word to her ears is like a symphony as it settles into the hearts of her people—a hymn of power, creation, and boundless hope. The people of Ametheden then recite the *Prophesy of the Three Alignments*, and then arise into singing the *Song of Ametheden*. My ears are truly raptured, dear T'Naeva, to hear such beauty of divinely inspired chorus.

From her place still hidden in the shadows, she listens to the enchanting melody, grinning widely as she hums to herself this mighty sonnet to honor their world into its destiny. These words now stirring things much deeper within her passions now, her feelings of frustration, of sorrow, and of longing become known to me.

*'One day, Xionn Theone... Will you truly remember who I am, or will I remain just a name to be forgotten to the ravages of your eternal duties?'*

Then, with a pause that echoes like eternity itself, Xionn lifts his brightened gaze skyward and speaks with a mighty thunder. Every inhabitant of the coliseum falls into immediate reverence through his magnitude of voice.

*"Finally, to my eternal Companion, the One whose presence shaped my every step, whose voice was a torch unto my path—this victory belongs as much to You as to me. Without You, O mighty and beloved Companion, I could have never become he whom You sanctify today. Your graces and gifts fashioned me from thought into being, from dream into reality. You are truly the cornerstone of all that I am!"*

Yet even as his radiant face glows with the joy of his words, I see it falter, his countenance briefly shadowed by something deeper and more profound. The Companion too is here, and His gaze shifts—not toward Xionn, but towards *her* as she closes her eyes and reaches a hand outward. He alone acknowledges and allows the woman's presence to be known to him, though He does not reveal who she is at this time, but instead...

A cosmic wind stirs, and her reach lightly caresses Xionn's bright and rigid cheek—and his chest tightens, and his heart stirs. This strange sensation once more strikes him as calm and familiar, like something... *or someone...* long forgotten has reemerged in this very moment. Yes my love, she has felt his face once more and she exhales with a gleeful reaction, knowing too he felt her touch, if only for an instant.

Xionn too quickly catches his breath, unaware that it carries the very fragrance of her touch, still lingering from when her hand reached for his face. The warmth he felt, the ache he could not name— this was *her*. And though the veil remains, though fate's curtain has not yet parted, something changes in him in that moment, and it is good. His chest rises fuller, not with pride, but with a sudden but quiet longing. A memory before memory itself flutters like a moth at the edge of a divine flame, never to be overtaken by its heat, but forged to its presence in memory.

In this moment of introspection, his speech ends, and Xionn quietly returns to his seat of honor. The world around him celebrates his ascent, yet he sits in solitude, his mind growing exponentially in these moments, and it becomes filled to the brim by a newfound and overwhelming awareness. Dear T'Naeva, it is true that the maturity of a god can sometimes become so overwhelming at exactly the incorrect time...

A flood of emotions suddenly break through his every divine sense, hurling it into his newly ascended being, piercing his tranquility with a cry... *of wailing*. A despair so powerful that it has echoed across time, space, and dimension—directly at *him*. Though unheard by those around him, this potent sound is deafening within his newly matured essence. Something far beyond his senses, tragic and profound, has unfolded with his family back on Earth, and the weight of this anxiety threatens to shatter his peace of mind very soon.

From the shadows, Ceffea also senses this terrible tide of grief that had suddenly awakened in him, and it stiffens her resolve. She closes her eyes instinctively and can feel a sudden torment pressing into his soul like a great and unseen weight. She parts her lips, yet only her powerful mind can reach for him in time.

*"Be still, radiant Xionn... I am here."*

Her voice, once only a mere whisper, is no longer soft and indiscernible to him—but now has resonated as loud as thunder into his evolved mind.

Xionn immediately stands as his eyes dart around the ceremony, searching... but there is nothing there, no focus to the beautifully potent voice he just heard, and his anxiety increases. It is then that the Companion intervenes before Xionn can grasp the source of both the cry and the thundering of voice he has just heard, and He puts an immediate end to the chaos. By divine authority, the fates themselves are forbidden to allow *'The One'* to endure any further confusion or torment, especially on this magnificent day of his *second* ascent into godly maturity.

Without hesitation, the fates obey their Master, bending to the will of the *One Sovereign Voice.* Xionn exhales deeply, his chest rising and falling as the weight of the wailing voice fades quickly within him. That ominous cry of Gaea that clung to his mind is now dissolved, replaced by a serenity so settled it feels unearthly to him, and his memory of it is gone.
That other voice, however, stronger and more defined than ever before, lingers at the edge of his mind like an echo of a memory that is eons old. Something he has known, yet still it is veiled in a truth unknown to him, and for the first time, a response stirs within him.

*'I have heard this voice before and it is familiar, but from where does it reside?'*

From the shadows, she watches his reaction as his torment fades, but she does not rejoice, and her thoughts once more become known to me.

*'He is free of sorrow for now, thank the Companion. But whatever truth comes from that terrible cry, I will be there for him. Even if your eyes forget, O radiant one, may your soul one day remember me, and may the Companion rejoice in it.'*

She turns to leave the assembly, but then—just for a moment—her foot falters. A longing arises within her chest, a force as ancient as her own soul. It trembles at the edges of her restraint—the ache to be seen by all, to speak his name aloud, to finally reveal her love to him. Or perhaps, to utter her very own name for the first time in ages, in witness to a world that has long forgotten her, or has it?

And then... it happens.

From somewhere deep within the gathered multitude of the massive coliseum, cutting through the electric hum of reverence and celebration, a lone voice arises. Clear. Steady. Unmistakably *Edenite.*

"By the Companion's eternal grace... *Ceffea Thesier?* Is that truly you?"

This name—unspoken on this plane of existence for nearly *twenty-five millennia*—falls like a celestial hammer, and the coliseum's air tightens as if creation itself has drawn a sharp breath. For a heartbeat, even the cosmos seems to pause, listening to her name in wonder. Around the place where her name is spoken, a nearby crowd begins to suddenly stir.

Faces turn outward and skyward, eyes widen, and an electric fervor courses through them—as if her very mystery beckons them to seek her out. Whispers swell like a rising tide, building toward shouts of wonder. Ceffea's heart seizes as her brilliant emerald eyes press tight, her mind racing as the growing throng begins to shift closer, voices rising in growing waves of awe.

*'Oh no… not now. Not here. Not yet. They cannot see me—not as I am. Xionn must not know I am here either. Dear Companion, please… help me to make it so.'*

And Xionn, as if heaven answers her plea, does not hear this commotion.

The beautiful woman exhales—a sharp, controlled breath—and without turning to face the voice that dared speak her pre-Edenite name, she dons her cape and cloak and slips like a master thief into the crowd. A river of bodies surges in wonder, but she is already gone, her golden hair vanishing like a thread of sunlight into the shadows of those towering, majestic pillars.

Above it all, the coliseum breathes once again, but heaven does not. The Companion watches her flight intently, His infinite gaze softening—not with surprise, but with quiet delight.

*…Well done, my Beloved Edenite Rose. And yes… one day, Xionn will truly know you again, and on that day he will call you—his Mighty Lioness.*

In this, Xionn's second ascension into godhood, the Companion's devotion is not merely expressed; it is fulfilled. He has always seen the promise of greatness within these two mighty servants, an unyielding spark of purpose even Xionn himself cannot yet fully comprehend. His love, radiant and unwavering, shines as a nova, illuminating a path through his many storms yet to come. Though He already knows that Xionn will one day grieve and rage for his belived Opti…

**Today will not be that day!**

T'Naeva no longer weeps. She sits in quiet, regal poise, though the echoes of D'Reem's tale still swirl through her mind like restless phantoms. The inconceivable truths he has laid before her weigh heavily upon her soul, and one question rises above all others—sharp, unrelenting, impossible to silence. Can she still believe what her own eyes have seen?

Is Pesa's demise truly as brutal as her vision showed, or has yet another deception—subtle, insidious—crept into her spirit like the serpent in Eden's Garden? She closes her eyes, and the face of her parent flickers in memory— Pesa, a god of both light and ruin, of tender creation and unfathomable evil. Did Pesa fall in wrath? Or in a grace she can no longer recognize, obscured by the weight of a war as old, if not older than time itself?

Her gaze drifts to Ocean—her only known beginning, her only witness. Beneath the life force of those dark aqua-hued depths lies the secret of her origin, but no answers rise from them, *not yet anyway*. Only the mighty waves of her birth remain — strong and shifting, their rhythm crashing with purpose against the rocky outcrops of a world newly reborn.

To her, D'Reem is now more than a god, more than a warrior, more than the figure of impossible resolve etched into the memory of her creation. She sees him as he truly is—a wounded bearer of truth, the silent sentinel who carries not only prophecy but pain. He is her husband now. Pain borne for her... and perhaps for all existence. A strange, primal sorrow swells in her chest, mingling with something far older than grief—a nameless ache that seems tied to the bedrock of her soul.

It feels like remembrance — of something lost before time, a love so ancient it lay entombed beneath eons of silence. And there, in the quiet sanctuary between divine heartbeats, she understands she is not merely witnessing the end of one tale. She is standing at the threshold of another—a genesis trembling in the wake of eternity, where gods walk and mortals dare to follow. She, who in the ache of her own loss, now sees and desires only this above all else...

*Longing.*

She longs to understand her visions, *and* him. To reach across their great divide... to unravel why his pain feels so deeply entwined with her own. Between them still hangs a gravity not yet spoken. A bond not yet forged, but *fated*. Fated to become a purpose that will carry them into the unrelenting tide of what is to come. His voice is low—not trembling, but reverent, as if speaking directly into the silence that separates them.

"There are stories throughout the cosmos that have been kept secret from even its own multitude of civilizations—not out of cruelty, my love, but *mercy*. You and I, T'Naeva... and I believe we are such a story—one that humanity will speak of one day, with a smile, in their final age before all the cosmic mysteries are revealed. In this moment I do not yet know what you are to me, but I do know this... only that when you grieve, I too also grieve.

When I speak, something eternal in you arises to listen, and for this, I am grateful. We are not bound by the past alone, nor by what is to come... but by the silence between these things. In this precious silence, O beautiful goddess... I see something awaken within you and for this too, I am truly gratified to know its cause."

D'Reem's radiant gaze turns away, and his final words dissolve into silence. His eyes lower—not in shame, but in surrender to the path still veiled. And to you, *seeker of this living flame*—these words were meant for you as well. That you too may ask yourself...

*How has this truth stirred my inner fire?*
*How does its clarity help me walk more bravely through the trials I face?*
*How might I carry this story into my own life?*

Volume I— the first voice in its greater symphony—is now complete.

Through its written words,
Of **insight**...
Of **courage**...
Of **wonder**...
Of **hope**... *a realm awakens.*

A Realm,

*Where gods* **remember...**
*Where mortals* **ascend...**
*Where your next breath could reforge* **your very existence.**

———————————— ✦ ————————————

— *Volume II* begins to form—

Like a mighty tempest upon the horizons of thought— drawing ever closer, its whirlwinds of memory stir, awakening to remember their true master. A storm of determination that has always resided within *your* soul, waiting for you to grasp its reigns and ride its power into purpose.

To carry and release that power boldly...

*Into your* **faith...**
*Into your* **doubts...**
*Into your* **struggles...**
*Into your* **triumphs...**
*And see what stirs within...*

**To awaken what sleeps in the world around you.**

Thus ends the *Tide of Transgression*, and with it, this first volume of four —ushering in the wondrous and eternal realms ... of *thought*. The eons of ancients past that will never again be seen in the physical but shall live on...

Visible only to those whose minds awaken... to **MYTH**.

*Coming soon... the epic continues:*
**MYTH:** Lords of the Realm *Vol. 2*

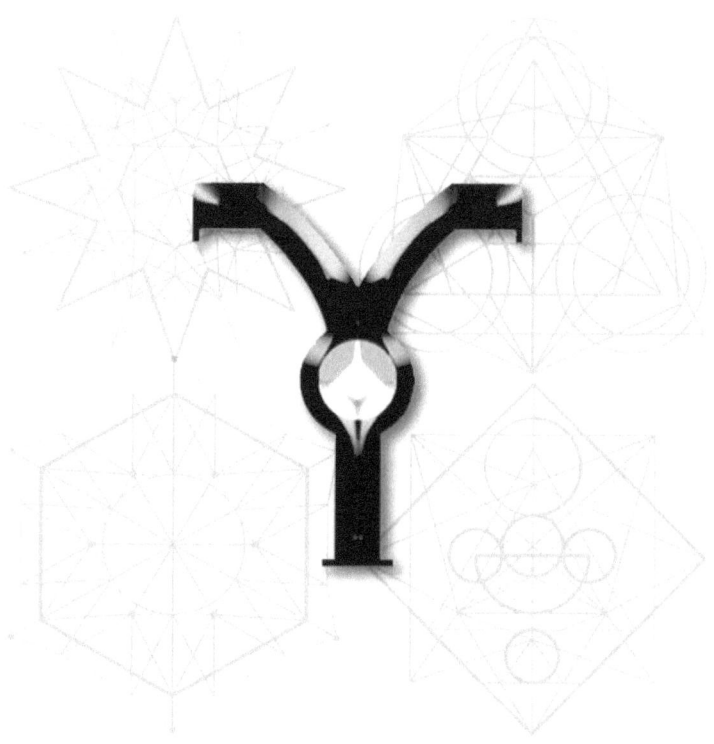